Wyldling Armor

Book Three of the Wyldling Dream Series

A.R. Grimes

A Cycle of Tehara novel

Copyright 2024 by A.R. Grimes

All rights reserved. No part of this publication may be reproduced, stored or transmitted in any form or by any means, electronic, mechanical, photocopying, recording, scanning, or otherwise without written permission from the publisher. With the exception of brief quotations used in a book review, it is illegal to copy this book, post it to a website, or distribute it by any other means without permission.

This novel is entirely a work of fiction. The names, characters and incidents portrayed in it are the work of the author's imagination. Any resemblance to actual persons, living or dead, events or localities is entirely coincidental. No artificial intelligence programs were used to write this novel.

Printed in the United States of America: First Printing, 2024

ISBN: 978-1-958718-04-9 (ebook)
ISBN: 978-1-958718-05-6 (paperback)

http://cycloftehara.com

Editors: Huckleberry Rahr and Weslee Imrisek
Cover art: GetCovers.com
Map designed using Inkarnate software (Inkarnate.com):
Ynys Lloches

For my friends in the Sun Prairie Writers Group
and all my Writer Pals.
Without y'all this book would never have been finished.

Put on the full armor of God, so that you can stand against
the schemes of the Devil. For our struggle is not against flesh and
blood, but against the rulers, against the authorities, against the
world rulers of this darkness, against the spiritual forces of evil
in the heavenly places. For this reason, take up the full armor of
God, so that you will be able to take a stand on the evil day and,
after you have done everything, to stand.

Ephesians 6:11-13 (Bible, EHV version)

Acknowledgments

If not for God's blessings and providence—in this case, the wonderful people He put in my life—I probably wouldn't have published any books at all. It's been a rough year with many changes. May God continue to bless my family for putting up with me through these difficult times. Ryan, Gabriel, and Michael: I apologize for being a continually distracted workaholic. Huckleberry, thank you for keeping me on track and pointing out plot holes. Thank you, Wes, for the encouragement, critique, and proofreading. Lawrence, thanks for being a sounding board and for making me laugh when I wanted to cry. Nikki and Elizabeth ... welcome to the madness! I will be forever grateful to the Sun Prairie Writers group—Gail, Dennis, Jennifer, and Mike—for helping me work through the Gordian knots of this behemoth's storyline. A shout-out to my ARC reviewers, Emily and Abigail, for giving of their time. For everyone else I may have forgotten to mention, whether friends from work, church, Facebook, or random passers-by, please know that I appreciate you. And last but certainly not least: thank you, Mom, for continually urging me to "finish writing that story, already!"

YNYS LLOCHES
NORTH
RECKONING POINT
ANCIENT GWERINDAWR CAPITAL
NEAR ATOLLS
LIMANI BAY
LAGOON COURT
CRESCENT ISLET
ROYAL PALACE
SPONGE BEDS

Sparks and Ash

When Toad opened his eyes, the world was in flames.

He drew in a sharp breath, then coughed as the acrid odor of smoke stung his nostrils and lungs. Blinking rapidly to clear his eyes, he discovered the forest around him was not, in fact, on fire. It had been the golden light filling his vision that made it seem like everything was burning. An effect of his wyld, rooted in the fire aspect of the Aethyr, that enhanced his eyesight so he could see in the dark.

Cautiously, neck muscles twinging, he lifted his head. He lay on his belly under the low-hanging branch of a spruce. That must be where the whatever-it-was—the nightstalker? —had flung him.

After Toad jumped on his face and set him on fire. A faint echo of rage pulsed through him at the memory of those glowing orange eyes. An angry smile tugged at his mouth.

I showed that joker who's boss. Serves him right for trying to grab the kiddo.

Toad's eyes widened and his breath caught. Annabelle! What in blazes had happened to her? Having come to Tehara through a portal from Earth, the girl wasn't much good at protecting herself—let alone fighting nightstalkers. Orange-eyed monsters ... His jaw clenched and his body shook. Why did the thought of orange eyes fill him with rage? He couldn't remember.

Criminy! Reminiscing can wait. I'd better find Annabelle before more trouble does. Commander Storm's counting on me to keep danger away from her. Get up, soldier.

With a groan, Toad got his limbs under him and pushed. They trembled with weakness. Nothing functioned as it should. Everything ached, but at least the pins and needles had gone away and his spine seemed intact.

"Stupid body," he seethed. He glared down at a pair of hands braced against the dark ground. Evergreen needles poked into his palms. "You *will* work."

Wait a minute ...

He froze, his heart's furious pounding ringing in his ears. Hands. He had *hands* again.

What the heck? Was this the dreamscape? Slowly, he rose up on his knees—yes, he had those, too—and held his hands before him, staring. Touching his head and face, he encountered a scruffy beard and hair tangling to his shoulders with twigs sticking out. He must look like a wild man. He barked a laugh. Not in the dreamscape, then, where he'd be clean shaven with short hair and wearing that incredible armor.

I suppose this means I'm Sir Thomas, again. Finally ... I'm me. *No idea how or why I changed back, but ...* Determination pushed speculation aside. *Gimme a sword, and I can actually make a friggin' difference in this battle!*

From the west came the distant sounds of steel crashing against steel, men shouting, and the rumble of moving earth—the Commander and the dwelfnim holding back their enemies. Nearby, crickets chirped from a copse of trees, and some other type of bugs were making a buzzing sound similar to the cicadas' whining keen during the day, only in shorter, softer bursts.

Before long, they'd be driving him crazy, but their irritating serenade informed him there wasn't anyone in the vicinity.

He peered through the smoke rising from his handiwork. No one living appeared to be around. The kiddo wasn't hiding in the trees, and there was no sign of her champion, either. Or his body. His special night-vision detected the cooling remains of three nightstalkers and the riding deer's corpse. He grimaced. Although it wasn't her favored mount, the kiddo was gonna be heartbroken. He wasn't looking forward to breaking the news to her.

Thomas crawled out from under the spruce tree, each wobbly movement bringing its own twinge of pain. Stupid joints. Was this how old people felt? *Darn it all. I'm not old; I'm only twenty!* He used a different tree—a less prickly one—to pull himself upright, groaning with effort. The nearest insects went quiet. Spruce needles poked his bare soles. He hung on to prevent himself from collapsing and stared at his feet, blinking in wonder.

I have two legs again.

He shook with silent, bitter laughter, and then he grimaced. For an entire moon, he'd been a toad, and now he was a man again. Why wasn't he ecstatic? This was what he'd wanted all along—to regain his humanity. What was wrong with him? Never mind; he'd worry about that later. He was a knight, and there was work to be done.

"The innocent must be protected."

That had been one of the first lessons Sir Rick taught him. It was part of the oath he'd sworn when raised to knighthood. Although he'd already failed at it so many times, Thomas would honor his late mentor in adhering to this principle. Sorrow quivered on the outskirts of his mind like an unwelcome guest. Roughly, he caged the emotion in the way Commander Storm had instructed during the mind shield training sessions.

Emotions could be dangerous. Indulging in sentiment caused mistakes. And mistakes led to death.

He looked down and snorted. For the love of all that was holy—he was as naked as the day he was born! He brushed spruce needles and other detritus from his beard and body, then paused as his fingers ran over scar tissue. Ridges lined his torso as if a huge cat's claws had raked him. Was that what happened? Too many missing memories.

Worry about the scars after you find the kiddo. They're old enough that they don't hurt and don't hamper your movement.

Thomas hobbled over to the corpses. Although he excelled at hand-to-hand combat, considering his current physical weakness, he'd feel much better with blades in hand. And boots on his feet. The dead nightstalkers didn't need theirs anymore, and the saddlebags ought to provide something he could use to cover his nakedness.

Digging through the saddlebags on the dead mount, he pulled out what appeared to be a pair of short pants made of thin fabric that laced up the front. In his haste to gird his loins, he nearly fell and ended up sitting on the dead deer's rump. What was its name again? Like so many things, he couldn't remember.

"Sorry, pal," he muttered, then flinched at the unaccustomed resonance of his voice. "Should know your name. You deserve better. At least you took one of those evil-eyed clowns with you."

He scowled as he fumbled tying the laces. This was taking too long. Stupid hands. They'd better work well enough to wield a sword. Deep within, the molten lava of his wyld still burned at a slow and steady rate. Although he hadn't exhausted his firepower, he must ration it. Passing out was not an option.

Gotta be strong for the kiddo.

He relieved a dead nightstalker of his weapons belt and clasped it about his waist. The enemy wielded a longsword as well as a shorter blade. He knew what to do with those. He found a pair of boots. Too big, but they almost fit ... Meh. Good enough.

"All right, kiddo, I'm coming," Thomas rasped.

Suddenly, all the bugs beyond the copse went silent. With his left hand on the grip of his new longsword, he drew on his wyld to fuel his eldritch vision. A heat image flashed between the trees in the distance, to the west. He went still, his gaze riveted to the corona of a biped figure that flickered like cold fire around the bole of a mid-sized tree. A human form.

He dismissed the possibility of it being one of the dwelfnim. Doubtless, they and the Commander were busy with the Battlecrows. They wouldn't abandon their posts. No, this was a foe who'd slipped past them. Another, slightly closer heat trace flickered in his peripheral vision, to the north this time. A flanking maneuver? His heart went cold.

They're going after the kiddo.

Red hot needles and icy shards pierced him. His breath came fast and shallow as he wound through the trees. It was going to happen again.

In his mind's eye, he recalled two swiftly moving giants in the darkness, shadows like forces of nature. They'd seized Enoch. One—Zakaar Ravenos, traitor and murderer—had taken down three troopers. Thomas had never felt so impotent as he had in that moment. He should have been able to protect the kid back then, but he'd failed. Because he was a toad. The resulting furnace of rage had precipitated one of his episodes of memory loss.

Was that the first time I used my wyld?

Thomas leaned against the slanted trunk of a fallen tree. The closest figure needed to pass by him if its goal was the waystone. Where the kiddo probably was. If her champion was down, then the enemy would find her easy prey. Fiery rage blossomed within his breast at the thought, and he caught a whiff of smoldering leaves.

He would not let it happen. Not again.

The innocent must be protected ... at all costs.

Bright yellow in the shape of a tall man burned in his vision. Too bright! He blinked to reduce his fire-assisted vision. The invader was close enough to make out from the way his moving form broke up the natural shadows and the faint sounds his passage made in the undergrowth.

Thomas concentrated on the inferno dwelling inside him, just like Balthazar Phoenixheart had taught him in the dreamworld. The Sage was an authoritarian taskmaster—no cozy chats while lounging against a reptilian elbow for Thomas—but the golden dragon-creature had painstakingly described the process of using his wyld to manipulate thermal energy.

Remembering his mentor's instructions, Thomas dipped into his reservoir and mentally rolled flames into a missile as if they were putty. Imagining crosshairs, he sighted his target. Nothing else existed.

He launched his missile. A lance made of fire sprang into existence and streaked toward the biped figure. He had a moment to glimpse orange eyes widening and then the world dissolved into heat and flame. The nightstalker howled and beat at his face. The reek of charred flesh filled the air. He chuckled. Nothing like a little nightstalker barbecue to spice up the place. With grim satisfaction, Thomas ignited the grasping hands with a thought.

Burn!

A wave of dizziness drove him to his knees. Cool, damp earth met his bare skin. Behind him, the anguished sounds abruptly ceased. Thomas disconnected from his inner fire and the flames on the man extinguished. No need to burn down the entire forest. He gave himself a moment to recover, then dragged himself over to check whether the nightstalker was dead. The charcoal briquette where his head had been assured him this was the case.

Let's see you get up from that, clown.

Something whistled through the air past his head. With instincts honed by training, he tucked his shoulder and rolled. *Blast it—the jokers must fight in pairs!* A male voice shouted in a consonant-heavy language that sounded like cursing. Thomas was up on his feet in a ready stance with the longsword at guard one and the shorter sword at guard three.

Darn it, legs, stop shaking!

The enemy blades retreated, then came at him again. He countered both with Cross Wind Low, and then resisted the subsequent attack with Parting the Reeds. His movements were mechanical, but clumsy, and his muscles screamed at the exertion. Light-headed, Thomas gauged his assailant.

Trying to overwhelm me so I don't flash-fry you, too, eh?

His opponent lunged, blades weaving in a pattern he suddenly recognized. Sir Rick had taught him. *This is the nehmwight style.* A chill ran through him as a pair of fiery orange eyes glared over the crashing blades from a gray-skinned face. The chill became cold fire. He'd seen features like that before— and not here, not in a swordfight. His scars prickled with ghostly agony as rage mounted within him like hungry flames. A stumble nearly lost him his right ear, and he barely raised the shorter sword in time to parry another blow.

Criminy. I can barely stand, let alone duel with this joker. Can't even go on the offense.

Jaw clenched, Thomas dodged his opponent's next thrust, feinted to the left, then lunged hard to the right with both swords raised in a cross block. Distantly, he noted that the blades made a nice set of crosshairs. Shouting curses, the nehmwight launched another series of dizzying thrusts and blows, and Thomas countered them. All but one.

Bright agony seared his left shoulder. Leering, the orange-eyed fiend knocked aside Thomas's second block. "You will die, wyldling. Kahntark Vespyrahl only wanted the maiden."

Wrath filled Thomas with renewed strength. He couldn't fail in this mission. Screaming wordless defiance, he lunged inside his opponent's guard, thrusting for the gut. The nehmwight parried the longsword. But the short sword found its mark.

Burn!

Thomas channeled the heat from his molten core through the blade and blasted his foe against a tree. The nehmwight shrieked, then spasmed and went silent as his head burst, jetting white-gold flames. The stench of scorched flesh filled the air. Wide-eyed, Thomas gaped as the fire winked out and his dead enemy slid to the ground.

Did I mean to do that?

"Doesn't matter," Thomas gasped. Satisfaction purred like a contented cat inside him. "Serves 'em right. Can't let those fiends ... take the kiddo."

He slumped to the ground. A piercing eagle-like shriek roused him. How long had he been lying there? His head swam and his stomach roiled. He attempted to rise. Pain shot through him. With a thready sigh, he clapped a hand over the wound.

Gotta stop the bleeding ... Cauterize the wound.

Eyes shut, he reached for his wyld. A spark remained. He pulled it up, forcing the flame into his own flesh. Agony flashed white and he nearly passed out again. For a moment, he panted, staring up into the black sky and the pretty stars. His throat felt raw and his shoulder throbbed. He found himself shaking with laughter.

Just one more scar to add to the collection. Good thing I'm ambidextrous.

Painfully, Thomas rolled to his feet, using the longsword for balance. He waited a moment for his head to stop spinning, then dragged himself toward the stone ring. At least it would be easy to find. An eerie light shone through the trees, but not the same as he remembered from the other waystones. This one's light shone bluer. His heart quickened. Was it time already? He ground his teeth against a fresh round of agony. *Heh. That's right. I have teeth again.*

"Kiddo better be there," he grumbled as he picked up the pace. "And the rest of them better haul their butts over here fast!"

Tree trunks stood out starkly like black bars, silhouetted by the glow ahead. Thomas skirted a boulder, and the stone ring came into view. A cloaked figure, head lolling, leaned against an upright stone. A dead nehmwight. The best kind of nehmwight. He tamped down a surge of vicious wrath, the desire to set the entire wood ablaze.

Keep it together, man. You have a job to do.

Squinting against the glare, he spied another tall, human form sprawled between the outer stones and the center. Two more figures huddled there, at the foot of a huge, glowing crystal.

Annabelle and her champion.

Thomas staggered toward the light. Only a stone's throw away from his goal—easily covered by a fit soldier in a short sprint—but his stupid, tired legs refused to work correctly. He paused, drawing in a sharp breath. "Kiddo," he called.

The girl stirred. Slowly, she lifted her head from the dog-man's chest and her eyes opened. Sapphire sparks and light-ribbons danced in the depths of the crystal behind her. Eyes fixed on her, he hobbled closer. "Annabelle. I'm coming."

She stared at him, lips parted, a frown wrinkling her brow. "Who are you?"

That's right; he wasn't a toad anymore. Why the hell would she recognize him? He grimaced at a stab of pain in his shoulder. Streaks of blue swirled in the opalescent light coming from the waystone. The light steadily increased. He crept closer, one hand pressed over his cauterized wound. "Kiddo," he grated out. "It's me. Toad. Er. Sir Thomas."

Her eyes widened as the confusion lifted from her face. "Toad!" Her sudden smile was like the suns coming out after a weeklong gloom of cloudy skies. As a strange warmth filled him—one that had nothing to do with his exhausted wyld—Thomas realized he would endure getting stabbed again, if it meant he was the reason for that smile. As he stumbled to the edge of the stone ring, an answering grin twitched at his lips.

I found her. I didn't fail. It's gonna be okay ...

The waystone flared, and he bit back a curse as he threw up an arm to block the light. "Annabelle!" Peering under his raised forearm, Thomas stumbled into the ring of standing stones. *Stupid legs—work!*

Annabelle reached for him. "Sir Thomas!" Panic threaded her voice.

He squinted as the waystone flashed again, a swirling vortex of sapphire light. With all his strength, he threw himself into the ring with one hand outstretched, shouting her name. As he crashed to the ground, pain drove away his senses. The glare winked out.

Did I make it in time?

"Kiddo?" he croaked.

Blinking away ghost light images, his gaze scoured the area between him and the waystone. A cold dread seeped into his very core and extinguished what little fire remained.

"No."

The empty space around the waystone mocked him. He'd fallen short. Because of his weakness, he'd failed in his mission. Just as he'd failed to save Enoch from abduction.

The girl and her champion were gone.

Walk on the Ocean

Sir Thomas! What happened to you?

Blue light dissolved into cold and darkness. One hand outstretched to a man who was no longer there, Annabelle hung, suspended, as heaviness engulfed her body.

Thomas ... He'd been ripped away from her. Just like Enoch had been. They were gone.

Desolation and terror squeezed her soul with icy tentacles. Panting, Annabelle suppressed the urge to break down and weep. No. This was neither the time nor the place for that. But where was she? She drew in a deep breath, trying to calm herself, and twisted from side to side. Everything flowed sluggishly, like molasses in February. Why did the air resist her movement? Pressure built in her chest and a thread of panic pulled taut around her heart.

Wait. Neither sensation belonged to her.

From above, light filtered through the dimness. She reached for it, but something was dragging her deeper into the darkness. Terror spiked. She looked down. On her hip, the last glimmer of Daar-Lûsin's faint opalescent light faded. Arms encircled her waist and bulging green eyes set in a black-splotched, white face stared up at her from the murk. Annabelle flinched. Her racing heart made it difficult to breathe.

Raeden! Bubbles burst from her mouth as she screamed his name.

He was sinking. Sinking? And ... bubbles? Holy cow! They were underwater. How was she not drowning? For a moment, she thrashed and clawed for the surface, her panic all her own.

But wait ... I'm breathing. I've been breathing this whole time.

Annabelle went still and remembered. She was a wyldling, the Weaver of Water. Using her imagination and the God-given connection to the Aethyr, she could manipulate water in all its forms. It naturally followed that she would be able to breathe within that realm. And then fear struck her anew.

Her champion possessed no such ability.

Annabelle grabbed Raeden's arms and kicked for the light above, pulling him along. Her muscles burned and her heart raced. The cuirass she wore dragged against her shoulders. She pushed back Raeden's terror filtering through their Oathbond. *Please, God, please help me. I'm not the best swimmer.* They rose quickly—more quickly than she believed possible.

Her head broke the surface, and she gasped, yanked up Raeden until his face was above water, then curled an arm under his head to keep him from sinking. He was so heavy—all dense muscle. At least she'd healed him, and he wasn't bleeding anymore.

Thank you, God, she prayed, *for Raeden's life and for delivering us from our enemies ...*

Their enemies. Oh, dear Lord. Were they in danger? An image flashed through her mind of a tall man wielding dual swords, his glowing orange eyes boring into her. He was going to kill Raeden, but then she'd—no! Annabelle shoved the memory away.

Trembling and clinging to her champion, she whipped her head around. No nehmwights here. Praise God! But also, nothing but ocean—she licked her lips and tasted salt—as far as her eyes could see.

"Water, water, everywhere, and not a drop to drink," as *Coleridge wrote. At least saltwater makes us more buoyant.* She let go of her champion with one hand long enough to rub water from her eyes, then paused, blinking through lenses dotted with moisture.

Thank God I still have my glasses! This time Toad— Thomas—isn't here to find them for me if I lost them ...

A half laugh, half sob escaped her raw throat as they bobbed like flotsam on the gentle waves. The cuirass dragged her down; she'd better remove the darn thing. Bracing her champion's head in the crook of her left elbow, she struggled to unbuckle the steel-braced leather armor with shaking fingers. Finally, the straps loosened. The cuirass caught on something, so she tugged until the stubborn armor ripped free and fell away from her. Immediately, she felt lighter.

She rested her forehead against Raeden's cheek, then froze. Wait. The Oathbond's song was muted. Raeden wasn't breathing. Panic—her own—filled her and her chest constricted. No, no, no. She couldn't lose him. Not her champion. Not her friend.

Under her prodding fingers, a pulse beat, slow and weakening. He still wasn't breathing. What about mouth-to-mouth resuscitation? She eyed his short, canid muzzle and contemplated how best to form a seal ... *Yuck.* But she would attempt it, for Raeden. If she could manage that while floating in the water. Ugh, no. They must get to shore. She glanced around wildly. Land humped up like a turtle's shell on the horizon, but it was far off. In between, she glimpsed what looked like a jumble of rocks. A reef, or a small island. But it would take time to get there.

Time Raeden didn't have.

With a sob, she bent her neck and touched her forehead to his, her mind grasping for answers. She knew a lot about human anatomy from her biology classes. It had aided her when she healed Raeden's stab wound. Surely, his respiratory system was similar enough to the diagrams she'd studied.

Please, God, one more time, please let me save him. She recalled the steps Lord Evanrudhe had taught her. How to consciously use her wyld—what she called the three C's.

"Calm the storm within. Concentrate on the desired result. Commit your wyld to action."

After taking a deep breath to calm herself, she concentrated on what needed to be done. First, his lungs must be purged of their suffocating weight. With the shining sapphire tendrils of her thoughts—her kythim—she delved along the natural conduit of the Oathbond. She visualized his lungs, their alveoli drowned in water, and imagined sucking the liquid out, like water traveling from roots up into a tree. Up through the minuscule, branching bronchioles, to the bronchi and then the trachea, past the larynx, and then—

Raeden convulsed, and she nearly lost him beneath the waves. She hugged him, propping his chin against a shoulder, and turned her head as he vomited water like a burped baby. He gulped air and shook with hacking coughs, his arms like steel around her, clinging to her. His thrashing threatened to drive them beneath the surface again. For a moment, panic drove out all reason; then, she recalled Commander Storm's lessons. She encased her mind in a bubble of ice, to block out her terror. It wouldn't last long, but in the meantime, she could think.

She took a deep breath and gathered facts from the swirling maelstrom of her thoughts. Fact: She was the Weaver of Water. Fact: she hadn't drowned, ergo, she wouldn't drown now. Fact: her champion couldn't breathe water like her. Fact: She needed to do something to keep Mr. Zero-Body-Fat from drowning. Fact: They needed a flotation device ... *but I can't just conjure up a rubber tube. What can I use?* Her calm fact-listing faltered, and panic beckoned with a toothy leer. She closed her eyes. *I'm the Weaver of Water. I can control the water, but there's nothing floating around here ... Ice!* Her eyes flew open.

Ice is just frozen water. You've made ice before, and ice floats. A memory surfaced of Dinah helping her to harness her new abilities. The dwelfnhad had made an interesting remark.

"Within the bounds of her Aspect, a wyldling is limited only by her imagination."

Determination flared. Imagination was something Annabelle had—in spades.

She reached for the sapphire pool at her core, concentrated, and envisioned a raft made of ice to buoy them. Nothing happened. Raeden thrashed, driving them underwater again. She fought panic—*you can breathe underwater, Ann!* —and kicked harder to propel them upward. *Please, God,* she prayed as she pushed Raeden's head above the surface. *Help me!*

"Ahdmerel," a deep, gentle voice spoke in her mind. Memories emerged of a blue dragon the size of three elephants and chained to a dais. Warmth and safety enfolded her as if she was cradled within his wings. But how could he be here? This wasn't the dreamscape.

Hadrien, is it really you? Help!

"I am here, child," he sent. "You are overreaching. An ice raft is an excellent idea, but you would soon succumb to the cold. I will show you how to build a raft without freezing the water. But first, you must calm yourself."

Images began flashing in the darkness behind her eyes. The Sage spoke in a soothing tone, describing the steps she must take.

Annabelle went still and allowed his silent words to shape her thoughts, from which she formed tendrils and sent spiraling down into her energy reservoir. She connected the sapphire pool to the water beneath her and Raeden and laid down a latticework of kythim in the pattern Hadrien supplied.

Water pushed against her legs and backside, flexible like a bubble, or an air mattress. Raeden's arms tightened. Hot breath fanned her neck. His entire weight squashed her as the buoyant structure popped them above the surface. She struggled to breathe, mentally calling: "Hadrien!"

All sense of her Sage had faded.

Hadrien?

Clouds swam in the blue sky, fire-rimmed black spots dancing sickeningly across them. Feebly, she shoved at her champion. *Get off me!*

Concern and confusion sang along the Oathbond. Another cough, and he rasped, "Anna?" He gasped, shuddering, and pulled his arms out from under her. Slowly, he pushed himself up. The raft wobbled, then settled as her champion went still.

Annabelle sucked in sweet air and stared into the green eyes blazing down at her. Water dripped from his disheveled, coppery hair onto her face. Anguish laced his voice. "Freylin!"

She forced a smile. "Hi. I'm okay. Are you okay?"

He reared up and then exclaimed something in his native tongue that sounded like a curse when the raft lurched.

Panic skittered along the edge of her mind, and she squealed, "Raeden, stop moving!"

Arms half extended, he froze. His chest heaved and he shivered as he stared into her face, with eyes round as saucers. Slowly, he lowered his arms and gazed all around. His eyes widened even more, his ears flattened, and a whimper escaped him. Anxiety crackled along the Oathbond. "Where did all the waters come from?" He looked at her. And then, eyes never leaving hers, he took three deep, steady breaths. Closing his eyes, he prayed in his native tongue, too soft and rapid for her to follow. Even if she understood the language.

Annabelle watched him closely, afraid to move. "Raeden," she ventured. "Is something wrong? Are you ..." She gulped. *Don't rock the boat, Ann.* Maybe a raft wasn't the best place to accuse a freaked-out kaenhir of being afraid. "Do you know how to swim?"

Her champion's eyes snapped open. They glittered wildly and his ears flattened against his head. He very pointedly did not look around. "*Nich,*" he replied, holding her gaze. "Your servant cannot—" he grimaced— "swim." He took a deep shuddering breath and bowed his head. "Here, he is like the duck in the desert."

"What?" Annabelle blinked at him. Did he mean "fish out of water?" But they were in the water! Hysterical giggles swelled in her throat. She swallowed them. If she started, then she wouldn't be able to stop. Water lapped against the edges of her raft. She felt her construct eroding, molecule by molecule. How long could she hold it together? Panic—she'd banished it only temporarily—licked at the edges of her mind. Raeden couldn't swim. And yet, somehow, they needed to reach land and find the others.

The others!

Annabelle inhaled sharply. Raeden leaned over her, concern replacing the mad gleam in his eyes. He reached toward her face, then drew the hand back, staring wide-eyed at the spelled water holding them up. "What is this?" Raeden pushed at the raft. Water sloshed as the surface gave, and his ears went back. "Freylin, this water is ... unnatural."

With her breath held, she couldn't respond as she concentrated on enhancing the surface tension of their bubble-raft so it wouldn't disintegrate beneath them. *There. Done.* She shivered. Had it grown colder? Releasing her pent-up breath, she glanced at her champion.

Raeden was in the midst of a breathing exercise. He met her gaze and his ears drooped. "Apologies. Your servant has failed you."

"No, Raeden, you didn't." Annabelle grabbed his hand. It blazed with heat as he pulled her up. Her head spun. He hissed through clenched teeth and his ears lifted. "Your hands are ice!" Carefully, they shifted around until she knelt facing him. She struggled to keep her head lifted.

Raeden chafed her hands, casting brief glances toward where the land and surrounding reef lay. "You are weary. Your servant must find for you a ... a safe haven for you to rest."

Feeling returned to her hands as he rubbed them. The dizziness receded. Annabelle frowned. "We have to find the others first."

"The others are on land," Raeden snapped, eyes flashing. She shrank back and his grip tightened. He shook his head. "Again, your servant apologizes, Freylin." With a final squeeze, he released her hands and then scrubbed his face. Taking a deep breath, he added, "He will master this fear. For you."

Annabelle bit her lip. She wanted to hug her friend, feel arms enclose and shelter her against the panic stalking on the fringes of her mind. But that would only freak him out even more. The Oathbond felt ... brittle. Gingerly, she touched one taut forearm. "It's okay, Raeden." She swallowed. Her voice trembled. "I'm scared, too."

His hands still covered his face. "Not like this," he groaned. "Not like this. Your servant has sworn to protect you. He cannot protect you here, on the waters ... from what could dwell in the water. He is ashamed, but he cannot hide how his fear makes him weak."

"You don't have to hide it from me. And you're not weak just because you're afraid." *I need to be strong for him.* Annabelle wrapped her fingers around his wrists. "Raeden, look at me." Terror quivered on the periphery of her thoughts, and her champion's fear compounded it. *Please, God, be with us.* She licked her lips, tasted salt. Darn it, she was thirsty. "Please, Raeden. We're all alone. I need my champion now. I need you."

Raeden lowered his hands from his face and met her gaze. She let go, her hands dropping to her thighs. She fussed with Daar-Lûsin, thankfully still in its sheath. "You know I'm a wyldling, right? Like Enoch, except I can do stuff with water, instead of wind." He nodded, and she took a deep breath, continuing in a stronger tone. She forced a smile. "Well, then, you don't need to be afraid of the water, so long as I'm with you, because I can control it."

Raeden's jaw tensed and his whiskers twitched. His gaze intensified. "Only the Almighty controls the Aspects. Take care, Freylin."

She winced, then laughed weakly. "Of course, God is in control of everything," she replied "I didn't mean to sound arrogant. It's not like I'm claiming to control *all* the water. Just a teeny bit. Enough to keep us from drowning, anyway." She grinned. "I made this raft using my power. Ability. Wyld." She was about to add that Hadrien had helped her, but then thought better of it. Raeden wouldn't take it well if she mentioned hearing voices. He still wasn't reconciled to the fact that the Sages weren't dead and one of them spoke to her in her dreams. And now, in the waking world. Somehow.

Closing his eyes, her champion took several deep breaths. "It is a very fine thing you have made," he replied, and opened his eyes. The terror and shame glittering in their depths receded, and the Oathbond reassured her with its warmth. "These tribulations are not what he would have wished for a little maiden, but the Threefold One knows best, and he has made you stronger." A smile quivered around his mouth. "Know that your servant is proud of you. Many thanks for saving this one's life from the dreadful waters." Fist to chest, he dipped his head in a bow.

"Um, yeah. Of course." Raeden was proud of her? Annabelle swallowed thickly. "I'm just sorry that we got separated from everyone else. How are we supposed to rescue Enoch now? Commander Storm's the only one who really knows his way around using the waystones, and now ..."

Raeden touched her shoulder, and she glanced up. "Pardon, Freylin," he said, eyes fixed on her face. "Your servant must pray. There is much to be thankful for, but he must also bring several petitions before the Almighty. Not least, that this raft finds its way to land very soon." He raised an eyebrow. "Perhaps the Almighty desires to hear from you, as well." Settling carefully back on his hams, he closed his eyes and murmured in his native tongue while fingering the crucifix around his neck.

A not-so-subtle hint that I should pray, too. Annabelle sent up a brief prayer of thanksgiving, a petition for Enoch's safety, and a request to reach land before her champion freaked out again.

When she looked up, Raeden was still praying. Good. She scanned their surroundings. Though the raft bobbed along the waves, the green and brown haze far off in the distance hadn't grown any closer, and neither had the rocky island between it and them. Unbidden, the refrain from a favorite song popped into her head about walking on the ocean, and she thought about Jesus walking on the Sea of Galilee. Too bad they couldn't do that here. Well, maybe someday she'd try it. Raeden would have a conniption if she attempted it now.

Annabelle frowned. Walking across the water wasn't an option, but perhaps she could use her wyld to make the raft move faster.

She closed her eyes and reached within for the sapphire pool of energy, then extended her kythim like tentacles, seeking a current. Something like a huge fist snatched up her awareness and swallowed it whole, dragging her rapidly into the depths. The immensity of the sea crushed her. Her kythim flailed, seeking purchase anywhere, but she was losing herself.

"Hadrien!" she screamed silently.

"Ahdmerel," his deep voice responded. "Calm yourself, child, and retract your kythim." Warmth encompassed her, pulling her back from the abyss and holding her secure, like a baby swaddled in a blanket. "I am here."

Annabelle drew in her kythim to cling to his great presence. "The current is so vast," she sobbed. "I can't harness it. How do I use it to get to shore?"

Hadrien's great wings shielded her from the cold and darkness. "Tapping into the gulf stream will only pull you further out to sea. You need not use one of the great currents," he soothed. "A lesser path along the island shelf will suffice. I will show you how to couple your raft to it, but it requires monitoring and occasional course corrections, lest you collide with the reef on the north side of Ynys Lloches." He sent more images of colorful threads woven into simple patterns.

What's Ynys Lloches? It sounds familiar.

She could wonder about that later. They needed to reach land. Annabelle focused on the steps Hadrien showed her. "I think I can do that," she replied. "Thank you." Reaching out, she coaxed strands of aquatic energy into the shapes she required, then held fast. She quivered with effort as she attached the weavings of water to her raft. "This takes a lot of energy."

"Indeed," he said, sounding strained. "The effort will tax your strength. But you are doing well. Remember, you can draw strength from the water itself. Once you reach Ynys Lloches, the gwerindawr will help you ..." His voice faded away again, like a radio moving out of frequency range.

The weavings took hold, little glowing threads hooking into her construct and stretching out toward the island. Annabelle grunted as the raft lurched. She reached out to the waters to replenish her energy. Vitality trickled inside Annabelle, and she redoubled her grip on the current. The water-threads she'd woven hooked in deeper, and this time they held, dragging the raft toward the rocky island.

She needed to get them to shore. And then they'd try to find the others—Thomas, Dinah, David, Peter, and Commander Storm—so they could continue their quest.

Annabelle fixed her attention on the current and clung to it with a death-grip.

We need to get to Y'Vasheirdenelle and find the answers we need: who's holding Enoch and where they took him. How else will we rescue him, otherwise?

Taboo

"Nobody's coming to save you, Milord Fancy-Jacket," William said, smirking. "So get used to the idea of being my prisoner." Grimacing, he rolled back his shoulders to keep the satchel straps from sliding down his arms on either side. Hidden under his burkheld—the robe worn by sorcerers and their apprentices—a portrait's edges poked him in the chest. Not that William needed reminding of its presence; the portrait's subject was never very far from his thoughts.

Enoch Northward, the erstwhile Acting Baron-Knight of the Northern Marches, crossed his arms and raised his eyebrows. "*Your* prisoner?" The Dreadlord had insisted Northward's fancy silver jacket and buckskin trousers be returned to him, but without boots adding to his height the bravado wasn't very impressive. His messily close-cropped hair and unshaven scruff didn't help.

Pointedly ignoring the heated glare of Zakaar Ravenos, the harkhurz assassin, the young knight made a show of looking around, and the band of soot-colored metal around his neck glinted in the lantern light. A derisive grin twitched at his mouth.

"Pretty sure this fortress belongs to the Dreadlord—your master's master."

He wasn't wrong. The Dreadlord had hired William's master to assassinate two Baron-Knights and capture a wyldling—tasks Tenebris had delegated to his assassin and his apprentice, respectively. At present, William stood with Northward and Zakaar in the courtyard behind the shield wall of Fastness, the Dreadlord's headquarters, a fortress the size of a small town built from mottled gray-brown stone. *Finally,* after eighteen days of traveling, they'd reached their destination. Now the real work would begin, and William's reward for capturing a wyldling for his master was in sight.

Speaking of ... William glanced around for the tall, black-robed sorcerer and sighed with relief; Tenebris was too busy directing the Dreadlord's minions regarding the disposition of his property to harangue William for dawdling. Aside from the servants, armored guards patrolled the courtyard, six of them full-blooded nehmwight warriors contracted to assist Tenebris. William caught the eye of Khalad, the squad leader, and they exchanged a nod. The respect of the elite warriors was an unexpected boon. He would be wise to foster it.

"And just because *you* believe no one will rescue me, Dulciber," the infuriating kadorei persisted, dragging William's attention back to him, "that doesn't necessarily rule out the possibility of me escaping." Tendrils of Northward's silver kythim—an aura that betrayed his moods—fluttered in an intangible wind while opalescent ripples pulsed outward from his head. Even after several weeks of captivity since the abduction, the fool still lived in hope.

William looked forward to squashing that hope; watching those ripples disappear and his kythim morph into flat gray lines, until it matched the collar binding his wyld. He blinked to clear his vision of Northward's aura, then loomed over the shorter youth with a broad grin. "Even if you could evade Zakaar and get past all the armed guards, the gates have a special locking mechanism and are heavily warded." He leaned closer. "To escape Fastness, you'd need the ability to fly. Oh, wait." He pulled a sad face. "The wyldling snare won't let you do that."

That got a reaction. An ugly snarl twisted Northward's mouth, and he tensed. Before he could move, Zakaar grabbed the prisoner and jerked him back. "Careful, Dulciber," the harkhurz said in heavily accented Tradespeak.

Northward tried to pull from his grasp while spitting curses at them both.

Zakaar's canine visage hardened, and he tightened his grip. "Remember, the warlock has battle training aside from his bound witchcraft. I think we should tie him up again, no?"

Doubtless a sly dig at William that he lacked such proficiency in the warrior's trade. But being an Arkhadahn, even an apprentice with only two circles, came with its own protections.

Scowling, he straightened and adjusted the straps of his satchels. "I warded myself against blunt-force trauma. If Milord Fancy-Jacket hits me, it'll rebound on him." The thought of Northward bending over and clutching bruised stones was enough to smooth away William's scowl. "And the Dreadlord said he's not to be physically restrained without an explicit order to do so. Oi!" He snapped, leaning over Northward and waving a finger. "Shut your suns-burnt mouth, you vomit-faced gutter-eel, unless you can come up with a better insult than 'son of a goat.' It's getting tiresome."

"William!" Tenebris roared, his bearded face contorted with fury.

Half-bent, William froze with his finger pointed at Northward, eyes widening as he glanced sidelong toward his master. His heart pounded like a hammer. Tenebris always harped on how much William owed him for saving his life from bloody sacrifice, for raising him to manhood after his mother abandoned him as a baby and training him to use power. But no matter how hard William strived for perfection, or how much he achieved, Tenebris always found something to criticize.

Merciful Valeshka, don't let Tenebris belittle me. Not here in front of everyone ... especially Khalad and his men.

Orange eyes blazing with perdition's rage, Tenebris strode across the courtyard, still shouting. "Quit bickering with the prisoner and deliver him to his cell, as you were told. And stand up straight," he said as he reached them. William hastily rose to his full height, but it still felt like his master towered over him.

"Did you secure the kaiber powder like I asked?"

William swallowed the whimper rising in his throat. *Burning suns! When he discovers I've consumed half our stock enhancing my Seeker's Web without his permission ...*

The master sorcerer arched an eyebrow. "Well?"

Not for the first time, William wished Tenebris's aura was visible to him. "Yes, M-Master," he replied in a small voice.

Northward snorted softly. His voice spoke in William's head. —*Sniveling coward*—

Inwardly, William screamed: *Oi! Shut it, Northward, or I'll have Zakaar wallop you.*

The captive flinched and his eyes bulged.

Ha! I was right. I can send as well as receive. He bit his lip to trap another whimper. *Void freeze it! What if Tenebris heard that?*

His Master's eyebrow arched higher, and he cupped a hand beside one pointed ear. "I must be getting old. I'm afraid I didn't catch your response, Arkhasuhl. You secured the kaiber powder, yes?"

"Er. Yes, Master," William responded. Tenebris must not have noticed the mental cry. If Tenebris had the ability to read minds, then William would've never gotten away with his resentful and treacherous thoughts. He doubted he'd still be drawing breath.

Speaking quickly, he added, "The kaiber powder ampules are in the rosewood chest under the spellform diagram." Minus the quantity he used and the three ampules he pinched yesterday. He already had an excuse ready if Tenebris questioned him further. The Dreadlord's special project required quite a bit of the potent narcotic.

Tenebris narrowed his eyes and looked down his nose. "You know I hate it when you mumble, William. As the sole Arkhadahn of the Thirteenth Order, I am the Highest. Show some blistering pride in your apprenticeship. Your blood may be impure—" William grimaced, his hands balling into fists. *Why did Tenebris always harp on that?* — "but you mustn't lower yourself to exchanging insults with the sort of barbarian kadorei filth who sired you." He sneered at the prisoner, who glared daggers at him.

"Kadorei aren't filth," Northward retorted. "I wish you blustering nehmwights could understand that we're all human beings, beloved of Lord Yshua—" The knight's voice cut off while his lips kept moving. Tenebris had muted Northward. Spell energy crackled and William shivered as a sympathetic tingle spread along the whorls of the two spelled circles inked across his shoulders. Thirteen circles allowed Tenebris to cast lower order spells merely with a thought.

William yearned for the day when he could do the same.

Still gripping Northward's arms, Zakaar's amber eyes glittered and his ears laid back. Spirals of muted orange appeared in his aura. The harkhurz grew uneasy whenever magic was used around him.

"That's better." Tenebris swung back to William. "You see? Instead of enduring his heckling, simply engage a muffling spell.

I know you're capable of that much." Leaning in, he hissed, "Don't make me regret rescuing you from the sacrificial altar. After all the Turnings I've spent training you in the ways of power, prove you're worthy to advance to the Sixth Order." Robes billowing, Tenebris stalked away to monitor the unloading of the wagon. There was a sensation like a cord snapping as the muffling spell ceased.

Northward snickered. "Witnessing that was worth being muffled." Zakaar shook him roughly, growling, but the knight chuckled.

William realized his fingers were still curled into fists, fingernails digging into his palms. Rage simmered like a potion over the fire, and he took a step toward the captive, who was grinning. By Villem's spear, he'd punch that smug expression off Northward's face ... Wait, no. An arkhadahn wouldn't sully his own hands. He had a better idea.

"Let go of him, Zakaar."

Brow furrowed, the harkhurz obeyed. Northward glanced back and forth between them, a frown replacing his mirth.

William stood rigid with his hands fisted at his sides. He schooled his expression into a blank mask. "Harkhurz."

Zakaar's ears lifted. "Yes, Dulciber?"

"The prisoner was impertinent to Ten ... to Master Tenebris. I give you permission to punish him—" he held up a hand when Zakaar moved with an eager gleam in his eyes— "Nothing permanent. Just something to remind him who holds the power here."

Northward lifted his chin. "The Threefold One." White streaks blazed in his silver aura.

Zakaar paused, uncertainty replacing the murderous glint in his eyes. One hand rose to touch a small bulge under his tunic.

Rolling his eyes, William groaned and rubbed his forehead. "Not this again. I've told you, Zakaar. You needn't worry about divine retribution. There are no gods. The Threefold One is a fairy-tale those lily-livered dwelfnim made up to keep the kadorei in line."

"You're a fool," Northward whispered. The white streaks faded to light gray.

"No, *you're* the fool, Milord Fancy-Jacket," William snapped, his hand creeping toward the opening in his burkheld. The wretched prisoner's idiocy had him craving whiskey. No. Not with Tenebris nearby. He forced his hand down to his side. "Foolish enough to get caught alone in the woods. A pampered and thuggish ignoramus with no conception of the power a wyldling actually possesses."

Despite his irritation, a smirk twitched at his lips. The power he'd have once he captured the pale maiden Northward believed he'd kept secret all this time. Recalling their meeting in the dreamscape made William's heart burn like a brand. His smirk vanished. Suns blister that maiden for the beguilement spell she'd cast over him! He'd pay her back for that.

Northward's brow furrowed. Ochre confusion spiraled through his kythim, mixing with red sparks of anger. *—What is this son of a goat up to? Regardless, I'm not rising to the bait—*

Hesitant, Zakaar glanced between them, clutching whatever trinket lay under his tunic. Even with the elixir suppressing his Blood Rage, the harkhurz had been panting for the chance to murder Northward over the past moon. He should be ecstatic. Why wouldn't he move now? The whole situation was irksome. William wanted to punch Zakaar, too. He wished he had the stones to go through with it.

Tenebris is watching. Must remain dignified.

William clenched his jaw and his entire body shook. "Burning suns!" he hissed. "Just punch him, Zakaar. Fold him in half and then lug him upstairs so we can dump him in his new quarters. Then we'll get something to eat."

The harkhurz shook his head as if to clear it. A vicious grin split his brown-furred visage, baring his fangs. "With pleasure, my friend."

Northward set himself, but Zakaar's eager fist hammered into his middle and doubled him over. Heaving the spluttering and red-faced youth over a shoulder, the harkhurz sauntered to the nearest bailey staircase.

As William turned to follow him, he inadvertently caught his master's gaze. Tenebris graced him with a slight nod. Satisfaction warmed the cold recesses of his heart at the Arkhadahn's rare approval, however slight. Usually, Tenebris loudly despaired of William ever advancing beyond the Second Order.

That all would change, now that they'd returned to Fastness. Tenebris had promised he would have six circles after undergoing the Arkhadahn's Trial. It was rare, but not unheard of for an apprentice to advance four orders in one go. He wasn't sure why Tenebris finally relented after holding him back over the past cycle. Perhaps his master finally recognized his potential.

William snorted softly, sweeping back his burkheld to keep from tripping over the hem as he ascended the staircase in Zakaar's wake. *Somehow, I doubt that's the reason he's putting me to the test. I need to proceed with caution. Make contingency plans.*

Zakaar mounted the steps swiftly. William glanced up, met Northward's furious blue-eyed glare, and experienced a frisson.

—I may be bound here and now in my body, but my soul will always be free. Unlike yours, nehmwight. The devil take you—

Don't react. William's lips tightened as he inhaled sharply through his nose and tried to keep his astonishment from registering on his face. It appeared the tessaramint was out of the bag. Northward knew William could read his mind. Or at least suspected and was testing it out.

Just like I would do, were I the prisoner in this scenario.

William was fairly certain that Northward couldn't actively read *his* mind. He'd caught himself thinking about the portrait and its subject around Northward—it was difficult not to, because the two had the same eyes, even if Northward's were often squinted in anger—and Northward hadn't reacted to William's musings.

This warrants further study and experimentation ... just not tonight.

Zakaar attained the landing. Bent over the assassin's shoulder like a sack of enraged potatoes, Northward switched from a mental to verbal barrage of insults.

William laughed. "Say that again. 'Scat of a verminous swine?' Better, but your delivery needs work."

"Your insults are no better than mine, you half-breed bastard."

Zakaar froze.

William paused with one foot on the next stair. Long ago and far away, a child wailed for its mother from the darkest recesses of his mind. William blinked and took a deep breath. His ears were ringing. Schooling his face to calmness, he breezily replied, "What did you call me?"

"Did I cut too close to the bone, *Dulciber?*"

William forced a smile, but it went crooked, so he banished it. "You say that name like it's an insult, or a taboo subject. It isn't."

Even if Tenebris meant it to be so. A constant reminder that a filthy kadorei barbarian had sired him. That William's nehmwight mother had abandoned him on an altar—a blood sacrifice to the gods—rather than confront that shame.

Affecting nonchalance, he climbed the rest of the stairs. "And no, you didn't cut me, to the bone or otherwise. I just wasn't sure I heard you correctly. Zakaar, I believe the

Dreadlord assigned Milord Fancy-Jacket the third room on the right. Toss him in, and we'll go find our supper."

He waved the harkhurz along, his eyes tracking Northward until Zakaar shoved him into his quarters.

Bastard. Half-breed. They were only words—words Tenebris called him all the time—and William wouldn't allow the words to hurt him. Even if they were the truth.

William hadn't realized how wound up he'd been until he stood inside his own room for the first time in moons. He breathed in the familiar scents of ink and parchment overlain with the dust of neglect, and the tension melted from his frame.

After sending Zakaar to fetch their supper, he stalked past Northward's prison—he didn't want to deal with the ignorant barbarian until after he had something in his stomach—then three doors down to his own chamber. He closed his eyes and reached out through his arkhabala. The tattoos prickled, crawling along his skin and forming new configurations as he sent his awareness questing, tracing the patterns of the wards he'd set before leaving a season ago.

As William expected, the spells had decayed into husks. It took little effort to dismantle them. He snorted softly. His constructions seemed amateurish compared with what he was capable of now. A determined adept could've broken into his chambers, but a careful scan revealed there'd been no intrusion.

He exhaled slowly. *One less thing for Tenebris to punish me for failing,* he mused as he unlocked and pushed through the door. *I'll reset the defense wards, stronger than ever.* It didn't matter whether there was anything worth warding against, or that Tenebris could easily bypass the wards and enter his rooms whenever he pleased. A master Arkhadahn expected his apprentice to maintain his wards in top working condition as a matter of pride.

Muttering a cantrip, William conjured a pair of orange werelights and sent the small, glowing orbs to inhabit the lamps hanging in opposite corners. One over his workbench and the other over his drafting desk. The chamber brightened. William smiled. He'd designed the lamps himself, with lenses to amplify the meager light.

He tossed one of two satchels on his bed. The other satchel—containing his personal anchor items, spell components, and several of his treasures—he placed more carefully on his workbench. Opening the satchel, William peered inside. The silver torc glinted in the werelight, and the strange, L-shaped weapons were there in their holsters. He already had in mind a good hiding place for the items he'd confiscated from the knight with the golden aura.

The one I somehow turned into a toad. As he fastened shut the flap, William shuddered at the memory. He still had nightmares about that man and his blazing sword even when he wasn't in the dreamscape.

Once freed of their burden, his restless hands immediately dove inside his burkheld, checking for several other treasures he didn't dare keep anywhere except on his person. *Of course they're still there.* Casting a glance at his door, he pulled out his flask, set it on the table—Empty, suns curse it—and then extracted a jar wrapped in wool, which he peeled away. He held the jar up to the light. Inside, something moved.

William grinned. "Welcome to your new home, Milady Blue," he said. After unscrewing the lid, he tipped the jar, shaking its contents into his waiting right hand. A moth the size of a sparrow landed on his palm, fluttering dark blue wings threaded with silver. He raised the moth level with his eyes. Feather-like antennae twitched as huge, glistening eyes regarded him from a furry visage. Odd, to think an insect could have a face and an expression. But this moth did. She seemed ... sad.

"Don't worry. You'll be happy here. The Dreadlord told me which nectar regina moths prefer, and you're in luck. There're plenty of lilies growing in the garden. I'll bring some up for you later." William gently dislodged the moth from his hand to crawl on a sprig of dried fragrant grasses sticking out of a bottle on his desk. A soft smile curved his lips as he admired the streaming tails of the moth's backwings.

She's very pretty, just like her namesake.

Heat rose to his face, and he cleared his throat, stepping back from the workbench. "Need to find more whiskey," he muttered, fingers brushing against the portrait. He found himself pulling it out of his sakkhelt and furiously jammed it back inside.

Villem's spear! You've got her features memorized; there's no need to look at it now. Unpack the anchor items and reset the blistering wards before Tenebris decides to barge in and harangue you for laziness.

He unpacked his satchels and returned items to their places while the moth hung around the lamp. Occasionally, he spoke to her, explaining his strategy for passing the Arkhadahn's Trial and advancing to the Sixth Order. "I don't know exactly when Tenebris plans to test me, but he said it would be soon." After stowing his spellform anchor items inside the pigeonholes dedicated to them above his workbench, he carefully gathered up the moth and put her back in the jar. "Can't have you blundering into my wardspell."

Just then, someone knocked on his door. William froze, heart in his throat. "Who's there?" he shouted.

"Dulciber, it is me," Zakaar replied, his voice muffled by the stout wood. "I have brought your supper."

Oh, that's right. I told the harkhurz to do that. With a sigh of relief, William opened the door. "Bring it in, then."

Zakaar entered the room with a serving tray, hesitated by the worktable, then set the tray down on William's bed. Turning, he cleared his throat. "Dulciber, Milord asked me to give you this." He pulled out a wax-sealed envelope from his jacket pocket and handed it to him.

William stared at his master's seal impressed in the red wax, trepidation and excitement sizzled along his nerves in turn. He was fairly certain of the message's contents. He worked moisture into his suddenly dry mouth. "Did he say anything else?"

"No," Zakaar replied. He peered into William's face, amber eyes alight with concern. "Are you well, my friend? You have not yet read the note."

Hands shaking, William broke the seal and unfolded the letter. He quickly perused the message's contents. "Master Tenebris has summoned me to be tested. Tomorrow. Midnight. On the northwest battlements. Burning suns!" That left him with less than a day to prepare. He looked up at Zakaar with wide eyes, panic scrabbling with cold little rat's feet. "I wasn't expecting it to be *this* soon."

"Are you worried about failing, Dulciber?"

Bridling, William examined his visage and kythim for any sign of derision. He found none. His shoulders slumped. "Perhaps a little. I've studied hard, and I'm prepared, but there's always that niggling doubt." He grimaced. "Tenebris always makes tests extremely difficult."

"Hmm." After gazing at him for several heartbeats, Zakaar reached inside his tunic and brought out a clattering collection of eight soot panther fangs tied on a string. With a quick jerk, he snapped the string and held it out to William. "Here. Take these. I have seen you use things such as these in your—" he grimaced— "magic. They will give you power, no?"

"Er, yes." William gaped, staring at the string of teeth. They were magnificent specimens. He'd coveted them since Zakaar extracted them from their dead owners' mouths. "But ...You killed those soot panthers. The fangs are your trophies. Why give them to me?"

Zakaar shrugged. "It is a small thing. I know how much you yearn for more circles drawn on your back. I hope these help you gain them."

Just like that?

Doubtless, Zakaar gave them to William now out of gratitude for the elixir that treated his Blood Rage. Or as payment for allowing Zakaar to beat up Northward. No one had ever just *given* William something before. Everything was transactional. Tenebris had taught him that. Items or services were exchanged for other items or services deemed of equivalent value. Sacrifices, usually of blood, and often of pain, must be made to obtain power. Power was everything, and nothing else mattered in light of that fact.

Head tilted and brow furrowed, Zakaar thrust the string closer. William snatched the fangs before the harkhurz could change his mind. Shoving them inside his burkheld, he snapped, "You're not getting these back, understand? I plan to make a talisman out of them."

Zakaar blinked. His whiskers twitched and humor glimmered in his eyes. "I do not expect the fangs to be returned, Dulciber. They are a gift—one friend to another."

"Oh. Well. Then. Um ... thank you." William turned and stalked over to his supper tray before the heat rising to his face showed, but the blistering harkhurz could probably smell his embarrassment. He waved a hand in dismissal. "Leave me. And don't come knocking again tonight. I'll be studying the rest of the night. And then I'll be sleeping."

With an Arkhadahn's Trial looming, he'd need as much rest as he could get.

Smoldering Shame

"Sir Thomas, wake up."

He'd recognize that implacable basso rumble anywhere. Commander Storm. From all around came the sounds of myriad frogs calling, insects buzzing and whirring, and the occasional feline screech. He parsed out the song of crickets and saliva sprang into his mouth. Crickets were tasty. Pungent herbal scents and wood-smoke filled the still air, although underneath he detected the decay-stench of a swamp. Heat baked the left side of his body but did little to placate the cold emptiness howling to be filled. Everything hurt.

Do I even want to wake up? With a groan, he opened his eyes, only to have white radiance stab into them. One of Dinah's lumen gems, holding the darkness of night at bay. He was sick of bright lights coming from crystals. Squinting, he turned his head away, toward the warmth. Something touched his wounded shoulder. He lashed out with his right arm. His arm?

That's right. I'm a man again. His heart felt like something squeezed it and he found himself gasping for air.

A hand grasped his wrist, arresting the movement with shameful ease. "There, there, now," said a shaky female voice. "Steady, Sir Thomas."

While taking deep breaths to steady himself, he focused on the person touching him. The dwelfnhad, Dinah, knelt beside him. Releasing his arm, she returned to spreading something cool and numbing on his shoulder. Her topaz eyes were red-rimmed. Dirt and worse smudged her beautiful face, streaked by tear lines, and perspiration matted black hair against the umber skin of her forehead. Dents peppered her rust-red and ruby armor—markings that hadn't been there when he'd last seen her.

"At least you've returned to your proper form," she added, with a wan smile. "That's a blessing. The healers did say the transformation could occur at any time, but the battle must have triggered it. How are you feeling?"

"Like something the Cat-Vulture dragged in," Thomas rasped, then frowned. Something was missing. It was dark, but he had no sense of the time. Was it still the same day? Where were they? His tunic clung to his skin. It hadn't been this muggy on the ridge where they'd made their stand at the waystone. And why was Dinah crying?

Then the knowledge struck him like a blow to his gut: *Annabelle's gone.*

Looking past Dinah, he met the troubled gaze of Commander Storm where he sat on a rock in the flickering firelight. The lumen gems surrounding their campsite clearly revealed his superior officer's fatigue. An emotion in his eyes Thomas had never seen.

Annabelle's gone. It's all my fault for being weak and slow.

He swallowed with difficulty. There was no point in apologizing. "Sir, I failed. They went through. I couldn't stop it. I wasn't fast enough—"

Without looking around, Commander Storm held up a hand, and Thomas shut his mouth. "The waystone activated ahead of schedule," the evainghir said in an even tone. "Either it reacted to the womanchild's wyld or to the relic she carried. Wherever they went..." Averting his gaze, he paused to clear his throat. "Wherever they went, it was not here."

"Wait." Thomas blinked. Despite the pain in his joints, he tried to sit up, but Dinah gently pushed him down with an admonishment to stay still until she finished. "Is there a chance the kiddo's okay? And what do you mean by 'here?' Have we gone through the waystone, then?" Belatedly, he added, "Sir."

"Aye." Commander Storm rested his forearms on his thighs, fingers dangling loosely between his knees. "The waystone brought us to the Sweltmire, which lies in the Ragenvue of the Southern Marches. We traveled to the edge of the swamps whilst you slept. You have been out of commission for several hours. As for the womanchild ..."

He sighed, slumping further. "Although nothing is certain, the womanchild holds Daar-Lûsin. Therefore, she and her champion were most likely delivered to a place of relative safety. Whatever their destination, it is not a place to which my vashenta grants access." He paused, tapping the shield-shaped amethyst pendant resting on his broad chest. Thomas's eyes went wide as he shook with a frisson.

The Commander's not wearing his armor. Has perdition frozen over?

"This means they went somewhere outside of the common waystone nexus," the Commander continued as his tone grew bleaker. Thomas opened his mouth to ask what he meant, but the evainghir went on. "That limits it to twelve possible locations on Tehara. Within the next eight days, we should arrive in Y'Vasheirdenelle. The nexus there has access to all waystones across the planet" Hollow-eyed, he stared at the fire, toying with the pendant. He didn't react when Peter swooped in, the breeze of his passage stirring Thomas's unkempt hair.

Unease curled in Thomas's stomach. Commander Storm had always been a pillar of strength and implacable resolve. He'd never seen the Commander look so weary, so ... defeated.

The syrax squawked, but even he sounded uncharacteristically subdued. "Still no sign of'em. They didn't come here." He sighed, ruffling his pink feathers, and raked his talons across the ground. *Scritch. Scritch.* "Lady Dinah, I brung them herby things you asked for, to keep the bugs away." Hanging his head, he muttered, "I still think we shoulda looked around more for Anna-belly and Dog-face, back where we come outta the waystone."

"Thank you, Peter." Dinah sniffled, extracting the limp plants from Peter's harness. She wiped her nose on her forearm and cast a glare at Commander Storm, speaking in a clipped tone. "I agree. But it's a moot point at present. We have a schedule to keep."

Turning aside, she rose to her feet. Her voice softened. "Excuse me, Sir Thomas, I must throw the vermin-bane on the fire, and then I'll brew medicinal tea for us." Her scabbard clicked against her armor as she moved away, just as her cousin strode into view, followed by two riding deer and his war elk.

Dinah gaped. "David, what in all of Tehara is that ... that *thing*?"

Stepping out from the darkness and into the radius of the lumen gems' light, the handsome dwelfnhir carried what looked like an alligator the size of a saddle under one arm. "A bog-lizard. Their skin is tough, but I managed to stab it through its brain." Sure enough, sticking out of the reptile's head, the hilt of his belt knife glinted in the light.

Peter's ears lifted and his eyes brightened. His tongue swiped around his beak. "Mmm. There's good eating on one o'them bog-lizards. Back before I fledged, my uncle on my mam's side useta catch one for the Grand Roost Festival. Dee-leck-tay-bull." He clacked his beak. "They taste like piggies, but better!"

Bending over the kettle, Dinah giggled. She shook her head. "Oh, Peter ..."

"Indeed, they do." David nodded, his lips twitching. "I thought so as well. Better not to waste the meat. The beast grabbed at Tinker's nose when he bent to drink from the pond back yonder." He jerked his head to indicate the direction; he held the reins of Annabelle's limping stag in his other hand. At least her riding deer—*Tinker! Remember the name!* —had survived, even if the other mount hadn't. Hopefully he'd see the kiddo's elation if they were ever reunited.

Thomas curled his fingers into fists. *When* they were reunited.

"Heya, Wart-bag," Peter said, his eagle eyes fixing on Thomas. "Glad t'see you're finally awake. Blessings on being all human-like again, and etcetera. I been meanin' to ask you about Anna—"

David interrupted. "Peter, may I borrow your beak and talons?" He set down his burden by the fire. Bracing a foot against the bog-lizard, he yanked out his knife.

"Okee-dokee." Tail lifted, the syrax trotted over to help with the butchering.

Eyes narrowed, Thomas tracked his progress. What had the crazy Cat-Vulture been about to say about Annabelle? "We'll find her," he muttered. "And I'll bring her back from wherever she's gone."

Even if it kills me. Criminy. I need to make up for my failure.

"Do not worry, Sir Thomas," David said as he stretched out the alligator-thing on its back. "If anyone can locate Miss Wells and Lord Raeden, it is the Caretaker of the Fortress of Living Stones." He crossed himself, and added, "Threefold One willing."

"If the Eldest will deign to speak with me," the Commander rumbled, as if to himself, as he stood, placing a hand on the pommel of the sword at his hip. "She and I did not exactly part on the best of terms."

Thomas grimaced. *That's right. This "Eldest" person we're supposed to meet has a beef with the Commander.* Even with an ambassador and Stonesingers along, she might not help them at all. "What's the problem, sir? I thought this elderly caretaker lady at the Stone Mansion was an ally who would assist us."

"The Eldest," Commander Storm replied, stressing the title, "is an ally." He gripped the sword, as if on the verge of drawing. "However, she and I had a ... disagreement ... regarding military necessity and priorities in times of war. She has not forgotten. And the fact that she refused to answer the last message I sent indicates she holds a grudge." Squinting into the darkness, he said, "Dire circumstances or not, the possibility exists: she may turn us away without a hearing."

Thomas leaned his head back and looked up at the stars. Grim resolve filled the cold hollow in his gut. "If that turns out to be the case," he rasped, "then I'll find a way to *persuade* this person to help us find Annabelle. I'll set her feet on fire if I have to."

That got the Commander's attention. "You will do nothing of the sort, Sir Thomas. You will accord the Eldest the same respect and courtesy you owe me as your superior officer."

Still staring into the sky, Thomas bit back a scowl. "Yes, sir." He could do as much—on the outside, at least. His innermost thoughts remained his own, where he pictured the Caretaker as a cranky old lady in a rocking chair, surrounded by cats, and waving a cane.

"Why do you call the Caretaker 'Eldest,' sir?"

"Because she is the eldest of the Sages' offspring still living."

"There're others aside from you, sir?" Thomas frowned. In his mind's eye, the cranky old lady grew scales and a tail. She still waved a cane, though. He tried not to snicker.

Releasing his sword, the Commander sighed. He ran a hand down his face. "Aye. Although her father was Ebenezzar

Earthshaker." He grimaced. "This is not a topic I wish to discuss, here and now."

Why is he so touchy about his family? I can't even remember mine. Dismissing that line of thought, Thomas nodded. "Understood, sir."

Commander Storm skirted the fire and came to hunker beside him. Whatever ailed him before, he seemed to have overcome it. His gaze was direct. "Do you deem yourself fit to continue, soldier?"

"Of course, sir," Thomas replied, raising his right fist to his chest. It took more effort than he thought it should. "Fit as a fiddle, and rarin' to go. Why wouldn't I be? Unless I turn back into a friggin' toad," he grumbled.

Back in Treehome, the dwelfnim doctors assured him he wouldn't once he returned to his human form, but they also admitted the spell had decayed to the point that they could no longer study it in detail. The doctors used a lot of fancy words to explain their conclusions. All Thomas derived from the mumbo-jumbo was that they were probably guessing about most of it.

"I remain confident that you will not." Commander Storm's reptilian visage betrayed nothing of his feelings, which settled Thomas's unease. They were back to business as usual. "Based on my examination once we arrived here, you will not revert. However, I remain concerned about the curse that transformed you into a toad," the Commander said. "Whether it shall have unforeseen effects. The spell work was something neither the Council nor myself had seen before. Dark energies, woven alongside Aethyric elements in a clumsy, yet potent fashion the healers feared to unravel, lest it do you lasting damage. Now that you are once again a man—"

"Sir," Thomas blurted. "Sorry, but hold on. Back up a minute. How do you know for sure I won't change back?" Jeremiah Bullfrog! How he'd *missed* having opposable thumbs!

The Commander's brow furrowed. "As the healers predicted, the malecto grammerye—"

"Malecto-*what?*"

"The curse that transformed you."

Commander Storm harrumphed. "If it will reassure you, lad, then I will examine you again." He leaned in, peering closely. Violet sparked in his eyes; it could be a trick of the lumen gems' light, but Thomas had long since concluded his superior officer possessed arcane abilities of his own. "As I stated, the curse has completely dissipated. You need not fear a ... reversion."

A weight lifted from Thomas that he hadn't noticed until it was gone. He closed his eyes. "Joy to the world and praise all the angels and saints in heaven."

"All glory be to the Threefold One," David intoned while he sliced away chunks of bog-lizard flesh, and Dinah responded, "Alleluia and Amen."

The Commander grimaced. "Despite this," he continued, "your transformation and the ordeal of the past hours has exacted its toll, and I guarantee there will be further physical trials ahead. Clearly, you require time to adjust to these ... changes. To recover, and rest. Under these circumstances, there is no shame in admitting to weakness, Sir Thomas. Or delegating your responsibilities to others."

Anger flared. *Oh, heck no. You're not leaving me behind.* He inhaled sharply. "I'm here for the long haul, sir. For Enoch. And Annabelle."

A memory of Enoch flashed through his mind, the first time Thomas recalled meeting the kid. Back when he was a toad. The kid stood on the trail back in the Darkenwood Forest, determination blazing in his eyes. *"I'm on a mission to find some missing people,"* he'd said.

Thomas clenched his jaw. Enoch was taken, and he couldn't save him because he was a toad and didn't realize he possessed a fire wyldling's power. But Thomas could have protected Annabelle. *I've gotta make this right somehow.*

Commander Storm regarded him for a long moment. "Let me make one thing very clear, Sir Thomas. My primary duty—and yours—is the security of the combined realms. The nature of this mission does not allow for delays. If I cannot wrest the lad from his captors before the moon turns, then we must shift focus to a war footing. Full-blooded nehmwights would never cooperate with Captain Wuya, and their presence near the last waystone cannot be coincidence." He shook his head. "No. The entire scenario smacks of something deeper. The lad's abduction could not have come at a worse time. With the might of the baron-knights reduced by half—and the Veils potentially failing—I anticipate that Vespyrahl will soon invade."

Vespyrahl. The most powerful of the nehmwight warlords. If he was responsible for what happened to Enoch ... Searing anger ripped through Thomas as he clenched his jaw and swallowed an oath. *I'll char broil Vespyrahl alive!*

"The political ramifications of the power vacuum have become dire." Dinah said in a small voice. "Based on the reports that refugees brought to Y'Dendordenelle, the Eastern Marches are in such disarray that the Council considers Fulcrum County a lost cause."

"Fulcrum County is the least of our worries," Commander Storm snapped. "The entire continent will fall into chaos and ruin whilst our enemy holds the last Sel Drayven prince like a sword over our necks."

Startled from his anger, Thomas's fractured memories clicked together like puzzle pieces. He'd known in his gut that Enoch was important—just not the scope of his importance. Now, a memory surfaced of Sir Rick on his deathbed—only they hadn't known it would be his deathbed at the time.

The elder knight had smiled at him from his sweat-stained pillow. "Thank you for coming so quickly, Sir Thomas. Before you rush off in search of those girls, there's a matter of great importance I need to share with you." He chuckled weakly. "Forgive me for the melodrama; this illness has reminded me of my mortality. If anything happens to me, I place the Northern Marches and guardianship of my ward in your capable hands. Above all, you must protect Enoch. He's the last of the Sel Drayven bloodline. The heir to the throne of Kellindashelle."

On his knees, Thomas gripped the Baron-Knight's trembling hand. He had no idea where Kellindashelle was, but he'd do anything for this man, who'd taken him in and trained him as a knight. "On the off chance that happens to you, Sir Rick, then I swear by all that's holy that I'll watch out for the kid. I'll keep him safe, and the realm, too." And then they both signed legal documents, which three of the Manor stewards and the garrison captain witnessed.

There was no way he'd break his promise to Sir Rick further by giving up now.

Facing his superior officer, Thomas cleared his throat. "Please, sir," he said. "I swore to Sir Rick I'd protect Enoch ... I must see this through. My strength will return; all it'll take is regular exercise and hard work. Which I can do as we travel. Allow me a chance to prove myself."

Commander Storm regarded him for a long moment. "Very well. Keep me apprised of any ... aberrations." He stood, turning to include the others. "Now," he continued after clearing his throat, "before we turn in for the night, I shall lay out our itinerary. Come, Sir Thomas, and seat yourself by the fire."

"Yes, sir." Thomas rolled on to his belly and struggled to get his elbows and knees underneath. His muscles burned, and his limbs trembled, but he pushed himself up on hands and knees with a pained grunt. He hunched over, panting and shaking.

Tears burned in his eyes behind a curtain of snarled hair. He blinked them away. Why was moving so blasted difficult? Thank God the kiddo wasn't here to see this. At the thought, shame smoldered throughout his entire frame.

The Commander's testing my fitness to continue. I'll show him I can!

When he lifted his head, the others were staring at him. David, having set up skewers of meat by the fire, was now on his feet with concern alight in his dark eyes. Poised in the midst of brewing tea, Dinah seemed about to jump up to help him. Even Peter had taken a few steps toward him, bog-lizard offal falling from his half-open beak.

Anger seared through Thomas alongside his shame. *I wish they'd stop looking at me.*

Eyes round and wide, Peter broke the silence. "Wart-bag, are you gonna be okay?"

Commander Storm surveyed Thomas with a trooper's wooden expression. "Sir Thomas, are you certain all is well with you?"

Swallowing his anger, Thomas forced a grin. "I'm just a little stiff. I'll be fine in another day or so. Should've stretched before I passed out, I guess." He barked a laugh. "That'll teach me to change shapes in the middle of a fight."

Dinah and David exchanged worried glances, and David stepped toward him. "Would you like a hand up, Sir Thomas?"

"No, thanks. I'm good. I'm just a toad-hop away," he replied with a laugh, shuffling to the log Dinah placed for him. His laughter sounded shrill to his ears. "You know, I'm used to being nearer to the ground. This brings back *fond* memories." Inwardly, he seethed at his weakness. The way they trembled, he didn't trust his legs to hold him up if he stood. How had he endured running around and fighting last night? Perhaps that was why he was so weak now.

Commander Storm waited for Thomas to settle on the log and receive a mug of tea from Dinah. "Ambassador, create a map of the region."

Dinah hurried over to the Commander and knelt, placing a hand on the ground. Her brow furrowed with concentration. Dirt and pebbles rose and shifted into shapes reminiscent of landforms, a bas relief representation of terrain in miniature. Thomas blew on his tea, whistling. Throughout their journey, Dinah had done this once or twice before—Annabelle had been delighted by it—and it still impressed him.

Commander Storm, who'd found a stick to use as a pointer, began speaking. The words of his preamble didn't register, rolling over Thomas as he basked in the fire's glow, its heat soaking into him like a restorative. Gradually, his aches and pains began to recede. Now, this was more like it. A bit like absorbing energy from the suns, if not as satisfying.

He carefully sipped the steaming tea, which tasted bitter despite the mint Dinah had added. It didn't seem as hot as it should; by all rights it should be scalding him. He watched the stick jab at salient features. The bog-lizard meat sizzled as its juices dripped, hissing, into the fire. An aroma like bacon, only sweeter, hung in the air, mixing with the pungent odor of the vermin-bane. Nausea twisted his stomach, and he swallowed with difficulty. The pork-smell brought him back to the battle, and the charred corpses he'd left in his wake. How he'd gloried in the destruction of his foes.

I really torched those nehmwights. But why was I so happy to kill them? That feels ... off. I don't believe I ever fought with such rage inside me before. He shook his head. He'd worry about that later. The Commander was getting to the important part.

"The next waystone lies a two-day's march north of here. We should arrive before it activates. After that, two waystones lie before us before we reach Y'Vasheirdenelle and the answers we seek. Based on what we discover there, two avenues lie open before us: either we follow our current course and rescue the lad, or we travel to the County of Mirrors, where we'll muster troops for the war against Vespyrahl." After a pause, he added, "Sir Thomas, I am uncertain whether you should continue on this journey without facing Phoenixheart's trials."

Thomas sprayed tea into the fire. "What?" *Criminy! I failed the Commander's test.*

David coughed, waving away steam.

Raising his brow, Commander Storm looked up from the rough map he was scratching into the dirt with a stick. "I find your ... weakness following the transformation concerning. Perhaps it would be wisest for you to sojourn in Y'Vasheirdenelle until you recuperate. The nexus there connects with the waystone in the Evergold Desert of Losaridos. You can face the Sage's trails—as he has offered in your dreams— and obtain the sourekghar hidden within the Crucible." He nodded toward David. "The Shepherd has offered to make the journey with you."

David nodded. "I have traveled through the Western Marches before, including the Evergold Desert, and I would be honored to accompany you. To assist in any way I can."

"Uh huh, thanks." Thomas narrowed his eyes at his superior officer. "What all would this entail, sir? How long of a sidetrack?" *And what sort of trials?* He suppressed a shiver. He had some idea of that part. Balthazar had told him.

"You must confront your inner demons, Helzarvenn."

Pushing that aside, he listened as Commander Storm explained the scope of his side quest. After passing through the nexus at Y'Vasheirdenelle, it would take two days to reach the Crucible, possibly several more days to obtain the sourekghar— he wouldn't say how long the Sage's challenges would take—and then another week traveling to yet another waystone that would send them back through another waystone within three days' walking distance of the Fortress of Living Stones, where the Caretaker would relay further orders from the Commander. Hopefully.

Thomas ground his teeth. *A week's delay, on top of Balthazar's trials, probably more due to the trials messing up my head*—after facing the trials to obtain Daar-Lûsin, Annabelle was distraught for a week and good for nothing—*after five days spent traveling to the Caretaker's Fortress? That's too blasted long. Annabelle and Enoch needed my help* yesterday. *I have to save them. I have to undo my failure, somehow.*

"With all due respect, Commander," he said, voice tight, "I'd rather continue on with you. The Crucible can wait until I find ... I mean, until we find the kids."

His eyes cold as dirty ice, Commander Storm went still. "So be it," he rumbled. "But if you have not sufficiently recovered by the time we reach the Fortress of Living Stones, I shall leave you behind with the Eldest until you do. Understood, soldier?"

The last thing he wanted was to be dumped off for some cranky old, scaled lady to baby-sit. Was this how Annabelle had felt when the Commander threatened to leave her at Treehome? Well, he'd just need to get stronger. Thomas exhaled noisily. "Understood, sir."

"Good." Commander Storm nodded, then grumbled, "I refuse to allow you to make a dog's dinner of this mission."

"We have reason to praise Lord Yshua for one thing, at least," David remarked. "Sir Thomas has been restored to his proper form."

Hanging his head, Thomas sighed. He'd failed Sir Rick by not finding those three girls. He'd failed to save Enoch from his abductors. He'd failed to protect Annabelle. Possessing his human body again hadn't brought him the fulfillment he'd long anticipated. All it brought was further pain. He pushed it down into the emptiness at his core and did what he had always done: mask the ache with sarcasm. "Praise away, Shepherd. God *really* came through for us. His timing was impeccable."

Dinah frowned. "Sir Thomas, you are a knight, sworn in Yshua's name. The Threefold One has blessed you so much in restoring your human body. How could you speak so ungraciously of him?"

Quite easily. If his return to a man was supposed to be a blessing from the Threefold One, then why didn't he see fit to restore Thomas's former strength, so he could protect those kids?

"A knight? Ha!" Thomas snorted. "Some knight I am. I had one task. One. Task. Protect the kiddo. You see how well that worked out."

Undertow

How could she have lost Daar-Lûsin?

Annabelle knelt; her damaged weapons belt sprawled before her like a dead eel on an alien shore. A boa constrictor crushed her chest, and her insides felt coated with ice shards. The magic dagger and its scabbard were missing, torn away at some point since they'd arrived in this realm. Lord Evanrudhe had entrusted it into her care, and now look what happened. This, after her success building and propelling the water-bubble raft throughout the day and night. She and Raeden had made it to land, but her discovery of the priceless artifact's loss eclipsed any joy she experienced.

It must've happened when I took off my cuirass, because I remember having it when we went through the waystone. Why didn't I notice it was missing before?

The rhythmic pulse of waves combing the shore failed to soothe her. Fingers hooked like claws, she plunged them into the brown sand. Agate pebbles and broken bits of shell dug into her palms. The discomfort seemed a distant thing while she struggled to control her breathing in the way Toad—*Thomas*—and the others had taught her. Frightening considerations swirled like flotsam and jetsam in a stormy sea.

Without Daar-Lûsin, how could she reforge her connection with Enoch?

Inhale. Exhale. Stop hyperventilating, Ann! But a serpent's coil of terror wrapped around her heart. If Daar-Lûsin brought Raeden and her to this place, then how would they get back to Commander Storm and the others?

"Freylin?" Raeden touched her back. Warmth seeped through the Oathbond, underlain by a spiky tension. From the tightness of his voice, it seemed he'd been trying to catch her attention for some time. "Freylin, the dagger must remain a problem for another day."

"No!" Annabelle pivoted and crawled toward the water. "I have to find it!" Her hands splashed in the surf and her anxiety died down to a dull whine, like a mosquito buzzing around her head. Was it possible to locate one little dagger out in the immensity of the ocean? *Maybe if I call Khinjara!* Envisioning the winged unicorn who was—somehow—the dreamscape embodiment of Daar-Lûsin, she extended her kythim, searching, calling for her friend ...

Raeden grasped her shoulder, halting her progress. "Freylin! Later, your servant will help you look. In the here and now, he scents danger."

"D-danger?" Annabelle shook out her trembling hands and brushed away grit on her damp trousers. *Can't we catch a break? I just want a meal and a dry place to curl up and rest!* Licking her lips, she scanned the beach empty of life apart from seagulls and then turned to her champion. "Is it nehmwights?" *Oh, God,* she prayed. *Please, no more fighting!*

"No." Straightening, Raeden gripped his hunting knife, ears pricked and nostrils twitching. "Durkvohnter stink of gathering storms and old blood. This is something much different. Your servant has never smelled sea brine and fish-scent coming from land before. It causes him unease. It reminds him of something ..." Sand and pebbles crunched under his boots as he stalked past her, sniffing the air and grumbling about all the water addling his senses.

Annabelle shivered. *Please, God. Let this be his typical caution and not a real threat.* She put on her belt. She imagined Commander Storm lecturing: *Waste not, want not.* Despite the broken frogging, the belt was still serviceable. "Um. How do you know it's dangerous? Maybe ... Maybe it's someone who can lead us to a waystone. And we still need to find Daar-Lûsin."

Raeden whirled, his green eyes wide. "Freylin, it is better to be secure now than to make apologies later." Returning to her, his ears canted back toward whatever he'd smelled. "Your servant will find a defensible place. Can you walk?" He half-knelt and extended a hand.

Annabelle grasped his wrist, and he hauled her up. The beach spun, shifting, and her legs folded like cooked spaghetti. "I guess not." She whimpered, clutching his sodden tunic.

With an exclamation of dismay, her champion swept her into his arms. "Forgiveness, Freylin. You did all the hard work in the waters. After that, you must feel like a punished egg."

Huffing a weak laugh, she replied, "If you meant I'm 'beat,' then I'm not arguing with that assessment." She rested her cheek against Raeden. Peppery cardamon mingled with the faint odor of wet dog, which was oddly harmonious. *Smells like safety.* His warmth soaked into her from the outside and merged with the Oathbond tied to her heart. Slinging an arm around his neck, she buried her face in his shoulder. Her father carried her when she'd been little, but this was ... different.

I don't know what I'd do without Raeden.

Her champion cleared his throat. "Your servant will find you fresh water and a safe place to rest. You must be famished. Perhaps he could hunt or gather berries."

Sounds good, Annabelle tried to say, but it came out as an incoherent mumble.

As he trudged up the beach, the ocean's strength retreated, and her light-headedness was joined by stomach cramps. "No," she murmured. "Please. Need ... to stay near water."

Raeden paused, tension and sour distaste crackling through the Oathbond. He sighed. "As you wish." She relaxed when the ocean's proximity spread over her like a cool balm in the freshening breeze. Raeden continued along the shore, praying in his native language. She drank in the words; they soothed her like the soughing of the waves against sand while she rocked back and forth. Were they back on the raft? No; her construct had disintegrated once they'd reached shore. Eyelids fluttering, she fought against the undertow of weariness.

Strange voices shouted and thunder rumbled. Was there a storm coming? Jolts went through Annabelle and her eyes flew open. The rumbling was her champion's growls, and the jolts came from his hastened gait. He clutched her tighter to keep her from bouncing too much.

She lifted her head, then gasped, "Raeden! What's going on?"

Raeden jogged, alternating between wheezing and growling. His breath rattled. Was he worn out, too? "Danger," he choked out. "Enemies."

Behind them, male voices shouted for them to stop. Nehmwights? *No ... not again!* Her heart constricted. "Somebody's chasing us?"

"Shach," he said. *Yes.*

Peering over his shoulder, she caught a glimpse through her smudged lenses of blurred human figures in pursuit, but they seemed to be painted in hues of ochre, pale green, and mauve. Odd, but not nehmwights, which were dark gray or ashen.

Besides, it was broad daylight. *Stupid, Ann. Nehmwights only come out at night.* If only she could think clearly! She swallowed. Her throat was dry. "What ... What are they?"

"Water sprites," Raeden snarled. "Your servant remembered the old legends of the folken, warning of their sea-salt and fish scent."

Annabelle frowned. That didn't answer her question. "But what are—"

"They are untrustworthy. Oathbreakers." Her champion skidded to a halt. "*Sturlz und drast!* They are in front, too."

He turned inland, then drew up short when an ochre-skinned man brandishing a spear blocked their way. Straight ahead, three men wearing linen kilts had emerged from the water and cut off their flight. Two were the color of coral and gripped tridents like they knew how to use them, though they seemed nervous. One murmured to the other. "What is that creature? It looks like one of those treacherous scout hounds from the historical murals."

Growls rumbled from Raeden's chest.

The man in front, with sky-blue skin and black straps crisscrossing his bare chest—*Are those knives in his bandoliers?*—held out his hands in a warding gesture and slowly approached, his expression wary. Water dripped from shoulder-length purple hair with dark green streaks. His eyes shone like burnished gold in the sunlight.

Annabelle gripped a fistful of Raeden's damp tunic. *That must be their leader.* She blinked at the man—youth? —drawn into his gaze like a toy boat in a whirlpool. His golden eyes were mesmerizing. Even with lowered brows and forbidding expression the young man was as handsome as David. But blue? Like a Smurf ... Ha! She swallowed hysterical laughter. Who ... What were these guys?

"Halt, in the name of the Brenin!" He declaimed in a resonant tenor. "Who-what are you?"

"Take care, Captain!" The ochre man said, leveling his spear at Raeden. "That must be a scout hound. They're blood-thirsty savages."

Annabelle tried telling them that Raeden wasn't, but her voice wouldn't work. And Raeden's growling wasn't helping their cause!

The sky-blue leader stopped. His expression darkened. "Scout hound, your kind is not welcome here on Ynys Lloches."

Did he just say "Ynys Lloches?" That's the place Hadrien mentioned. She shuddered as another question arose to trouble her. *What will they do to us, since Raeden's "kind" isn't welcome here?* Indignation flashed through her. *That's not fair! He hasn't done anything wrong.*

"He did not come here by choice," Raeden growled, squeezing her. Annabelle cried out.

The captain's eyes widened as they fastened on her. "Vile rogue! Release the damsel into my care, at once, or face the wrath of the Howling Tempest. We have you surrounded. Worry not, fair damsel," the youth intoned, placing a hand over his heart as he bowed. "My Howling Tempest will free you from your vile captor."

Annabelle began warming toward him; no one had ever called her "fair" before. But the blue guy probably meant the "pale" definition of the word, because of her light complexion. Yeah. That made more sense.

She frowned. *Wait. Does this guy think Raeden's holding me against my will?*

"Um, thank you, sir," she said. "But I don't need to be freed. Raeden's not a 'vile captor;' he's my champion, and he's carrying me because I'm tired. You see, we're lost—"

"As the protectors of Ynys Lloches," the young captain continued, "we cannot take any chances with a scout hound, fair damsel. Allow me to introduce myself. I am Mordred

Dwylocyflym, called Quickhands, of Ynys Lloches, Twywysog and Captain of the Howling Tempest, son of Morgan Brenin, king of the gwerindawr, and brother to Rhiannon Merchetifydd, heir to the Sanctuary Throne."

Gwerindawr! Annabelle's eyes widened. At Treehome, Dinah had mentioned them as a peaceful and hospitable race of merfolk—*real live merfolk! Wow!*

Her brow furrowed. Dinah also said there was blood feud between the gwerindawr and Raeden's people. And ... Mordred? That name left a bad taste in her mouth. In the legend of King Arthur, Mordred had been one of the villains. *But that was on Earth. Maybe this guy can help us find the waystone. Wait ... did he say his dad was a king?*

She blurted, "You're a prince?"

"Yes, fair damsel." His voice grew coaxing. "But you may call me Mordred. How are you called and where are you from? Would you honor me with the holding of your name?"

I see no reason not to share that much. "My name's Annabelle, and I'm from Wisconsin. You can call me Ann—"

Raeden's arms tightened around her. He growled, "This water sprite will hold nothing of yours, Freylin." A steady anger burned through the Oathbond, scorching Annabelle's heart. "Do not try to deceive her with pretty words, water sprite." Raeden twisted, turning her toward the water and away from their challenger. "The little maiden is under this one's protection. Your tempests may howl all they want, but he will never place her into your 'quick hands.' Those whose ancestors betrayed the folken during the *Kreigenrechtsallen* cannot be trusted!"

"Raeden," Annabelle said, but the question on her tongue died away. Her eyes settled on several colorful people bobbing in the waves, all watching her and Raeden. Some carried polearms or spears like the men on the beach. Whatever happened here, there'd be no escaping out to sea.

"Cwensgowt filth," said an ochre-skinned man on Raeden's left, then spat into the sand. His grip tightened on his weapon. "Be wary, princeps. Scout hounds cannot be trusted. They betrayed us at the Battle of Twisted Fans."

That's basically the same thing that Raeden said about these ... water sprites. Is that the reason the gwerindawr and the wensallen-kaen hate each other? I have a bad feeling about this. Annabelle shrank against her champion.

"Peace, Lladdhe," the blue princeps murmured, his eyes still on Raeden. "I remain on my guard against this savage." Squaring his shoulders, he declaimed, "Scout hound, no one need be harmed. Release the Lady Ann, then remand yourself into our custody." He sneered, and suddenly knives were in his hands. "The next time I speak, it will not be with words. And my knives never miss their targets."

Annabelle shivered. She patted Raeden's chest. "Please, Raeden. Just do as he says. I don't want a fight." *I don't want him to get hurt again.* Her breath quickened as an idea blossomed. If these 'water sprites' attacked, perhaps she could protect them both. "Put me down ... in the water."

Raeden stiffened. Beneath her hand, his heart pounded fiercely. "Freylin," he said, sotto voce, "your servant will never submit to the demands of water sprites."

Annabelle met the "water sprite" leader's gaze. In his golden eyes, she read the death of her champion. She touched the arm cradling her. Raeden quivered; his arms felt like steel cables around her. "Then do it for me," she whispered. "Because I asked. Please."

Raeden froze. The Oathbond conveyed a sense of ... dreadful focus. "As you wish. But your servant begs you to follow his lead. Do nothing—how does one say it in this cursed speech? Ah, yes—Do nothing rash," he whispered in her ear.

She patted him. "I won't."

The kaenhir's grip loosened and she slid down until her sodden boots squelched in the sand. She really ought to remove her boots before her feet rotted. They were probably all shriveled up like prunes. An incoming wave splashed up over her legs and soaked her trousers anew. It felt like waking up again.

Refreshed though she was, Annabelle clung to her champion's arm. "There, your Highness," she called. "He put me down. I'm sorry if we trespassed; we didn't mean to. All we want is a waystone to get out of here. Can we please go now?" She offered a tentative smile.

Mordred raised his hands, gripping knives by the blades. "Damsel," he said, albeit in a gentle tone. "Pray, step away from the scout hound, and I shall escort you to my father."

Eyes wide, she gripped Raeden tighter. *Is he going to throw those knives at Raeden the second I move?* While pondering her next words, Annabelle reached out with her kythim to the beckoning waves. A whisper of what she'd commanded while out to sea answered. She lacked the strength to do anything with it, but at least it was still there. She began to refill her depleted reservoir.

"She will fall without support," Raeden snapped, shifting until he stood between her and the leader. His fingers rested on the hilt of his hunting knife. "Arrogant whelp! Did your mother not teach you manners?" The youth stiffened, his expression darkening further, but Raeden went on. "You who call the folken savages! Why do you introduce yourself with knives bared?" Taking his hand away from his weapon, he fisted it against his chest. "This one is called Raeden von Bleistaff, of the Black

Forest clan." But he did not bow as he normally would have done.

Heart racing, Annabelle stepped around her bristling champion and into the water. Cooling energy bolstered her legs so she could stand on her own while the conduit between her reservoir and the ocean strengthened. Her wyld reservoir filled steadily. Almost enough to do something, if necessary.

"And like I said, Your Highness," she offered, "you can call me Ann. I'm from Wisconsin."

Mordred stepped forward, beaming. He tapped his forehead and his heart. "Greetings and well-met, Lady Ann of Wisconsin." He spoke the name of her home slowly and uncertainly, then brightened. "Be welcome to Ynys Lloches." He extended his right hand. "Come along with me. I shall take you to see the Brenin."

Raeden stepped forward and put himself between her and the youth. "This one has sworn to protect Freylin, and she remains with him, always." His tone was cold and formal, but underneath it all the Oathbond twisted and seethed like a nest of vipers. "This one demands an audience with your king."

"Very well, scout hound." Mordred grinned, but it didn't reach his eyes, which went harder than the metal they resembled. "Howling Tempest. Take him into custody."

As one, the colorful guards leveled their spears and tridents at Raeden. More men erupted from the waves, their spearheads glittering in the sunslight. They'd crept closer while she'd been preoccupied with gathering waterpower—and observing their leader—and now her champion was surrounded by a ring of ... was that obsidian? Whatever it was, the pointy ends would jab right into him if he moved.

"Why are you doing this?" Annabelle glanced between her champion and the gwerindawr leader. Mentally, she began gathering skeins of sapphire energy from the ocean. "He didn't do anything wrong!"

"There is no reason to fear," Mordred drawled, sauntering nearer with his hands held out. "I shall escort you into the Brenin's presence, Lady Ann. As a precaution against any ... misunderstandings, my men will accompany your champion."

Raeden's green eyes found hers, conveying an unspoken warning. What was he trying to tell her—to attack? Refrain from doing anything? The Oathbond sizzled with tension and made it difficult to breathe. Or hold on to the slithering strands of water she'd gathered. They kept slipping free of the pattern she tried to weave.

Her champion's ears flattened and he bared his teeth, snarling. A warm hand encircled Annabelle's arm. She whipped around to glare at a blue chest crisscrossed with black leather. Should she try to grab one of his knives? *No, Ann, remember—he's faster than you!* While she dithered, Mordred gripped her other arm and held her fast. She tried kneeing him in the groin. He deflected it with a thigh. "None of that now, damselfly," he reproved in a mild tone.

Glaring up into the princeps's handsome features, she struggled to pull away. "Let go!" She reached for her wyld, but it retreated from her grasp. Mordred tightened his grip. Fear shot through her like a lance as he ushered her toward the beach.

Black flames consumed the Oathbond. *Oh, no.* Roaring something in his native tongue, Raeden plunged through the spearmen encircling him. Crimson bloomed across his tunic.

No, don't fight! Annabelle screamed, but no words emerged, only inarticulate horror.

Her champion's eyes blazed emerald fire as he drew his knife and slashed at Mordred, slicing through a bandolier. A line of blood welled up. The princeps cried out and sidestepped, yanking her into the water. She staggered, splashing, but his grip was like steel on her right arm, bracing her up. His other hand became a blue blur. A black knife hilt jutted from Raeden's left shoulder.

The kaenhir barely flinched as more crimson spread around the hilt. His beige tunic had turned almost completely red and the rents in his black vest gaped open. "Release her, water sprite!" He slashed Mordred's fingers on her arm. The gwerindawr let go with a curse and stumbled, falling. Raeden reached for her, but then froze. His eyes went round as saucers.

The Oathbond ... flickered. A cold desolation swept through Annabelle. One of the guards had thrust a trident into Raeden's back. *They've killed him!* A dark image of a nehmwight stabbing a sword into his middle flashed through her memory. Somewhere, someone screamed in denial. It sounded like her.

"No! No! No!" Annabelle shrieked. "God, please. Help me." Heat flared in her core. Everything in her sight turned blue. Power surged forth from her reservoir. There came a noise like thunder as the water rose from its bed, and a shining wave engulfed them all.

Raeden can't die! God, save us.

Clarity returned to Annabelle's mind in the silence of the water. She knew what to do. She'd healed Raeden before. She could do it again. Surrounded by water, her kythim followed the iron-salt tang of blood to its multiple sources. She located the worst wounds and quickly stanched the flow, then moved onto the next. *Thank God! I'm getting better at this.*

There wasn't time to heal Raeden completely—and the results wouldn't be pretty—but at least she could save her champion's life. She panted, felt the strain rising, and let go.

The water receded to reveal shocked faces. Spears and tridents lay scattered on the beach, their obsidian points shattered. Marine life squirmed, flopped, and wriggled all around them; she felt remorse for stranding the poor creatures.

And at her feet sprawled her sopping wet champion—with newly healed scars peeping through his torn clothing. Stunned, but alive. Blessedly alive.

Thank you, God. Annabelle sank to her knees as weariness fell over her like a blanket.

"Freylin?" Raeden stared at her. Next to him in the sand, a fish gulped the air. "You ought not to have done that."

"You've gotta be kidding." With a snort, she picked up a purple sea star and tossed it back into the ocean. "Not save your life?" Crawling along the beach, she continued tossing sea creatures back into their element.

"No," Raeden replied. "He has gratitude for that, Freylin. But you should not bring the sea to the land."

"She is the Ahdmerel," one of the coral-colored men said. The whites of his eyes shone around his purple irises. "She can do as she pleases, scout hound."

Ahdmerel? Pausing in her mission to save the sea animals, Annabelle gasped. That's what Hadrien called her. How could these gwerindawr know that title? She stared at the coral man, then turned to Mordred. "What ... What is he talking about?"

Rising, Mordred fingered the ugly, reddish-purple line of his hastily mended injury. In the confusion, she'd healed him, too. "Ahdmerel will heal you with living waters," he whispered in a rapt tone. It sounded as if he was quoting. He gazed at her. "I am healed. You truly are the prophesied Ahdmerel." Right fist against his chest, he dropped to one knee and inclined his head. "Forgive me for manhandling you, Lady Ann."

"Uh ... sure. But what—"

"The prophecy is being fulfilled!" The man who'd stabbed Raeden stared at his erstwhile victim. "Even the cleansing waves obey the chosen of Rainblessed."

All the gwerindawr guardsmen faced her. As one, they placed right fists over their hearts and bowed. "Honor to serve the blessed Ahdmerel," they chorused.

"Huh?" Annabelle paused in her labors, her mind reeling, trying to make sense of it all. "Why are you all bowing?" Her voice rose an octave. "What's this about a prophecy?"

Anxiety moaned along the Oathbond. Raeden coughed. "Freylin ..." He no longer appeared stunned, and his eyes glittered like emeralds. "Take care with your wyld. The water sprites believe you are a god."

"Not a god, scout hound," Mordred said, raising his head. "The gwerindawr are not heathens. But we hail the Ahdmerel as one sent by the Threefold One to bring us glory." He fixed her with his golden gaze. "Lady Ann, I must honor you as the one prophesied and awaited by the gwerindawr. As princeps of my people, I cast down my shield at your feet."

Holy cow! Annabelle stared at the blue-skinned man kneeling before her. What was going on? Everything seemed surreal. If it weren't for the suns overhead and the shadows their light cast, then she'd believe she'd fallen into the dreamscape.

Trivial Pursuit

William stared unseeing at the open book on his worktable. His fingertips drummed a nervous staccato against the wooden surface. A parchment half-filled with notes on the Dreadlord's monograph about manipulating the dreamscape sat atop his spell journal while his reedpen lay idle beside the ink jar.

I wonder if Milady Blue's asleep right now. Should I attempt the Dream Trance as described in the monograph?

A movement distracted him from his deliberation. Landing on his elbow, the other Milady Blue folded her indigo wings and crawled up to his shoulder.

William raised his eyebrows at the moth. He snorted a laugh. "So much for a bit of light research to pass the time until Tenebris carves four new circles into my back." Three and a half hours to go. Freezing Void, but he wished the suns-burnt test was over and the etching was already done.

He hadn't slept a wink since receiving his master's message. His mind had been too busy. He'd finalized his plans. The densely scribed sheets scattered about his room served as a mute testament to his productivity. It was only in the past half hour that his mind had begun to drift.

He ceased tapping a mindless rhythm and reached into the sakkhelt pocket where he kept his whiskey flask. And the portrait of Annabelle. He hesitated, uncertain which item he wanted to bring out. Neither. The blazing flask was empty, and there was no good reason to look at the pale maiden in the green dress. No. Suns burn that beguilement spell!

It only proves Tenebris was correct—that all females are foul sorceresses to be avoided.

Grimacing, he yanked his hand out empty and slammed his fist on the table. Disturbed, the moth flitted from his shoulder to the vase of flowers he kept for her nourishment. He'd need to water them soon, or gather fresh ones from the garden ...

Focus on the plan! The Dreadlord had approved his scheme to lure Annabelle near Fastness, where she could be easily snared. And then William would harvest her power with the wyld-siphoning apparatus he was building.

He dragged over a parchment on which he'd scribed a list and snatched up his reedpen to add some final thoughts. *First, I must come up with a way to separate Milady Blue from the winged and horned equine guarding her dreams.* He'd learned from his studies that the creature was an hisanabyad, a race of void-proficient shapeshifters believed long extinct; presumably annihilated during the last battle of the Oblivion Wars. Apparently at least one hisanabyad had survived. How the voidrunner had ended up Annabelle's protector perplexed him. But that mystery must wait for another day.

William chewed on the end of the reedpen and reviewed his list. *Before I can even approach Milady Blue, I need to disguise myself so she and the cursed knight—and that awful bard—don't recognize me. Something awe-inspiring. Even scary—but not too scary for Milady Blue. Then I need a shield against her enchantments and a fiery sword. Some kind of armor I can infuse with defensive spells ...*

Straightening in his chair, he opened a book about the Aethyr to a spot marked by a scrap of parchment and flipped to the next page.

His eyes settled on an ink drawing of a magnificent, formidable creature, and a grin spread across his face. "Hello, what's this then?" He chuckled as he drank in the illustration's details. "The solution to my conundrum—that's what." On the page opposite the illustration were some references to a battle between the Evaingynon and the Hollow. He frowned. Who or what was the Hollow? He made a note to ask the Dreadlord about it later. No time now for idle research.

According to the Dreadlord's writings, William didn't need to use a spellform to create a disguise in the dreamscape. The milieu of the Aethyr was malleable enough for a versatile mind to craft into nearly anything without tapping into his arkhabala.

Including the facsimile of a Sage from out of the legends.

Ha! It worked!

Purple mist drifted around William beneath a midnight sky jeweled with stars. Concealed by his new form, he crouched in his dreamscape tower and grinned at the mirror he'd conjured. A black-scaled visage with glowing orange eyes grinned toothily back at him. Six pairs of horns crowned him, one pair curving down parallel to his jawline while the others twisted backwards from his head. He raised his hands to touch his new features, then paused, gaping at talons the length of his actual fingers and twice as thick. His grin broadened. *Zakaar's not the only one with finger-daggers—and mine are even better!* He tapped them against wide scales across his chest like plates of steel. Armor that could be imbued with defensive magic.

"Now to try out the two charms I crafted!"

William flinched at the voice booming out of his mouth. It held a new depth and greater resonance. He'd need to tone that down, so he didn't scare Milady Blue. He spoke, familiarizing himself with his voice before he tried casting spells.

He sang a cantrip that tested the limits of his musical talent—admittedly, that had never been anything to brag about—and then gasped at the chill soaking into his scales like the waters of a mountain stream. There. That should keep Annabelle from bewitching him further. Feeling a drain, he drew on the Aethyr around him as the Dreadlord's monograph instructed. Violet light flashed. He inhaled, breathing in the purple mist, and energy flooded into his Aethyric reservoir. His newfound strength made him giddy. He suppressed the feeling.

If only I could've used this power during my Arkhadahn Trial. Once I master this in the waking world, Tenebris had better sleep lightly. I wonder ... Could I send him nightmares?

Filing that idea away for future reference, William intoned a second, simpler cantrip, and his shivers subsided as the protection spell settled over him like a warm mantle. It enhanced his disguise's natural physical defenses while adding heat and flame resistance. Now the scarred knight couldn't penetrate his scales—not even with his burning blade.

Hopefully. Better to avoid him and not put that to the test.

A sensation akin to his arkhabala stirring drew his attention to his back. Vaulted over his ducked head were batlike wings the hue of the night sky. *Excellent! I can't wait to try those out.* It was time to venture out into the wider dreamscape and do just that. He dismissed the mirror and dropped to all fours. That was how wyrmkin walked along the ground; doubtless Evaingynon moved in the same manner. But first, he needed to ensure he knew how to use his new parts.

It wouldn't do to embarrass himself in front of other dreamscape travelers.

After finding the muscles that controlled his wings, he spread his webbed pinions. He laughed. Just like another pair of arms!

This would take some practice ... or was it instinctive? Instead of concentrating on the process of making his new limbs move, he envisioned the result. Muscles flexed—it *was* like spreading and flapping a second set of arms. The mist eddied wildly in response to his wingbeats. He filed away the mechanics into a new headspace he'd developed for this new form's muscle-memory, then furled his wings.

Elation's glow warmed his insides as he ambled toward the crenelated wall of his tower. His backside ... twitched ... and he stumbled. Glass shattered as a black, whiplike and spiked *thing* lashed out at his potion-brewing apparatus. A startled roar escaped his jaws, and he turned to glare at the long, spiked appendage scraping against stones. It felt ... weird.

Burning Suns! How could I forget that I have a blistering tail?

With a thought, William cleared away his laboratory and study materials until the tower stood empty of obstacles. He needed more space to practice using his Evaingynon disguise, until he moved as majestically as he looked.

Once satisfied that he had his limbs under control, William spread his wings and leaped from the tower wall. "Envision your goal!" He growled a spike of fear into submission and continued with the mantra. "You can fly. You won't fall. You shall soar across the dreamscape with ten times an eagle's magnificence." Shakily, he drifted through the purple mist—Aethyric essence—swirling around him. He inhaled more of it, then leveled out into a glide. He roared in triumph at his flight. Relying on his form's instincts, he soared over a dark forest toward a familiar glade beside a stream.

Northward used to be able to fly—but now he can't. Ha! Next chance I get, I'll grind it into his face.

William miscalculated his momentum upon landing. He splashed in the stream, bellowing curses. He looked around as he crept ashore. Had anyone seen that? Merciful Valeshka! He was alone in the clearing. But surely, Annabelle and her equine protector would be along soon.

William sat on his haunches to wait. He ticked through his list. Yes, he was ready. The stars wheeled overhead, but the patterns they formed were strange.

Getting up, he paced the clearing as he went over his plans again. His claws ripped furrows in the mossy earth. "Where is she?" he muttered. "The timing works out. I went to all this trouble—"

Violet light flared, blinding him. A voice boomed: "How dare you use that semblance here!"

Valkor's Scythe! It's that cloaked bard—the Dream Traveler. I'm doomed.

Eyes shut, William covered his head with his wings and trembled. Reflexively, he primed his arkhabala, then moaned when the spelled tattoos didn't respond. He was blocked from the Arkhabadh. This had happened the last time he'd encountered the Dream Traveler, when the cloaked bard had made him dance to his music like a puppet on strings.

If I ran, would he come after me?

Wait. William had armor now, and better control over the dreamscape. He'd specifically warded himself against these sorts of encounters. His spelled armor would protect him. He must confront his fear and overcome it. The impressive creature he'd become wouldn't cower like a scolded child. Neither would a true Arkhadahn; he could hear Tenebris yelling at him to stop slouching.

Annabelle could be watching. She'd never respect a craven.

William forced his wings apart and straightened, looking down his fanged snout at the pathetic worm standing before him. He needed to tilt his head back to manage it, because the "worm" was the Dream Traveler, and his lambent, gray-lavender gaze was right at William's level. His cowl was lowered and for once William got a good look at his face.

The Dream Traveler was a dwelfnhir, and aside from the scar, the revealed features resembled the Dreadlord's. Despite his resolve, William's limbs quaked, and he back-pedaled, nearly tripping over his tail.

"Whatever the disguise, you cannot fool me ... nehmwight's get." The bard stalked him, his scarred face twisted in fury as fingers danced over the strings of his lytarra. "I care not if you use the form of an Evaingynon, but you must not use *that* one!"

Music flowed over William. Although he clapped his hands over his fan-like ears, a humming filled them as his scales writhed and his horns ached.

My wards failed. That cursed bard's destroying all my hard work!

"Stop!" William splashed across the stream, but the bard pursued him without even dampening his feet. "I'll change it— only stop!" He roared as the vibration of his scales reached a crescendo.

Suddenly, the onslaught ceased. The buzzing in his scales died away. William shook, staring wide-eyed at his tormentor as he slowly lowered his hands to the ground.

The Dream Traveler sneered. "Fear not, *battle mageling.* You still retain your protections. I merely altered your appearance."

William examined the visible parts of himself. His scales were now a dark gray, like his skin, although his arkhabala adorned his flanks and wingbacks in inky black. The horns that had curved along his jaw now jutted backward with the rest. Everything else seemed the same. He didn't mind looking different from the drawing, but the bard's reaction seemed needlessly violent for such minor alterations. As if William's choice in scale color was a personal affront. Perhaps the bard had a weakness he could exploit. He wished he could read his kythim.

William swallowed, then lifted his head. "What's wrong with the way I looked before?"

The instrument faded from view, and the Dream Traveler crossed his arms. He seemed to have calmed down. "You have no right to use Shadowveiled's form. Should you don it again, I will make the dreamscape your own personal perdition." He smiled thinly. "I'll lead Helzarvenn right to you. And your 'Milady Blue' will learn who holds her heart-brother captive."

"No, you can't tell her!" William blurted, then cursed himself as the bard's smile widened.

He laughed. "Ah, I have your measure now. One little uttering, and all your well-spun plans to entrap Ahdmerel unravel." Stepping forward, the bard tapped between William's eyes. "Aye, nehmwight's get, all your little schemes are transparent to me." He tapped again.

Of all the insufferable—

"Suns burn your eyes!" William snarled, lunging at his tormentor. Violet and orange light crackled between his talons. Without seeming to move, the bard eluded him. Overbalanced, William fell forward, catching himself on his hands. Steam rose and the light winked out. William stared at the scorched moss, his anger fading.

That ... was interesting. He sat back on his haunches, warily eyeing his companion. Why wasn't the bard attempting to control him like he did before? *Are my spells holding him off?*

Beyond his reach, the Dream Traveler held the lytarra and idly plucked a stray note, then dismissed the instrument. He tilted his head and squinted at William. "Your powers are growing—as is your foolishness. How about a friendly wager? I'll even grant you a boon."

"There's no such thing as a friendly wager." The spikes along William's back rose like an enraged cat's fur and his voice roughened into a growl. "I'm not the fool you think I am. I don't gamble unless I know what's at stake." He paused. "What boon would you grant me?"

"I'll answer one question pertaining to your ... quarry. One honest answer. No strings attached."

Excitement crackled through William like lightning. He dampened it. Could he trust anything this scarred dwelfnhir told him? Probably not, but it wouldn't hurt to hear him out. This was his chance to rid himself of the pale maiden's enchantment. Then he wouldn't be plagued by stray thoughts about her anymore, or odd emotions robbing him of his concentration when he needed to think clearly.

I need her hooks out of my mind!

He schooled himself to serenity and met the bard's sardonic gaze. "How do I break the beguilement curse Annabelle cast upon me?"

For a heartbeat, the Dream Traveler stared at him, then doubled over in mirth. William scowled. Why was that so blazing funny? He'd thought about asking the Dreadlord for help with the beguilement spell, but now he was glad he hadn't. The last thing he needed was to appear ridiculous in the eyes of his master's employer.

William slammed his tail down, then flinched at the spray of water. "Well, Dream Traveler? I asked a question. Hysterical laughter is not the answer I sought." He scoffed. "You don't know the answer, do you?"

Straightening, the bard's guffaws died away as he wiped away tears and the hostility receded from his eyes—but William kept his guard up. "I haven't laughed like that in ... a long time. As for your 'curse,' lad ..." The bard shook his head. "Oh, I *do* know. I know very well. Your master has kept you cloistered, or you'd recognize the pangs you suffer as those common to any youth who fancies a comely maiden. These 'hooks' are not the Ahdmerel's fault." He chuckled. "If anyone is to be blamed, tis yourself."

"What?" William gaped. The Dream Traveler's archaic speech took some swift translating, but it wasn't difficult to discern his meaning. "*Fancy* her? That's ridiculous! I don't believe you. It must be a suns-burnt *spell*." All he wanted was her power. Once he sorted out the harmonics of the Aethyric crystals in his wyld-siphoning apparatus, he would drain her magic into gems and claim it for his own. Then he'd be done with her, and they could go their separate ways.

Why must the thought of not seeing her again bother me so much?

The Dream Traveler grinned. "I saw how you looked upon her, when you caught her trespassing in your tower—before she even had the opportunity to summon her wyld."

"And that's another thing," William snarled. An urge to savage the smug fellow with fangs and talons had him flexing his fingers. "You had no business invading my tower and whisking her away. Anything in my territory belongs to me. Milady Blue's magic is mine to harvest—"

"Wrong." His expression flat, the Dream Traveler's voice went soft, but vehement. William experienced a frisson, recalling the power his companion held. If only William could get that suns-burnt lytarra away from him!

"Believe whatever pleases you," the bard murmured. "But you are wrong." He shook his head again, and tsked. "Such potential, wasted on a covetous fool in a trivial pursuit. And here I thought to teach you the ways of dream traveling ... should you take my wager."

Before William could interject, he raised a hand and continued, "If you are set on this reprehensible path, know this:

to strip Ahdmerel of her wyld would mean her death." His eyes hardened. "Tell me, nehmwight's get. Are you as ruthless as your master? Are you prepared to kill a wyldling for their power?"

Kill Annabelle? William stiffened. Armored scales or not, he felt like the bard had punched him in the gut. The ability to breathe eluded him. Memory presented the image of the knight with the golden aura, bound and bleeding on the table. All that screaming, and the metallic tang of blood ... Tenebris pressing the knife in his hand. Delivering the death-stroke to a sacrifice was an honor seldom entrusted to an apprentice—unless his master tested him for advancement.

William had failed. One slash of a knife. Such a simple task, and he'd been incapable. What sort of Arkhadahn would he be if he couldn't finish off a sacrifice? He glanced at his hands, strange with their scales and claws, but more powerful than in the waking world. He envisioned them closing around Annabelle's neck, claws digging into the pale flesh, the blood welling up, her blue eyes closing forever ... Perhaps her death was the only way to end her hold on him.

A voice inside him shrieked in protest, but he silenced it, squashing it down deep. He swallowed bile. His hands shook.

No. I must conquer this. I won't fail again!

His gaze piercing, the Dream Traveler whispered, "I thought not."

William bristled. "Now *you're* wrong," he growled, stretching his neck until he was taller than the Dream Traveler. "I'm trained as an Arkhadahn by the highest of them all. I'll do whatever it takes to acquire power—to surpass him."

To get out from under Tenebris's thumb. To be his own master at last. And it's not like he'd be slicing into Annabelle. The wyld siphoning process was bloodless. He'd designed it to be that way. Hopefully it was painless, too. After witnessing the knight's torture, he knew he wouldn't be able to abide *her* screaming.

The Dream Traveler regarded him with a faint smile. If looking up at William bothered him, he gave no sign. "Your goals require you to get close to your quarry. To accomplish that, you must gain her trust. And her sympathy. This is a campaign best carried out with honesty—not disguises. What happens when she sees through your deception? At best, she will be displeased with you for pretending to be one of the Evaingynon. I think you may have greater success approaching the maiden as yourself."

"I already have a plan to befriend her. And she *won't,* because I'm not making any such claim." William's tail spikes rattled against river stones. "What do you know about Milady Blue, anyway? I suppose you're great friends with her." He sneered. The very idea made his stomach twist in knots. *Milady Blue and her power belong to me.* He itched to slash the dwelfnhir's face and give him some new scars.

"Temper your jealousy, little mage." The Dream Traveler chuckled. "You have no right to it. Here is my wager: Convince Ahdmerel to be your friend in the span of a moon's turning. Should you succeed, you may thrice call upon me for aid in your endeavors, and I shall come to help you. If you cannot gain her trust and affection, then you forfeit any dominion within this realm. I shall cast you from the dreamscape as I see fit."

William narrowed his eyes. The Dream Traveler had demonstrated his ability to expunge him from the dreamscape previously. If only he could grab that blistering lytarra! "How do I call you? Just holler for the Dream Traveler, and you'll come running?"

The Dream Traveler smiled. "An Age ago, I was christened Remiel. Call me by this name, and I swear by Lord Yshua I will come." He traced a cross over his heart. "This is a binding oath for me, if not for those like you who follow false gods."

"Remiel. I'll remember that." William smirked as he laughed inwardly. Remiel. What a silly, pompous-sounding name. "You may as well address me by my name—if you know it." He was heartily sick of being called "nehmwight's get."

"I do know it," Remiel replied, with a sly smile. "William Dulciber, the only begotten bastard son of a nehmwight—"

"Oi!" William interjected, lifting his wings. "You don't have to rub it in. I am what I am, and I'll make no apologies for it. Furthermore, I'll have you know I follow no gods, false or otherwise."

Remiel frowned. "Everyone follows a god. Whether they know it or not. Look to your histories and you will discover the truth about those whom the nehmwights call gods. Not all records from the Oblivion Wars were lost."

"I could care less," William retorted. "Gods are make-believe nonsense for superstitious ninnies." He dug his claws into moss and mud. The way it squished soothed the agitation rising within. He pretended Tenebris's face was beneath his talons.

The Dream Traveler sighed, shaking his head. "The Threefold One is quite real. In time, perhaps the maiden of your fancy shall convince you otherwise. Farewell, child of two worlds." With a nod, he stepped to one side ... and vanished.

For a moment, William gaped at the place he had been. Then he snorted. "Fancy Annabelle? Ha! What rubbish. Nearly as rubbish as his talk about gods." Doubtless the maiden cast the beguilement to make him weak and control him, just as Tenebris had warned him females did. In mucking about with William, Annabelle played a dangerous game.

His eyes narrowed as he kneaded the sodden ground like a cat preparing its bed. *And in this game, turnabout's fair play.*

Let's see how Milady Blue likes it when I cast a spell to enthrall her.

Before the next moon, he'd have her 'friendship' and win the wager. Although he couldn't care less about Remiel's aid, he relished the prospect of expanding his own dominion of the dreamscape without the meddlesome bard's interference.

It was time to return to the waking world. William reluctantly shed his reptilian disguise and armor. Too bad he couldn't bring it with him for use during his Arkhadahn's Trial. That would certainly wipe the condescending sneer from Tenebris's face. But William still had a surprise in store that was certain to win him his circles. And with them, more power. Grinning, he returned to consciousness and the anticipation of agony at his master's hands.

Banked Embers

No pain, no gain.

Thomas's aching arms trembled and burned with fatigue as he struggled to finish his exercise. Morning birdsong from trees surrounding the clearing mocked him with its cheerfulness. They were worse than the tree frogs and the bugs in the Sweltmire a day and a half ago. Crazy birds; they'd woken him two hours earlier with their chirping and they were still going at it, louder than ever.

No wonder this time is called Lark Watch.

Perspiration slicked his skin under the oversized tunic he'd pilfered from Raeden's belongings—everything Thomas wore was borrowed and ill-fitting. At least David did a decent job as a barber and helped rid him of his beard. Grunting and cursing under his breath, he collapsed on his stomach, then rolled on his back and wiped his face on the tunic sleeve.

I hate being so weak!

Flexing his legs, he rocked himself into a sitting position. "Criminy," he gasped, cradling his head in his hands. "Sir, I can't ... do ... any more ... than ... forty-two." That was awful. Commander Storm told him he'd been able to do at least a hundred, before ... all this. "And here I thought ... I was getting stronger." Pushing his damp hair back from his forehead, he glanced over at his spectator, then grimaced. It wasn't the Commander, as he'd thought—it was Dinah.

Well, crud. That made it even more embarrassing.

The dwelfnhad looked up from where she knelt before a firepit, laying out kindling. She'd rolled up her tunic sleeves. It was still early enough that she hadn't yet donned her armor. "The Commander is helping Peter scout the path ahead, Sir Thomas. I don't believe he slept last night; he's concerned about problems lying ahead. Maybe even bandits."

Frowning, Thomas scratched his chin. If the Commander feared them getting waylaid, then why hadn't he said something last night? They could've made plans for defense.

I may be physically weak at the moment, but I've a good head for strategy, and Sir Rick trained me well in the art of battle.

Dinah continued, "Commander Storm expects us to join him at Sparrow Watch by the ruins of Fort Arwydd." With a sigh, she brushed bits of bark from her hands. "And don't worry; your strength will return in time. Working yourself to exhaustion isn't the answer." She tilted her head, her expression carefully blank. "Could you reconsider your decision? Obtaining the sourekghar from Balthazar's Crucible would be the fastest way to regain your strength."

Dark fingers of foreboding slid up his spine. *Smoke fills his lungs, choking him. He screams soundlessly as the burning wall collapses, right on top of—*

No. Stop! There's no time to deal with this. His heart hammered and his insides grew cold. *And I don't want to see it.*

Thomas squeezed his eyes shut and shook his head. That memory fragment was probably what Balthazar meant when he mentioned facing inner demons. He rubbed damp palms along his trousers, then began stretching out his tired muscles.

"David says he's amenable to accompanying you to the Evergold Desert." Her brow puckered and concern filled her voice. "Sir Thomas, are you ...?"

Thomas flinched. "No, Ambassador. I have not reconsidered. I'm going with you beyond Ee—vah—sha—uh, that stone fortress place. Locating Annabelle and Enoch comes before weeks of journeying to Balthazar's Crucible." And whatever demons the Sage wanted him to face. He needed to divert the conversation. "Um. I was wondering. Just how can the Caretaker help us find Enoch and Annabelle anyway?" Commander Storm's touchiness about the Caretaker piqued his curiosity about her abilities and potential weaknesses.

"Sir Thomas, can you tell me the difference between a wyldling and a souretholim?"

Okay, so the Ambassador was in teaching mode. Frowning, he watched her shred birch bark for tinder. "Yeah," he replied after a moment's thought. "I heard you and Annabelle discussing it on the road." The kiddo was curious about how magic functioned. Previously, Thomas couldn't care less—so long as the magic actually worked when he followed the steps—but Annabelle's enthusiasm had awakened a thirst in him to learn new things.

He swallowed a surge of grief and cleared his throat. "Uh. Wyldlings can make things happen with their aspect just by thinking of it. Souretholim need to touch whatever they're working with. So, I can create a ball of fire, but you need to be touching the ground, rocks, or whatnot to make them do anything."

Setting aside the flint and steel, Dinah nodded. "Correct. Now, keep in mind that whatever souretholim can do, the Sage's children can accomplish on a much grander scale. I shall demonstrate my meager skill in earth-sensing, which is a form of surveillance." She offered a ghost of a smile as she turned and placed her hand upon the ground. "You've seen one use of it before—when I created the map from soil."

Her brow furrowed, red light flashed in her eyes, and ripples spread out from her hand through the dirt, plants and detritus shivering as they passed. Thomas froze in the act of touching his toes, staring at the rings of raised earth as they swept toward him, then grimaced as the wave rolled beneath and past him. "What the—"

Dinah slumped and exhaled shakily. Perspiration bedewed her forehead. After a deep breath, she said, "Each life form has its own special energy signature. I just scanned the soil beneath us for poisonous scorpions. Just within this clearing, there are four hundred and twenty-three. But don't worry," she added when he hastily got his legs under him, "The scorpions are far too small to pose a danger to us."

"Well, that's reassuring ... if creepy." Pensive, Thomas stared at the ground. His skin crawled and he fought the urge to scratch. "So, with this earth-sense, you can concentrate on something's energy and seek it out. Something like, say, a wyldling."

"Yes, Sir Thomas. Each human possesses a unique energy signature. Souretholim and wyldlings stand out because they possess a special 'shine,' in a manner of speaking, due to their manipulation of the Aethyr."

The dwelfnhad sounded tired. Glancing up, he asked, "Are you okay? That seemed to take a lot out of you."

"I'm fine. Thank you." Dinah brought out a handkerchief and wiped her face. "My sensory range is quite limited. Merely searching this small area saps my strength. David is stronger—he's older than me and has more experience—but his strength peters out after a mile or two."

A hope that had begun glowing flickered and died. "So, you and your cousin couldn't find Enoch or Annabelle?"

She shook her head. "Only if they were nearby. David and I together could, at our best, extend our range to a ten-mile radius, and it would take hours to complete. By combining our efforts with every Stonesinger in existence, we could possibly survey half of the Imerinthian continent within a moon's span."

Raising his eyebrows, Thomas whistled. "That's impressive, Ambassador. And I suppose with the Caretaker's coordination, all of you Stonesingers could scan more land even faster?"

She gave him a wry look. "Certainly. Although the Stonesingers need not take part in it. With the aid of her Farseer, Lady Delwyr's sensory range encompasses the entire planet. She could locate Enoch Northward in a day or two."

"Criminy," Thomas said. "That must take real focus and discipline." He frowned, pondering. An idea began to take shape. "Energy signatures. Huh. I wonder if I could do something similar. Come up with my own fire-based method to find Enoch and Annabelle."

"It's possible, Sir Thomas," Dinah replied, sitting up taller. "You know ... as a wyldling, you have the option of seeking them in the dreamscape. I believe you and Ann discussed meeting in the dreamscape to train, at one point. Back when ..." She cleared her throat. "Forgive me. Back when you were a toad."

He met Dinah's inquiring gaze. Her eyes were bright and her lips pressed tightly together.

Is she going to cry again, about Annabelle being gone? I sure as heck hope not.

Thomas straightened. "You don't need to walk on eggshells. Yes, I was a toad. I'm not anymore. As for me searching the dreamscape ..." He scrubbed a hand through his hair. "Technically, the idea has merit."

But if I do that, then I risk ending up in that caldera with Balthazar. I don't feel like enduring another lecture about how I need to confront my fears. And yet ...

"I'll definitely try. Again, I mean, and this time seek energy signatures. I haven't succeeded yet in finding Annabelle in the dreamscape. Even before she—" He broke off.

The dwelfnhad had settled back on her heels, biting her lips and staring at the flint and steel. Her eyes shimmered with unshed tears.

Oh, good grief. For the love of bullfrogs everywhere, she needs to pull herself together. Thomas sighed as he continued his stretches. Because stretching was something he could *do*.

Sniffling, Dinah wiped her eyes. Then she spoke, her voice firm. "Will you make another attempt to find her tonight? If you still can't reach her ..." With a shaky breath, she pasted a smile on her face. "Regardless, there is still time, if you decide to change your mind about the Evergold Desert." Taking out steel and flint, she struck sparks into a pile of fluffy tinder.

Thomas squinted at the falling sparks. *Why is she laying a fire here? There's already one back in camp.* "Ambassador, if you wanted a fire lit—"

Dinah spoke in a clipped tone, like a no-nonsense nurse. "You're already exhausted, Sir Thomas. Do you want to make things worse for yourself?" She bent and blew on the tiny flames.

Thomas was suddenly reminded of the first time Annabelle had struggled to light a fire, back when he'd been Toad. He'd helped her, though she hadn't known it. The effort of growing and sustaining the spark she'd struck had worn him out. Once he'd learned that lying in the suns would replenish his reservoir, he'd found himself capable of much more.

He peered upward between leafy branches. *And here we are, under overcast skies. It hasn't helped matters that I haven't been able to soak in the suns' energy.*

"But why're you building a fire? Would you like me to juggle lit torches or balls of fire—maybe make them different colors?"

Thomas sniggered. "If I'm too worn out to create fire, then I'm sure as spit too worn out to do any tricks with it."

"No tricks necessary." Dinah gave him a tight-lipped smile, which seemed at odds with her beautiful face. "I built this fire for a purpose. Did it not occur to you to wonder why Commander Storm insists on having a fire whenever we stop to rest, despite it being high summer?"

"Heh." Thomas snorted. "Of course I do. Kinda hard to cook meat and boil water without one." At Dinah's arched eyebrows, he held up his hands. "Okay. I'll stop kidding around. The fires are so I can absorb energy."

She smiled. "David and I were debating your limits as they pertain to extracting energy from fire. I think we should test them."

He shrugged, then scratched his bristly chin. Time to shave again. "I'm all for pushing the limits of my abilities." Even if it hurt, he needed to get stronger. For the sake of the kids.

Dinah fed the flames. Soon, the fire burned steadily. With a satisfied nod, she straightened, then rose, waving a hand at the merrily crackling blaze. "Now, Sir Thomas. I'd like you to draw the heat from this fire into your reservoir." Rising to her feet, she quirked an eyebrow. "Do you need a hand up?"

"No." Thomas scoffed. "But thank you." His limbs trembled as he stood and shambled to the fire. Even as he concentrated on not stumbling, the flames drew him like a starving man to a banquet, tugging deep in his gut. Closing his eyes, he leaned over the fire. Heat licked his face. *It feels so good.*

"Careful!" Dinah grabbed his arm when he teetered, nearly collapsing into the fire.

Thomas sank to his knees, staring at his hands, unmarked by blisters or burns. "Should've let me fall," he mumbled. "My wyld is fire. I probably would've been fine."

Letting go of him, Dinah sighed. "Are you absolutely certain you won't get burned?" She shook her head. "Never mind. This is not the time to test that out."

"Enough chatter." Thomas rubbed his hands together, then braced them against his thighs. "Let's just do this." Narrowing his eyes, he peered into the flames and extended his awareness as tiny tendrils—kythim, Enoch and Annabelle called it. His kythim gravitated naturally toward the fire. A pulse of warmth trickled into his core. He grinned. "It's working."

Thomas *pulled*, and the heat entered him in a rush even as the flames diminished to embers. He rocked back with a grunt. His body vibrated and his head threatened to break free from his neck and float away.

"C-Criminy!"

Electricity zinging through him, Thomas leaped to his feet, and Dinah backpedaled with a yelp. And then the buzzing sensation subsided to a dull glow deep inside him.

Dinah gaped, and Thomas grinned sheepishly. "Sorry, Ambassador. I guess I extracted a little *too* hard. I hope that didn't ruin your experiment."

The dwelfnhad blinked and drew in a shuddery breath. She forced a smile. "On the contrary, Sir Thomas. We both learned something here. You demonstrated how quickly you can draw energy, and that doing so extinguishes a fire."

"And you learned to keep your distance." Thomas chuckled. "Now, if only we could package a fire and bring it along with us." Dinah tapped her lips, looking thoughtful as he circled the smoking remains of the fire. "Here's another upside: now I can walk. And finish my exercises." He glanced at his feet. "Oh. And before I forget ... thank you, Ambassador."

This time, her wan smile seemed less forced. "You are welcome, Sir Thomas." She inclined her head slightly, then took another step backward, fidgeting with her belt pouch. "If you don't mind, David and I have our devotions now. And breakfast." Gently she added, "You are welcome to join us"

He waved at the pack he'd left sitting on a rock under a tree. "No, thank you. I brought my own breakfast." Besides, listening to their devotions made him itch inside his head and feel even more inadequate.

"Devotion only takes a few minutes." She hesitated, then met his gaze directly. "I think it would help with your ... problem."

Oh, no. Not this again. He bristled. "What problem is that?"

"Your temper. And blaming yourself ..." She swallowed. "... for what happened."

But losing the kiddo *was* his fault. What good would reading Bible verses do? It wouldn't bring her back, and it wouldn't make him less angry. *I'd rather do five hundred push-ups. At least that way I'm* doing *something.* Thomas swallowed the snarky comment before it passed his lips. Dinah didn't deserve that. She'd been kind enough to build that fire, and she'd helped him come up with the idea to use energy signatures to seek Annabelle and Enoch in the dreamscape.

When he didn't immediately respond, she persisted. "After your reaction to losing Annabelle, David and I are very concerned. So is Commander Storm, though he would never admit as much." Black hair had come loose from her braid, and she pushed a stray lock behind a pointed ear. "You should speak with him. David, I mean." Her topaz eyes grew sorrowful. "We're your friends, Sir Thomas. We only want to help you."

This is embarrassing. How do I deflect her concern? I don't need *that kind of help.*

Glancing at his feet, Thomas shrugged. "Uh ... thanks for that. I suppose it couldn't hurt to talk with the Shepherd. Tell him I wouldn't mind a quick spar, once we reach the fort." He took a deep breath. If they wanted to help him, then maybe they would have some ideas as to how he might control where he ended up in the world of dreams. "And when we get underway, I want to pick your brains about locating Annabelle in the dreamscape."

Dinah blinked, looking confused, then her expression cleared, and she smiled. "Yes. Of course, Sir Thomas. Sounds like a splendid plan."

Watching her walk back toward camp with a spring in her step, he mused: *I'll convince them there's nothing wrong with me that hard work, plenty of practice, and finding Annabelle and Enoch won't fix.*

Octopus's Garden

Clinging to her champion's arm, Annabelle tried looking everywhere at once. The garden to which Mordred led them rioted with colorful blossoms, pleasant floral scents, singing birds, and humming bees. Lined by flowers, a canal meandered throughout and widened into pools like crystal beads on a silver necklace. Fruit-bearing trees of exotic types grew around these cisterns with low, stone benches placed to take advantage of their shade. There was even a small pavilion with a palm frond roof in the middle of the orchard.

However, Annabelle found it difficult to fully appreciate the garden's natural beauty. Guards surrounded them, their spears angled toward Raeden, and his uneasiness seeped through the Oathbond. After Raeden had given his word of honor that he would not attack them again, Mordred allowed Annabelle to hold Raeden's knife. She experienced a pang as she attached it to her belt where the Dagger of Moonlight had once hung and nearly went into a panic attack.

What if I never find Daar-Lûsin?

Patting her hand, Raeden bent to whisper in her ear. "Fear not, Freylin. Threefold One willing, your servant will not leave you to these ... tricksome water sprites. He will make their king hear reason and see sense." His uneasiness subsided, buried under a wave of warm reassurance, followed by steely determination.

While they walked up from the beach, the guards had alternated between staring at her and murmuring in awe and grumbling about the "scout hound" being punished for harming the princeps. *But I healed the damage! That should count for something.* Would the gwerindawr king—the Brenin— lock up her champion in jail anyway? Annabelle's grip tightened on Raeden's arm and tears burned in her eyes at the thought of being separated from him. There were other things to worry about, too. Her mind ping-ponged between two thoughts: what was this crazy prophecy the gwerindawr had about the Ahdmerel, and how could she convince the merfolk to bring them to their waystone?

We need to get back to the others. Can I use this prophecy to our advantage somehow? As much as she hated the idea of manipulating the reverence of the gwerindawr toward the 'blessed Ahdmerel,' escaping from this place must be a priority.

The handsome princeps wouldn't speak about the prophecy, claiming that was the province of the archimandrite— who was most likely with the Brenin at his Court. The answer was the same when she asked about the waystone: She must wait until they met the king.

Mordred paused beside one of the pools. Yellow and pink water lilies floated languidly on its surface. Annabelle's eyes were drawn to the fountain feature at the far end. She gasped as elation filled her.

Raeden glanced at her with concern. "Freylin?"

"It's Hadrien!" Grinning, she pointed at the stone figure rearing up on one end of the pool, wings spread, and forelimbs extended with palms facing outward. Water trickled from his eyes and jetted from his clawed hands.

"Why do you stop, water sprite?" Raeden asked their guide. He made a show of looking around the garden. "One does not see any king here." He nodded at the statue of Hadrien. "Unless your king is that stone Sage." Her champion's whiskers quivered in mirth as he cast her a sidelong glance. Annabelle giggled, clapping her hands over her mouth.

Mordred looked at him incredulously and several of the guards laughed. Unlike Annabelle's, it held a mocking note. "Ignorant beast," one of the others muttered.

"He was joking." Annabelle frowned at all of them. *If Raeden can retain his sense of humor, then everything will be okay.*

"A joke in poor taste, but what else can one expect from an uncouth scout hound?" Mordred scoffed. Raeden growled. Tapping at his knives' hilts, the princeps narrowed his eyes. "To answer your question, we have stopped here so that you can refresh yourselves before I present you to my father." He beckoned one of the guards. "Lladdhe, please apprise His Majesty about our guests."

The ochre-skinned man bowed, handed his spear to another guard, then turned and dove into the pool with scarcely a ripple in his wake.

"What the frumious bandersnatch..." Staring at where he'd disappeared, Annabelle approached the pool with Raeden close on her heels. "Is there a ... portal in there?" *Maybe their waystone is underwater. Could we get out of here that way? If only I had the dagger!*

"Not quite, Lady Ann." Mordred chuckled as he sauntered to her side. "An underwater tunnel system connects all pools and shelters across the island."

So much for that idea. But still, the pool looked so fresh and cool. The lilies bobbed serenely, and the water beckoned her with a familiar tug at her gut. Raising the tide on the beach had drained her and she needed to soak. She drifted closer.

A hand on her shoulder halted her at the edge and she whirled around. Ears laid back, Raeden's green eyes were wide as he hissed, "Careful, Freylin. One cannot know the dangers of this place."

Mordred stiffened. "There are no dangers here for the Ahdmerel. The pool is shallow at this end. She is free to drink from the fountain without harm."

Annabelle laughed shakily. "It'll be okay." She patted her champion's hand, gently dislodged it from her shoulder, then sat at the pool's edge. It would be nice to rinse off the salt and sand she'd accumulated since removing her boots and trekking up the beach. "You must be thirsty, too. Why don't you drink some water from the fountain?" She smiled, nodding toward the statue. "I'm sure Hadrien won't mind."

"Indeed, he would not," Mordred said, smiling. "Rainblessed is generous with his gifts." He sat down and dangled his legs into the pool.

Eyes fixed on the princeps at her side, Raeden squared his shoulders and clasped his hands behind his back. "Your servant will wait until you finish washing." Disheveled though he was and surrounded by trident-toting men, the kaenhir exuded a natural poise and dignity like he hadn't a care in the world. The black thread of rage stitching through the Oathbond while he glared at Mordred told a different tale.

Annabelle's grin faltered. *I hope he can keep himself together like that when we're standing in front of the king.* "Okay. This shouldn't take long." After rolling up her trousers, she scooched to the pool's edge and swung her feet over, then slipped into the water. Beneath her feet, the pool's bottom was pebbled and sloped toward the center.

When Mordred slipped into the pool, Raeden inhaled sharply. The Oathbond trembled but he said nothing. Had one of the men stuck him again with a spear? Her heart skipped a beat as she recalled the attack on the beach. *No!* She whirled to confront them.

None of the guards threatened her champion and he stood as he had before, unharmed. He tilted his head. "Freylin?" He spoke while Mordred asked, "Lady Ann?" The two men glared at one another. The guards tensed. Slowly, the princeps retreated until he was sitting on the edge of the pool, his golden eyes darting between her and her champion.

Please God, no more fighting!

Annabelle forced a smile and shook her head. "Nothing's wrong."

Mordred waved and the other gwerindawr relaxed and began talking among themselves. Laughing inwardly at her paranoia, she returned to her enjoyment of the pool. Cool water encircled her waist as the water lilies danced away from her on the ripples she created. She scooped up water, scrubbed her face, and smoothed back her straggly hair.

I wish I had a comb.

With a sigh, she wriggled her toes and gazed at the weeping Hadrien statue. She leaned back until she floated, soaking her hair. Part of her yearned to sink deeper into the pool until the water closed over her head, but Raeden would probably freak out if she did. Although he'd praised her for bringing them all the way to land on the bubble raft she'd created, he still seemed uneasy about both her connection to Hadrien and her wyldling abilities. A line creased her brow while she stared up into the sky. A wispy cloud drifted past. Why did it bother him so much that she was for all intents and purposes a water mage? Was it because he couldn't swim? That was easy enough to remedy. There was plenty of water around to practice in.

Annabelle stood up and squeezed out her messy braid. Water tinkled musically back into the pool. "How much longer until we can see the king?" *And get some answers.*

Mordred sat on the edge to her right, an arm-length away, and dangled his blue legs in the water. He flashed her a dazzling smile. "It will not be long, Lady Ann. Lladdhe should return it three flicks of a lightning bream's tail."

Behind her, Raeden grumbled about the diabolical nature of the Trading Language. She chuckled. "Where I'm from, we say 'two shakes of a lamb's tail,' but you're merpeople, so I guess you'd use water-based idioms. I suppose you don't have sheep here." Something tickled her left leg. A minnow? Water weeds? She shifted her feet further to the right.

The princeps tilted his head and frowned at the sky. "No, Lady Ann, we do not." After glancing at her champion, his golden eyes returned to her with an intensity that made her heart flutter. "Will that be a problem?"

"No. I was just ..." A muscular tendril snaked up along her left calf. Squealing, she backpedaled until her back struck the pool's edge. She gasped, "Something touched me!" Mordred moved toward her, but her champion reached her first.

With a shout, Raeden grasped her under the arms and hauled her out. He set her on her feet, and she stared at the pink and yellow blooms surfing the waves she'd created, but nothing burst out. Her heart pounded a million miles a minute. "Oh, my gosh! Are there lampreys in there?" Just the thought of a jawless eel latching on to her like a giant leech sent a shiver down her spine.

Baring his fangs, Raeden snarled. "What vile trick is this, honorless water sprite? You put her in danger!" He pulled Annabelle in close, and she sagged against him.

The guards leveled their tridents at her champion. "Release the Ahdmerel," demanded one with fuchsia skin and indigo hair.

"Hold, men!" Mordred cried. He'd half turned with hands lifted, one leg still in the water, and the other tucked under him. "There are no lampreys in our waters, Lady Ann."

She sighed. "Thank God! What was it, a snake?"

"No." Raising his eyebrows, Mordred gave her a confident grin while he gently splashed in the water, then stuck his arm straight in up to the elbow. "Lady Ann, I'd like to introduce you to a friend of mine. Aha!" His laughter was joyful and carefree. He rose, pulling his arm out of the water, then sauntered toward them.

Raeden tensed, turning to one side to shield Annabelle. "What is that little creature?" He snuffled. "This one has not scented it before."

Beaming, Mordred held out his arm. "This is Wesleyen. Don't worry; he's harmless." Something mottled green and orange the size of a softball clung to his wrist like a lumpy bracelet. Bulbous eyes with slotted pupils peered at her with curiosity and intelligence.

Oh, my gosh, it's a little octopus! So freaking adorable.

A thrill running through her, Annabelle let out a squeal. "Cute!"

Her champion relaxed and loosened his arms. "Is it then not a threat?"

Stepping away from him, Annabelle laughed. "No. Otherwise, why would Mordred bring it out here?" She reached out to touch the creature, then hesitated, glancing back at Raeden, then at Mordred. "Can I ... Can I hold it?"

Mordred chuckled. "Of course. Go on, Wes. Greet Lady Ann properly." The octopus pulled several of its tentacles off Mordred's arm, twined them around Annabelle's wrist, and crawled into her hand. Its skin rippled, shifting from mostly orange and green to acquire dark blue splotches with lighter blue stripes on its tentacles.

"Freylin ..." The Oathbond quivered with a warning.

"It's okay, Raeden. Hello, Wesleyen," She crooned. "Who's the prettiest octopus in the world? You are." Wesleyen stared at her while its arms writhed like a nest of blue worms. It was less slimy than she anticipated, more velvety and slippery. The suckers prickled against her skin as its muscular tentacles explored her fingers, palm, and forearm. She giggled. "That tickles!"

"This is excellent," Mordred said. "Wes took to you more quickly than I thought he would. Usually, he's more reserved."

"He's wonderful." Annabelle laughed, cringing a little as Wesleyen pulled himself up to her left shoulder and began poking in her ear. "Eee! Not there." She offered a finger for Wesleyen to wrap a tentacle around and coaxed him into her right hand. Colorful patterns flickered across his skin. "I'm just amazed there are species of freshwater octopi here. I didn't realize they were so adaptable. I thought they can only survive in saltwater."

"Our octopus companions can live in either." Smiling, Mordred moved nearer until she could feel his body heat. "Do you know, Lady Ann? They can survive out of water for more than an hour. They're remarkable creatures, loyal friends, very clever, but often bent on mischief." His expression fond, he petted Wesleyen's head. "Soon after he hatched, Wes would climb out of his mother's spawning garden every morning and crawl across the courtyard to my sister's basking pool. The little blighter would steal her breakfast berries right off the serving platter and then hide them inside the water lilies. It drove Rhia to distraction."

Annabelle giggled. "That's hilarious. You're so smart, Wes!" she said, stroking between the cephalopod's eyes. She looked up into Mordred's friendly countenance and then shrank back. The afternoon suddenly felt too warm for the handsome princeps to be standing so close. *And I'm a mess. I hope I can take a proper bath soon.* She focused on the octopus. "Um. I remember you mentioning a sister when we first ... met. Her name is Rhia? Are you two close?"

"Yes." Mordred grinned. "Her name is Rhiannon. She's preparing for her duties when she becomes queen, which takes up much of her time, and I am quite busy as the Captain of our Howling Tempest. But we remain close, despite her being three cycles my elder. She's always been like a mother to me; after our mother went home to Lord Yshua when I was four, Rhia took charge of my care."

"Oh." Eyes wide, she met Mordred's gaze. "I'm sorry you lost your mother." *Nine years difference in their ages. That's the same as between me and my baby sister. At thirteen, would I have been able to raise Drew and Amy?*

Touching her arm, he smiled. His golden eyes drew her in. "You have a kind heart, Lady Ann. But there's nothing to regret. I don't remember my mother."

He seems like a nice guy. Maybe he'll help us, once we've spoken with his father.

Grumbling something in his native language, Raeden drew up beside her and cleared his throat. "Freylin, perhaps you should return the little blue creature to the water."

"Okay," Annabelle whispered, shaking herself. Mordred's smile vanished and he stepped away, the spell broken. At the pool's edge, she hunkered down and extended her arm into the water. She looked at the octopus and felt a pang at leaving him. "Alright, Wes. You'd better get back home to your family." *At least he has that option. I'm not sure when or how I'll get home, after I save Enoch.* It probably wouldn't be too bad staying on Tehara. She had friends here. And yet ... Tears stung her eyes and she blinked them away.

The cephalopod stared up at her. His tentacles gripped tighter. He wouldn't budge.

Annabelle lifted him from the water and looked into his bulbous, slot-pupiled eyes. "You want to stay with me?" His skin shifted completely to dark blue, and ribbons of aqua blue rippled along his tentacles as Wesleyen crawled up her arm to perch on her shoulder. She laughed, feeling a bit lighter. "Alrighty, then."

Rising, she turned to find the gwerindawr men staring at her, slack jawed. "Just like in the prophecy," a coral-skinned man breathed. Mordred nodded. "As the current flows, so shall it be," he murmured. He made an undulatory gesture with his right hand, then bowed. "Lady Ann."

Annabelle groaned. "Now what did I do?" Rolling her eyes, she sought her champion, whose expression was darkening as the Oathbond grew prickly.

Water splashed behind her and the ochre gwerindawr, Lladdhe, clambered from the pool, brushing off a water lily. "Captain," he announced, scanning them all. His eyes widened as he took in Annabelle and the blue octopus. "Uh. Well." He swallowed, and his gaze shifted to Mordred. "Your Highness. The Brenin and his heir are eager to receive the blessed Ahdmerel in the Royal Courtyard."

Swallowing sudden fear, Annabelle straightened her spine. Ready or not, it was time for her to meet royalty.

Risk

It was time to meet his fate.

William glanced into the void above. According to tradition, every Arkhadahn's Trial took place under the cold and silent regard of the midnight stars. When the constellation Valkor's Scythe attained its zenith, Tenebris would come out to challenge William's spellform. If he could endure his master's onslaught for longer than fifteen minutes, then Tenebris would add to his arkhabala by tattooing four more circles into his back. If William couldn't endure, then ...

He clenched his hands into fists. *Don't even think of defeat!*

The grit he'd scattered on the pitiless stones of the parapet in preparation crunched as he shifted his weight. Chalk- and blood-stained fingers clenched and unclenched, itching for the flask he hadn't dared bring up here and instead left with his burkheld and sakkhelt, back in his room. What he wouldn't give for a sip of whisky right now.

He swallowed the curse that rose to his lips. *Hold it together. You've studied and bled for this. Even devised a trick or three. You're ready.*

Pride's warm glow filled him as he gazed at his spellform. It was his own design, an amalgamation of fragments gleaned from nearly a hundred spells he'd studied over the past season and put together in an entirely new way. The grit—crushed beetle carapaces, spider legs, and snail shells mixed with sand and a bit of his blood—was an innovation. Something Tenebris wouldn't be expecting.

He could feel the string of soot panther fangs he'd hastily sewn on the inside of his trouser waistband, the teeth warm against his skin. Perhaps they also would aid him, as Zakaar hoped. Zakaar's gifting of the teeth still flummoxed him.

I still can't believe he just gave *them to me. They were supposed to be trophies to commemorate his kills. He said he gave them to me because I'm his friend, and he knew I wanted them. Is that what friendship means, then?*

William tensed as the wooden door of the fortress keep creaked open and Tenebris strode out into the night toward him, black robes swishing around his ankles. He halted a pace away from the boundary of William's spellform. Stroking his chin, the Arkhadahn stalked the perimeter of William's construct, his carnelian gaze raking over the chalk patterns.

Arkhabala coiling in readiness, William turned to keep his master in view. Both his countenance and gray kythim remained still, giving nothing away.

William unclenched his fingers and forced himself to breathe evenly. *You won't find any errors, Tenebris. I've triple-checked my calculations; painstakingly scribed every rune and drew every line with precision.*

Tenebris stopped, frowning at the memory rune. William's breath caught in his throat. Had his master found a weakness? Was the spellform mucked up, after all? He swallowed, then squared his shoulders. At his sides fingers curled to form fists, nails digging into damp palms. With an effort, he loosened them. *Suns burn it! I want my whiskey flask. Let's get on with this, Tenebris.* His right hand hovered near the hilt of his bone knife. A breeze from the southeast fanned him, chilling the sweat on his back. Hopefully it wouldn't disturb the grit he'd laid down.

Finally, his master's eyes flicked up, gleaming. "A marriage of simplicity and complexity. Two moons ago, I never would have expected this of you, William. But now ..." A faint smile curved his thin lips. "We shall see if you possess the necessary mettle to advance. Remember, you cannot tap into the Aethyr for this."

I don't need to cheat in order to survive your battle spells, Tenebris.

William bit back the scathing reply rising to his lips. "I know, Master. I never intended to." He flexed his fingers and his arkhabala prickled as he sent energy into the tattoos.

His master snapped his fingers, and a sand timer limned with orange light appeared on the periphery of the spellform. Eyes flashing, Tenebris snapped, "Ivektormahl!"

The timing glass flipped, and the sand began its slow and steady trickle.

It begins.

William tensed, Ripping out his knife from its sheath as his master raised a hand surrounded by a black mist and flickering orange lightning—a third level Pain Hex, as he'd predicted. He muttered a cantrip, slashed the blade along his forearm, and flung droplets of blood into the pattern chalked at his feet. A three-layer advanced battle shield sprang into existence around him just as Tenebris released his spell. The angry cloud ate away at the two outer layers, then disintegrated when it contacted the third.

William frowned at the tingling sensation coursing through his arkhabala. He'd earned his third circle, but his master's offense packed a punch and the impact had weakened the shield more than he'd anticipated. Tenebris was playing dirty. No worries. William had expected that. Now, Tenebris was probably expecting him to complain about it. He blurted, "That was a Fifth Order Pain Hex!"

"Indeed, Arkhasuhl." His master replied with a thin smile. "Did you think this was going to be easy?" He waved a hand as he circled the spellform. "Quit whining. Your shield held. You've acquired your third circle." He sounded disappointed.

William allowed himself a tight-lipped smile. *You expected me to buckle, didn't you, Tenebris?* While his master paced, William reinforced his battle shield. So far, all went according to plan. Instead of binding his self-inflicted wound, as he normally would, he allowed the blood to flow in a warm trickle down along his hand and fingers to drip upon the stones as he moved along a slow, spiraling path from the center of his spellform. His gaze never left that of his master's. Time seemed to slow, but a quick glance at the sand timer informed him otherwise.

Holding his battle-shield steady, William tensed in preparation. To earn his fourth circle, he'd build a physical construct while maintaining a shield that would withstand a round of his master's offensive spells. Time to conjure his golem. He kept his face carefully blank; he'd added a creative twist. Murmuring the words of the cantrip he'd adapted from a similar spell, he unleashed the potential in the blood he'd scattered. In a blizzard-like flurry, the grit rose and congealed into the shape he'd devised just as Tenebris gathered black clouds and orange lightning between his palms—more and larger than before.

William barked out a verbal command, and the construct solidified into an arachnid monstrosity. The black spider pushed up on jointed, bristly legs to about the height of his waist, its glowing orange eyes fixed on Tenebris. Purple antennae quivered as it clicked fanged palps. Moth's wings unfurled from its back, dark blue traced with threads of silver. He gasped for breath. Pain quivered along his arkhabala.

Burning suns! That expended more energy than he'd calculated. Unease burrowed like tiny worms through his gut, but he couldn't back down now.

Tenebris frowned, peering at his construct. "What manner of shape did you choose for your golem, William? It's unnatural." Between his master's palms the dark cloud had grown threefold the size of the previous hex.

I thought that was obvious!

"A moth-spider hybrid." William wiped his forehead and scowled. "You said my golem didn't have to be naturally occurring so long as it was some sort of beast." Tapping its front legs rhythmically against the stone and fluttering its wings, the construct chittered in what sounded like approval.

Tenebris shuddered. "Well, I hope the energy expenditure is worth it, because that thing is absolutely hideous."

Despite his fatigue an exultant grin spread across William's face. He patted one bristly leg. *Don't listen to Tenebris, Milady Blue*, he soothed the hybrid creature, squeezing more blood from his wound to feed the spell that would increase the construct's size. He panted, fighting a surge of vertigo. *You're worth every drop. And you're not hideous—you're magnificent.*

On impulse, he'd given his familiar the same appellation as the maiden he hunted in the dreamscape. He wasn't sure why the idea appealed to him so much, but he'd imbued the construct with the same warmth he'd observed in Annabelle.

At least this Milady Blue can't beguile me. And it'll do as I say.

Black tendrils from Tenebris's arkhabala crept up his neck and into his face like war paint. The stench of ozone filled the air, nearly drowning out the coppery reek of freshly spilled blood. William's stomach twisted, and he swallowed nausea. From the palpable build-up of energy around him, he assumed that Tenebris was preparing to launch another magical assault.

A Master Arkhadahn of the Thirteenth Order had no need to utter cantrips.

That'll be me one day ... when I defeat him in the Arkhadahn's Challenge and absorb his power by rite of conquest. "We keep what we kill," just as Tenebris had taught him.

The energy on the parapet attained its peak. Bobbing up and down, the golem rattled its palps in warning as Tenebris released his next magical assault. As before, the black cloud spread across the orange barrier, and William grunted, driven to his knees. *I must endure this or forfeit the trial.* He sent more energy into his circles to reinforce his shield and felt vine-like offshoots of the tattoos writhing along his back, up his neck, and down his arms. His defense strengthened as his arkhabala tingled with pins and needles. Its potential had drained to a dangerously low level. His unease turned to fear.

My next trick better work, or I'm done for ...

Head spinning, he slapped his palms against the bloody runes and spat out a cantrip, straining to bend the power to his will. *Come on!* Unlike before, the spellform absorbed the energy from the lightning as it crackled along the shield. Both the barrier and the chalk-lines briefly flared orange.

Power infused his arkhabala, recharging his circles' energy to full capacity. *It worked! I passed the Fifth Order trial.* Feeling like he'd shake apart, his lungs labored as the overflow passed through him and into the construct. His spider-moth golem swelled, doubling in size, and the fracturing sensation subsided. Panting, he stared. Midnight blue wings fanned out and eight legs tensed, poised to spring. A thrill went through William when Tenebris's eyelids twitched and his jaw clenched.

"Ha!" he gasped. "All that, and no wounds. Weren't anticipating that, were you, Master?"

Tenebris sneered. "Is that the largest golem you can conjure?" He snorted. "Pathetic. Just what I'd expect from a half-breed."

William flinched. The spell layers faltered as he nearly lost control. His arkhabala seared with a flux of power and he felt as if he'd been scalded from the inside. A snarl twisted his lips.

I won't let him grind me down.

Milady Blue chittered and braced him up, bristles poking his bare skin. Two huge, round eyes stared at him. He felt a wave of warmth and concern from—it? Her? Her. Fascinating. A newfound determination filled him.

"It's all right, Milady Blue," he rasped. "I've earned my fourth and fifth circles in one go." Grasping her proffered leg, he pulled himself up to his feet, glaring at Tenebris the entire time.

His master arched an eyebrow. "Milady Blue?" he remarked in a mocking tone. "Is this some sort of jest?" Blazing eyes narrowed. "Be serious. You've earned five circles, but with that cavalier attitude, you won't attain acolyte status tonight."

"I am completely serious." Pushing past his fear, William squared his shoulders as he stood tall beside his golem. "You won't defeat me, Tenebris. I'll have my circles—all six."

I won't fail.

"That remains to be seen." With a grim smile, his master accumulated the dark energy cloud for another offensive spell, twice the size of the previous one. "Because that was all apprentice level, I've gone easy on you thus far. But I won't tolerate mediocrity in an acolyte. Prepare yourself, William. Show me you can be excellent." Eyes glowing, he muttered an incantation.

Jaw clenched, breath hissing through his teeth, William reassured himself that the shield still held, and his golem was stable. To earn his sixth circle, he'd launch a Sixth Order assault on his master. He applied himself to the spell before Tenebris built up enough energy to attack again. Doubtless, the final part of his trial would be a barrage of Pain Hexes. Tenebris might be powerful, but he wasn't terribly creative.

William's fingers curled tighter around the hilt of his knife, and he set the blade to his scarred forearm, drawing fresh blood. Still watching Tenebris, he let it drip as his mind reached out for his golem.

Prepare yourself, Milady Blue.

She sidled closer, brushing against him. Warmth and a fierce protectiveness washed over him in an overwhelming wave. His awareness fractured, and part of his awareness hurtled backwards in time and elsewhere in space. He was sobbing, clinging to a woman's neck, his tears wetting her hair. Honeysuckle wreathed him with its scent. Soft fingers stroked his head soothingly. The woman's voice whispered: *"Hush, baby. Don't you cry. I'll keep you safe, my sweet William."*

William snapped back to the present with a gasp, shivering and slicked with sweat. What in all the nether perditions and outer darkness was that? Another hallucination? This was neither the time nor the place! Had Tenebris snuck in a delirium spell while he was building his golem?

Shaking himself, he redoubled his surveillance of Tenebris. As if no time had passed at all, the dark cloud building between his master's palms was no larger, but it appeared denser with a subtly different shade. William frowned. What was Tenebris conjuring this time? It didn't look like a Pain Hex. Could it be ... Would he dare break tradition to punish him with *that* spell?

Yes. Yes, he would.

Fear's cold talons twisted William' stomach into knots. His shield wouldn't hold against a Seventh Order malecto grammerye—in this case, a paralysis curse. Luckily, he had his backup plan. He reached for the connection to his golem and sent instructions.

Milady Blue lifted her wings and rattled her palps in response, sending back firm resolve and reassurance. When the shield went down—given the potency of Tenebris's spell, there was no preventing that now—she would make sure that none of Tenebris's attacks touched him, leaving him free to launch his counterstrike.

Good girl. We're not out of the fight yet. He rattled off the cantrip and felt the drain on his arkhabala as Milady Blue swelled, the top of her leg joints at William's shoulders.

With a snarl, Tenebris unleashed his assault. The dark energy exploded outward, splitting into myriad streams which struck like vipers at multiple points of William's defense. Agony seared through his arkhabala as the shield fell. It burned like all three suns.

Milady Blue sprang in front of him. Sparks flew and she shrieked like a teakettle. He staggered and fell on his backside with a grunt, clenching his jaw to prevent a cry from escaping. Blood gushed from his lower lip when his teeth ripped it. The metallic tang coated his tongue, and he spat.

William grinned savagely. Thanks to his master, he was accustomed to such discomfort. He glanced at the sand timer.

Let's roll the bones.

If his master could cheat by using Seventh order spells, then so would he! Pushing aside nausea, William seized the power from his shed blood and snapped a command. Energy surged. His golem expanded again, to the size of a mammoth, then split into three. Through the haze of pain and crackling lightning, he saw his master's jaw drop.

Despite the warning throb of his arkhabala, William chuckled. "I've got you now!" Blood dribbled down his chin. "Go, Milady Blue."

Two constructs darted in opposite directions while the third hunkered over its creator with wings spread wide. Hand trembling, William touched the fuzzy carapace. *Feels like a poison peach.* He grinned, more blood trickling from his cut lip as he pushed up on his hands and knees, panting. Sweat dripped to the stones; too bad he couldn't use that to recharge his spellform. He wiped the blood from his chin and traced a rune of reinforcement. More energy flowed from him into the constructs, waning dangerously. *Just a little longer.*

William panted, his heart beating a staccato against his breastbone, and gasped out the attack cantrip. Pain lanced through his arkhabala and power backlashed piling into him like a giant fist. Milady Blue uttered a piercing screech. Arms boneless, William grunted and nearly collapsed flat on his face. A sense of aching loss hollowed him out. Grit pattered down like rain on the spellform.

Tenebris must've destroyed one of the constructs.

"Suns curse it," he rasped, slapping a hand on the spellform's lines. "That's a third of my power gone." The blood-infused grit made the golem more real, hence the impact of dissolution was stronger than it would have been otherwise. He'd known it would be a risk going into the Trial, but if he could endure, then the gamble would pay off.

I must lay Tenebris out flat with my next attack.

From beneath his primary construct, he watched the other engage Tenebris. Wings beat at the Arkhadahn while it darted at him with fanged palps at the ready. But Tenebris managed to keep it from landing a blow or a bite, shielding himself even as he gathered energy for another devastating offensive spell.

At least he's distracted enough not to throw it at me.

William spat blood. "Attack, Milady Blue." The golem chittered uncertainly, sending a wave of concern regarding his safety. He swallowed his annoyance. "I didn't conjure you to play nursemaid. Just do as I say and *attack*."

"Problems, William?" His tone almost jovial, a fierce grin split his master's face as he evaded the golem, all the while building up another crippling curse. Milady Blue's duplicate kept hitting a shield, sparks flying when she tried to strike him. "Are you certain you're ready for six circles? An Arkhadahn who cannot compel his own golem's obedience is hardly an Arkhadahn at all." With a casual flick of the wrist, he threw the spell at the construct menacing him. Black lighting coursed over the copy golem. She shrieked as her wings shriveled and her body shook and steamed.

It's now or never.

William shook off his sickened fascination and barked out a command, reinforcing it with a mental goad. This time, Milady Blue obeyed, skittering forward with wings flapping and her forelegs raised—just as her twin exploded. Aftershock ripped through William with invisible knives, searing along the tattooed swirls of his arkhabala.

Merciful Valeshka, it hurts!

Wracked with agony and shuddering, William collapsed upon the spellform, trying not to whimper. The world spun sickeningly as his original golem battled Tenebris. Through their connection, he sensed her ferocious determination and grinned through the pain and blood coating his teeth. He'd crafted his construct well. Milady Blue was splendid. But against Tenebris and his Seventh Order attacks ... how long would his golem endure?

Have I failed?

No. That wasn't an option. William closed his eyes. Just for a minute. Aside from his right arm, he couldn't move. And he was so tired. His vitality ebbed alongside Milady Blue's, and he suppressed an urge to weep in helplessness. Inside, the violet pool beckoned, tempting him. But he mustn't tap into the Aethyr. Not during the Arkhadahn's Trial. Tenebris said the Aethyr was ... unclean. William would lose all the ground he'd gained over the past season. No more circles, even though he'd clearly earned three tonight.

With only two circles on his back his strength was insufficient to snap the connection to the golem and reverse the power drain. All his carefully laid plans were for naught. He'd crafted his golem too well. In overestimating his own endurance, he'd taken too great a risk.

I chose to roll the bones, and I lost. He grimaced, swallowing the bitterness of defeat. *If only I had a talisman to provide a new conduit. Something. Anything.*

Wait. William's eyelids fluttered open. He remembered. He *did* have something.

Zakaar had given him the soot panther fangs. With his trembling right hand, he dabbed at his still oozing wound, then seized hold of the string of teeth with blood-smeared fingers. A talismanic invocation of protection sprang to his lips. His arkhabala flared white hot, like flames across his back. The shield crackled to life around him. He severed the connection just as his golem disintegrated under Tenebris's relentless attacks. Grit that had once been Milady Blue fell all around him and the aching loss inside redoubled. His eyes burned; surely, that was from the dust in the air. No other reason.

Teeth gritted to keep a scream from escaping, William held his shield with all his fading strength. Black lightning snaked across the stones to arch over his prone form. Breath hissed through his teeth as he observed the dark energy writhe inches from his face with clinical detachment. He recalculated. Perhaps he had a chance. As long as his shield held.

Provided I survive this ... Embrace the pain!

Abruptly, the onslaught ceased. William's ears hummed as a ringing silence descended. Was it over? Soot panther fangs jabbed his palm, and he realized he'd clenched his hands into fists. His grip loosened, and his entire body sagged with weariness. It was all he could do to concentrate on breathing. His entire form seemed to want to melt into the chilly stones beneath him. The coolness was a soothing balm against the feverish heat of his expended arkhabala. Likely, he'd need more than a day's rest to replenish it.

Tenebris stood over him with an unreadable expression. "That was a foolish gamble, William," his master remarked in a dry tone. "You are fortunate to continue drawing breath, after expending your life force on that enhanced golem. I am both appalled and impressed."

He narrowed his eyes and stroked his beard while something like a smile tugged at his lips. "Splitting the golem was a clever innovation. And your use of the soot panther fangs to empower a new shield was resourceful. It reminds me of my own Trial for the seventh circle. And yet, after all your defiance, here you lie. Nothing left. Helpless at my feet." He paused, continuing to stare in silence.

Stop toying with me, Tenebris!

William was too spent even to quiver with outrage. "Burning suns, master! My sixth circle ..." He inhaled sharply. "Before you end me—or I expire from exhaustion and humiliation—tell me ..." Shuddering, he swallowed tears, then added, "Just tell me." Tenebris arched his eyebrows. He hunkered beside William, grasping his shoulder with fingers like iron. Leaning closer, he gave him a shake as a shark-like smile spread across his face. "Congratulations, Acolyte. You passed the Trial ... barely. Once you've caught your breath, I'll etch your circles. All *five* of them." His eyes gleamed as he grinned outright. "Prepare for a great deal of pain."

Temper Flares

Thomas breathed deeply, inhaling the cinnamon aroma of flowering vines that festooned crumbling stone arches in the overgrown courtyard of Fort Arwydd. He tried to ignore the fatigue burning in his muscles. The jolt of energy he'd sipped from the spent fire was beginning to wane, and the sky still hadn't cleared. Blocking David's off-hand thrust, he completed the Fisher Crane form to parry the longsword and danced back out of reach to catch his breath. His boots crunched in the dingy gravel of ancient pathways as he shifted his balance, poised to transition into the next attack form—Striking Viper. Both arms trembled as he turned, observing his circling opponent.

No pain, no gain. I need to get stronger.

Hadn't he said something like that to the kiddo? Fat lot of good he'd done for Annabelle. And he'd done even less for Enoch. If only he had been a man, and not a toad, when Enoch's captors had taken him ... A pang pierced him like slivers of obsidian sliding into his heart.

Stop thinking about it! There's nothing you can do to change what's happened.

Sweat dripped down his brow, and his knuckles ached from gripping the hilts of borrowed blades. Too tight. He could almost hear Commander Storm admonishing him to stay loose.

Thomas scowled. *I've gotta leave this pity party. There's work to be done.* He took a deep breath and prepared to continue the exercise, but then swallowed a curse. *For the love of all that's holy! I've forgotten the next stance.*

"Sir Thomas?" David paused. "I know it's been awhile since you've practiced. Do you wish for me to go over the next form with you?"

"No, I'll get it. Just stand back while I figure it out, and then we'll continue."

With a nod, David returned to center, and Thomas backtracked through the last five movements. He shouted a warning, and eyes alight, David snapped into a ready stance. Thomas attacked, launching into Striking Viper, movements jerky at first. David defended, blocking and parrying carefully to compensate for Thomas's weakness. It chafed him, but as his body remembered and found its rhythm, the movements came naturally, and David sped up.

Gaining confidence, Thomas matched his speed, meeting David blow for blow, driving him back. Concentration furrowed the dwelfnhir's forehead and his breath quickened even his lips curved into a broad smile. He began to counter Thomas's attacks in earnest.

Great; he's taking me seriously. Let's see what I can do.

Their swords clashed in a silvery rhythm as they moved in an intricate dance around the clearing. Thomas observed his opponent narrowly all the while, looking for weakness, an opening in David's defense. Finally, he saw one. He blocked David's longsword and lunged in, pressing the edges of both their blades against David's neck. Hooking his right leg around David's left, Thomas swept his feet out from under him.

David rolled away and then rocked up on his feet again with limber grace. "Nice counter," he said, still grinning. "Your ability with the sword is remarkable, Sir Thomas. And you're a canny opponent. It's been a while since anyone bested me like that. Except for Commander Storm, of course."

"Really?" Thomas panted. Once he got his breathing under control, he said, "You weren't just going easy on me?"

Solemnly, David shook his head. "After you found your stride, I stopped holding back and gave it my all." He rapped a fist against his chest. "Warrior's oath," He added, then smiled. The sheen of perspiration imbued his handsome face with a healthful glow. He always seemed in a better mood after sparring. The dwelfnhir was a natural fighter. Too bad he'd decided to leave the warrior's path to become an ordained minister. It seemed such a waste.

Thomas returned his smile. "Thanks." Relief filled him; he *was* stronger now. There was no reason for the Commander to leave him at Y'Vasheirdenelle, after all.

Sheathing his swords, David snorted. "I believe we've both had enough sparring for one day." He wiped his forehead.

Thomas frowned. "I'm fine. Just needed a minute to catch my breath. I'm ready to go another round." He rotated his wrists to keep them limber. *I must push myself harder.* He smirked at the dwelfnhir. "Unless you're afraid I'll beat you again."

David burst out laughing. "I'm already properly humbled. You'll not entice me that way, Sir Thomas." Recovering his composure, he cleared his throat and glanced at the sky. "It's getting on toward Raven Watch. I should check with Dee; she'll have finished her assessment of the enhancements necessary to make this old ruin siege-worthy."

Sheathing his swords, Thomas blew out a puff of air. "Siege worthy?" He frowned. "We shook off the Battlecrows when we came through two separate waystones. And there's been no sign of human activity anywhere along our route. Does the Commander expect the local wildlife to mount an attack?" The paths they'd taken thus far led through Veil-protected areas that kept out the most dangerous predators. However, Commander had mentioned that the Veils were failing. Encountering vicious beasts may become a grave concern.

David chuckled and clapped a hand on his shoulder. "All I know is Commander Storm will expect us to be prepared to defend the fort, should anyone attack tonight."

Thomas snorted. "Fair enough."

They followed the sound of a voice softly singing in dwelfnic and found Dinah outside mending a huge crack in the south-facing wall. Thomas stared as the stone flowed like soft clay molded by unseen hands to fill the gap. As they approached, Dinah turned from her work and smiled, the stone's progress slowing.

David said, "Dee, is our gift ready?"

The dwelfnhad brightened. "Yes. I put the finishing touches on it while you sparred. Just a moment." She resumed her airy song and finished the wall after a few bars. Then she hurried over to a lightning-blasted tree that had fallen near the southwest bastion. A small globe streaked red, gray, and beige sat on a buttress root.

Thomas faced David with a quizzical frown. "What's this about?"

David arched a black eyebrow. "The reason you shouldn't have snapped at my cousin this morning."

Rubbing the back of his neck, Thomas grimaced. "Touché. But I did apologize."

Smiling, Dinah came over, holding up the tri-colored globe. It was the size of a muskmelon. Small holes surrounded a stem with a loop, through which a dull metal handle threaded. "This is yours, Sir Thomas. David and I made you a firepot. Now you'll have a source of energy at any time of day, regardless of the weather."

The reddish globe tugged at him. Thomas realized he was already reaching for it. He drew back, but Dinah stepped forward, thrusting the firepot closer. Taking it, he cradled it in his hands. Weighing a pinch less than Murder Stick, it felt smooth like polished stone and cool to the touch. He sensed the heat inside that called to him. "Wow. You made this for me?"

"Of course, Sir Thomas." Dinah chuckled. She patted his arm. "Sang it from that boulder at our last camp—the striped one you said looked like a big cat stretching. We can't have you exhausting your reservoir, now, can we?"

"It's well-insulated," David explained, tapping the handle, which felt metallic but was supple like leather. "You can attach it to your sword belt, or Tinker's saddle. To add tinder, unscrew the lid."

Glancing up, he met their warm, topaz gazes. He swallowed past a sudden thickness in his throat. "Thank you. This ... this means a lot to me."

"You're very welcome," the cousins spoke in unison. Looking at each other, David smiled while Dinah laughed outright. "That's five in less than a week," David murmured, punching Dinah lightly on the shoulder. "And we don't even possess an alarimet bond."

Thomas eyed them sidelong. *They're so in sync. Almost like twins.*

An image rose, drifting like vapors through his mind and superimposing itself over the dwelfnim—*a laughing girl with dark auburn hair and eyes the hue of a summer sky sits across a table strewn with playing cards. She leans over with a toothy grin and punches him in the arm. "Jinx! You owe me a soda."*

Thomas froze, dropping his gaze to the firepot in his hands. The girl's playful blow left a phantom impression on his right bicep. What the heck? Barking a laugh, he shook his head, as if to dispel the image ... memory?

There's no time for a trip down memory lane right now. Keep it together, man.

Pushing aside all speculation, he unbuckled his belt and strung it through the firepot's handle, so it hung beside his right hip, beside Murder Stick, which was roughly half the longsword's weight. He'd test out how the firepot influenced his balance.

Up on the ramparts of the ruined fortification, they found Commander Storm waiting for them. His fingers drummed restively against the pommels of his scimitars as he gazed eastward, where a hill rose from surrounding trees, a ring of standing stones adorning its summit like a crown. Beyond it, Lachesis sank behind a bed of puffy clouds like stuck-together cotton balls.

Thomas frowned. While they traveled, the kiddo had been a fount of seemingly useless trivia. What had she called that type of cloud? Something that sounded like cumin. Accumulate? Cumulus? He shook his head. This was no time to let his mind wander.

"Sir," he greeted the Commander. "The walls are all fixed now."

"Very good." Commander Storm grunted. "I sent the buzzard to catch our supper. We'll stay here for the night and use the waystone when it activates half an hour before firstdawn. Shepherd, Ambassador, get some rest. Sir Thomas will wake you when supper is ready."

David clapped Thomas on the shoulder, then he and Dinah went to seek sleeping spots inside the fort's walls. Thomas raised his eyebrows. "There's no sign of human activity. Are you worried about bandits?"

The reptilian warrior turned to regard him with a gaze as sharp as the steel he bore. "No sign of bandits, but, regardless, I am filled with ... disquiet. Over the generations I have learned to trust my instincts." He gripped his swords. "And they're telling me something is amiss."

"Sir?"

Just then, Peter came flapping in from the northwest, carrying a goat-like creature the size of a small deer. He swooped to deposit the corpse at the Commander's feet, then landed in a flurry of pink feathers and fur atop the ruined battlements. "What's the word, Cat-Vulture?" Thomas called, unable to suppress an acerbic tone. "And you'd better not say—"

"Lawks!" the syrax exclaimed with a gleeful twinkle in his eyes, and Thomas cringed. Wings flared wide, Peter coasted down to the ground, alighting near his kill. "I got a nolkibara, Dukey—ah, Commander," he amended, shrinking back when the evainghir swung around to glare at him. "Their meat's real sweet."

Thomas stood on the rampart between the north and west bastions of the fort, gazing out into the darkness. Bundles of wood were stacked on top of each bastion. Commander Storm had been pleased to discover a copse of cinder pine; apparently the wood contained flammable oils and burned faster than other conifers. Before Lachesis set, they'd chopped down a number of trees, split the logs, and assembled the makings of four bonfires.

They were prepared to hold off any enemies until they could make a break for the waystone on the next hill.

With his left hand on his longsword, Thomas surveyed the eerie forest below, for once glad that Annabelle wasn't with them.

Poor kiddo's got too much imagination for her own good. She'd see monsters in every shadow and tree.

Something moved. For a moment, he wondered if his own imagination was running away with him, but then he saw a pair of glowing orange eyes. And another. And another.

Criminy. The Commander was right. Now that there was a clear and present danger, Thomas felt almost relieved.

Commander Storm barked an order, and the dwelfnim cousins lit the oily wood. Bonfires ignited on the parapet of each bastion.

Men's voices spoke in a harsh, consonant-rich language and a wave of blackness swept toward them. Pairs of lambent orange lights flared in the darkness under the trees, all around them. The eyes of predators. Nehmwights! Tremors shook Thomas to his marrow. Flashes of memory assaulted him. Orange eyes and whorls of darkness on a gray-skinned face. The sting of a sharp blade slicing through his skin to create slits of agony ... his scars. Blood. So much blood. Then there'd been a bright flash, nausea, painful contortions ...

Who had done all this to him? His fingers curled into fists.

I don't know, and I don't care. Nehmwights were part of it. The pain will go away once all those orange-eyed jokers are reduced to cinders and soot.

Thomas reached deep inside to tap into the pyre at his core. While he picked out targets, rage seethed like a knotted nest of vipers. His lips skinned back from his teeth in a broad grin as he drew his sword. He would make them pay.

You will all burn.

He drew energy from the fires. Turning in a half circle, he thrust out his sword, blade aglow, and swept it from one side to the other, igniting a wall of flames that rolled toward the nehmwights rushing the fort. He fed the fire with his wrath and it flared hotter. Men screamed. Skeletal shadows danced jerkily inside the inferno he'd unleashed. Heat fanned against his face, and the sweetish, nauseating reek of burnt flesh filled the air. Part of him, a small, distant part, felt like vomiting. The rest of him was shaking so hard in exultation he thought he'd fly apart.

Another wave of tall figures in black armor emerged into the firelight from the wilderness, all holding either swords or axes. They were everywhere! Their eyes glowed like the yawning gates of perdition. Thomas would send them down there, where they belonged. The world constricted until only he and his foes existed. Rage, hot and bitter, pooled in his gut. Thomas reached out with his kythim and seized upon all sources of fire.

He drew from the bonfires then held out his hands as if offering a gift. All the heat in his body coalesced into a sphere above his palms. "Here comes the sun!" With a roar, Thomas hurled the sphere toward the orange-eyed warriors. He flared out his fingers, and the sphere expanded. Pivoting on his heel to spread the wealth, a grin spread across his face as ravenous flames engulfed ten armored figures and the explosion sent others flying backward.

Gotcha. Burn, you jokers!

But there were survivors. He must kill them, too. Thomas strained, but his reservoir was empty and cold as a barren hearth. His fire-enhanced vision faded. Aside from the shivers wracking his frame, he couldn't move. Knees buckling, he began to list sideways.

No ...

Thomas sucked on the fire still devouring his foes, drawing in more power, then pushed himself upright. Flames guttered out and the clearing plunged into darkness. No matter. The golden light allowed him to see. Energy seethed and roared inside him like a beast. A tiger. Yes. He could see the beasts inside him, great cats made of fire. His grin widened. He would release the flametiger to immolate all the orange-eyed fiends. Burn the forest to ashes and their enemies along with it. That's the way it was done.

Ashes, ashes, and they all fall down.

Giddiness swelled through him, and he giggled. Someone was hollering at him to stand down, but he couldn't. He wouldn't, not until all the nehmwights in the world were reduced to charcoal. Only then would it be safe.

I'll burn them and scorch the earth where they stand before they hurt anyone else.

Thomas realized he was laughing. "Burn, you jokers! Burn!" As the wall of flame died, he noticed there were more nehmwights. He would kill them, too, but his reservoir was emptying fast. Ah, but he had the firepot at his belt that Dinah gave him. Threading his kythim through the flames, he sucked in energy. Everything glowed golden. Commander Storm shouted something, but he couldn't make it out. What in blazes? Never mind. He would deal with that later. Right here and now there were nehmwights to fry.

He drew on his power again and sculpted flametigers from living magma. One, two, three ... that was all he could manage. Three would have to do. He watched the great cats manifest, tails lashing, bright golden-white with stripes of blue fire lighting up the night like a sun come to life. They stood in thin air and looked at him with eyes like twin furnaces, awaiting his order.

Thomas pointed his burning sword at nehmwights attempting to draw back into the shadows. *Blasted cowards.* "Get them!"

With a roar, the flametigers descended and pounced on the fleeing warriors, raking them with claws like daggers while blazing jaws closed around their necks. The nehmwights burned to ash, and the flametigers bounded after others, reducing them to ash as well. They were incinerating the last three warriors when the great cats began to fade.

At least I took out those orange-eyed jokers before they hurt anyone else.

The fire along Thomas's blade died away. A searing pain spread through his hand, and he cursed as his fingers opened to let the longsword fall. Swaying in his seat, he stared at the palm of his hand. Shouldn't there be blisters? His vision wavered and shrank to a tunnel surrounded by gray shadows. The world was tilting, tilting ...

Strong hands caught him and set him on his feet. The Commander's voice rumbled like thunder, "While I do not lament the lack of enemy survivors, I expect you to obey me, Sir Thomas. Did you not hear my order to fall back? We must head for the waystone."

Thomas shook his head. "No, sir," he whispered. "I heard nothing."

David stared at him with a grim expression. "Those nehmwights were in full retreat, Sir Thomas. The waystone activates in five minutes. We could have escaped them."

Sword in one hand, reins clutched in the other, Dinah gaped at the smoking corpses of the enemy scattered among the rocks and scorched trees. She was shaking and making little whimpering noises. "He ... *laughed.* Burned ... them ... all."

Commander Storm nodded. "Aye. He did, indeed. And now we need not worry about them ambushing us later."

Thomas blinked owlishly at the charred remnants of thirteen nehmwights. *What happened? Did I just torch over twenty nehmwights?* Trembling, he stared at his hands. After such fury, they should be scorched to a crisp. Sir Rick must be rolling in his grave. This wasn't how a disciplined knight fought. Never while consumed with anger—or so eager to kill his opponents. Fear curled in his belly.

What is happening to me?

Sea of Sorrow

With the octopus clinging to her neck like a squishy pendant, Annabelle trotted in Mordred's wake to compensate for his long-shanked strides across a narrow walkway spanning a moat wider than Commander Storm's impressive height. *Why is everyone on this planet so freaking tall? Aren't there any short people aside from me and Enoch?*

Ears drooping, her champion stalked immediately behind her, and the armed guardsmen of the Howling Tempest followed, singing in harmony to a martial beat. Far from a howling throng, they sounded like a men's choir. Her heart lifted and she found herself joining in: "Though storm-waves crash and break the strong ... While outsiders preach that right is wrong ... When a sea of sorrow drowns our song ... Lord Yshua leads us on, leads us on ... To sanctuary."

Distress tingled along the Oathbond, then was quickly suppressed. Annabelle glanced over her shoulder. Raeden was shoving wax plugs in his ears with a pained expression. Her voice faltered. *Oh, that's right. He gets overwhelmed when people sing. I wish there was something I could do to make him feel better ... Should I hold his hand? It would make me feel better, too.*

Stepping down from the bridge on the other side of the moat, she thrust her arm back and wriggled her fingers. After a moment, she felt Raeden grasp her hand and step down beside her. She squeezed and sent a wave of reassurance and affection Raeden-wards along their bond. Shock, then gratitude flowed through to her, but she sensed he held back stronger emotions, like wild animals on a tight leash. How upset must he be about the gwerindawr? She wished she had his control, then grimaced ruefully. She had a recourse, though it had been a while since she practiced the mind fortress and emotion-dampening exercises Commander Storm taught her. Unwise, but too much was going on.

One hand in her champion's, the other bracing Wesleyen's head, she hurried after Mordred, passing through orchards and gardens as before with the guards fanned out to surround them. Approaching a tall hedge, they came upon a vine-enshrouded gate rearing over their heads, where Mordred stopped. His eyes narrowed at their linked hands, and he frowned. His expression cleared as he addressed her. "Lady Ann, I've brought you and your champion along the landbound path to my father's court, and here is where it ends." He lifted his chin and met Raeden's gaze, his lip curling. "Beyond this gate is a lagoon in which my father holds audiences. A raised walkway wide enough for one, as a courtesy for those who fear getting wet, will bring you to a dais where our people voice their petitions and criminals face the Brenin's judgment."

Low growls rumbled in Raeden's chest. "Your Highness." He bit off the words. "This one does not fear getting wet. And he does not approach the king as a criminal."

"Raeden's no criminal." Annabelle gripped his hand tighter. The growls subsided. Wesleyen crawled to her left shoulder, and she reached up to stroke a tentacle. In a softer tone, she asked, "How deep is the water, Mordred?"

Turning to her, Mordred's sneer transformed into a warm smile. "No higher than your waist at its deepest, Lady Ann. Not a hardship for the Ahdmerel, I'd wager. Nor even for your champion."

Wade awkwardly through the water in front of a king and all his courtiers? She scowled. *I don't think Raeden's dignity can withstand any more blows today.*

The princeps watched her with concern. "I could carry you, if you are weary."

Feeling the Oathbond flare with her champion's ire, Annabelle squeezed Raeden's hand in warning, then let go. "No, thank you, Mordred," she replied, her cheeks growing warm at the image her traitor brain presented. She pushed it aside. *There's no way I'll let this smug, pretty Smurf boy embarrass my champion. What I wouldn't give to be able to walk on water! Wait ...*

Raeden stiffened. "There is no reason to fret over milk on the floor. Your servant would rather go into the water with you, Freylin, than walk a path of shame."

"You won't need to do either," she said, slowly, as she envisioned the patterns she'd need to employ. "Because I'll weave a new path for us." Suddenly uncertain, she glanced up into her champion's furred visage and solemn gaze. "If you trust me?" *I'm not sure I trust me!*

Placing a fist over his heart, Raeden bowed. "Your servant trusts you, Freylin. His life is already sworn to you."

Annabelle gulped. *No pressure, then. Please, God, let this work.* Heart racing, she turned to Mordred. "Open the gate, please."

His expression unreadable, the princeps did as she asked, pulling the two halves of the gate inwards to reveal a semicircular platform of pinkish stone large enough for their entire group. Beyond lay an expanse of placid water sparkling in the sunslight as it lapped against the porch, and a narrow, pinkish stone path extending out into a lagoon roughly the area of two football fields—if a football field could be ovate.

Instead of a statue of Hadrien, a throne made of dark blue stone and draped with flowering vines stood in the center like an imperious island. A broad-shouldered, blue-skinned man wearing a long, white linen kilt, and not much else sat on the throne. He was too far away to see details of his face, but his beard and hair were the same purple with dark green streaks as Mordred's.

Is he all by himself? Where's the rest of his court? But then she saw movement and brightly colored gwerindawr in the water at the throne's base. As she watched, a woman with the same coloring as Mordred and the king heaved herself up to sit on a submerged ledge at the king's feet. *And that must be Princepsa Rhiannon.* A burgundy man pulled himself up beside her on the ledge, shoulder to shoulder. They both shaded their eyes. Annabelle stared.

So many colors ...

The princeps made a sweeping gesture, like a gameshow host presenting a prize. "Welcome to Morgan Brenin's Court." He straightened, then frowned. "What do you plan to do, Lady Ann?"

With an effort, she pried her gaze from the people on the throne-rock. She huffed a laugh. "Uh ... Make a path across the lake."

Can I do it? Hands cupped around Wesleyen's soft head, Annabelle shut her eyes and took a deep breath. *Please, God. Be with us. Grant me the strength and endurance to do this.*

It was now, or never. She unfurled her kythim—putting her in mind of Wesleyen's tentacles—and reached out to the water, gathering sapphire energy. She recalled Hadrien's lesson from when she built the bubble raft, then wove a tight pattern to increase the surface tension of the lake alongside the path as far as she could—nearly halfway to the throne. *I'll need to build the path as we walk.* When she tested it, the path gave under her prodding foot. She concentrated on the water nearest the gate until the surface firmed to the consistency of a moss-covered forest floor, though it looked like glass. It held when she stepped out on it. She released a blustery sigh.

The guardsmen all gasped and murmured in awe. Mordred clapped and laughed in delight. "An outstanding feat, Lady Ann."

Happy to entertain you, Your Highness. Annabelle snorted. "I'm here all week. Er ... for the foreseeable future." Mentally, she surveyed her work. The lattice was holding. Now for the difficult part. She held out her left hand to Raeden. His eyes locked on hers, he gingerly stepped out onto the lake. He wobbled, the Oathbond keened with his terror, and his hand trembled in hers, but he came to her. Like Peter walked across the Sea of Galilee to Jesus.

"Freylin," he rasped. "Remember. You are not Lord Yshua."

Did he read my mind? Startled, she almost lost her grip on the skeins of water. "I know," she snarled through her teeth. "Stop distracting me."

He winced, glancing aside. "Apologies, Freylin. Your servant will control his fear." The Oathbond went silent.

Must be nice. I wish I could shut down my emotions like that. Stop it, Ann. That's not fair. Annabelle grimaced and softened her tone despite the tension running through her body. "Sorry. Just hold on and stay right by my side. I'm not sure how far I can extend this ... bridge thing. It's trickier to maintain than the raft was."

"You are doing well, Freylin. Your servant trusts you."

Buoyed by his faith, Annabelle smiled. "Alrighty then. Let's go." She took a step. And then another. The surface held. With her lower lip caught between her teeth, she sent her kythim ahead of them to knit together water-threads into a road just wide enough for two. To her left, Raeden prayed under his breath, although no distress leaked through the Oathbond.

Once the pattern was laid, she lifted her head and set her eyes on their goal: the gwerindawr king on his throne. Mordred and his men followed. She glimpsed flashes of light blue, ochre, and coral as they porpoised through the water on either side. Were those ... *tail fins?* She almost lost her grip on the water-threads again.

Annabelle bent her attention on reaching the patch of open water between the throne-islet and the platform at the end of the pink stone path. Once there, she focused on weaving the strands of water energy tighter and then fastened them in place. There. Now she didn't need to concentrate on it. But she didn't let go of Raeden's hand; she wasn't sure whether the water would hold him up otherwise.

The Howling Tempest guards flanked her and Raeden. Mordred's head and shoulders emerged on her right. He looked at his father, seeming uncertain, his bravado vanished. After casting a glance her way, he licked his lips and straightened his spine, although the scar Raeden had inflicted remained hidden. The hauteur returned to his expression. "Father," he declaimed in a pompous fashion that made Annabelle's nose wrinkle, "I have brought you the Ahdmerel of prophecy."

On his throne, the king's eyes narrowed as he examined Annabelle, and she tried not to fidget. In turn, she examined him. Morgan Brenin wore a bronze torc. As her eyes passed over it she thought of stagnant water. Weird. An ornate scepter held loosely in his right hand lay across his lap. He looked like an older, sterner version of Mordred with a beard, but his golden eyes lacked his son's warmth. His handsome face hardened, and his lips thinned as his gaze settled on their linked hands.

Annabelle fought an impulse to let go and gripped her champion's hand tighter. Raeden returned her squeeze and the Oathbond radiated a steady hum of ... readiness.

The couple sitting waist-deep in the water seemed friendlier than the king. After casting a distrustful glance at Raeden, the woman observed Annabelle with curiosity shining in her golden eyes and a faint smile curving her generous lips. Seated beside her, the burgundy man stared at Annabelle and grasped the woman's arm. "Rhia—just like my vision foretold," he whispered. "Ahdmerel walks on the sea, and beside her is a scout hound."

Oh dear, Annabelle thought. *He must be talking about the prophecy. Is Raeden wrapped up in this somehow, as well?*

"Captain Mordred," announced the king in a rich baritone. "You say you have brought the Ahdmerel, and I cannot help but believe it is so, because she strides across the waters as the landbound do on solid ground. Introduce her to us, so we may be well-met."

Mordred lifted his chin. "Your Majesty," the princeps replied stiffly. "I present to you the Ahdmerel, Lady Ann. With her is her champion, the scout hound Raeden von Bleistaff. Lady Ann, it is my honor to introduce my father, Morgan Brenin." He gestured toward the gorgeous woman, and his tone warmed. "My sister, Rhiannon, princepsa and heir to the Sanctuary Throne," he indicated the burgundy man with another wave, "and this is her consort, our archimandrite, Sawel."

Blushing, Annabelle hunched her shoulders and raised her free hand in an awkward wave. "Hi. It's nice to meet you. Um. Your Majesty. Your ... Highnesses."

Morgan Brenin inclined his head, and his expression softened a fraction. "Be welcome to our Sanctuary Isle, Ahdmerel."

Annabelle waited, but the king said nothing about her champion. *No welcome for Raeden, then?* Her stomach began a slow descent to her feet. She sensed nothing different from the Oathbond, so she glanced sidelong at Raeden. His ears laid back and his gaze riveted to the king. This didn't bode well.

Sawel's dark eyes flickered to Wesleyen wrapped about her arm. He gasped, "A companion of Rainblessed's color! Just like in the prophecy!" He heaved himself from the water to a higher ledge, as if this would help him get a better look at her. Annabelle gasped, staring wide-eyed at the purple and silver tail, like a metallic scaled sheath over his legs, and the webbed flukes he had instead of feet.

That's right! The gwerindawr are merfolk.

"Mackerel's scales, Sawel!" Laughing, the princepsa hopped up beside him and swatted his shoulder. Her caudal apparatus shimmered with scales of cobalt blue and violet, like jewels. "You're frightening the poor thing, and she's already pale as a wobbegong's belly."

Sawel glanced between Annabelle and his wife. "But Rhia ... the prophecy stands before us in the flesh. We are blessed to see it fulfilled during our lifetimes."

That darn prophecy again. Annabelle trembled. Though she wanted to ask questions, the king's stern gaze dried her mouth and robbed her of speech. She felt as if she was about to shatter like an icicle falling from a roof.

"Your Majesty," Raeden said. He fixed the king with a baleful stare. "One hears of a prophecy concerning the Ahdmerel. It brings her great discomfort not to know what it is about. Will you now explain?"

Annabelle bit her lip. *Thank you, Raeden!*

Morgan Brenin sneered. "Impertinent scout hound. You talk out of turn. What is it you are called again?" He scowled at their joined hands. "And what is your relationship to the Ahdmerel that she allows a beast to ... speak for her?"

Raeden bristled. He lifted his chin and squared his shoulders. "This one is called Raeden von Bleistaff, and he has sworn the Defender's Oath before the Threefold One—"

"He's my champion," Annabelle blurted. "And he's *not* a beast. He's a gentleman."

"A gentleman?" An ochre-skinned guard protested. "Captain. Please, forgive me for this indiscretion, but I cannot remain silent. Your Majesty, this scout hound assaulted the princeps!"

Rhiannon gasped, and her husband put an arm around her. She clasped her hands over her heart. "Dred, is that true?"

"Orcwith!" Mordred snapped, his eyes blazing as he shot a glare at the guardsman.

Annabelle blinked. *Why is he so upset with his guard?*

The guard flinched. "My Captain ... princeps." He lowered his head. "Forgive me. The demon drew your blood. He must be punished." Several others nodded, muttering among themselves and casting dark glances Raeden's way.

Morgan Brenin's gaze bore into the kaenhir. "Did this foul beast lay hands upon you, my son? If this is so, then he must be sequestered on Crescent Islet for the protection of our people."

Oh, no. We can't be separated! Despite the raft's stability, Annabelle felt her heart plummet. Beside her, Raeden stiffened. The Oathbond flared with rage, but his countenance gave nothing away. He was taking a deep breath to speak when the princeps cleared his throat.

Mordred rose higher in the water until his entire torso was exposed. "He did not lay one hand upon me, Father, and my knives found their mark."

Annabelle eyed the princeps narrowly. *I thought Mordred hated Raeden. Why does he seem to be defending him? Or is this some sort of macho man thing?*

Mordred rolled back his shoulders to display the scar more prominently. His sister gasped. "Don't worry, Rhia. What you see is the remnant of a mere flesh wound delivered by his blade. It barely stung, and the blessed Ahdmerel healed it immediately."

"Yes, I did," she put in, grateful for Mordred's curious behavior—whatever its reason. "Your Majesty, it was all a misunderstanding. Raeden thought he was protecting me. Please don't separate us. If you plan to imprison my champion, then you'll have to sequester me on this Crescent Islet along with him."

Mordred gaped, shaking his head. His sister and her husband both began talking at once, and the Howling Tempest muttered among themselves.

"I forbid it!" Morgan Brenin proclaimed, leaping to his feet and raising his scepter. Everyone fell silent. The king furrowed his brow. "Our blessed Ahdmerel, left alone with a male scout hound?" His family joined him in scowling at Raeden. "That would be the highest impropriety. No." He leveled the scepter at Annabelle. "The Ahdmerel shall guest with my daughter here on Ynys Lloches, until she fulfills the prophecy."

"Nich!" Raeden drew her close to him. "If this one causes such offense, then he and Freylin must leave this place. Where is the waystone, water sprite?" He growled. "There must be one here, for the dwelfnim come—"

"Silence, beast!" the king bellowed, his face flushed a darker blue. "Why should we tell you anything? You who are of the deceitful ilk who betrayed our ancestor in the Battle of the Twisted Fans! Guards, seize that scout hound and take him away to Crescent Islet."

"No! Stop it!" Annabelle screamed, and water shot straight up in geysers between them and the approaching guardsmen. The water pillars collapsed in a heavy downpour. Raeden ducked his head and cursed. Her raft shuddered beneath their feet until she reinforced it with her will. The gwerindawr cowered under the impromptu rainfall, except the king, who stood still as a statue and stared at her with a frown, like a disappointed parent.

Now she had their attention. Glaring at each royal gwerindawr in turn, Annabelle fought back tears. "Please. What the heck do you want from me? Will someone explain this prophecy?"

If I knew the prophecy, then I could figure out how to fulfill it. And the sooner I fulfill it, the sooner Raeden and I can leave.

Sawel seemed to recover from his shock first. He blinked as if waking from sleep. "I can do that, Lady Ahdmerel." He turned to the king. "If I may, Your Majesty? How else will Ahdmerel know what she must do?"

Morgan Brenin nodded, his face expressionless. "That is sensible. It is her right to know."

Beaming, the archimandrite turned to Annabelle. "The Threefold One blessed me with the vision about your coming, over three moons ago. It came to me in rhyme." He cleared his throat and began singing in a clear, pleasant baritone. The royal siblings raised their voices to sing along in harmony after the first verse, but Raeden moaned and gripped her hand.

"Commanding the waves, Ahdmerel walks on the sea.
Bound at her side is our old enemy.
Glory will come if one bends the knee.
Seeking the tempest, she's drifted astray.
A shard of the moon may light her way.
Glory is yours if she chooses to stay.
She mourns what was sundered, hopes to weave bonds anew.
For her sake a companion dons Rainblessed's hue.

Glory beckons with tendrils of blue.
Amid living waters, she heals the most grievous ill.
The darkest of hearts she can't bear to kill.
Glory eludes those who scorn Yshua's will.
Into the depths she dives in love's name.
Armored by faith, the triumph she'll claim.
Glory attends those who hope for the same.
Break curse's vile chains to free a world held in thrall.
Rainblessed's scion holds the key to it all.
Glory may follow if you heed the call.
A sea of sorrow awaits, should Ahdmerel fall."

Annabelle stood riveted as each phrase washed over her. Commanding waves, seeking tempests, weaving bonds, healing, diving into depths, and breaking curses—She was expected to do *all* those things? *Some of it I know I've done, but ... And I might fall? What does that mean? I'd bet a lifetime's supply of cheese curds the prophecy doesn't mean what it appears to mean.*

A chill ran through her as she recalled Grecian myths. For those heroes and heroines, little good came of foretelling the future. Prophecies brought only grief. She shivered. And what was to become of Raeden? His hand trembled in hers. She looked up into his grim visage.

She licked her lips and faced the stern-looking monarch. "Your Majesty, I'd be happy to do what I can to fulfill this prophecy, but couldn't you please let my champion go?"

"We are all bound by law, Ahdmerel. For the crime he committed against the princeps, the scout hound will remain imprisoned until he is executed."

Executed—for a scratch that's already healed? Annabelle felt as if she was plunging into an abyss. *I can't let that happen!*

"No, please," she begged. "Don't kill my champion. I'll do anything—"

Urgency quivered along the Oathbond as Raeden interjected, "Freylin, do not speak so! They will take it as a promise—"

"Please!" Annabelle shouted over him. "There has to be some other way—short of death—that he or I can make restitution."

"Because you are the Ahdmerel, I will be merciful and commute the sentence of death to imprisonment. However ..." Pausing, the king raised his scepter. Dismay prickled down her spine like a spider's legs. "However," he continued, "Raeden von Bleistaff shall remain a prisoner here until the blessed Ahdmerel fulfills the prophecy and leads our people to glory."

Annabelle gaped. *That could be twisted around to mean anything!*

"Your Majesty. Please give me some ... parameters. How do you define glory?"

Morgan Brenin stared right into her eyes. "That is not for us to determine, but for the blessed Ahdmerel to puzzle it out."

Head lowered, Raeden sighed. "Better your servant dies, Freylin. Now the water sprites have bound you here to serve them."

Annabelle swallowed a nasty word. What had she done?

Bakkharat

"Valkor's burning Scythe!" William cursed as he slammed the book closed, taking care not to lean back on his freshly etched arkhabala. His mind reeled from the implication of the information he'd gleaned from various texts in the Dreadlord's library. "I still can't believe it. That cursed Dream Traveler was on to something."

It had taken hours of research, and there hadn't been much, but he'd finally parsed out vague references to both the Hollow and the powerful sorcerers whom the nehmwights worshiped as gods. Although he still wasn't certain how the two groups were related, they'd all been either destroyed or banished to the Sundered Realms by a spell gone awry at the close of the Oblivion Wars. Along with the Sages ...

Brow furrowed in thought, he toyed with a speculation that had been forming over the past week. If Northward and Annabelle could reach their Sage mentors through the dreamscape, did that mean William could find a Sage, too? Perhaps Jethro Shadowveiled would be willing to teach him more about reading minds and his affinity to the dreamscape in exchange for his freedom. Or something.

William snorted. To perdition with that twaddle. *I already have two masters breathing down my neck. I don't want a third.* The way things were going, he'd be bound in service to Tenebris for another generation. When he was six winters old and became Tenebris's apprentice, he'd sworn the blood oath that all apprentices made: to serve and obey his master until he advanced to mastery himself. Of course, William had quickly discovered and exploited loopholes in the oath, but its essence secured him firmly under Tenebris's authority.

As he carved the circles into William's back, Tenebris freely admitted the only reason he'd advanced William now was because his plans to exact revenge upon Warlord Vespyrahl—Tenebris's father—were coming to fruition. His master needed an Arkhadahn at acolyte level to aid him in the Grand Working meant to utterly break the powerful warlord. The entire process would take roughly three Cycles. Tenebris made it clear there would be no more circles for William until after Vespyrahl and his entire faction was scoured from the face of Tehara.

Stupid blood oaths! I was too young then, but now I know better. I'll never swear another blood oath again.

Grumbling, William closed his eyes and massaged his temples, forcing himself to ignore the crawling in his skin and the sudden vagueness in his head. Now that he'd scratched the itch of his curiosity, he must concentrate on the real task laid before him—designing the mirror-maze with which he'd trap the hisanabyad guarding Annabelle's dreams.

A smile spread across his face. *Leaving Milady Blue vulnerable. And with my new armor to repel her charms, she'll be an easy—*

Pain erupted through the five circles recently etched into his flesh. The one he'd carved himself on his chest under Tenebris's supervision was the worst. Heat radiated from his arkhabala to encompass his entire torso, as if Tenebris had cast a Nettle Sweep over him.

"Suns burn me to ash! Confounded circles—settle down, already!" He leapt from his seat and flung off his burkheld, exposing his spelled tattoos to the cool, dry air of the library. Spluttering maledictions, he seized a pitcher off his luncheon tray and splashed water on his chest before dumping the rest down his back. The riot in his arkhabala subsided.

The latch clicked and William froze, panting. Alarm stirred his heart to frenzied pounding. Had Tenebris awakened already and come to punish him? *Should've locked the suns-burnt door, never mind that the Dreadlord forbade me to.* Crackling potential filled the air and his arkhabala's writhing resumed as he mentally assembled a Fourth Order stun spell.

William gasped, nearly swooning at the power coursing through the spelled tattoos like fiery ice. He must grow accustomed to that. Lifting a hand and gathering dark lightning within, he glared at the door. "Who's there?"

"It is I." Zakaar entered the library. "Come to remind you ..." He paused, squinting. "Dulciber, why are you all wet?"

It's only the harkhurz ... William slumped and sank into his seat. He negated the spell. But instead of dissipating entirely, a ring of energy pulsed outward like thunder without sound. The door slammed shut behind Zakaar. Bookshelves and scroll cases shook, dust puffed in the air, and the watch glass mounted on the wall shattered. Glass tinkled as purple sand gushed out to pile on the ground.

William exhaled a pent-up breath. Eyes wide, he met Zakaar's startled gaze in the silence that followed. Bright green starbursts and jagged yellow lines flashed in the harkhurz's kythim. He shot to his feet, knocking over the chair. "Freezing Void, Zakaar!" He slammed his fists on the table. Parchment, ink bottle, and reedpens rattled. "Blistering knock next time." He trembled. *So. Much. Power.*

Zakaar stood frozen. He blinked at William's onslaught, shivered all over, and then glanced around the library. "What were you doing that required privacy? This is not your bedchamber, Dulciber. It is for—how does one say it?—public use."

Muttering, William set his chair upright and collapsed into it, then shot to his feet with a yelp. *I need to learn my new limits before I really muck something up.* He shook a finger at the harkhurz assassin. "That's not the point. Never startle an Arkhadahn. You'll live longer."

"I shall follow your very wise advice." Zakaar put a fist to his chest and bowed as indigo ripples spread through his kythim. Humor glittered in his eyes and his whiskers quivered. He indicated the brown robe William had dropped upon the floor. "You may wish to put that on. Remember? Half-past Thrush Watch, you and the warlock are to join the Dreadlord in his conference chamber." A snarl curled his upper lip and black tinged his aura. "The warlock was not in his room, or I would have brought him to you."

Northward. May the suns scorch his stones. William snatched his burkheld off the floor and gingerly shrugged into it, hissing through his teeth. How could he forget? The Dreadlord had given Northward freedom to roam inside Fastness, with only a few exceptions. That figured. Just when it would inconvenience William most, the wretched barbarian would take up the Dreadlord's offer to explore the vast fortress.

"Where in blazes did that addle-pated twit wander off to?" He muttered, hurriedly putting away books. "Do you have any ideas on where he might have gone?"

The assassin shook his head. "I have not, or I would have brought him." He clasped his hands behind his back and tilted his head to one side. "How are your circles, Dulciber?"

William scowled while shoving his notes and materials into their assigned satchel compartments. *Now that you mention it, my back and chest blistering itch and burn like all the world's fire ants are crawling under my skin. Thank you so much for reminding me.*

Keeping his face blank, he looked up from his satchel. "My circles? They're healing up nicely." No reason to tell the harkhurz about the periods of dizziness, fever, and euphoria he'd experienced since the expansion of his arkhabala. Why reveal weakness? Those side effects would soon pass, as they had before. "Why do you care?"

Zakaar crossed his arms and scrunched his brow. "Do you not recall? I am your friend. Inquiring about your welfare is something a friend does."

What an asinine practice. Is that ... normal? Perhaps I erred when I believed the harkhurz returned to sanity.

William gave his companion a dubious look. "I told you, I'm fine." He surveyed the harkhurz for signs of madness. Zakaar was well-groomed and wearing a clean, black uniform with shiny brass buttons, like the Dreadlord's soldiers. His eyes were clear, his ears lifted, and his bearing was relaxed. No madness, despite his abiding hatred of Northward. William's elixir was still working. A warm glow grew behind his breastbone and under his most recently etched circle. Zakaar was back to his old self, before the Blood Rage symptoms began.

"I am glad," the assassin replied with a brief nod. He raised his eyebrows. "Dulciber, do you not notice? Your trousers are wet. There is still time; we can go back to your rooms so you may fetch a dry pair."

William carefully slung the satchel from his shoulder. Yes, he could feel the dampness, but it wasn't aggravating—not like the burning itch of his tattoos. "There's not enough time for that. We need to find Northward." As he strode toward Zakaar and the door, he spared a glance for the glass and sand piled on the floor. The broken watch glass was Zakaar's fault for startling him.

After they found Northward, William would send the harkhurz back to tidy up the mess.

Zakaar stepped aside and held the door for him. "I can track the warlock, if you wish." His black nose twitched. "Outside his room, the scent was less than an hour old."

"Merciful Valeshka! I'm surrounded by lack-wits." William stopped in his tracks and pinched the bridge of his nose. After taking a deep breath, he turned to the harkhurz. "Zakaar, if you could sniff out Northward, then why didn't you track him down before you came to me?" At his companion's confused look, he growled, "Go on, then. Find him. Now."

Zakaar's furry ears lifted. "As you wish, my friend. I shall find the warlock for you."

"See that you do," William grumbled as Zakaar prowled down the corridor, sniffing. He had no doubts about the assassin's ability to locate Northward. Once set on his quarry, he never failed to carry out a mission.

This put him in mind of his own mission to capture Annabelle. He hadn't much luck in reaching her lately in the dreamscape. Didn't she sleep anymore? She *was* traveling ... He should check at various times of the day. Frustration woke his arkhabala to humming as he caught up with Zakaar at an intersection. He was eager to confront the maiden in his new disguise. Thinking back, he wasn't certain the Northward mask he'd conjured had completely fooled Annabelle; she'd seemed suspicious near the end of their ... meeting.

Heat crept up his neck. *No. This happens every time. Don't think about her. Focus on solving the problem around her. Although the hug felt rather nice. I wouldn't mind another ...*

"Dulciber, do you have a fever? And why do you smile so, like a man who dreams of his beloved? It looks very strange on your face."

"No, I don't!" William stammered, the flush rising higher. "And I wasn't! Smiling like that, I mean. I was just thinking about ... about ... what it would be like to have thirteen circles, like Tenebris. How powerful I'd be."

What is he on about? Beloved? William scoffed. *That's impossible. I don't care what the Dream Traveler said about "fancying her." It's a suns-cursed beguilement spell!*

He leveled a glare at the assassin, who'd halted beside a flight of stairs to goggle at him like a witless looby. "And for the record: my face isn't strange—yours is. Now, shut it. You're supposed to be hunting down Northward. Fulfill your duty, harkhurz."

Zakaar chuckled. "Apologies; I was concerned that you were ill. I will be quiet now."

William growled, irritated by the amusement lingering in Zakaar's canid features. "See that you do. Babbling buffoon." *What does he know about anything? He's as dim as a cave on a moonless night.* Aloud, he muttered, "I should send you back to clean up the broken watch glass. If I didn't need you to locate Northward, I would."

After a solemn fist-to-chest salute, Zakaar resumed the hunt in silence. William descended a flight of stone steps in his wake, then they went down a corridor that led outdoors into the central courtyard. As they approached, the crash of steel against steel and shouts came to his ears.

That's Northward's voice!

"Villem's bloody spear," William exclaimed, lengthening his stride to pass his companion. "What's going on?"

"Do I have permission to speak?" Zakaar asked, trotting to catch up. "If I do, then I would tell you that the warlock is sparring with Marshal Incendo."

William swallowed a curse as he skidded to a halt and stood framed by the entrance to the central courtyard. If there was someone he loathed more than Northward—and Tenebris, for that matter—it was Marshal Incendo, the Dreadlord's adopted grand-daughter. Ever since she and her cursed pet had pummeled him nearly to death a Cycle ago, William steered clear of the woman. They'd broken his arm and left him battered and bleeding. When Tenebris patched him up afterwards, as a punishment he made sure the healing process hurt worse than Incendo's fury.

So what if I said she resembled a half-baked heifer's haunches? She had no call to sic her blistering wyrmkin on me and then come after me with a pair of ironwood staves.

Crickets chirped and a sweet smell wafted in from the flower garden beyond. Lungs tight, William scanned the grounds but saw no one. Incendo's yellow-eyed beast wasn't lying in wait to ambush him.

He jumped when Zakaar touched his arm. "They are most likely inside the hedge maze."

"It's a labyrinth," William snapped. "There's only a single path to the center. A maze has multiple ways and branching paths. Get it right."

"My apologies, Dulciber." Zakaar held up his hands. "I will lead the way."

William knew the labyrinth; not only was it a single path, but the lilies he gathered to feed his regina moth grew in the center. However, he allowed Zakaar to lead. William followed him into the hedges, seething as they wended their way to the center and the sounds of battle.

Provided Incendo hasn't already slain Northward, he'd let Zakaar use him for a punching bag for putting him through this! That kadorei oaf knew about the meeting with the Dreadlord.

The labyrinth path straightened with a clear view of the center, where two warriors performed a deadly dance inside a circle of bare ground surrounded by blood lilies. Their swords flashed in the rosy light preceding Lachesis-set. Northward's silver aura blazed with electric blue spots outlined by brown tendrils, and he was grinning as he went on the offense against his opponent—a slender kadorei woman, not much taller than Northward, who wore chitinous black armor and a black war-cap over braided, dark auburn hair. Her aura was a steady flicker between bronze and gold, shot through with thread-thin cyan spikes and light blue streaks. The kythim of both rippled and flared. William gaped. Incendo had a vibrant aura like Northward and Annabelle, and it was similar in color to that cursed knight who'd chased him through the dreamscape. While he watched, a golden tendril from Incendo spiraled away to somewhere to his left, and her kythim shrank. A faint growl came from that direction.

Never far from its mistress, Incendo's wyrmkin sprawled out on the verge, wings half-furled and tail stretched along the hedgerow. Gold-bronze mist hovered around the beast, then winked out. Its eyes flared golden. What had he just witnessed? The thing growled again. William stiffened, but the creature made no move to rise. Zakaar stepped between him and the wyrmkin. It lifted a lizard-like head to glower at him and hissed menacingly. Funny, he hadn't noticed the intelligence in its gaze when he was younger; but that was probably because it was bashing him with its tail at the time. Now he could see the resemblance between the creature and the illustrations of the Sages he'd found.

William gave it a wide berth. "Oi," he shouted. As he stalked along the garden path toward them, his hastily donned burkheld gaped open. "What blithering imbecile entrusted our prisoner with a sword?"

The combatants paused, then fell back into a more relaxed posture, Incendo with all the poise of a coiled viper.

"I did, boy," she remarked in a tone as chilly as her pale blue eyes. She sneered at him. Perhaps her burned face wouldn't allow her to assume any other expression. Chills raced down his spine. Something about her pale-eyed glare reminded him of a recent nightmare.

"Master Northward found me here practicing the sword dance and offered to spar. For that, he required a blade." She shrugged. "So I gave him my practice sword. Don't worry, its edges are dull." Sheathing her weapon, she turned to Northward and placed a fist against her armored chest. "It was a good bout. Your Swan Stance is rusty, but with regular practice you'll soon be in fighting form."

Northward didn't seem at all put off by the hideous burn scars marring the left side of her face. Offering her the practice blade on outstretched hands, he bowed. "Thank you for instructing me, Lady Marshal." After she reclaimed the sword, he straightened. "I'm honored that you indulged me. You probably rank within the top five best sword-dancers I've ever met, and I was taught by Commander Storm."

Incendo raised her right eyebrow. "High praise indeed." The right side of her mouth twitched into the ghost of a smile. Perhaps with her, it was the closest she'd get to smiling. "Sadly, it seems our training session is at an end for the day. I believe the Dreadlord wished to see you at this time. I have business with him as well, so I shall accompany you." Then she glanced at William, and any good humor vanished. "That is why you and your pet assassin are here, isn't it ... boy?"

Zakaar stiffened. William bit back a caustic retort. "Er. Yes, ma'am."

"Well, look lively, boy. The Dreadlord won't appreciate your dawdling." As Incendo swept past between William and Zakaar, she beckoned to the wyrmkin. "Here, Fiskra." The wyrmkin rolled to its feet, stretched like a cat, and padded after its mistress with a baleful parting glance at Zakaar and William.

"Zakaar, we're done here," William said. "Go clean up your mess in the library."

Zakaar opened his mouth as if he was about to protest, then shut it again. He bowed. "Of course, Dulciber. I will see you at dinner." Ears laid back, the harkhurz stalked off through the labyrinth, leaving William alone with Northward.

Stepping carefully over the blood lilies, the youth approached William. He was smiling, the insufferable wretch. "I don't think the Marshal likes you much. Not that I blame her."

"Incendo doesn't like anybody." William scowled. It could cause problems for him if Northward had found an ally in Marshal Incendo. "But apparently, you're not anybody. Come on, Sir Fancy-Jacket."

Northward's eyes widened as they settled on his seventh circle. "What in perdition ... is that a sorcerer tattoo?" He grimaced, and dark green colored his kythim. *—So that's what the evil things look like. What a disgusting way to maim oneself. And it's lopsided! —*

"It's part of my arkhabala, yes," William snapped. "Now let's get going." He spared a surreptitious glance at his chest. *Merciful Valeshka, is my circle asymmetrical? After all that work with the blistering compass!*

"Looks painful," Northward said, falling in beside him. "No wonder you're always so ..." His comment dissolved into laughter. "I see you couldn't make it to the garderobe in time!"

"It's water," William growled as he fastened the ties of his burkheld properly. "I splashed myself while I was shaving." Why did he even care whether this kadorei thought he wet himself?

"You're old enough to shave?" Northward grinned. "Maybe just barely. You must not be very good at it. From that ugly circle cut into your chest, it looks like the razor missed. Just like you missed the garderobe."

"Try again, Northward. You almost hurt my feelings with that one." He rolled his eyes. *I've seen sixteen winters. Just because I only need to shave every other week ...*

Shaking his head, Northward snorted. "Not worth the effort. What's this meeting about?"

William sneered, resisting the urge to shove the other youth down a stairwell as they passed it. "What do you think? The Dreadlord's going to make you an offer you can't refuse."

"Why am I not surprised? I figured he had you drag me out here for some reason. Whatever it is, I'm not sure it's worth the life of Sir Rick." Northward began describing all the laws Tenebris had broken the moment he set foot in the Darkenwood Forest. William tuned him out, only half-listening.

What he'd told Northward wasn't far from the truth. Yesterday, the Dreadlord had summoned William into his private study—ostensibly to play a game of bakkharat. While William tried to ignore the burning discomfort of his new etchings and offer at least something of a challenge, the Dreadlord explained his plan to use Northward as a sort of catspaw—and how William would assist.

Help Northward? That didn't sit well with him. Then the dwelfnhir warned William not to react to any insults, accusations, or demands for justice that Northward hurled at him, even if the Dreadlord appeared to agree with what the kadorei youth said, and grant concessions to William's disadvantage.

"If it helps, William Dulciber," the Dreadlord had said, using his archimandrite in a gambit to block William from castling. *"Think of my plan as a bakkharat game. A game on a global scale, in which I am positioning vital pieces meant to take down Warlord Vespyrahl before he devastates an entire continent."*

Thereby placing the Dreadlord in a position to fill a power vacuum and rule from the shadows, William recalled with a smirk. Admirable goals, really. If you enjoyed that sort of political nonsense. All Tenebris cared about was exacting revenge on Vespyrahl.

And all I want is power enough to escape Tenebris. To be left alone. I don't care to play games—at least not at the Dreadlord's scale.

He shuddered. The problem with playing games was that you risked losing. He'd already risked losing his magic during his Trial. Fortunately, for that he'd had the information he needed to succeed. Here, he wasn't certain he knew enough about the players or the stakes to estimate the costs and benefits. And if the Dreadlord allowed Northward too much leeway in dispensing justice, then William could find himself dangling from a noose. He realized he was rubbing his neck and forced his hand down.

Northward was still harping on about his dead friends and obtaining justice. He really needed to get past that and focus on what was important. Like shutting up and doing whatever the Dreadlord told him instead of vexing William with his inane drivel. Ah, *finally*. The little prig's rant was winding down.

"So ... Dulciber," Northward concluded, emphasizing the name. "Other than poisoning beloved elders and covering up the crimes of child murderers, what's your role in all of this?"

"Oi, what's this now? My role? This isn't a play, Sir Fancy-Jacket." William laughed. "But I suspect the Dreadlord will tell us to work together on some sort of grand scheme."

"Work with a serpent-tongued miscreant like you?" Northward scowled. "I'd sooner take a bath in a cauldron of dirty dishwater and rotten vegetables."

Eyeing him approvingly, William gave a low whistle. "Now that was a proper insult." Then he frowned. "What're vegetables?"

Northward gaped. "Are you serious? You don't know that?"

"Of course I know!" William snarled. "Now hurry up before I call Zakaar. He's been wanting to use you for a punching bag again." *Vegetables?* So what if he didn't know what those were? He'd simply go to the library and look it up later. Or maybe Zakaar could tell him. He'd been living with kadorei for a while and probably knew all about their disgusting habits.

The Council Chamber lay in the interior of Fastness with a view of the central courtyard and gardens. A pair of guards—hulking kadorei men—stood on either side of double doors. Incendo stalked down the hall. William remained a cautious five paces behind her. Kythim tinged with a light orange color, Northward gave him an odd look and moved closer to her.

Inwardly, William shrugged. *Cozy up to the termagant if you like. It's your funeral, Sir Fancy-Jacket.*

The Marshal crashed to a halt before the doors, brandishing a message tube. "Announce me!"

"Yes, sir!" One soldier hastened to open a door and stuck his head inside to murmur, "Marshal Incendo to see you, my lords." After receiving a further order from within the room, he opened the door and bowed.

Incendo swept past him and the larger man shrunk away from her, flashes of terror in his kythim. William met his gaze as he passed. The soldier assumed a wooden expression.

William sneered. *Too late. I already know she scares you spitless.* Incendo's wyrmkin decided to curl up against the wall across from the door. Good. The horrible beast could terrorize the soldiers.

Northward followed Incendo in, then stood with his back against the wall. William paused just inside the chamber to take it all in. Ah. That was the reason for the plural "lords." On the other side of a room dominated by a huge table, the Dreadlord and Tenebris sat across from one another at a small square table near the window, through which a patch of sanguine sky was visible. Outside, crickets chirped, and a floral scent wafted in from the gardens beyond. Bathed in lantern-light, the table surface was made up of alternating black and white squares and set with game pieces of the same colors. Bakkharat. He grinned.

The Dreadlord maneuvered a white piece to capture one of Tenebris's black. The Ventnor Defense. *Nice move.* Studying the board, he saw that the Dreadlord would defeat Tenebris in five turns. William smirked. His master was merely average at the game. How that must gall him. Cycles ago, Tenebris had taught William the rules, then refused to play anymore after it became William's favorite game. Tenebris claimed he must learn to give up idle enjoyments if he wanted to achieve mastery.

But the real reason is that I surpassed him.

Incendo stood beside the Dreadlord, unburnt hand on his shoulder and whispering in his ear. The Dreadlord unscrewed the tube. He turned from the board and unrolled the message scroll. His eyebrows twitched and he grunted softly as he read.

William frowned. To elicit any physical response from the dwelfnhir, that message must contain news of great import. Did it pertain to this meeting? What he wouldn't give to be able to read the man's kythim!

—I need to see that!— Northward stepped from the wall, his eyes fixed on the message. Apparently, they agreed on that much.

Crushing the scroll in his fist, the Dreadlord rose and faced his opponent. "Yvres Tenebris, we shall finish this game tomorrow. You may go. I'll keep you apprised of the situation." The sorcerer nodded, his expression bland. He didn't even glance at William, but he felt the promise of his master's impending wrath as he passed by.

I didn't even do anything this time! William hunched his shoulders, cringing from an imagined blow.

Northward's glare followed Tenebris, then he caught William's eye. *—he really has you cowed, doesn't he?* — Oddly enough, there wasn't any venom in his mental voice. He sounded almost ... sad? His silver kythim dulled to light gray.

Doubtless, the kadorei wretch tried to catch William reading his mind again.

Eyes narrowed, William was about to deliver a scathing comment when the Dreadlord rose. "Thank you, Marshal," he said, smiling down at her. "You have executed the mission admirably, as always."

Lavender streaked through her kythim; a color William rarely saw and hadn't yet labeled. Something pleasant? A smile contorting her burnt face, she saluted. "I only do my duty, sir."

"I shall not detain you from your responsibilities, then." He dismissed her with a wave of his hand. Incendo exchanged a cordial nod with Northward. As she exited the room, her cold-eyed gaze swept over William, and he repressed a shiver. It was like a storm had passed without unleashing its fury. His fingers curled into fists at his side.

One day, when I attain mastery, that suns-cursed woman and her pet will get their comeuppance. And if Northward allies with her, it'll be to his ruin, regardless of the Dreadlord's plans for him.

"Thank you both for joining me," the Dreadlord began.

Northward snorted softly. *—for all the world like he hadn't hired two murderous sons of goats and an insane child-killer to drag me here—*

The Dreadlord smacked a palm on the table, and Northward winced. "Doubtless," he continued in an even tone, "you are wondering why I brought you here and it is time to disclose my plans." He gestured at the table. "Please. Take a seat."

Fists clenched at his sides, Northward stiffened. "It's bad enough you abducted me, but I refuse to discuss any plans that involve me working with murderers."

Smiling, the Dreadlord met Northward's defiant glare. William watched with interest; how long could Northward bear up under that fathomless stare? After a moment, the youth inhaled sharply, and his eyes dropped.

Ha! Weakling. William grinned.

The Dreadlord glanced between them, eyebrows raised. "Sooner or later, lads, you will abandon your mutual animosity and work together. For the greater good." He pointed at the table and his voice cracked out like a whip. "Sit. Down."

Despite himself, William flinched.

Northward stiffened, then rushed to grab a seat. *—He sounds just like Commander Storm! —*

"Of course, Your Eminence." William hesitated a beat, waiting until the other youth was at the table before moving himself. He chose a spot that placed his back toward a wall and kept the others in view. Aiming for nonchalance, he drew out the chair and eased into it. He suppressed a grimace as his new circles flared with a fresh spate of itchy tingles. Hopefully the Dreadlord would get to the point and reveal what was in that scroll so that William could return to his research. And his whiskey flask.

"Thank you." Slowly the Dreadlord paced around the table, tapping the scroll in his palm. "According to reputable sources—and my own personal reconnaissance—the protective Veils and wardspells across Tehara are breaking down. I believe you both know the danger their loss poses to human communities everywhere." Holding up fingers, he ticked them off. "Cave bears, soot panthers, lykharim, duskprowlers, and terror birds, to name but a few."

"You forgot the worst of them all—nehmwights," Northward muttered, cutting a glance at William. *—vile, murderous fiend—*

Crossing his arms, William looked down his nose at him. *I won't let you rile me, Lord Priggish.* He leaned back, then jerked forward with a hiss of pain.

"Aye, nehmwights." The Dreadlord conceded with a chuckle. "I did not forget them. However, the danger of nehmwight invasion into kadorei lands pales in comparison to the threat lurking on the horizon."

This was ... different. William expected him to immediately mention wiping out Vespyrahl's faction. That was a sure way to sway Northward to his cause. There must be a larger-scale game afoot. William needed more information. It was probably in that scroll. Despite himself, he exchanged a puzzled glance with Northward.

"Excuse me, sir," Northward said. "I know about the Veil collapsing. But all human communities have mundane protections as well. The Council mandates that all villages build durable shield walls and are also associated with a garrison. We're provisioned to withstand sieges of a Cycle or longer. Our soldiers are well-trained, and Commander Storm is the greatest military mind on the planet." His blue eyes narrowed. "What's coming that could overcome all that?"

The Dreadlord arched an eyebrow. "Tell me, Enoch sel Drayven, what do you know of the Hollow?"

William froze. Had he heard that right, or was his discomfort with his flaming arkhabala causing him to hallucinate? *I was just reading something about the Hollow! Is he going to explain what they were?* William leaned forward.

Northward's tone grew scornful. "Those bogeymen? I know they're just folklore. They don't really exist."

Chuckling, the Dreadlord placed the scroll on the table. Fingers twitching, William eyed it. When would he find out what it contained? Was it about the Hollow?

"Folklore is often based on fact," the Dreadlord remarked as he tapped the ends of the scroll. "Actual events. Real people. However, the historians may choose to ... cleanse their records and present a sanitized version of history. The truth is forgotten. If the kadorei are to escape from their chains, then you must learn all that the Council has concealed, Enoch sel Drayven. One of those things is the fate of the Sages and their enemies, the Hollow, who were once of their number. Over an Age ago, their wars devastated the planet."

The Hollow were once among the Sages? William frowned. That cast his research in a new light.

"The Oblivion Wars," Northward said. "Named as such because nobody remembers exactly what happened. And I'm to believe that you do ... sir?"

"Very good, Enoch sel Drayven." The Dreadlord nodded. "I do refer to the Oblivion Wars. And I never said I *remembered*. But I know the truth of what happened, despite the Hollow's efforts to conceal it. The leader of the Hollow was a mind mage—perhaps even greater than Jethro Shadowveiled—who cast an Oblivion Net to ensure the survivors forgot a great many details."

He chuckled. "But he missed several individuals. Then, after the Hollow were banished to the Sundered Realms, the Dwelfnic Council completed the task of purging their records. Perhaps they meant well; believing ignorance of the spells involved would prevent the return of the Hollow. Or perhaps they wished to hide a shameful secret. However, accurate histories exist, and I discovered them. Feel free to peruse my collection in the library, both of you. I know William Dulciber has already done so. And I trust you have found them illuminating?"

"Er, yes, Your Eminence. Quite illuminating."

Turning to Northward, the Dreadlord described all the wonders and horrors the Hollow had wrought during the Oblivion Wars. Without the intervention of the Sages, it was easy to imagine the havoc the Hollow could wreak.

"And now," the Dreadlord concluded, "the Warlord Vespyrahl seeks to release the Hollow from the Sundered Realms."

Ah. William's eyes narrowed. *I see the entire playing board now.*

"Vespyrahl?" Northward's eyes went wide as saucers as he leaned forward, intent on the Dreadlord. Whatever he'd been expecting to hear, that wasn't it.

"Indeed. Vespyrahl craves ultimate power, and he believes his gods—the Hollow—can give it to him. He cares nothing for the ruin that will surely follow. Join me in preventing the escape of the Hollow, Enoch sel Drayven, and I shall give you everything the Council has ever denied to you."

"Such as?" Northward's kythim flared with red sparks. "Why should I work with someone who sanctioned the murder of the only father I've ever known ... by this scum and his henchman." He jabbed a finger at William.

This was too much. He'd only done as he was told. Mixing a potion didn't count as murder. Leaping from his chair, William planted his fist on the table. "Oi! I never killed anyone, you sanctimonious windbag. That was—"

His furious gaze fixed on the calm dwelfnhir, Northward shouted over William. "Nothing you could offer me would convince me to join you."

A wan smile curved the Dreadlord's lips. Triumph glinted in his eyes. "Enoch sel Drayven, I know where your sister lives.

Your only surviving blood relative." He patted the scroll in front of him. "Work with me to save the world from the Hollow, and that knowledge becomes yours—and the freedom to act upon it."

So, Northward had kin! *That's* what the Dreadlord was offering him? William swallowed his derision. *Family. Bah! Were I in his boots, I'd hold out for a better bargain. My own mother abandoned me to be sacrificed to a made-up god. Family is bad news.*

And if what he'd read so far about that Hollow was true, then what the Dreadlord offered was a death sentence in exchange for useless information.

Northward stared at the scroll. He licked his lips. "Give me some time to think about it. First, I'll need to research those histories."

William eyed him sidelong. *Is he just buying time or is he actually considering it?*

"Very well," the Dreadlord replied. "I depart to monitor several business interests on the morrow at firstdawn. When I return in five days, I expect to hear your decision. In the meantime, William Dulciber can show you the library. I believe he wishes to return to his studies and the answers he seeks." He rose from his chair. "Do not allow me to detain you, lads." He gestured toward the door in what was clearly a dismissal.

Once they were outside the room, William rolled his eyes. "Oi, come along, Sir Fancy-Jacket. The library's this way." Did Northward even know how to read? There were times when William doubted the other youth's intelligence. However, surely even Northward wasn't stupid enough to believe the Dreadlord would ever let a wyldling go free.

Caster of Flame

Here, in the dreaming place, Thomas would find the answers he sought. He'd put into practice what he'd worked out with Commander Storm, David, and Dinah. All it took was reaching out with his kythim to locate energy signatures, then following them to their source.

Under the clear blue, sunless sky, Thomas stalked toward the cluster of decaying and moss-covered walls of a long-abandoned garrison town—doubtless remnants of a forgotten war. He'd last seen his prey—the source of one of those energy signatures—scurrying in this direction. If that nehmwight thought he could hide in those ruins, then he had another thing coming. The joker could run, and he could hide, but sooner or later ... Thomas would find him.

He bared his teeth in a feral grin. The youth's terror was palpable; he could almost taste it. Like barbecue. He pushed aside the discomfort roiling in his stomach.

Run, boy, run. But you'll never escape me. And if you don't tell me where you're hiding Annabelle and Enoch ...

He wasn't sure why he needed to kill the youth, only that the raging inferno inside him demanded vengeance. Was it something to do with the scars on his chest? He could puzzle that out later. Right now, he was looking for some clues as to the kiddo's whereabouts. Doubtless, the orange-eyed clown he chased knew something about that.

The energy signatures had different ... scents? Flavors? Colors? Perhaps a combination of all three. Thomas had discovered echoes in the dreamscape that reminded him of Annabelle—a flash of blue and the scent of a spring rain mixed with citrus—but she hadn't been around.

Instead, he'd discovered the nehmwight boy lurking about.

He'd better not have done anything to her.

Thomas raised his left hand, and his wrath coalesced into a golden sword, the hilt cool against his palm. Flames ignited along the blade. Anticipation shivered down his spine.

There! A flicker of movement between the lintels of a weather-beaten arch. A glimmer of violet light. Thomas broke into a run. Dead, dry grass crunched under his boots. He barked a laugh. The entire grassland was ripe for a wildfire. He contemplated setting everything ablaze, driving the joker out into the open, but the smoke would hamper his vision. Besides, Caster of Flames or not, he'd learned that he was as vulnerable to smoke as anyone else.

His grin settled into a grim smile. Not a problem. There were other ways of dispatching his target. A flaming sword would do nicely for that. And the sourekghar would shield him from any retaliation. With a thought, he brought the sourekghar into being and felt himself enveloped in the gold-chased armor from head to foot.

My fury made solid.

Violet mist billowed out from the stone arch, concealing whatever lay beyond. Thomas slowed several paces shy of the opening and eyed it warily. Doorways had a special significance here, or so Commander Storm said. Destinations weren't always what they seemed. Step through without your goal firmly in mind, and you didn't always end up where you wanted. And they worked both ways. *Things* could come through them. Dangerous things, made of fangs and flame. He'd extinguished every last one of them. In light of that, what was a little fog—even if it was an unnatural color?

He snorted a laugh. "You can't scare me. I'm the bogeyman here. Did you find a good hiding place? Ready or not, clown, here I come!"

Tightening his grip on the weapon and galvanizing the resolve in his heart, Thomas squared his shoulders as he strode through the mist-shrouded arch. He went with the blade held before him like a torch, but it illuminated nothing. Dense purple fog swirled like a living thing, lit by eldritch light and strangely dry. It smelled of varnished wood and some kind of resin. A haunting melody drifted around him, reminding him of something ... Warmth and love, followed by an aching loss. Tears pricked his eyes and his vision swam.

He shook his head. *No! I won't be side-tracked!*

"Nice try, clown." Thomas gritted his teeth and pressed forward, holding his sword in a crossguard. Suddenly, he broke through the dry, violet mist as if through a slight resistance and stumbled into the center of a courtyard fenced in by crumbling stone walls. In counterpoint to the music, his sabatons thudded against cracked pavers overrun with sickly weeds as he regained his balance, scanning his surroundings, prepared for an assault.

Who was playing that music? It sounded like a guitar, but sharper somehow. He'd heard that instrument before. He turned in a circle, then blinked. Where'd the blasted nehmwight go?

"You will not find your quarry here, Helzarvenn."

Thomas spun, blade flaring brighter with golden flames. His eyes widened. Criminy! Was there no end to the surprises in this crazy place? He spluttered, "You!"

Limned in violet light, a tall, cloaked figure stood where he'd sworn there was no one a moment before. A cowl hid its face, and it held a guitar-like instrument—the source of the music he'd heard—long fingers plucking the strings in a mocking tune reminiscent of Ring Around the Rosey. A pleasant baritone sang: "Ashes, ashes, we all fall down."

Thomas settled into a ready stance. *I've seen this guy before ... I think.* He frowned. "Who the hell are you?"

The cloaked musician chuckled and covered the strings, silencing them. "I am known by many names, although those I encounter in the dreamscape often forget me." He shrugged. "To their loss and detriment. I am the traveler of dreams, the questor of nightmares, the wandering bard who has no place to rest his head. My true name is not for you to know." He strummed a chord. "But you may call me the Dream Traveler."

"Dream Traveler, eh? Suits you." Thomas snorted. "But I think I'll call you Mr. Cowl." He narrowed his eyes. "Where'd you hide that orange-eyed filth?"

"The one you seek is not in my custody."

"But you know where he is."

"Oh, yes." A smile colored the words and amusement emanated from beneath the cowl. "Here in the dreamscape, I know where many things are." He plucked out a descending chord. "But many things here are not what they seem."

Oh, don't I know it! Thomas straightened. "Tell me where the nehmwight went. He's a criminal who needs to be brought to justice." *Do I know that for sure? Doesn't matter; he's a nehmwight and he's sniffing around where Annabelle was. He's guilty of* something. Hurriedly, he added, "And he has information I need."

A booming laugh echoed around the ruined courtyard. Shaking his cowled head, the Dream Traveler muttered, "Justice? Revenge, more like. But the time will come for him to face the music. His wretched father, too." The bard plucked out seven descending notes. Louder, he said, "Lives must not be bartered lightly. I cannot provide you with information regarding the lad's whereabouts."

Oh, really? Thomas lifted his chin. "Cannot, or will not?"

"Will not." The bard chuckled. "Everything comes at a price, wyldling. There are so many things I could teach you, places I could show you, people I can find for you—if you purchase the right to learn."

Thomas scowled. What was this joker's game? "Purchase. Huh." He grunted. "With what friggin' currency, Mr. Cowl? I've got no cash on hand." No pockets, either.

The Dream Traveler scoffed, and his playing took on a derisive tone. "I have no interest in coinage or gems. Such has no meaning here, in the dreamscape."

"What do you want then?" Desperation fanned the flames of his anger. *I need to find Annabelle before that nehmwight does.* Voice tight, he said, "Name your price."

"If you can best me in a swordsman's duel—to first blood— then I will lead you directly to your prey. I will even tell you the location of the Windblade Master and the Water Weaver."

How did he know I was looking for Enoch and Annabelle? Had Thomas said something out loud that he shouldn't have? Or had Mr. Cowl been spying on him?

"A duel, huh?" Thomas drawled. "That sounds right up my alley." He examined his adversary. Mr. Cowl was a big guy, as tall and almost as broad as Commander Storm, but he was a *musician.* What did a bard know about fighting? On the other hand, he wouldn't have suggested a duel if he didn't know one end of a sword from the other. And he had no idea what was under that cloak. No. Thomas had better be wary, and certain he understood the terms.

"Let me get this straight. If I win, you'll take me where I want to go and tell me whatever I want to know." The cowled head dipped in a nod. Heart racing, Thomas affected nonchalance and raised an eyebrow. "Do you really know where Enoch and Annabelle are? And how I can free them from whoever holds them?"

"I do. And I will freely share ... everything I know, should you overcome me."

Thomas snorted. "Easy enough to promise. But what happens if *you* win? You'll kill me?" Not that he worried about that. Thomas was a skilled fighter, trained by the best and most renowned warriors on the continent. His armor was iron-clad and he possessed a blade that was *on fire*. Heck, he could conjure a second one if he wanted to. The dreamscape was malleable that way. Whatever advantages Mr. Cowl had, Thomas had them, too.

The Dream Traveler laughed. "Merciful Yshua, no! Snuffing out your existence serves no purpose whatsoever." His tone darkened. "As I've already said, I do not barter with lives lightly. Unlike my brother, I do not dance with death and deal in bloodshed. If you lose, Helzarvenn, I will simply set you loose in the dreamscape, to drift wherever you will." He raised a hand and waggled his fingers. "Like ashes falling to the ground."

Brow furrowed, Thomas eyed him, incredulous. Was this joker out of his gourd? *I doubt he has that power.* But he needed information to complete his mission. He frowned. "Take off that cloak, first. I'm not agreeing to duel a man whose face I can't see."

"As you wish." Laughing softly, the Dream Traveler unfastened the amethyst clasp at his throat. The cowled cloak dropped to the cracked stones and faded away, revealing a brown-skinned dwelfnhir clad in chitinous armor similar to Thomas's sourekghar, only chased in violet instead of gold.

Black eyebrows raised, the Dream Traveler regarded him with a sardonic smile. Like every dwelfnhir Thomas had met, he was flawlessly handsome—or would have been, without the pale, puckered scar running from his forehead, through an eyebrow, and down his right cheek to his chin. His eyes were an odd pinkish-gray color, and half of the right iris was pinker than the other half.

Thomas suppressed a grimace. No wonder the Dream Traveler wore a cowl. That scar was one of the first things you noticed. The damage looked like it was dealt by a sharp blade.

Like all those scars on my chest. He shivered. *Well, that scar is proof that someone bested him, at one time or another. I can do it, too.*

He cleared his throat, swallowing the ire that attempted to rise. He must remain cool and clear-headed if he meant to duel for answers. Borrowing a phrase from the kiddo, he said, "Alrighty then. I agree to your terms, Mr. Cowl. Let's dance." As he shifted into the challenger form that opened every swordsman's duel, he took in the instrument still cradled in the bard's arms. "Uh, you did say this was a swordsman's duel. Where's your weapon?"

The Dream Traveler's smile turned fond as he patted his guitar-thing. "This lytarra is my best and truest weapon. However, you are correct. For a swordsman's duel, I require a sword." The instrument vanished, and in his left hand the bard held a blade equivalent to his own—except that the flames flickering around it were violet instead of golden.

He assumed the defender's fighting form. "And yes, despite my scar, I know my way around a blade well enough." Thomas flinched, and the dwelfnhir chuckled. "The course of your thoughts are clear, Helzarvenn, and the scar is rather a prominent feature of my facial landscape." He grinned, something like madness glittering in his strangely colored eyes, but it was quickly gone. "Shall we begin?"

I've got a bad feeling about this.

Too late to back out now.

"Yeah, let's get this over with." His eyes on his opponent, Thomas cautiously circled the Dream Traveler, who paced him with enviable grace. He wondered if the dwelfnhir really was left-handed, like him, or equally good with both. It didn't matter. Thomas had to beat him. "I need that information," he muttered.

The Dream Traveler narrowed his eyes. "I find it decidedly odd that a wyldling must ask for help in locating other wyldlings," he remarked, as if musing aloud. "Did you know, Caster of Flames, that the term 'wyldling' derives from the dwelfnic root wyld'to'allein, which translates roughly as 'forger of bonds' in the Trading Language?"

Oh, great. He's one of those jokers who tries to distract his opponent by yammering about random trivia. I'd rather listen to Annabelle drone on about the difference between a lamprey and a hagfish. Jeremiah the ever-lovin' bullfrog! They're both freaky eels!

"No, I didn't," he replied testily. *Don't let him get to you.* He took a deep breath. "You gonna fight, or would you rather chat over tea and crumpets?"

Eyebrow arched, the Dream Traveler retorted, "Are you not proficient enough with the sword to carry on a conversation whilst dueling?" Thomas attacked in lieu of a reply, and their blades met in a spray of gold and purple sparks. The Dream Traveler parried without effort. "Struck a nerve, did I?"

Thomas sprang back, watching his footing. "I don't see what a language lesson has to do with finding Enoch or Annabelle. Not to mention that nehmwight scum." The Dream Traveler eyed him sidelong, smiling faintly as they circled one another, saying nothing. Thomas ground his teeth. *I'll burn that self-satisfied look off his scarred face.*

"Will you, now?" murmured the Dream Traveler, violet flames reflected in his eyes while they danced around one another. "That question remains unanswered, as yet, Caster of Flames."

Is that know-it-all fiddler reading my mind? With a shout, Thomas resumed his offensive. It had the desired effect: the Dream Traveler shut up. For several moments—or whatever passed as such in the dreamscape—the combatants' fiery blades clashed, and the scream of steel was the only sound while Thomas took his measure of the Dream Traveler's skill.

It was more than equal to his own—better even. The Dream Traveler was faster and stronger. He held himself back; Thomas knew it in his bones. His stomach sank, but he battled on. What else could he do? The only way to gain the information he needed was to cut this joker. At least in the dreamscape he wouldn't grow weary.

Thomas frowned. The style in which his adversary dueled was eerily familiar. Each swordmaster possessed his own signature, his own flair, so to speak. And Commander Storm had taught him to riposte in exactly the same, no-nonsense manner.

The Dream Traveler laughed. "Of course," he cried, gaily, like a man at a carnival as he fended off blow after blow. Gold and violet sparks rained down like fireworks, yet nothing caught ablaze. "And who do you think helped teach *him* the sword dance?"

What in blazes—?

Thomas nearly stumbled when his foot caught in a crack. He recovered quickly, but not before the Dream Traveler thrust past his guard, nicked his chin, then slammed the sword hilt against Thomas's left wrist as he danced backward. Thomas's hand went numb. He barked out an obscenity as the flaming sword fell from nerveless fingers.

Grimacing, he squatted and raised his arms in a cross-block, willing his helmet to protect the exposed areas of his face. The sourekghar would ward off blows from the Dream Traveler's blade while he recovered his own weapon. *I hope.* Seeking his sword—where *was* it? —he tensed in anticipation of the downward strike. Inside the helmet, blood trickled down his neck. His cut chin stung like the blazes.

"Don't bother," his opponent drawled, his own hands empty. "Your sword has vanished. First blood goes to me. You've lost." He tsked, sounding ... disappointed. The Dream Traveler lunged toward him and struck the heel of his palm against his forehead. "Farewell, little Caster of Flames."

With a grunt, Thomas fell back ... and kept falling. *Criminy!* His stomach lurched sickeningly. The dreamscape whirled around him in gray-green streaks, then receded into purple fog that smelled of dank stone, followed by wood-smoke. Thomas spun away. Into a void.

Rage filled him, burning his insides, and he wept tears like flame. "Get back here, you fiddling coward!"

"Never mind Jethro's wayward firstborn," a deep voice commanded, filling the emptiness. "Come to me, Helzarvenn."

Thomas felt an urge to vomit that had nothing to do with weightlessness.

Oh, God. Please ... no. I can't deal. Not now. Not with him. Not Balthazar Phoenixheart.

Tears of a Dragon

The water globe shimmered in the hazy air of the dreamscape. To Annabelle, it resembled a flower bud at the end of a slender stalk of water that extended from the dark blue surface of a river. With a surge of intent, she detached the basketball-sized globe from its tether. It came to hover beneath her outstretched hands. Could she make it look like Hadrien Rainblessed? Since losing the Dagger of Moonlight in the waking world, she'd also lost Khinjara in the dreamscape. This meant she had no reliable method of reaching Hadrien. She missed him.

However, as much as she'd like to see the Sage, crafting the details of a real dragon was probably beyond her skills.

I should stick to smaller things, for now.

Pensively, she sucked her lips over her teeth and turned to the Dalmatian sitting on his haunches beside her. "What do you think, Dallas? Should I make a family for you, and we can re-enact Amy's favorite movie?" The dog whimpered and tilted his head. She chuckled. "Don't worry. I'll cut Cruella DeVille out of the script."

She'd fallen asleep expecting to find herself in the dreamscape and arrived there with the purpose of seeking out Enoch. Knee-high grass colored in pastel hues of green, yellow, and pink whispered around her armor-clad legs as she walked alongside a dark river. While following its path through the pastel grassland, she paused to create an animal companion. Naturally, Dallas had sprang to mind. Who better than the pet of her childhood? His black-spotted white coat reminded her of Raeden, so it was almost like her champion was there in spirit, fulfilling his oath to protect her.

Guilt pricked Annabelle, thinking of Raeden all alone on the islet where the gwerindawr had imprisoned him. Morgan Brenin hadn't backed down on his decree. He allowed her to visit him for an hour every morning and evening, but that wasn't enough. She missed her champion.

"At least I have you here with me, Dallas. You'll keep me safe, won't you, boy?" The dog woofed softly, and she forced a smile, balancing the ball over one hand while stroking his head.

Dallas looked at her with soulful eyes and wagged his tail. He lifted his ears and panted. Annabelle squinted into the rippling water as an idea took shape. "You know, the gwerindawr have pet octopi. I think I'll make one of my own, to keep here in the dreamscape."

With her hands cupped around the water-ball, Annabelle concentrated on the image of Wesleyen—from the shifting colors of his skin pigments to the suckers on his tentacles. Slowly, water formed into the shape of the little blue octopus. Tentacles grew from the sphere and the creature took on lifelike features, even moving its appendages. She sent her water construct to hover over the stream and tethered it there with an umbilicus of water. Ears pricked at attention, Dallas stood and stared, softly growling.

"It's okay, Dallas," she soothed, scratching behind his ears. "I'm not replacing you with a cephalopod." She smiled at the octopus. "I think I'll name him Kraken. You know, like: 'release the kraken!' in the movie." She chortled, peering at her creation undulating in midair. "I wonder if I could make a kraken to free Raeden from his prison. Or scare the gwerindawr into letting us go." Her laughter died and she grimaced. "No. I'd feel terrible, threatening people like that."

But you still want to do it anyway, the nastier side of herself whispered. *And it's not as if you'll actually hurt anyone.*

Dallas whined, then resumed growling. Annabelle frowned. "Hush, boy. Don't tell me you're afraid of a little octopus! It's not like I actually made a kraken ..." Her voice petered out. The dog wasn't looking at the water construct, but rather off into the distance. "What *are* you growling at, Dallas?" Rising to her feet, she squinted across the river, seeing nothing aside from the pastel grasslands. However, the quality of light had changed. As if a sheer, tinted veil had dropped between her eyes and her surroundings. Was it growing darker? Usually, the sourceless light of the dreamscape remained the same.

Uneasy, she turned. Her eyes widened. Water rose up in globules and melded with her creation, increasing its size. What was going on? Her breath caught in her throat. She wasn't making the water do that! The cute blue octopus swelled into a huge, baleful monster with spiky black and mucous-green skin, its tentacles as big around as her body. Annabelle tried to concentrate on shrinking the creature down to its original size, cursing herself for thinking about krakens ... because that was what the octopus was fast becoming.

"Stop growing, Kraken!" she demanded in an unsteady voice, trembling as she rose and backed away. "You're big enough." It kept accreting mass from the stream and grew to the size of an elephant.

Annabelle reached where Murder Stick normally hung but noticed with a sinking sensation that although she wore the dark blue sourekghar, she wasn't wearing her weapons-belt. She visualized the sword in her hand. It wouldn't appear. She tried again. Nothing materialized. What the heck?

"K-Khinjara?" she called, looking around wildly. The hisanabyad hadn't shown up since she lost Daar-Lûsin. But there was someone else she could call upon for help. A knight who'd promised he'd protect her in the dreamscape. The warm glow of hope filled her. Maybe if she screamed loud enough, he would find her.

Taking a deep breath, she hollered: "Sir Thomas!"

When Thomas didn't appear, Annabelle swallowed tears. Her breath came quick and fast. *Okay, Ann. You'll just have to deal with this yourself.*

Dallas moved in front of her, hackles raised and growling. "No, boy, stay back." She reached for his collar, but the dog charged Kraken, barking. The creature burbled. A huge tentacle wrapped around Dallas and yanked him up above its bulbous head. Dallas yelped.

"Kraken!" Annabelle clenched her fists. "That's not for you. Drop him—now!"

Ignoring her, the beast dragged Dallas under its mantle and used several more tentacles to stuff the thrashing dog-simulacrum head-first into its beak. Color leached from Dallas's writhing body until he returned to his amorphous, transparent water state.

Just like that, her dear pet was gone.

"No," she wailed. Her knees buckled. "Dallas!"

Horror shot icicles through her. And then came stabbing grief. It wasn't Dallas, not in truth, but it still hurt. Why, oh why hadn't either of her constructs listened to her? The water was supposed to obey her. She was the Ahdmerel.

Raeden's warning echoed in her mind: *"You do not control the water, Freylin. That is for the Almighty to do."*

Annabelle shuddered. *Was I playing God? I need to undo my mistake!* Well, if Kraken refused to obey her, then she must cut him off from the water. Maybe then he'd shrink. hiccupping sobs, she searched in the gathering gloom for the umbilicus connecting the creature to its source of energy. Where was it? Oh, dear God, there were hundreds of threads pumping water into him! There was no way she'd sever them all before—

Finished with its meal, Kraken swelled even larger. Bulging eyes fixed on Annabelle.

Her heart skipped a beat. Would he eat her next? What would happen if she died in the dreamscape? Khinjara had told her it was possible, but didn't know how death in the dreamscape translated to the waking world.

I don't want to find out. I have to escape!

Sobs wracked Annabelle. Panic stripped her of reason. She tripped as she fled, falling on her rear. Terror set its barbs in her flesh as two tentacles snaked toward her.

"Stop!" Screaming, she raised her arms to block out her impending doom. "Oh, God, please save me!"

Light flickered, and she peered out from under her sheltering arms. Orange and purple lightning struck Kraken, and the tentacles withdrew with a jerk.

"Oi!" a resonant male voice shouted. "That's my wyldling. Shove off, water-spider!" A dark, monstrous form with bat-like wings descended between her and her rogue creation.

Annabelle gasped. Was that a dragon? Did God just answer her prayer?

Wings furled, the draconian newcomer reared on its—his? — hindquarters and partially blocked her view of Kraken. Tall and slender, he was larger than Commander Storm, but nowhere near the size of her Sage, Hadrien.

Annabelle scuttled to one side to avoid being struck by a long spiky tail and watched, heart racing, as the winged creature raised scaled and muscular forelimbs. The lightning streaming forth from his talons intensified and a stringy black fog surrounded the tentacled monster. Annabelle shuddered; it felt like ice spurs were twisting in her gut and she suppressed an urge to vomit.

Like Dallas, Kraken lost all color, shivered all over like Jell-O, then sizzled into steam. Drifting through the air, moisture refracted the orange and purple light like prisms. Full night had fallen, and the lightning show formed a corona around the dragon who had just fought off the Kraken with ... lightning bolts? Her construct exploded into a fine mist and small water globules that went flying everywhere.

Cringing, her savior threw up his forelimbs—arms? —to block his head. "Merciful Valeshka," he cried, shaking his wings. "I just had a suns-cursed bath last week!"

The ice at Annabelle's core melted away. So did the nausea. Warm water sprinkled down like rain, dampening her hair and beading on her armor. Despite the circumstances, she barked a laugh at the sight of a dark-scaled dragon the size of her dad's Jeep stamping and cursing. Her mind careened from one question to the next.

Is he a Sage? Where did he come from? His voice sounds familiar ...

"And good riddance," her rescuer grumbled with one last shake of his limbs. The dragon dropped on all fours and spun, the dangerous tail whipping behind him. He staggered, then froze, as if startled. After glaring at the spiky appendage and muttering, he turned to face her.

Annabelle's breath caught in her throat as his lambent gaze met hers.

The dragon has orange eyes like one of those monsters!

Propped up on her elbows, she froze in the act of rising. Her head spun. Heart racing, she recalled scenes of darkness, smoke, and blood. The same sort of eyes, blazing with inner light and promising her death. And then, she'd used her wyld—

Annabelle forced away the memory. *Focus on the present, Ann. A dragon just destroyed your kraken. A dragon, of all things. Wandering around in the dreamscape. He rescued me. But ... why? And why am I not terrified?*

His eyes dimmed. Starlight revealed a surprisingly mobile reptilian face surrounded by bone-white horns tapering back toward his long neck. Aside from the horns, his head was shaped like Hadrien's, with similar fan-shaped ears. Her heart pounded as admiration mingled with astonishment.

The creature scowled. "Burning suns and freezing void," he snapped, shaking his entire body, scattering water droplets. "That water-spider was a potent construct."

Water-spider? Annabelle blinked in confusion as she pushed herself up with her hands and stared, craning her neck to look at him. She tried to speak, but her throat was too tight after the loss of her pet. She should be able to create Dallas again ... Right?

Focus, Ann! There's a freaking dragon here, for goodness' sake!

"Creating two golems at once is foolhardy." The dragon crouched beside her, lowering his snout to within inches of her face. She shrank back. He narrowed his eyes. The purple irises reminded her of amethysts. Wait ... hadn't his eyes been orange before?

He shook his head. "And here I had you pegged as a cautious, clever maiden. Are you trying to get yourself killed, Milady Blue?"

Golems? ... Milady Blue? Her brow scrunched. Somebody called her that, once. Was it this dragon? When did she meet him? *I think I'd remember meeting a dragon, of all things! But on Tehara they call them Sages.*

Her throat worked, finally producing sounds. "Who ... What ..." She took a deep breath. "Are you a dragon—I mean, a Sage?"

"I'm not a Sage." The dragon smirked, reinforcing the feeling of familiarity. "So by process of elimination, that means I must be a dragon." He settled back on his haunches, looking smug as her little brother with a handful of cookies.

She pushed aside that impression. "There really are dragons on Tehara?"

He snorted. "Of course there are, Annabelle. But only here, in the dreamscape."

She gasped. *He knows my name! Who is he, and should I be freaking out right now?*

Aside from her initial frisson of shock, no such sensation emerged. The dragon didn't radiate the same menace as the nehmwights who'd tried to kidnap her. Despite his size, he was skinny and seemed ... awkward. Young. It might simply be his passing resemblance to Hadrien—and the fact he was a dragon— but she felt drawn to him.

"I ..." Frowning, Annabelle slowly pushed herself to her knees. Raeden had warned her she needed to be more wary. Not all feelings can be trusted. Just because this dragon looked a bit like Hadrien didn't mean he was safe. She licked her lips. "You know my name. Have we met before? Who are you and why did you save me?"

He rolled his eyes. "Of course we've met. How else could I know you? I saved you because you're, uh ... we're friends."

Light-headed, Annabelle rested her fingertips on her temples. "Friends? Since when? I don't think I'd forget being friends with a dragon." She reached for her wyld, but it slipped from her grasp like a wet garden hose.

With a grimace, he raked talons through the moss between them. "Since last time when you asked for my help in finding your brother. Don't you recall?" Pausing, he stared at her, then glanced aside, snarling in a consonant-heavy language that made the hairs rise on the back of her neck. Annabelle made out the words "Dream Traveler" amid the thorny tangle of words.

My brother ... Does he mean Enoch? A wave of dizziness swept over her, and she braced her hands on her knees. It was getting harder to concentrate. "Hey. I can't understand you. What're you saying?"

Not quite looking at her, he fussed with torn bits of moss. "Er. That the dreamscape is unpredictable. It was too much to hope for—you remembering me."

His head drooped and he looked so dejected Annabelle found herself leaning toward him, hand extended to touch his snout. Eyes widening, he flinched and jerked back before she made contact. With a little yelp, she overbalanced and toppled over.

Black talons shot out and grasped her shoulders, arresting her fall. Her gaze locked with his purple eyes. Then a bolt of black-blue energy traveled straight to her core, and the nauseating ice spurs returned.

"Mother of the Outer Darkness!" The voice was his, but it seemed to come from inside her head. "What ... How ... A sympathetic resonance between my magic and hers?"

What's going on? Annabelle's mind reeled. A child's cry for his mother rang in her ears. She smelled honeysuckle and tasted lemons. *That's not my thought!* Panic lanced through her as she thrashed against the dragon's claws. One flailing hand smacked his nose.

"Argh!" Wincing, the dragon grunted, and his grip loosened. He shook his head. "Suns burn it, Annabelle! There's no need to hit me."

She whimpered, shaking her stinging hand. Both dragon and dreamscape spun around her. *I have to get out of here. Away from .... Just away.* Struck by vertigo, she swayed when she took a step backward.

The dragon grabbed her shoulders and steadied her. His purple eyes were wide with pupils dilated, streaming tears. She must have imagined the orange before. All those fears and nightmares about nehmwights ...

"Don't try to move," the dragon said, breathless. "You're depleted from creating that water-spider golem."

Still holding her in place, he glanced back between the crooks of his folded wings—what must it be like to have six limbs, plus a tail, to keep track of? —and the spikes along his back bristled. "Catching up can wait, Milady Blue. We need to leave before the golem reforms."

Annabelle blinked until there was only one of him. "Huh?"

"It's still feeding off your wyld," he replied. "That's why you're so weak. Once you leave, the energy will dissipate completely." His tone grew urgent as brought his face level with hers. "Unless you want to become that thing's dinner, come along with me. We'll go somewhere safe, where there aren't any water-spiders."

She laughed weakly. "Water-spider? That's cute. Actually, it was an octopus."

Visage twisting into a scowl, he thumped his tail on the ground. "Aqua-whatever it's called, the blistering thing wanted to eat you. We should go before it reforms and tries again."

Annabelle frowned. "I don't know—"

With an exasperated groan, the dragon gathered her up in his arms—forelegs? —and then launched himself into the air. He smelled like ozone, dried blood, and faintly of honeysuckle. Shock rippled through her, driving away her dizziness. How dare he! Annabelle pounded a fist against the broad scales of his chest; the other arm was trapped against her side. "Let me go!"

She kicked, but her legs were held firmly together by his other arm.

"You really don't want me to do that, Annabelle." His voice rumbled in his chest. He sounded strained. Was she too heavy for him? He was kind of scrawny. Steady wing beats sounded above her, but she didn't feel the passage of wind. "It's a long way down, and I'm not sure where you'd end up if I dropped you."

With a tiny "eep," she went still. How high up were they? Her stomach lurched. She was afraid to look down.

"Where are you taking me?"

"I'm bringing you to my tower."

Of course, the dragon has a tower. Where else would he imprison helpless damsels?

Annabelle suppressed a sudden urge to weep. She wasn't helpless. She was a wyldling, and Christ's beloved child. Her power would replenish in time, as it always had. And with God on her side, she needn't fear anything. Hadn't she prayed for help? This dragon had come to her for a reason. Perhaps he really meant to help. But what did he expect in return?

"God," she murmured, clinging to the dragon, "thank you for delivering me from my own folly. Grant me wisdom. Please give me strength and courage. Keep me safe and don't let me fall. Your will be done. Amen."

"What are you babbling about?" His arms stiffened. "Are you casting a spell?"

"No!" Annabelle smacked his chest in time with her words. "I'm not babbling—or casting a spell—I'm praying." Jaw clenched, she hit him again, for good measure. She clutched at him again, as the sob threatening to escape fought its way free. "I'm afraid of heights."

"I won't let you fall." He sounded defensive. "And I won't hurt you. I told you—we're friends."

Friends. I'd like to believe that. Wearily, she laid her head against the smooth scales, nice and cool against her warm cheek. She closed her eyes and listened to his heartbeat; it seemed too rapid for such a large creature. "You say we're friends," she murmured. Some of the scales on his chest were colored to form a circle. She traced a cross inside the circle. "But how can that be? I don't remember you. I don't even know your name."

"Call me Varazslo," he growled, then shuddered. "And stop doing that. It ... tickles. I'd rather you hit me again."

A frisson of recognition shot through her. That name—she'd heard it before. But why couldn't she remember the dragon? She was just opening her mouth to ask when he landed, and her feet touched solid ground.

Varazslo's grip loosened. "Welcome back to my tower, Milady Blue."

Backing out of his embrace, she found herself standing in vaguely familiar surroundings with the stars blazing down from a pitch-black sky. "Yeah," she whispered, looking around. "I think ... I've been here before."

He leaned back on his haunches, then shifted around as if uncertain what to do with his tail. "I've made some changes since you were last here. Can you spot them?"

Exhaling loudly, Annabelle quickly stepped away while keeping a wary eye on her host. She held her right hand at her side and imagined gripping her short sword. Nothing happened.

Is he messing with me? I suppose I'll play his game. But he'd better not try anything nasty. Or Murder Stick will be putting in an appearance.

Varazslo chuckled. "Don't worry, Milady Blue. You're perfectly safe here." He spread out his wings. The dragon wasn't all black, more of a dark gray with lighter gray chest scales and the patchy black circle over his heart. Along his flanks black swirled like a mackerel tabby's markings. A rather pretty pattern.

His eyes glittered like amethysts. "As you can see," he said, "there's no water-spiders. No need for instruments of murder."

Annabelle shook her head. *Why do I feel like he can read me like a book?*

After giving him a strange look, she scanned the area. Indeed, it all seemed vaguely familiar. A crenelated stone wall circled the space, which resembled an odd combination of library and laboratory. There was a telescope mounted between two crenels, and a single chair in front of it. At least there weren't any chains lying around, and no manacles attached to the chair. Her eyes narrowed. It was far too small for Varazslo, and where would his tail go?

"Why would you need a chair?"

Varazslo smirked as he coiled his tail around his foreclaws. He raised his eyebrow ridges and spoke in a patronizing tone that made her hackles rise. "Chairs are meant for sitting, Milady Blue. We're going to have a nice long talk, you and I. You may as well be comfortable." He nodded toward the furniture. "Go on. Take a seat."

"Talk about what?" She crossed her arms. "What do you want from me, Varazslo?"

The dragon sighed. "Fine. Don't sit." Averting his gaze, he scraped his talons against the stone. A nervous habit, no doubt. "You asked for my assistance in finding Enoch Northward." He peered down his snout at her. "I know where he is ... if you still want the information."

Annabelle froze, feeling like her heart skipped a beat. She didn't recall asking for the dragon's help, but he'd found Enoch! She swallowed her immediate response and pushed down rising hope. There had to be a catch. Nothing was ever given for free. Especially when dragons were involved. She'd learned that from all the stories she'd read.

"You know I do. But what are you expecting in return?"

Looking away, he scuffed at the floor again. He was going to chip his talons if he kept that up. "An even exchange of answered questions over the course of two hours. We'll arrange to meet every night going forward. Tonight, I tell you where to find your brother, and in exchange, you answer a question. For one thing, I want to study your magic." He glanced at her, then examined his claws. "The golem you created was quite impressive. I was hoping ... we could help one another learn. Grow in our proficiency."

Annabelle's heart leaped. That didn't seem so bad. Discussing magic can't do any harm, right? She wasn't losing anything—so far as she could tell. It reminded her of group projects in school, where students shared information and worked together for mutual benefit. But how to prove Varazslo actually knew Enoch? *I need to test him. Quick! Think of some weird detail.* Drowning her elation, she asked, "When did you last see Enoch? I miss the way his green eyes sparkle when he smiles. Does he still favor his left leg?"

The dragon snorted. "Don't try to trick me. Northward's eyes are the same color as yours, and he doesn't have much to smile about right now. And he doesn't limp."

Arching an eyebrow, she crossed her arms. "I won't agree to anything until you give me something concrete."

"I was under the impression that I just did." Varazslo's tail lashed out and slammed against a cabinet, rattling glassware. He snarled, grabbed his tail, and shook it like he was throttling something. "Villem's bloody flail! Why won't you behave and lie still?"

Cheese and crackers! This guy's a hoot. I wish I could trust him. Annabelle barked a laugh, then covered her mouth. "Do you usually talk to your ... appendages?"

"Uh, no ... just this one," Varazslo muttered darkly as he dropped his tail. "Suns-cursed thing has a mind all its own." He rolled his eyes. "Alright, fine." He muttered something, and Enoch appeared, albeit translucent like a ghost. And scowling.

Annabelle gasped. "That's him!" She reached for the image. It winked out before she made contact. *At least Enoch looks okay, if not exactly happy.*

"Told you." The dragon sneered. "Last time I saw him, your heart-brother was alive and well in the Western Marches, kept in a stronghold called Fastness. That's in the Ingaraik mountain range."

"But where ..." Her heart plummeted. "How do I get there? Are you holding out on me?"

His violet gaze grew sullen. "No, Annabelle, I'm not." He waved a hand and a translucent map like a hologram floated in the air, showing mountain ranges and the outlines of lakes that looked eerily familiar—like the Great Lakes back home. "This is the Northern Marches."

"Wow." Varazslo made it look so easy. "How do you do that?"

He smirked. "After manifesting a water golem, creating a simple image shouldn't be difficult. And here's the Western Marches." He made a swiping motion, and the lakes slid to the right. A line of stylized mountains came into sight. "The Ingaraik Mountains." Then he flared out his claws and the view zoomed in on a glowing orange dot that appeared in the midst of the triangles. "Fastness is right there. And I happen to know which waystones you'd need to get there from the Northern Marches."

She watched as the map zoomed out, her eyes growing round. Little purple lights appeared, scattered across like stars. And then her shoulders slumped.

But I'm not on the same continent anymore.

Rubbing her forehead, Annabelle sighed. "Thank you, Varazslo. I suppose there's not much I can do with this information, anyway—so long as Raeden and I are stuck on Ynys Lloches. And I'm not sure where that is on Tehara."

Unless she found Sir Thomas in the dreamscape. Then she could pass along the information to him. If he was still with Commander Storm, the evainghir might recognize the name of the stronghold. He'd certainly know where the Ingaraik Mountains were. Hope flickered like a candle's flame in the darkness.

"Ynys Lloches?" The dragon's snout wrinkled. "Lucky for you, I've been studying maps of Tehara. That's an archipelago way off the western coast of Imerinthia." He widened the scale until a series of islands slid into view.

Annabelle's heart sped up. Ynys Lloches sort of looked like Hawaii.

"I'm counting that as two you owe me." Varazslo waved his talons. The map vanished and a large hourglass filled with orange sand hovered in midair. Grumbling, he glared at it. The sand turned purple. With another wave, the hourglass flipped over, and sand trickled into the bottom half. "Our first session begins now."

Time to hold up her end of the bargain. A quivery excitement filled her. Varazslo seemed knowledgeable. Maybe he could help her figure out the gwerindawr prophecy! She pulled the chair closer to the dragon, then sat down. "Okay. What're your questions?"

"I'm still mulling over my second question." Spikes rattled as his tail twitched. He glared at it, then peered at her sidelong. "Regarding the first... I told you I wanted to study your magic. Not so much a question as me describing something I'd like you to do with your wyld, so I can observe your methods."

She frowned. "You saw what happened with my Kraken. How it was drawing from my wyld." *And ate Dallas ...* Shuddering, she hugged herself. "I don't want a repeat of that."

The dragon grunted. "I'm not asking you to make another blistering water-spider. What about that other creature you had with you—the one it ate—the white thing with black spots?"

Annabelle swallowed past a lump in her throat. "That's called a 'dog,' and he wasn't a thing." She looked down. "He was my pet, Dallas."

Varazslo sat up straight and fixed her with a measuring look. "Make the Dallas, then."

Could I create him again? What if I can't? Does it mean Dallas is dead all over again? I don't want to start blubbering in front of this dragon.

Her voice small, she replied, "I don't know ..."

He huffed out a sigh and rolled his eyes. "Just try it. Even if you don't succeed, I'll still see what I need to see."

But what if she wept when she failed? She squared her shoulders. *Focus, Ann! Who said you'll fail? You made a deal, now you need to honor your side of it.* Whispering a prayer for God's help, she concentrated on the image of Dallas, then pulled sapphire threads from her reservoir. A water blob coalesced between her and Varazslo.

The dragon leaned closer, ears fanned out, his eyes gleaming. The black swirls on his scales moved and sprouted tendrils like vines. That was distracting. As was the nausea roiling in her belly. *What the heck?* Was this a new symptom of overextension? Clutching at her midsection, she dropped her eyes to the water blob as it lengthened and grew a head, four legs, and a tail. A water-dog golem stood before her, transparent and featureless as glass.

Please, be Dallas!

Try as she might, she couldn't make the construct look like her childhood pet. *Oh, God! The kraken killed him for good!* Tears stung her eyes. She whimpered as the nausea intensified, and then suddenly the sensation was gone, like strings snapping.

Sagging, she struggled to remain in her seat. The water-dog shivered and began to come apart.

"Alright, I've got it."

Dallas! She reached out, but the construct disintegrated into a blue mist. *No. I have to bring him back ...* Her entire body trembled. Everything went watery.

"Oi!" Varazslo shook her. She blinked. His reptilian visage snapped into focus. "I said I've got it. Stop straining yourself, Milady Blue. And quit that crying. Freezing void! It's just a sunsburnt golem."

Wiping away tears, Annabelle shrank back in the chair. She swallowed a waspish retort and measured her words. "A real friend would realize I loved that dog. But maybe a dragon doesn't understand human feelings."

Gaping, Varazslo settled back on his haunches. He eyed her narrowly. "Maybe I don't, Milady Blue, but maybe I'd like to." Then he bared his fangs in a wide grin. "I've decided on my second question."

"Okay." She sniffled and rubbed her nose on her forearm. The sooner she answered his question, the sooner she could leave and find a hidden spot to sob her heart out. "What is it?"

His gaze dropped to his talons scraping at the stone floor. "My experience with maidens is ... severely limited. I admit to not understanding you. But I'd like to know you better." He grimaced, peeking into her face. "How do I become your real friend?"

Annabelle managed a watery smile. The absence of her friends—Enoch, Dinah, Khinjara, and Thomas—was a constant ache squeezing her heart. She could always use another friend. Especially in the dreamscape.

Scars and Soot

Golden light flared, brilliant as the second sun, Lachesis. Like magic, it drove away the nothing surrounding Thomas. As swiftly as it had departed, gravity returned, and so did the ground beneath his feet. He staggered, throwing out his arms to maintain his balance. Heat caressed him, and he stared in disbelief at his bare arms and scarred torso. His armor had vanished.

Was he still in the dreamscape? He stood in the middle of a forest populated by trees with flaming crowns that weren't consumed, gave off no smoke—and nothing smelled burnt— while ash floated down from the clear blue sky like gray snow. A familiar place to which he'd dreaded coming.

"Criminy," he muttered. "I'm near Balthazar's Crucible."

So much for finding his missing friends.

"Helzarvenn," the voice boomed all around him like thunder, and he flinched. "You have not yet experienced my crucible—not in the waking world. Come to me. You have much to learn."

Whatever you have to teach me had better be pertinent to my mission, or no dice, Phoenixheart.

Not that Thomas dared say that aloud. Commander Storm had nothing on this guy when it came to sternness.

"I am able to sense the tenor of your thoughts, child." Neutral in tone, the Sage's voice came from everywhere and nowhere all at once.

Thomas grimaced. "Sorry, sir. I mean no disrespect." He'd better be careful.

"I pardon you," the Sage responded. "After all, the young are often impatient. They prefer to focus on the coals smoldering at their feet and remain insensible of the inferno consuming them."

Thomas rolled his eyes. *I get it. I'm Helzarvenn, the Caster of Flames. But this guy lays it on a little too thick with his fire metaphors.* He braced himself for a reprimand, but if the Sage heard his present musings, then he chose not to comment.

Straightening, Thomas groaned as he scanned trees with foliage made of fire that blazed against the backdrop of a serenely blue sky. The ashfall gathered in fluffy drifts as high as his ankles. Thomas concentrated, trying to summon the sourekghar and his burning sword. Nothing happened. He sighed. He doubted he'd find answers here. Not to the questions he asked, at any rate. The Sage had his own ideas regarding what Thomas needed and what he should be doing. Balthazar Phoenixheart made that perfectly clear at their last meeting.

He shuddered. Balthazar Phoenixheart wasn't at all like how Annabelle described Hadrien Rainblessed. *There'll be no cuddling with* this *dragon and chattering about feelings while he cries armor-forming tears over me—that's for sure.*

"What keeps you?" The Sage bellowed: "Come, Helzarvenn!"

Criminy! Maybe he did *hear me.* Thomas flinched. "Yes, sir!" he blurted. "Just stretching out the kinks. Now I'm coming." Jaw clenched, Thomas strode forward, kicking aside ash as he went. *Where's a broom when you need one?* He was on a sort of pathway between ranks of fire-leaved trees and bushes with flaming foliage. It didn't matter in which direction he walked. He always ended up at a caldera filled with bubbling lava that blazed like an inferno but did not burn him. Muttering to himself, he said, "But I'm only answering his call because I want my armor back."

"You cling to vapors," the Sage replied. "The sourekghar you don in the dreamscape is but a seeming. Tis not the real thing."

Waving ash from his face, Thomas rolled his eyes. He bit back the sarcastic remark that rose to his lips. "Sir, with all due respect, isn't everything 'but a seeming' here in the dreamscape?" Movement caught his eye. Something blaze-orange mottled with gold scuttled under the bushes on his left.

"Not all. Events transpiring in the dreamscape have lasting repercussions. For example, some wounds acquired here transfer to the waking world."

Thomas reached up to touch his chin, but the Dream Traveler's winning touch no longer bled or stung. All that remained was a divot where the blade cut him.

Heh. Another scar.

Catching a glimpse of movement, he squinted under bushes as he passed them. The leaves blazed, but the fiery glow didn't reach beneath their branches. Yellow eyes gleamed in the darkness. Hundreds of them. And weird squeaky, squelching noises, almost like frog calls, came from the undergrowth.

Unease prickled along his spine. "Those weren't here last time. What's hiding in the bushes?" He waited, but aside from the frog-like sounds, no answer came. "Sir?" Nothing. "Phoenixheart!"

His only response was the cessation of ashfall, and the creepy squeak-squelch chorus increased its volume. He sped up his pace. Not because he was scared—not at all! *I just want to reach the caldera and get some answers before I wake up.*

Flat-bodied, orange and gold lizards crawled out from under the bushes ahead of him. They were about the size of his feet. As they gathered in droves, squeak-squelching, the ash tumbled away from the path to reveal the black basalt of an old lava flow. The lizard-things assembled into ranks ten deep on the cleared surface, blocking his path. They went silent and stared at him with burning yellow eyes, bobbing up and down. Their golden spots began to dance along their smooth skin and glow, then burst into white hot flames.

Thomas stopped in his tracks and glared at this latest obstacle. "Great," he muttered, fisting his hands at his sides. "Salamanders. Now I have to deal with flaming critters. Why is it always something?" When he tried again to summon the sourekghar and his burning blade, he met with failure. He laughed without humor, then shook a fist at the sunless sky and hollered, "You could've at least given me a fire extinguisher!"

As one, the salamanders rushed him, crackling with heat. Thomas snarled, "Oh no, you don't." He reached down into the magma boiling at his core, then raised an encircling curtain of fire. It probably wouldn't kill the beasts, but it might slow them down. Pushing forward at a run, he laughed as salamanders bounced off his shield. "Woo-hoo! How do you like that? Ashes, ashes, and they all fall down."

He needed to get through, but there seemed to be no end to the salamander swarm. Soon, the flaming creatures covered the fire shield and Thomas's advance slowed to a crawl. And then, the little beggars started eating through his curtain, licking up the fire like honey.

"What the ... No way!" Thomas reached into his reservoir, drawing up more fire for his curtain, but the lizard-like creatures only gulped faster, their eyes blazing brighter.

Several salamanders fell through the holes they'd made. Thomas choked out a curse. He braced himself, but when their sticky, flaming bodies touched him, it was like lightning bolts lancing through him. The shield dropped and he charged ahead blindly, slapping the beasts off him and kicking them aside. He fell to his knees. Shame burned hotter than the salamanders piling up against his body. He was failing again.

Somehow, he managed to form words from a throat grown raw from screaming. "Phoenixheart! Help me, please. Help!"

There was a sensation like thunder without sound. A bright light flashed. Cowering, Thomas squeezed his eyes shut. The pain vanished, but shame remained like a heavy, burning mantle weighing down his shoulders.

"Rise, Helzarvenn."

With a shuddering breath, Thomas pushed himself up. A light and warm substance slid easily from his bare skin, but something still clung to him. He opened his stinging eyes and made a face at what they beheld.

I'm sitting in a pile of ash. What's this black stuff—soot? The charred corpses of those salamanders? Yuck.

Thomas brushed away the greasy soot that clung to his scars, blinking away tears and scanning his immediate surroundings. He sat upon gold-streaked marble, the stone cool against his skin. Heat made the air shimmer and sweat pop from his pores.

Right in front of him was a dais, and a huge, golden-scaled foot, its finger-like toes tipped with heavy, brown claws. The foot was attached to a muscular, golden-scaled leg shackled and chained to the marble. His gaze followed it up, past the broad chest with scales like plates of golden armor, and wings like giant fins folded against his body by chains.

Eyes swimming with tears traced the length of a swan-like neck draped with metallic feather-like scales until they focused on the saucer-sized, human eyes set in a crested, golden head with a beak-tipped snout and flaring nostrils, from which steam issued. Feathery tendrils growing around his maw like whiskers floated in the air as a bestial visage that blended avian and reptilian features peered down at him.

The visage of Balthazar Phoenixheart, his teacher and tormentor.

Hard as stone though his face was, the dark eyes were not without sympathy. "Tis a difficult lesson, learning when to ask for aid. But you have done well, child."

Thomas gasped. "Sir, please. I need ... my armor."

Balthazar sighed, fragrant smoke blasting from his nostrils and rolling around them, smelling of incense. He flared his crest and shook his great head, the feathery whiskers fluttering around his mouth and along his lower jaw. "Still, you persist in chasing after vapors. But I shall humor you."

Inhaling sharply, the golden Sage reared his head back, his chest expanding. Then he lowered his head and exhaled. Golden flames shot out, surrounding Thomas, cleansing him of soot and clearing away the rest of the ashes. The fire flowed like wax where it touched his body, and then solidified. Unlike the salamanders, this fire didn't hurt. It strengthened him.

He stood, examining the sourekghar with grim satisfaction. "Thank you, sir." He frowned. "But why send the salamanders after me? I thought you wanted me to come."

Chains rattling, Balthazar settled back on his haunches. "I did not send the salamanders to obstruct you, Helzarvenn. You brought them upon yourself."

Thomas forced his expression to a trooper's blankness, but inwardly he scowled. "Why would I obstruct my own progress, sir? And with hordes of salamanders." He snorted. "What was the point of that?"

"You burden yourself unnecessarily."

"With what?"

"Anger. Guilt. If you are not protected, Helzarvenn, they will eat you alive. Such things are possible in the dreamscape."

"But I have the armor now." He held out his left hand and concentrated. The burning sword appeared. "And my weapon. That's protection enough."

Balthazar's eyes narrowed. His ears and crest flattened against his skull. Chains rattled as he slammed his tail against the dais. Thomas staggered, and the flames on his sword flickered out. "Stubborn youth," the Sage rumbled. "Stop being obtuse. What have I told you? The armor you wear here is only vapor. Here, your only shield is faith in the Threefold One, and that you sorely lack. You have not yet endured the trials and confronted your inner demons. Come to my Crucible. Only then will you obtain the sourekghar in truth."

Thomas straightened his spine. In a tight voice, he asked, "And what about my mission to rescue Enoch? And I have to find Annabelle. She was under my protection when—"

Balthazar glared down his snout at him. "Ahdmerel has a champion to protect her. Your concern for her is laudable, but there is naught you can do for her at present."

This Sage was maddening! Thomas clenched his jaw. "Sir. Please. I've tried seeking Annabelle and Enoch on my own, but I haven't had much luck. Do you know where they—"

"Helzarvenn, you are asking the wrong questions." Balthazar heaved a sigh, and golden smoke puffed from his nostrils. Slowly, the Sage sank on his haunches, as if gravity pulled him down, the tip of his finned tail twitching like an irritated cat's. "Listen, child. The Caster of Flames bears a special burden, as his power is most ruinous. He must not allow his anger to master him. Until you have passed through the cleansing fires and burned away your dross, you cannot be of use to either Ahdmerel or Skelsdaran. Or your companions. First, seek out my Crucible in the waking world, and face my trials."

"And how long will that take?" Thomas flung out his hands. "I know traveling to and from your place in Losaridos will take a few weeks—which is already too long—and roughly how to get there. How about the trials? What do those entail?"

Annabelle hadn't said much about the ordeal she'd endured in gaining the Dagger of Moonlight, but she'd been pretty upset about it for nearly a week afterward. Thomas couldn't afford to be incapacitated by grief or depression.

"I have told you what the trials entail: you must face your inner demons. You must come to terms with your past and lay your guilt for any wrongdoing at Yshua's feet. Trust in him to cleanse you with redeeming fire. Apart from that, I cannot say until you stand before me in my Crucible, for I do not know what events lying hidden in your past have so crippled you. The memories are as veiled from my sight as they are from yours."

Crippled? Thomas snorted. "Perhaps I'm a little weak, sir, but I wouldn't call myself crippled. I just need to work harder."

"'Tis your mind that most requires healing, Helzarvenn." Balthazar continued, "As for how long your trials may last ... Hours, perhaps days. It depends upon how stubborn you are. How quick to learn and adapt. But you shall have the sourekghar in the end."

"I don't have time for that!" Thomas raked his hand back through his hair; he wanted to tear it out. He breathed deeply to calm himself and moderated his tone. "Enoch and Annabelle need me *now*, sir."

A nehmwight sorcerer was involved in Enoch's abduction—they knew that much. Where Annabelle had gone remained a mystery. He needed to find her! Her champion might be enough to protect her from the dangers they encountered in the waking world, but the kaenhir had flat-out admitted he couldn't do anything for her in the dreamscape. Then there was Mr. Cowl, and that nehmwight had been sniffing around ...

"For all I know, they're being tortured by nehmwights." All because Thomas had been cursed to take the form of a toad.

Hanging his head, he clenched his hands into fists. Shame rose up hot and bitter in the back of his throat. It only made him angrier. "I need to know where they are to fulfill my mission."

Balthazar stamped his foot, rattling his chains and shaking the dais so Thomas had to catch his balance. His sword disappeared. The Sage thrust his snout an arm's length from Thomas's face. "And are you so certain tis *your* mission to emancipate Skelsdaran from his captors—wherever they may be? Your responsibility, alone, to search all Tehara for Ahdmerel?"

Criminy! He's huge.

Heart racing, Thomas wiped steam from his cheeks. "Do you know where they are?" he asked, trembling. "For God's sake, Phoenixheart, tell me!"

Balthazar's fan-shaped ears flattened and his lips peeled back from his fangs. "I do not know where the other wyldlings are. Here in my prison—" he rose on all fours to his tallest as the chains allowed, which was a half-crouch, then settled back on his haunches with his tail curled around his forepaws— "I perceive nothing of the outside world, save what knowledge you have brought along."

Despite the terror pulsing through his veins, Thomas straightened his spine and met Balthazar's gaze. The adrenaline rush made him bold. Biting off the words, he said, "Then what good are you?"

"Impudent child!" The Sage's eyes blazed with sudden fury. "You have closed off your mind to guiding wisdom and your heart to salvation's message. Leave me, and do not return until you are ready to learn."

With a flick of his tail, Balthazar sent Thomas sailing through the heated air. He plunged toward the lava surrounding the Sage's dais. As he fell, a giant flametiger emerged from the molten rock, mouth gaping wide to swallow him whole. *No! I haven't found the kids yet!* As he flung out his kythim, seeking energy signatures, Thomas braced himself for pain—

He woke, eyes wide and gasping. Sweat plastered his hair flat against his skull and his tunic clung to him as he sat bolt upright on his bedroll. A shadow passed in front of a faint orange glow. *Enemies!* With a hoarse cry, he took hold of the sword he kept unsheathed at his side and rolled to his feet. Or tried to. His knees decided to buckle, and gravity did the rest.

Thomas lashed out with his sword as he landed on his backside. Steel rang out as the force of the blow vibrated down his left arm. "You won't take me alive!" Rage boiling, he seized hold of his wyld ... then blinked as golden light enhanced his vision, illuminating the blade that had blocked his, and David's concerned expression.

"Sir Thomas, it's me." David backed away, blade held warily before him for a moment before he sheathed it.

"Did you find Annabelle, Sir Thomas?" Dinah approached from behind her cousin, holding a crystal that she coaxed into giving off light. She stifled a yawn. "It seemed like you had a nightmare. You woke us with your muttering and thrashing."

"Not Annabelle." His hands trembled as he sheathed his sword. "A nightmare. It was a real doozy. I had to fight someone."

And I lost. I wish I could remember who it was. Somebody with a scar ... He accepted David's assistance in rising. "Thanks." He managed to grin. "Stupid legs can't be trusted."

David's lips twitched in a wan smile. "You faced battle in the dreamscape?" he asked, drawing back as Thomas gained his bearings. The dwelfnhir's eyes gleamed in the crystal's soft, white glow as he looked him up and down. "At least you don't appear to be injured, praise Yshua. What were you fighting?"

Thomas grimaced. "I don't want to talk about it now. Anyway, I can't remember." Turning away, he walked carefully toward their mounts. He rubbed his chin, his fingers pausing when he felt the divot. *Something cut me, but all that remains is this scar. Balthazar said ...* And then he stiffened. He remembered *something*. His eyes widened. Jeremiah Bullfrog! The nehmwight in the dreamscape!

"Commander! We have to reach the Fortress of Living Stones. We need to find Annabelle. She could be in terrible danger!"

Commander Storm rose from where he hunkered beneath a tree, hidden behind David's battle elk. "I am here." His eyes grew steely. "Report."

Peter flew down from his perch, squawking about Annabelle, and the dwelfnim cousins hurried over. They crowded around him, while the Commander stood with his arms folded, his face a mask. Heart in his throat, Thomas related all he could remember of his dreams, carefully avoiding any mention of the Sage. They didn't need to know about that right now. He fingered the scar as he spoke.

When he came to the end of his recital, the evainghir narrowed his eyes. "But you cannot recall who you fought?"

"Commander," Dinah all but sobbed. "That's not important. Did you not hear what Sir Thomas said? A nehmwight in the dreamscape is after Ann!"

David sighed. "Are you certain you saw a nehmwight, Sir Thomas? In the dreamscape things aren't always what they appear to be." His gaze was direct and probing. "I'm not saying it's impossible ... but you seem rather fixated on nehmwights."

"And killin' them with fire!" Peter asserted in a cheerful tone.

Ignoring the syrax, Thomas scowled at David. "Are you saying I imagined the guy? I know what I saw!"

"That's enough," Commander Storm rumbled. "Sir Thomas, the Shepherd is correct to be skeptical; nehmwights cannot enter the dreamscape. I don't know who or what you saw, but it could not have been a nehmwight. But if you believe the womanchild is in danger ..." He shook his head. "There will be no more sleeping tonight. We might as well move along—and with all possible haste. The next waystone is only half a day's march from here." The evainghir's piercing regard seemed all too knowing. Thomas had to avert his gaze. It must have been a trick of the light, but for a second, violet sparks had danced in the Commander's eyes.

It struck him, then. Purple mists surrounding him in the dreamscape. A cowled figure offering him deals. Violet fire along a blade wielded with an expertise beyond his own. If it couldn't be a nehmwight ... Had whoever he fought pretended to be a nehmwight? But why would anyone do that?

I'm missing something important.

As Thomas climbed into the saddle, he resolved to find out what. There had to be a way to fix his broken memory without facing any demons.

Mortal Combat

Orange light flickered. William's voice shook as he chanted the fifth cantrip for a malecto grammerye—a curse meant to target the mind. He watched Tenebris, who stood across a spellform with a diameter over twice his height. Vine-like tendrils spread along his master's contorted visage like shadows cast from the depths of perdition. When he gained his thirteenth circle, would his arkhabala move into his face? He couldn't help but speculate what it felt like.

Probably like spiders crawling, but it looked impressive enough. Would Annabelle like it? She'd seemed fascinated by the swirling of the arkhabala on his dragon's scales. The blistering things still itched, but not as badly as in the waking world. He quickly suppressed an image of Annabelle scratching them. Merciful Valeshka! That was a sure way to lose the battle against her beguilement spell.

He shook his head, scowling. *Forget* her. With an effort, he shoved all thoughts about Annabelle, every scrap of memory, into the new headspace he'd created and slammed it shut like a room with a door. This time, he triple-locked it.

There, that ought to hold her. Now, focus on the suns-burnt spell before Tenebris realizes that your mind is wandering.

It was the first time he and Tenebris combined their efforts to create a spellform of this magnitude, constructing a mind-fog curse to strike down the Western Baron-Knight. Now that he had seven circles, William possessed the capacity to assist his master in a Greater Working. Tenebris claimed it was an opportunity to prove that he could collaborate with other Arkhadahns and not only as a solo practitioner.

I couldn't care less about that last bit. But I'll snatch all the crumbs Tenebris throws at me. Whatever it takes for my power to grow.

Grateful that Tenebris was too absorbed in the spell to bark out instructions he didn't need, William picked up his knife. He slashed along an old scar on his left forearm. The familiar sting grounded him as he spilled his blood into the grooves. While intoning the sixth cantrip for enhanced connection, he reached through his arkhabala to ensure adequate power was still coursing through the spellform.

Agony spread in a sheet over his back and gnawed like a beast at his chest. He embraced the pain like an old friend as his circles expanded to conduct the energy Tenebris sent, and then directed the flow counterclockwise around the spellform.

He frowned. Tenebris's design was inefficient. Maybe if he tweaked that flow and opened a conduit there ...

His feet flew out from under him and a sharp pain exploded at the back of his head. Moisture spattered against his face. Groaning, he opened his eyes. A flurry of orange lights danced above him amid the raindrops. "What pretty stars," he mumbled. "Is it raining?" And then Tenebris's furious visage eclipsed them.

"Fool!" His master grabbed him by his burkheld and hauled him up. "What did I tell you about letting your mind wander?"

"My mind wasn't wandering," William retorted, trying to get his feet under him. Why wouldn't the floor stop moving? How could it be raining indoors? "There was a flaw in the—"

Tenebris snarled, shaking him. "Do not finish that sentence, William, if you value your tongue. What do you know of higher-order workings? My designs are closer to perfection than yours will ever be. Gah!" He shouted as the water droplets changed into a torrential downpour, then shook him until his teeth rattled. "William, you idiot. What have you done?"

Tenebris let him go, and William slumped to the floor. "Master, I ..." His voice died away and his jaw moved soundlessly as he stared at the water drenching everything. *I have no idea.*

"Enough," Tenebris spat as inky vines swirled up his neck to coil around his jaw. He snarled out the ending cantrip and William's entire body tingled with the surge of power.

The rain ceased. His master glared down at him. "Fortunately for you, the spell functioned as it should. I stabilized the spellform and enacted the malecto grammerye ... before you decided to experiment."

William swallowed thickly. He clutched his head, hair squelching and dripping water down his neck. "Master, uh, I thought ..."

"You *thought.*" The Arkhadahn snorted. "You think too much. Since you think you know so much about the Arkhabadh already, perhaps you wish to explore other disciplines."

William suppressed the urge to vomit. He tried to deny, to apologize, to beg for mercy, to say anything at all, but all he managed was an undignified squeak.

Burning suns and freezing void, I made it rain indoors! What's my punishment this time?

Tenebris bared his teeth in a too-wide grin. "Tomorrow, you train with the warriors," he said with relish. "May Valeshka have mercy on your pitiful soul ... because your body is about to go through perdition."

Gratitude and relief flooded William when Zakaar offered to accompany him to the training hall at the tail end of Heron Watch, just before he typically ate dinner. He spent the next five minutes trying to suppress the feelings. They made him weak.

The harkhurz sauntered alongside William as he stalked down the main corridor, where the Dreadlord exhibited all manner of expensive treasures. He'd won them all by right of conquest ... often without tapping into his Aethyric skills.

William fought down panic while his companion burbled on and on about the myriad styles of martial arts in which he was proficient. Tenebris had forbidden William from tapping into his arcane abilities—even for self-defense—during his new training regimen. Then he bound up William's arkhabala until Lachesis rose. His master claimed he'd never learn anything by taking short cuts, or cheating.

Cheating? William dug his fingernails into his palms, distracting himself with pain from the *absence* on his back and chest. *There's no way I can survive, let alone win, any real fight with the warrior-trained. Not without using magic.*

"... And then I will teach you how to grapple in the way of the folken," Zakaar concluded. Light blue outlined kythim tendrils streaked with lavender and his ears stood upright. Clearly, the assassin was pleased with this turn of events.

William was not. He glared at a priceless vase displayed on a plinth in an alcove. Pushing down the desire to smash it, he gnashed his teeth and growled, "Fine."

Zakaar eyed him sidelong, sniffing. "Dulciber, you reek of fear. Do not worry, my friend. This is your first time. The warriors will go easy on you. There will be great pain and much falling down, but I will make sure you do not come to grievous bodily harm."

William snorted. "Thank you so much for the vote of confidence, Zakaar. I'm not afraid of pain. Or being knocked down. I always get right back up again."

Zakaar's brow scrunched, and his short muzzle wrinkled. "Then why do you smell of burnt feathers and carrion? What is it that frightens you so, if not the pain and the falling down?"

Blistering everyone seeing me fall. Over and over again. And not being able to retaliate with my greatest asset.

Fortunately, they arrived at the training arena before he could formulate a plausible lie that didn't make him look weak. William hesitated at the entrance, a set of double doors made of a dark wood carved in serpentine patterns. From the placement of the hinges he could tell they opened inward. A gouge marred the top panel on the right-hand side, but it had been varnished over. Had an ax done that? He licked his lips. Sounds came through the closed double doors that did nothing to calm his nerves—the crack of wood on wood and the rattles and bangs of metal crashing together.

"Here we are," the harkhurz said, extending an arm. "Do you wish for me to announce you, Dulciber?"

He whirled and snarled, "Villem's bloody spear—no!"

Zakaar chuckled. "You will do well. Hold on to that anger, Dulciber. But loosely. Do not let it blind you."

His nerves writhed like vipers. He took a deep breath. "Right, then." *Time to roll the bones.*

William glanced both ways down the corridor. Good. No Tenebris. He pulled out his whiskey flask and took a large swig, ignoring Zakaar's tsk. The whiskey was essential for bolstering his fortitude. Inhaling deeply, he placed trembling hands on the right-hand door, then pushed. It didn't budge.

What? He wasn't *that* physically weak. Lugging around Tenebris's gear ensured he had decent upper body strength. He could lift one fully armored Northward and maybe two

Annabelles without armor—*no!* That insidious thought was going right back into its dungeon. *Quadruple-locked.*

Muttering a curse, he shoved the training room door again. This time, Zakaar's brawny arm provided the impetus necessary, and the door swung open with a creak. The scent of male sweat, oiled steel, and cedar rolled out.

"Thanks," he growled. It was more fitting for the servant to open the door anyway.

Zakaar held it open for William as he stepped over the threshold into unexplored territory. Points of egress—good; multiple ways to escape—interrupted each wall along with racks of torture devices—among them he recognized swords, spears, and axes. Some blades were made of wood and meant for training while others were metal and might hold an edge. He surveyed the five Golorum: elite warriors, all bare-chested, well-muscled, and armed to the teeth. They moved like dancers, boots thudding on the wooden floor, trading blows and calling out insults or encouragement in equal measure.

That'll never be me.

An undignified squawk escaped William's throat.

The men stopped and looked at him. Cruel humor glinted in their orange eyes. One made a joke he couldn't quite make out—something about fresh meat—and the others laughed. Behind him, Zakaar murmured something.

William gulped. *I ... am ... going ... to* die.

A hand clapped on his right shoulder, and he swallowed a yelp. The nehmwight squad leader, Khalad, stepped around him into the room. "Ah, you have finally arrived," he said in the Trading Language. "Welcome, Arkhasuhl. Your sparring partner will join us shortly."

Zakaar's eyes narrowed. "Who?" He gestured at the Golorum. "Another of those?"

"No." Khalad chuckled. "My men and I are not in the business of torturing untrained youths. The Dreadlord has assigned someone ... a bit closer to his level."

William choked on saliva. *Oh, no ... this might be worse.*

While Zakaar pounded his back, the Golorum squad leader made a sharp gesture and barked out a command to the others. Saluting him, the warriors put away the training weapons, retrieved their tunics and uniform jackets, and then filed out another door on the other side of the room. Before they passed out of earshot, one said, "The Arkhadahn's lackey will make a splendid mop for our sweat." And the others laughed.

William clenched his jaw. Khalad patted his shoulder, grinning. "Do not mind them, Arkhasuhl. This is how warriors talk. Often, teasing is a sign of ... affection."

In my experience, insults are usually a prelude to a beating.

William sighed. Also speaking in Trade, he said, "Let's just do this, Golor Khalad." He trudged to the middle of the room. Behind him, a door opened. "Tenebris put a seal on my arkhabala until mid-Frog Watch. I'll stand over here, and you can hit me with one of those sticks until I beg for mercy."

Zakaar growled. Footfalls echoed in the training hall. William turned, then let out a groan.

Fantastic. Sometimes I hate being right. But this has got to be better than taking on the Golorum.

Northward halted halfway across the floor. "Hit you with a stick? Sounds good to me," he said, smiling. There was a feral gleam in his eyes. The skin around the wyldling snare looked raw, as if he'd been prying at it.

His baleful amber gaze never leaving the kadorei youth, Zakaar leaned against the wall and crossed his arms. "Say the word, Dulciber, and I turn the warlock into a new satchel."

Northward's lip curled. "And what makes you think I'd let you touch me ... child-killer?"

Zakaar snarled and Northward's right hand drifted toward his hip—doubtless reaching for his sword that was no longer there. William kept the weapon locked inside a chest at the foot of his bed. *Mine by right of conquest, for capturing him.*

Frowning, Khalad looked between the youth and the harkhurz. "Arkhasuhl," he murmured in the nehmwight tongue. "The assassin should leave before the session begins. Or I shall place him in restraints for the duration."

William rolled his eyes. As much as he relished watching Zakaar punch Northward for his sass, the Dreadlord wouldn't like it if anything happened to his precious wyldling cat's paw.

"Oi, Zakaar!"

His ears came up. "Dulciber?"

"Go fetch us some dinner. Wiping the floor with Sir Fancy-Jacket here should work up my appetite."

Northward snorted.

For a moment the harkhurz didn't move, but then he pushed off the wall. "As you wish." Zakaar sauntered for the door. William tensed as he passed close by Northward, who stood glaring at him, but didn't budge—not even when Zakaar leaned over and growled in his face.

"That's enough, Zakaar."

Shooting William an offended glance, the harkhurz left the training hall. Khalad went around to lock the doors.

William released a pent-up breath. He shook his head, muttering, "Stupid harkhurz."

Northward looked right at him. *—Ravenos needs to be put down. Otherwise, one day he'll kill someone you care about—*

Averting his gaze, William shrugged out of his burkheld. "Oi, Northward. Stop mucking about. Go choose your weapon."

The sooner this was over, the better. The silence of his skin was driving him insane.

But the other youth just stood there with his arms folded and lips pursed. William couldn't wait to punch him.

"We are now private," Khalad said, taking his robe. "And there will be no weapons. Your first lesson should be in hand-to-hand combat."

"Is it true your magic is blocked?" Northward asked. "I don't have to worry about invisible fists smashing me to the floor?"

"Yes. Tenebris sealed it for the next hour." He scowled. "After that, watch out."

Khalad nodded. "I give you my word of honor, one warrior to another, Enoch Northward. The Arkhasuhl is bound."

Northward squinted at Khalad, then nodded. "I believe you."

—The Dreadlord still needs me for something, and this nehmwight serves him—

He took off his fancy jacket, then removed his tunic. Although shorter than William by a foot, the youth was still wiry; captivity hadn't softened his physique. Northward chuckled. "Praise Yshua; the Festival of Lights came early this Turning." Grinning, he cracked his knuckles. "Time to teach you a lesson."

"Whatever," William grumbled. "I'm going to punch you in the face." He waggled a finger. "One rule: Below the belt is off-limits."

Northward shrugged. "Alright. No trauma to the groin. I give you my word. But there *is* armor for that, you know."

—unlike yours, my word can be trusted—

Heart racing, William removed his sakkhelt and under-tunic, then hesitated. The wyldling snare was tucked into an inner pocket of his breeches. Should he add that to the bundle? No ... That could be useful. Maybe Northward wouldn't have the upper hand in this fight. He stifled a smirk.

Khalad gave him some advice, explaining how to make a fist while Northward stretched. Then the youth stood half crouched with his feet shoulder width apart and his arms bent, prepared to grapple. Trying to calm himself, William calculated the angles and the amount of force that could be brought to bear—

"You have the advantage of height, Arkhasuhl, but that can be used against you as well. Let's see what you know. Go at him. Throw a punch. Don't think. Just do it." Khalad slapped his back, propelling him forward.

Curses rattling through his head, William lunged at Northward. There was his target: that smug face. He made a fist with his right hand—just like Khalad had taught—and launched it at his nose.

Something knocked his arm aside. White light blossomed in his head and pain radiated from his jaw. William reeled, backpedaling.

That sneaky little dolmagh punched me!

"You overextended," Khalad said, from off to the side. "And you kept your arm out for too long. Punch, then immediately pull back."

Northward waded in and swept his legs out from under him. William stumbled, falling on his backside. His fingers dipped into his breeches and caught hold of a metallic strand. And then Northward was coming at him.

Before William could react, the shorter youth was on him, knee in his gut and fingers digging into his throat. "Make one move, and I rip out your trachea," he said in a conversational tone, then smiled. "Got you."

Choking, William bared his teeth. *No, you don't!* As Northward's eyes widened, he positioned his hand to whip out the snare.

Grasping the strand of wyldling snare, William struck. He reached for the violet light, but it glimmered out of reach. He spat a curse. Northward gaped as the snare encircled his arm. *Ha! Who's got who now?* Northward released William's throat and seized the soot-gray cord. His eyes flared silver. *What?* Then the end in William's hand writhed and lashed around his wrist. Cold shot up through his arm, up his neck, and spiked into his head. He couldn't move. All senses winked out like the world had vanished.

This can't be happening, this can't be happening ...

William felt like he was falling. His awareness plunged inward. Bits of him became unraveled like threads strung with shining beads. Colorful images shone inside the beads, some of them moving tableaux, while others were static or contained only voices and other sensations. *My memories!* He reached for them, trying to pull them back, but one slipped through his fingers as if made of vapor. William as a child, curious about the locket, followed by Tenebris beating him for touching it.

No! You can't see that, Northward!

As he watched helplessly the bead slid down the soot-gray of the snare into the silver vortex. It was followed by another of similar ilk, and yet another. Then there was one that always confounded him— one that wasn't based on sight, but sound and scent—a woman singing in Tradespeak and the scent of honeysuckle. She was sobbing.

Make it stop ... Who was she? *Stop!*

He strained for his arkhabala. Nothing. He could see the amethyst pool, but it remained out of reach. A soot-gray cord lay between it and him. He grabbed it.

Icy agony spiked in his mind. William screamed.

Other sensations returned, but paramount was pain. It always was. Suddenly, the pain diminished to a minor pulse inside his skull, and he realized he could feel other things again. His cheeks were wet. He smelled something acrid and tasted blood. He'd bitten his burning tongue.

His ploy with the snare had failed. And he was laying on the wooden floor of the training hall, at Northward's mercy.

And now he'll kick me while I'm down.

Eyes squeezed shut, William tensed his muscles for the inevitable blow. It never came. He opened his eyes and flinched back from something brown and blurry. A bludgeon?

Abruptly, the fuzzy brown object swam into focus—Northward's hand extended toward him. William stared at it, then his gaze traveled the length of Northward's arm to his face. In those earnest features, he read no sign of triumph, derision or scorn. There was something strange in those blue eyes. Something other than the color that reminded him of Annabelle. For a moment, he almost recognized it ...

And where in perdition did that strand of wyldling snare go?

The moment passed. Northward raised his eyebrows. "What're you waiting for, you sad sack of a beggar—a formal invitation?" He flexed his fingers. "C'mon, I'll help you up."

Really?

William grabbed his wrist. For an instant he was tempted to yank Northward off balance and send him sprawling, but the other youth immediately backpedaled while grasping his forearm in both hands. William had little choice but to get his knees under him and rise or let Northward drag him across the floor. Like a suns-cursed *mop.*

Northward rubbed his collar. Was it thicker than before? Valkor's Scythe, the snare strand had merged with the snare around his neck. William felt like Northward's knee was still digging into his abdomen.

How many memories did the wretch steal?

While Khalad explained everything he'd done wrong, William split his awareness and sorted through his mind with one half while listening and responding with the other. Yes, the memories were still there. Had he imagined everything?

"I'm impressed," his erstwhile opponent remarked, for all the world as if nothing untoward with the snare had occurred.

"Fighting at that level of handicap takes serious stones, Dulciber."

He rubbed his jaw and grunted. Northward had a wicked left hook. "I'm just glad you refrained from smashing them again."

—Adding insult to injury isn't exactly sportsmanlike. And this isn't the battlefield—

William narrowed his eyes. Northward was fishing again. The kadorei youth grinned. "Why did your master block your magic and send you to the training hall, in the first place?"

"Because I keffing made it rain indoors."

Speechless, Northward stared at him, then burst out laughing.

Fire Extinguished

It was raining.

Staring off into the drizzle, Thomas scoffed. *But when doesn't it rain, in the Mistenholt Range?* So far, his impression of the northernmost edge of the Western Marches left much to be desired. Chief among them: a cozy shelter with a blazing fire in its hearth.

With his expression set in a trooper's blankness, Thomas drew Tinker along the mountain pass, in line behind Dinah and her mount while David brought up the rear with his war elk. Commander Storm and Peter led the way half a mile ahead of them. The trail often proved too narrow and uneven for riding. On the surface, Thomas exuded a stoic calm. Inside, he wrestled exasperation and weariness as he hugged the cliff wall and carefully placed one foot in front of the other.

According to Commander Storm, this was the final stage. They'd arrive at the Fortress of Living Stones before midnight. Dinah kept telling him that the Caretaker and her Farseer would provide the long-awaited information regarding the whereabouts of both Enoch and Annabelle. Information Balthazar Phoenixheart couldn't give him. Thomas's hand flew to the short sword at his hip, reassuring himself it was still there; that it hadn't disappeared like the burning blade in the dreamscape.

Increasingly, he'd been reconsidering his position, mulling over his encounter with Balthazar and the chastisement he'd received. The golden Sage's remarks burned inside Thomas, no matter how he tried to smother their flames. He didn't want the thoughts rattling around in his brain anymore, poking and jabbing like caltrops.

Not that he had much else to think about at the moment—aside from worrying about Enoch and Annabelle. Every topic his mind pursued concerning them tended toward the dark and depressing. And the weather provided no solace. The rain kept coming down, a constant chill drizzle that soaked through his leathers and clothes straight through to the skin. Jerking his head, he flipped a sodden hank of hair from his face, then rubbed his itchy nose on his bracer. He grimaced. Gah! Everything was wetter than a bullfrog's backside.

I've forgotten what it's like to be warm and dry. He shivered as he wiped moisture from his brow, then glared at the fog surrounding them. Technically, it was a cloud. They were still in the upper altitudes.

"What's the deal? I thought we'd be descending by now. Stupid rain." He muttered to himself as he and Tinker rounded a bend on a trail.

Maybe the kiddo would appreciate this weather, but I sure don't.

Thomas snorted, a smile curving his lips as he imagined Annabelle's lecture about how the rain was good for the farmers' crops, improved children's complexions, and encouraged world peace in the never-ending cycle of life. Or something equally convoluted that involved mermaids, unicorns, and dragons.

He paused and glanced back at Tinker's empty saddle. His smile died. Tinker shook his head, flinging droplets from his ears and antlers as he gazed at Thomas with huge, sad eyes.

With a sigh, Thomas tugged on the lead and continued walking. "Yeah, Roast Venison. I know. I miss her too."

Shepherd David came around the bend, his war elk in tow. His lacquered helm glistened with beaded moisture.

David regarded him from beneath the visor. "Something amiss, Sir Thomas?" His expectant gaze seemed to invite confidence. Throughout their journey—as the terrain allowed—the Shepherd had coaxed Thomas to share his troubled thoughts. After every denial, he expressed his willingness to wait for Thomas to be ready.

He suppressed a bitter laugh. The Shepherd was in for a long wait.

David was still watching him, so Thomas shook his head. "Just checking on Roast Venison, here. Nothing's wrong."

Liar, he thought. *Everything's wrong. It's been wrong since Sir Rick died and went even wronger when you went into the woods looking for those girls, and went wrongest of all when something, somehow, changed you into a friggin' toad and wiped away your memories.*

Giving Tinker an awkward pat on the neck, he swallowed his bitterness and resumed his painful trudge. The path grew steeper. Brown and gray stone dampened by rain slid past. Occasionally, he caught sight of rocks containing slightly different hues. He counted them to pass the time and to distract himself from his burning muscles and rasping breath.

Oh, look. It's the ninety-ninth brown rock with red streaks. And that other one is banded in a slightly lighter brown. Variety! Oh, joyous day!

Abruptly, the white-furred haunches in front of him stopped. Thomas halted, reached for his longsword, then hesitated. Dinah was moving down the trail toward him, but her gait and posture were relaxed. He squinted into the misty rain at the dwelfnhad. "What's the hold up?"

"There's a bridge ahead," Dinah replied. She wore a helmet like David's. Lucky duck. Must be nice to have armor that fit like it was made for you. "Commander Storm wants us to wait here while he reconnoiters."

David came up behind. "Does he believe we'll have company?" he asked, humor curving his lips. Did the man never get upset? He always seemed so ... even keeled. Based on that smile, perhaps he was spoiling for a scuffle with bandits or wild beasts.

I know I am. Something to break up the monotony. So long as it's over quickly; we need to keep moving.

Thomas snorted. "In this lovely weather? Unlikely. Even so, we'd make short work of them." His right hand strayed to Murder Stick's pommel. Yep. The weapon was still there.

Stroking her mount's neck, Dinah lifted her chin and her tone cooled. "Unlikely, but not impossible. We'd rather be safe than sorry, Sir Thomas. There's no reason to fight unless we need to." Her demeanor suggested that, as a knight, he ought to know better. It irked him.

That's right, Ambassador. Keep looking down your nose at me like a haughty, pointy-eared princess. Pretty soon you'll keel over backward, and then I'll laugh ...

A memory of Annabelle's sorrowful gaze suddenly flashed before his eyes and guilt's needles pricked him. Dinah was her friend. He ground his teeth.

Okay, kiddo, I'll laugh on the inside, while I help Dinah up. Like a gentleman.

Thomas cleared his throat. He needed to stop being so crabby. Raising his eyebrows, he swallowed his urge to deliver a scathing comment. "You're right, of course," he said, blithe as a summer day. David chuckled and shook his head.

Pebbles clattered, and then Commander Storm came around the bend.

Thomas bit back an "I told you so" when he noticed the tension in every line of the Commander's burly frame. He stiffened, every sense on alert. "Sir?"

"It's time we moved on but stay sharp."

Dinah peered beyond the evainghir, then glanced at the sky. "But Commander. What about Peter?"

At the mention of the syrax, Thomas felt stirrings of pity. *Poor Cat-Vulture. He must hate this weather worse than I do.*

"He hasn't returned." The Commander's visage hardened. "We haven't the time to linger. Come, we must keep to our schedule." His glance briefly settled on Thomas. "Every moment we delay, the womanchild remains in peril. I reckon the buzzard is merely delayed by water-logged wings but be prepared for anything. We dare not let down our guard."

With the Commander far in the lead, they ascended, and the thunder of river rapids filled Thomas's ears. The path opened up to a flat area large enough to accommodate the entire group. Tinker's ears lifted as he trotted after Thomas, and then they both drew up short. The rocky platform ended in a sheer drop-off. Commander Storm stood near the precipice, where two posts indicated the beginning of a suspended bridge across the chasm. One large hand gripped each post as he stared intently out into the fog. Violet light flashed briefly, then a spark raced from the posts along suspension cables so slender that he hadn't noticed them at first.

Typical. I swear, everything is "hurry up and wait" when we should just be hurrying.

Thomas straightened his spine and forced a crooked smile. "Well, boys and girls, shall we see what we're up against?"

He hadn't yet turned to take a step when David clapped a hand on his shoulder, arresting his movement. His eyes on the Commander, the dwelfnhir bent close to his ear and said, "Wait for the 'all clear,' Sir Thomas."

Thomas squinted. The Commander hadn't moved. "What is he doing?"

"Checking for surprises," David replied, withdrawing his hand. "Tampering or traps."

Was tampering a concern? Were we worried about that?

While David spoke, two pulses of violet light shot along the cables and terminated at the posts. Commander Storm flinched, then took his hands off the posts, clenching and unclenching his fingers as if working out stiffness. He shouted, "The way is clear of traps. Shepherd, Ambassador—I need whoever is most efficient at sensing fractures in eversteel."

David exchanged a glance with his cousin. "That would be you, Dee."

With a nod, the dwelfnhad hastened over to the bridge. Commander Storm's mouth moved as he gestured at the posts. Dinah crossed her arms in salute, then moved to stand between the posts with a hand upon each.

Thomas sighed, tugging on Tinker's halter. The roar of the water increased. Nudging David, he asked, "What's eversteel? Never heard of it." He eyed the slender cables as they approached. "Could a sword slice through it?"

David nearly smiled. "I know what you're thinking," he shouted, "but I wouldn't waste a good blade attempting to cut through these cables." Stepping up beside Dinah, he rapped a gauntlet against the post, and it sounded like he struck metal. "A joint invention of the Sages, Ebenezzar and Balthazar. They wrought the entire bridge of eversteel, which they forged from sky-iron using a method long lost to us since the Oblivion Wars."

"It sounds like a lot of knowledge was lost. One of these days, you'll have to tell me about these Oblivion Wars and the Sages. Ebenezzar must have had the patience of a stone." Thomas scoffed. "I can't imagine anyone wanting to work with that overbearing, fire-breathing old coot."

David blinked. "According to legend, the Sages often collaborated to create marvels. Balthazar as readily as any of them. Their greatest accomplishments were all joint ventures."

Balthazar must've gone sour since ancient times, Thomas mused, then shrugged. *I would too if I was chained to a stone dais over a pit of boiling lava.*

His eyes cut over to the dwelfnhad, and the Commander, who stood off to one side with his arms crossed, watched their back trail. David monitored his cousin. Thomas pursed his lips. Why was this taking so long?

Moments later, Dinah shuddered, then let her arms drop to her sides. "The bridge is sound!" She took a step back, staggering, and her cousin caught her before she fell. "I'm well."

While the Commander conferred with David, Thomas swiftly assessed the dwelfnim, noting the strain around Dinah's eyes, and how David hovered over her. Clearly, the sensing thing she'd done took a lot out of her. And her cousin would be distracted over her well-being. There was no way either of them could take point. The Commander oversaw all their plans and shouldn't be risked. With their primary scout missing, there was no telling what might lie ahead.

Of them all, Thomas was most expendable. It would have to be him.

Jeremiah Bullfrog! The things I do for the kiddo.

"Sir," Thomas shouted. He indicated the chasm. "I'll go first."

Commander Storm turned from the dwelfnim, glancing from Thomas to the bridge and then back again. "We shall follow at intervals on the count of thirty. And Sir Thomas?" Narrowing his eyes, the evainghir loomed over him. "Do not go charging ahead without us."

Criminy! I've gotta stop acting like a green recruit.

"Yes, sir. Of course not, sir."

David touched his arm. "Lord Yshua go with you."

Thomas's cheek twitched. He nodded. "Yeah, you, too, Shepherd."

At first glance, the structure appeared too delicate to hold their combined weight. The narrow path and slender cables faded from view before they reached the other side. It swayed slowly, creaking. Darkness yawned below it like a hungry mouth, and unseen water roared like all the world's lions. He didn't fear heights, but his stomach lurched. Images filled his mind, of planks breaking under their boots and cables snapping to spill them all into the ravine.

Thomas caught himself making a rhythmic gulping noise in his throat. *Stop that! What's wrong with you? You're a knight—not a blasted toad anymore.*

"Joy to the world." He laughed bitterly. "Simply wonderful. Just what I always wanted—an opportunity to plummet to my death."

Commander Storm lowered his eyebrows. "The bridge is perfectly sound, Sir Thomas." His basso rumble was audible even over the water's roar. "No one has tampered with it. But remain vigilant."

Remember, you're doing this for the kiddo.

"I was only joking, sir." Thomas clicked his tongue and tugged on Tinker's halter. "Come on, Roast Venison." He tried to ignore the squirming unease in his gut. Up close, the bridge appeared sturdier than he'd thought at first. He exhaled noisily and felt himself relax.

Legs don't fail me now. Thomas kept his eyes forward as he strode across the creaking bridge. He counted: "one, one thousand ... two, one thousand ..." Mist swirled. The river's steady roar helped to orient him. As he advanced, details of the opposite side began to resolve more clearly. Rocks, as usual, but also the dark green tops of redwood trees began to emerge.

Great. More damp and poorly lit forests. There's no end to them on this blasted continent.

He checked the draw on his blades and extended his kythim to touch the embers inside the firepot swinging from his belt. All seemed good to go. Tinker's hooves clicked a steady rhythm while he counted. "Twenty-three, one thousand ..." The ubiquitous gray-brown boulders and shaggy conifer branches grew more distinct. The path ahead lay empty. Gravel crunched under his boots as he stepped off the bridge and he breathed a sigh of relief.

With a hand on his longsword, Thomas took another step, leading his mount off the bridge. He scanned his surroundings, taking care to look up, as well. Nobody jumped out at them from behind the rocks. Nothing plummeted from above to rake him with its claws or snatch him up into the sky.

Commander Storm had warned them about flying, scaled and feathered creatures called wyrmkin that lived in the mountains of Mistenholt. Apparently, some grew large and strong enough to carry off David's war elk. Even worse, they were highly intelligent. From the way the Commander described the wyrmkin, they resembled the dragons Annabelle had chattered about on their journey, and by extension, the Sages.

Thomas snorted a faint laugh through his nose. Knowing Annabelle, she'd bounce in the saddle and grin at the prospect of glimpsing wyrmkin.

Whereas, if I kick the bucket and never see any, then I'll die without regret on that account.

Frowning, Thomas kept surveying the tree line. Speaking of predators descending from on high, where was the Cat-Vulture? There was no sign of a pink syrax, either. Under the roar of the rapids, he heard the tell-tale crunch of gravel behind him.

It was Dinah. "The trail is wide enough to ride from here."

Thomas managed to grin. "Hey, finally some good news. Now if only the suns would come out." The dwelfnhad laughed.

David and Commander Storm made it over the bridge without incident. At their raised eyebrows, Thomas shook his head. No sign of Peter. Commander Storm frowned but kept his own counsel.

The dwelfnim mounted up, and with the Commander leading the way, they continued along the trail, which remained flat for a time and then sloped downward. Thomas worked his jaw and swallowed to make his ears pop. The mist swirled and began to thin as they descended. Even better, the cursed rain slackened and finally stopped. By the time they reached the bottom of the pass, it seemed lighter.

Thomas stared up into the sky. Was the overcast clearing up? He leaned back on the reins, and Tinker halted. "Well, well, well," he breathed, squinting as the clouds thinned. "Wonders never cease. Looks like the suns are coming out."

"Praise Yshua," David murmured as he reined in his elk beside Thomas. "Give thanks to the Almighty Threefold One, for he is good, for his mercy endures forever."

The mingled rose-golden rays of Lachesis and Atropos burst through and bathed the travelers with their light. Thomas closed his eyes and tilted his head further back. He could feel the damp evaporating from his clothes and the energy soaking into his skin. A smile spread across his face as the guttering spark in his reservoir slowly began to grow. He hummed.

A heavy tread thudded beside Thomas. He didn't bother opening his eyes. "Just give me a second, sir," he whispered. "Please. I need this." Even while he spoke, a shadow fell over him, and he groaned as clouds rolled in to conceal the suns once more. So much for filling his tank.

If the worst comes to worst, at least I still have the firepot.

Commander Storm cleared his throat. "We must move on, if we mean to reach the far side of the range before the morrow." He handed Thomas a small canister of grease paint. "Your mask has worn off." Without the paint, his pale skin would stand out like a beacon. Thomas reapplied it.

For several hours, they traveled across a rugged valley choked with lush growth, the air close and still under gnarled branches dripping with moss. The patterns in the bark of the old trees resembled leering masks and grotesque faces. David and Dinah stayed close, and Thomas was glad for their company. Just when he believed the creepy forest would never end, the trees thinned out and the ground began to rise. So did his mood.

Maybe we really will reach Ebenezzar's fortress before tomorrow.

They stopped and dismounted for a brief rest in a clearing as the daylight began to dim. Peter joined them, descending suddenly with his fur and feathers bushed out. His hazel eyes were wide, and he kept his wings unfurled. "Dukey," he hissed, digging his claws into the mossy ground. "Dukey!"

"Peter!" Dinah wiped tears from her eyes. "Oh, praise Yshua. You're okay."

Commander Storm crashed to a halt, scowling. "Where have you been, Buzzard?" he growled softly.

The syrax opened and closed his beak several times. "You're never gonna believe it, Dukey, but—"

Commander Storm's eyes narrowed. "Spit it out." He sniffed, then tensed, drawing his right-hand scimitar while scanning the gloom. "We're not alone. Delta formation, now." His left hand made a hooking gesture, clenched briefly in a fist, and then drew his other sword.

Thomas looked around. *What did that mean? I've never seen that Battle Sign before.*

Mind reeling, he pushed aside his confusion as he moved into a triangle formation with the dwelfnim on either side, all senses alert as they followed their leader's example. Dinah inhaled sharply, ending in a whimper. David murmured something in another language—probably the dwelfnic tongue. Dinah echoed him. A shivery tingling sensation ran up Thomas's legs and through his body, making his hair stand on end for an instant, then subsided.

What in blazes? The dwelfnim must've done something ... stone-singerish. It was similar, yet subtler than the sensation he received when the kiddo had used her wyld. Frustration burned low in his gut; he didn't dare expend his reservoir or tap into the firepot to increase his visual acuity in the rapidly fading light.

Peter cowered, ears wilting.

Oh, for the love of ...! Every muscle tense, Thomas gripped his sword hilts. "Messenger Peter," he barked. "Report!"

The syrax flinched. "It's the Battlecrows," he squeaked.

Shock jolted through Thomas. He stopped wondering about what Dinah and David were doing. *Battlecrows? Out here in the Western Marches? How?*

"Lord Yshua, be with us," David whispered.

"Well, Buzzard?" Commander Storm bit out the words, but his tone conveyed annoyance rather than anxiety. Or astonishment. Did nothing surprise him? "How many foemen? In what positions? Give me information, or by the Great Below, you'll be the first casualty in this battle."

Peter wailed. "I'm so sorry, Dukey. I dunno how I missed 'em. An' then I saw ... *him.* I got confused for a while. Forgot what I was doin'. They must be usin' magic."

"Him who?" Thomas asked, but neither of them paid him any attention. He set his jaw, then took a deep breath, loosening his death-grip on the swords.

"Magic." The Commander growled, rotating slowly as he scanned the deepening shadows. He muttered under his breath, then said something that sounded like "ron-doll-voor-den." Violet light sparked in the evainghir's eyes. Thomas started; this time, he wasn't imagining it.

Like Mr. Cowl from the dreamscape? What gives? He shook his head. Who? Once more, the memory eluded him.

Peter scrambled up a tree and crouched on an overhanging limb. "There ain't that many, this time. Mebbe three, four platoons, sitch-ee-ated between us and the fortress."

Not that many. Only sixty to eighty warriors waiting to make mincemeat of us. Heart pounding, Thomas settled into a waiting stance with his longsword angled in front. He glimpsed hulking bear-like figures alongside human shapes moving in the shadows.

"Criminy! Commander ... the jokers are all around us."

"Aye," the Commander replied, rolling his shoulders. He sounded far too composed. "Steady, lad. Buzzard!" he snapped. "Your report is not finished. What else did you see—or did you forget that, too?"

Peter yowled another apology. "I counted twenty Dagger-tongues. And ... and somethin' else. I think their captain's with' em, 'cause I saw ...him." He gulped. "R-Rook. They're never apart." He moaned and covered his eyes. "Say us a prayer, Shepherd, otherwise we're done for."

Why the melodrama? Thomas snorted. "What's a Dagger-tongue? And how ..." His voice trailed off when he glanced around, looking for the other two legs of the triangle. Where had David and Dinah gone? The ground beneath his boots shivered.

Rage flared in Commander Storm's eyes as he tracked something unseen beyond the clearing. Thomas pitied whoever was on the receiving end of that glare.

"The wraithcloak may deceive others," the Commander growled, "but you cannot hide from me. Show yourself, Wuya."

Thomas's eyes widened as a form separated from the shadows, flowing from them like ink into a humanoid shape. Black armor adorned it from helmet to sabatons and a half cloak of black feathers fell from its pauldrons. A helmet with a crest of feathers and a corvid mask covered its face.

On his right prowled a massive syrax twice Peter's size—the black raptor half doubtless the source of the feathers on the cloak—its leonine half dark gray with black stripes. On the warrior's left stalked another winged and feathered menace of comparable size to the syrax, but this creature's body was predominantly covered in reptilian scales, with a head shaped much like Balthazar's. As the creature surveyed the clearing, its eyes settled on Thomas, then narrowed before moving on.

Thomas shivered at the malevolent intellect in that gaze. *Is that ... a wyrmkin?*

The syrax opened its hooked beak and hissed.

A low, feminine voice chuckled as the black armored warrior stroked the menacing syrax's neck. "Now, now, Rook. Is that any way to greet an old friend?"

Waterfalls

Annabelle pressed her hands against her churning stomach. Her encounter with the dragon in the dreamscape weighed on her mind, but that wasn't the reason for her discomfort. Not directly. Much to the contrary—it was because of that meeting that she now knew where Enoch's captors had taken him. Once she found a way back to her friends, she could pass that along. But now she also had a moral dilemma on her hands.

Should I tell Raeden? No ... it'll only upset him.

Her champion had enough to worry about. Better to let it lie until they were able to do something with the information. There was a festering sensation to the Oathbond whenever she spoke of the dreamscape. It disturbed Raeden that he couldn't protect her there. While not outright forbidding her, he'd strongly suggested she not venture into the dreamscape since she'd lost Daar-Lûsin and its protection. She hadn't bothered arguing.

Raeden hadn't liked her meeting Hadrien, and he wouldn't be happy about her talking to yet another dragon. Though Varazslo seemed nice enough. And he had saved her from her own folly. Despite her indisposition, Annabelle smiled, recalling the dragon's awkward request for lessons in friendship. It was ... sweet. She'd agreed to meet him again.

He saved me from the kraken, and he knows a lot about the dreamscape. I see nothing wrong with making friends, so long as I don't trust him too much.

A keen yearning for her former traveling companions stung her like tiny slivers under her fingernails. She missed Dinah's comforting presence. David's calm mien and unwavering faith always soothed her anxiety. And she could really use some of Peter's cheerful optimism. She even missed dour, old Commander Storm. Even though he didn't like her, he was steady and strong. Like a rock she could lean on. And Toad ... Sir Thomas. She sniffled.

Does he miss me as much as I miss him?

Surreptitiously wiping her eyes, Annabelle glanced at her current companions, whom she hoped would become friends as well. Presently, she sat with Rhiannon and her handmaid, Portia, beside a deep pool fed by a cascade of waterfalls. One waterfall dropped at least fifty feet—or so Portia said—from the highest point while on the other side a series of three interconnected falls descended in stepwise fashion like a watery staircase. It was a breathtaking sight.

Twelve gwerindawr youths hauled themselves up on river stones as they ascended the cliff leading up to the terraced waterfalls. It was a game called "king of the river;" a race to the summit. And this was the secondary reason for Annabelle's tummy troubles.

The roar of the whitewater hummed in her ears. She watched as the gwerindawr plunged several body-lengths from the top tier to the next lower one, and dove again until they reached the bottom, and then attempted to swim—or climb the rocks— up the series of waterfalls to the top.

The young men had their swimming tails to propel them upward against the water until they could grab hold of another protruding rock. They used their galamerdhe to brace themselves. How were they not slipping? As she watched, a green-skinned boy halfway up lost his grip, and she gasped as he dropped into the pool below. He emerged with a "whoop" to climb again; she closed her eyes and thanked God. When she opened them again, the blue-skinned fellow—Princeps Mordred—was nearest the top. Her heart beat faster. Although the young men showed no apprehension, she felt enough for the lot of them.

"How the heck can they do that?" Annabelle gaped.

"Seasons of practice," Rhiannon said, selecting a morsel from the tray Portia held out to them. "They'll be fine." She chuckled. "Dred never seems to tire of the game."

"Perhaps it's because the scamp always wins," Portia said.

"They must have incredible upper body strength." Not trusting her upset stomach, Annabelle shook her head at Portia's offer of food. "Maybe later."

Portia had packed them each a seaweed packet containing sticky barley, raw fish, citrus, radish, and pickled ginger. Similar to the breakfast Annabelle brought to share with her champion, she thought of them as "sushi sandwiches." She found them tasty, but Raeden refused to eat anything the gwerindawr prepared for him. He claimed their food made him ill and that he could hunt or forage.

Annabelle worried that the kaenhir wasn't eating enough. In the brief time they'd been on Ynys Lloches, his fur had lost its luster and he'd grown rather gaunt. He needed more protein. That morning, despite his protests, she used her wyld to capture a large salmon-like fish for his breakfast. Last night, she'd created a pond for him on the prison islet and stocked it with fish.

Now if only I can convince Raeden that Rhiannon and Mordred could be allies.

After taking a sip of fruit juice to wet her dry throat, she frowned, leaning forward and shading her eyes. Mordred had attained the summit and flung himself across the rapids toward the single, straight waterfall. A thrill of fear shot through her. "Will he jump from there? It's too high!"

Portia shook her head and sighed. "Our princeps can be a mite reckless, when he feels he has something to prove." She glanced at Annabelle sharply. "Or someone to impress."

Annabelle snorted. "Oh, it's impressive all right."

Impressively reckless. Now I have another stubborn male to worry about. Why must boys act so stupid?

Just the thought of leaping from such a height made her muscles clench and her heart skip a beat. How Rhiannon could be so blasé about her brother risking his life was beyond her ken. What if Mordred snapped his neck or cracked his head open? Could her wyld even heal that level of damage?

She shuddered and forced back tears at the image of the princeps, broken and lifeless on the rocks. *Please God, don't let me ever have to find out.* While Mordred positioned himself for a dive, she reached down into her reservoir of sapphire energy, then extended her awareness through the water below. Just in case something bad happened.

"There he goes," Rhiannon intoned, her voice warming to fondness.

Heart in her throat, Annabelle tracked Mordred's descent, his blue form plunging into the pool. The turbulence of the churning waterfall messed with her senses, but then she experienced something like a tickle along her spine. Had Mordred survived? She shivered as the sensation intensified, and Rhiannon put an arm around her, disrupting her concentration.

"Cold, dear?" She chuckled. "Don't worry so much about my brother. See?"

A sleek dark head broke the surface a stone's throw away from where they sat, and Annabelle released her pent-up breath.

Grinning, the princeps swam over and placed a melon with a blue-striped, purple rind on the rock jutting out into the pool where Annabelle sat and then heaved himself up beside her. He basked in the praise of his sister and her handmaid, then turned to Annabelle.

"I brought you a watermelon, Lady Ann. They only thrive under the waterfalls here."

She swatted his shoulder. "You think bringing me fruit will make up for nearly giving me a heart attack? That was foolish. You could have died." Behind her, Rhiannon and Portia murmured in amused tones.

His grin faltered, but his golden eyes danced as he took her hand and enfolded it between his own. "Were you concerned for my safety, Lady Ann?"

Annabelle blushed. "Of course I was concerned. I don't like when my friends put themselves in danger for no good reason."

"No good reason?" His eyebrows rose. "But, Lady Ann, this is our way of determining who is the best. How else can I prove I am strong and capable enough to court the Ahdmerel?"

"Court me?" Cheeks burning, Annabelle jerked her hand from his. Based on his solicitousness since she'd arrived, she'd wondered if things were developing in that direction. His insistence that she drop *his* title, and the way he waited on her, serenaded her with ballads of his own composition ...

But she'd scolded herself for wild imaginings. The cute, popular guys at school never looked at her twice. Mordred reminded her of them. Back home, he'd be a prep or a jock. She was a nerd and a klutz. Why would a handsome prince be interested in her?

Oh dear. That's right: I'm the "blessed Ahdmerel." Is it because of that prophecy? And what will Raeden do if he finds out? Even the *scent* of Mordred made the Oathbond black and prickly with rage.

"You can't court me," she blurted. "I need to return to my quest. Besides, we barely know each other."

Rhiannon laughed. "Lady Ann, that is the purpose of courtship. Getting to know one another better. Sawel and I came together in this way."

"But you knew each other all your lives," Annabelle protested. "You had time to become friends and fall in love before you married."

"Fish piddle." Rhiannon pouted and flicked a hand. "Love can develop in an instant, like a stroke of lightning. I can tell you already like my brother." Her tone seemed to imply: and how could you not love him?

Mordred's warm gaze captured hers. "I know it has only been a fleeting time, but I know my own heart. I care for you, Lady Ann. It would be my honor to serve and protect you."

"Um. Wow. I do like you, Mordred," Annabelle stammered, her heart doing flip-flops. Why did he have to be so cute? She wrung her hands. They were cold as ice. This was proceeding way too quickly. She'd never even dated anyone before. In this world there was no playing the field. Courtship led directly to marriage. And this guy was a freaking prince. Whatever their prophecy claimed, she was basically a nobody.

Besides, eventually I need to go back home to Wisconsin. My family.

She licked her lips. "I care for you. As a friend. I don't know if I can ... court anybody. Not right now. I'm not ready. The mission to save my brother ... My friends need me. I'll be leaving soon, and ..." Her voice trailed off.

Did they need her to complete their quest? Commander Storm had been reluctant to bring her along from the start. Without battle training or survival skills, Annabelle was dead weight. She'd learned some, but ...

What if God brought me to Ynys Lloches to serve a different purpose? Is the prophecy a sign that I should stay here?

Her chest tightened at the thought of abandoning Enoch to his fate. The brother of her heart. How could she do that? And these people hated her champion!

Instead of looking disappointed at her reservation, Mordred smiled. He thumped a fist against his chest. "I'll wait for you to be ready. And I'll prove myself to you with feats of strength and endurance—"

"Please, Mordred," she interjected, "don't go diving off waterfalls anymore. You don't need to prove anything to me." Her face felt like it was on fire. "I'm already impressed. Just ... not ready for courtship. Let alone marriage."

He touched her cheek, frowning. "Surely, there must be a difficult task I could complete to win your favor."

She pulled his hand from her cheek and gripped it, his warmth soaking into her cold fingers. Here was an opportunity to test him. "You want to win my favor? Fine. Let Raeden go. He didn't do anything wrong."

Mordred's expression went flat, and Rhiannon gently said, "That is the one thing he cannot do, Lady Ann. Our father has expressly forbidden it."

"Then show me where the waystone is—the one I know you have. My friend Dinah and a bunch of other dwelfnim have been here before."

Annabelle cast a pleading glance at Rhiannon, but the princepsa remained silent. Her full lips thinned as she scrutinized the remnants of her meal.

Mordred squeezed her hand. "I don't even know where the waystone is." He sighed and his expression grew dreamy. "I wish I did. Then I could leave Ynys Lloches. Travel the world beyond the endless ocean. Do something noteworthy and prove myself to my father." His teeth flashed in a grin. "Seek out the prophesied glory by your side, Lady Ann."

Annabelle ducked her head to hide her bewilderment. However, she wondered. Could she use the prophecy to enlist Mordred's aid in finding the waystone? But that meant defying his father's decree. *I don't want to get him into trouble.*

"Dred," his sister admonished. "You are being too forward. Please forgive him, Lady Ann. He knows not the meaning of moderation."

Annabelle glanced at their entwined fingers, pale blue and pale pink. What would her parents think if she brought home a merman as her boyfriend? And if they married, what would the children look like? She bit back a bubble of laughter. This was ridiculous. She should be thinking of ways to get off this island and return to her quest.

"I need to figure out the prophecy."

Rhiannon touched her arm. "Lady Ann, my husband knows the prophecy from stem to stern and back again. If you wish, I'll tell him to assist you in your studies."

"Thank you." Annabelle smiled as relief filled her. Rhiannon was trying to help, and Sawel seemed like a nice man. "That would be awesome!"

The prophecy! Like flotsam, a line emerged from the maelstrom of her mind: *"A shard of moon may light her way."* Could that be a reference to Daar-Lûsin? An idea took shape. A way to put off Mordred without offending him while also helping her and Raeden.

She squeezed his hand, let go, and met his earnest gaze. "Okay. Maybe you can prove yourself in another way, then. Do you think you can find the place where Raeden and I came through? I didn't see a waystone ring, but maybe it was on the ocean floor."

The princeps nodded. "I've been exploring around Ynys Lloches since I first grew my galamerdhe, and the Howling Tempest patrols the waters regularly. There are four stone rings on the ocean floor roughly half a day's swim from the main isle—one each to the north, east, west, and south. Those might be waystones. My men and I check them for activity while on our long patrols. Until now, they've remained quiescent."

Portia frowned and leaned forward to peer into her face. "Lady Ann, you are not thinking of returning the way you came." Her hazel eyes narrowed, and she sounded disapproving. "The Brenin has decreed you must fulfill the prophecy."

Rhiannon looked crestfallen. "Is our hospitality not to your liking?"

"No, that's not it," Annabelle hastened to assure the princepsa. She glanced among them, suppressing a flash of irritation at Portia. "You all have been very kind. I'm grateful for all you've done, and I won't leave until I absolutely have to."

But what if this is where God wants you to be?

Shaking off that concern, she fussed with a strand of hair that had come loose from her braid and then faced Mordred. "When I arrived here, I lost a special artifact somewhere in the ocean. It's called Daar-Lûsin, and it's a dagger with an opal-like stone down the center of the blade. About yay long." She held her hands a foot apart, then smiled. "Could you please find it?"

Brightening, Mordred grabbed her shoulders. Excitement gleamed in his eyes. "I'll begin the search at once, Lady Ann. My men and I shall scour the ocean floor around these waystones. Rest assured, I'll place Daar-Lûsin into your hands before the moon wanes."

He saluted her with a fist to his chest and, without a solemn nod, whirled and swam back to the falls. He hollered a command. The other youths ceased their games and began to rally around their captain.

Scorched Earth

Thomas gaped. The captain of the Battlecrow army was a woman? Well, that explained the Commander's anger. He didn't appreciate females "playing at being soldiers," as he phrased it.

Rising to his full height, Commander Storm's visage became a mask of granite and steel. "You presume much." He rotated his wrists—the signal to keep an eye on their flanks. "Too much, for a garrison captain who forsook her duty." His eyes narrowed. "*Traitor.*"

Okay, Thomas mused as he scanned the clearing, *maybe the Commander has a reason other than the captain's sex to be ticked off.*

"I merely followed the example of my superior officer." Wuya's voice hardened as a gauntleted hand tapped out a rhythm on her companion's neck. "Where were you, *Commander,* when Dunkelnost's horde attacked Nervashi?"

The syrax—*Rook?* Thomas sneered. *What a ridiculous name*—fluffed his black crest and cooed like a giant pigeon. The woman continued speaking. "Where were you when Warmaster sel Drayven fell and the barrier went down?" She snapped her fingers. "Rook! Secure the messenger."

No longer being petted, Rook's baleful gaze settled on the pink syrax, crouched frozen and wide-eyed in the tree like a terrified cat. Quicker than thought, Rook swarmed up the tree and was upon Peter, wrestling him from his perch.

"Where were you, Storm," Wuya said in a venomous tone while the syraxim yowled and spat. Placing a hand on the other creature's—the wyrmkin's—neck, she drew out her next words. "Where were you when the harrows laid. My. Town. To. Waste?"

Whoa, lady. Monologue much? Thomas glanced between the black-armored mercenary and the Commander despite his orders to monitor their surroundings. He snorted, then muttered, "And here I thought *I* had a major chip on my shoulder."

Staring at him with creepy white eyes, the wyrmkin growled softly. Its nostrils flared.

The evainghir stepped toward the mercenary captain, who had battle-axes in her hands before he advanced further. "Don't try anything, Storm." The crow-helm turned, and Thomas flinched when the beak pointed his direction. "You either, *boy* ... whoever you are. Or my Rook dispatches your pink popinjay." Rook's bulk pinned the smaller syrax, and he growled with his beak clamped around Peter's throat like wicked black scissors. Peter trembled and keened.

Poor Cat-Vulture. Thomas winced, but Commander Storm appeared unmoved.

Wuya's head swiveled from side to side as if searching the clearing. "Now, where is the albino child? And I thought you had two Stonesingers in your little party."

Albino child? Thomas scowled. "Who the he—"

The mercenary made a dismissive gesture with a weapon. "No matter. My Battlecrows have you completely surrounded. We'll find the little wyldling—wherever you've hidden her. Drop your weapons and surrender her now, and no one needs to get hurt."

Thomas inhaled sharply. The Battlecrows *were* after Annabelle! For once, he was glad that she wasn't with them.

Commander Storm settled back on his heels, swords lowered and looking at his ease. His eyes narrowed. "And what leads you to believe that you have the upper hand in this scenario?"

"The evidence before my eyes."

"Then your eyes deceive you."

Wuya laughed. "I disagree. I have you, your messenger, and your squire at my mercy, Storm. Allow me to prove it to you."

Thomas scowled. This was too much. "Hey, lady! Who're you calling a squire? I'm Sir Thomas, Knight of the Northern Marches."

The beaked helm turned his way. Wuya tsked. "Hush now, boy. The adults are speaking." She snapped her fingers, and the wyrmkin backed away, the eyes never leaving Thomas.

Why does it keep staring at me? And where is it going?

Thomas moved until he was back-to-back with Commander Storm. "Sir—there's a wyrmkin. Did you see?"

"I saw, lad. Remain vigilant. It will come after y—"

With a hoarse cry, Wuya banged a battle ax against her chest, and odd creatures with long heads, stocky legs ending in huge claws, and scaly bodies shambled into the glade. They looked like the freakish offspring of an armadillo and an anteater—if such animals ever grew to the size of cattle. Soldiers with slight builds rode upon their backs, armed with spears and battle-axes. From a quick count, Thomas determined there were six or eight beasts, all with riders.

"Really. That's what you've got—a posse of giant naked anteaters?" Thomas barked out a laugh. The ground trembled. David and Dinah must be planning something big. Readying his blades, he grinned. "Bring 'em on."

"Concern yourself with the wyrmkin," growled Commander Storm as Wuya shouted more orders. Dropping his voice, he added, "And whatever happens, do not use your wyld."

"What? Why not?"

"That's an order, trooper!"

Wuya hollered. "Torchbearers!"

"Wuya is a shadow-jumper," the Commander hissed. "She could come at you from any shadow, so keep an eye out for her, as well."

"Got it, sir," Thomas snarked as he surveyed the shapes moving in the trees. "I'll grow eyes all over myself and watch everyone and everything then."

Commander Storm grunted a laugh. "If you think it will help, then I won't stop you."

Thomas blinked. *Did the Commander just make a joke?*

Firelight flickered beyond the trees, and heat flared in sympathy deep inside Thomas. His grin widened as six soldiers emerged from the forest, each holding a torch mounted on a tall pole. Just his luck! *Don't mind if I do.* He extended his kythim, reaching for the energy, then stopped. Hadn't the Commander given him an order not to do that? Cursing, he snatched the tendrils back.

Commander Storm bellowed. Metal rang against metal. Ululating cries filled the glade.

On his left periphery, a creature bounded up, and Thomas whirled to confront the odd-looking beast and its howling rider. The creature lifted its tubular head, and something shot out, striking Thomas's fingers before darting back. It broke his concentration. "Ouch!" He dropped the longsword, then shook his stinging hand while cursing. "What the... Did that thing *bite* me with its tongue?"

"Where's your bravado now, sir knight?" The rider laughed, baring her teeth in a savage grin. "You look like a fool." She tugged the reins. "Hyah!" The beast rose up on its hind legs and raked at him with claws like curved knives. With an inarticulate cry, Thomas ducked and stumbled back, then rolled to one side to avoid a spear point in his gut.

"How do you like my Dagger-tongues?" Wuya gloated, prowling around the clearing. The torchlight shed shafts of light on the battleground, but it also amplified the darkness in between. Seeming to fade in and out of the shadows, Wuya bounded from root to root, her feet never touching the earth. "Their tongues shoot out fast as arrows. I hope they are enough of a challenge for you, *squire.*"

"Stop taunting the lad." Commander Storm was engaged in fighting two of the beasts and their riders, who jabbed at him with spears.

"But it's so easy!" Wuya flowed through the shadows beneath the trees with her axes at her sides, observing the fray and shouting out orders. "Mind the Stonesingers, my daughters!"

Her daughters? Does she mean the beasts or their riders?

"Nasty old bird," Thomas grumbled, shaking his hand. It had gone numb. *Well, that's useless. But I'm not down for the count yet.* Tucking the arm behind his back, he raised Murder-Stick and danced to one side to avoid the Dagger-tongue's rush. It wasn't difficult; aside from the shooty-stabby tongue, the creatures were neither terribly fast nor nimble.

"Sir Thomas—ware the wyrmkin!" Commander Storm's blades wove their deadly dance.

Panting, Thomas scanned the glade, the forest, the shadows. He could use his wyld to enhance his vision, but Commander Storm had told him not to. Things moved around, but all he could make out were the Dagger-tongues, their riders, and the torchbearers positioned on root buttresses, where their feet needn't touch the ground. The fire called to him.

No, I mustn't.

A beast made a gargling, wailing cry and collapsed. Its rider sprang from the saddle, screaming—another woman? —threw aside her broken spear and charged the Commander while brandishing war axes. He made short work of her, pivoting on a heel and whipping her aside with his armored tail as he turned to deal with his next opponent. Behind him, the soldier struck a tree and slid to the ground, unmoving.

Wuya's form resolved from the darkness on the far side of the clearing. "Laxir!" Her voice was anguished, like a mother watching her child die. "Perdition take you, Storm!"

"You never could handle loss, Wuya." Commander Storm replied as he ducked a darting tongue and cut down the second beast. "Victory comes at a cost. If it bothers you, then stop sending those whom you most value to their deaths. Come out from the shadows and confront me yourself."

With the short sword held defensively, Thomas assessed the situation. Perhaps he'd miscounted. There were only six beasts in the clearing, including the two Commander Storm had dispatched.

Wuya must have noticed the discrepancy as well. "Naylor! Kimura!" She called out several more names, then made an exasperated sound. "Where have they gone? Farula, never mind the elk. Gehenna is taking too long. Find that wyldling!"

On Thomas's right, David's mount alternated dodging and kicking another Dagger-tongue while its rider attempted to lasso the war-elk. After Wuya gave her order, the rider shouted an acknowledgement. Her mount backed off, lifted its head, and then the elk staggered. Skirting him warily, the Dagger-tongue shambled off into the shadows with its nose to the ground.

Inwardly, Thomas smiled. *Good luck with that; you won't find Annabelle.*

Tinker was protecting Dinah's riding doe, charging at any scaled beast that approached, but his efforts slowed, and his movements grew clumsy. Something was wrong with the stag. However, Thomas couldn't intervene because he had his own ugly scaled creatures with shooty-stabby bits. And he couldn't feel his left arm. What the heck was on that thing's tongue?

Movement flickered. Another tongue struck him with a glancing blow on the right cheek as he spun to guard his flank, where a Dagger-tongue dashed toward him. His face stung for a second, heat trickled, then it went numb. Was its saliva some kind of paralyzing agent? Or poison? *Am I going to die? I need to warn the Commander!* Fear ripped through him. Thomas opened his mouth, but his tongue wouldn't cooperate. All that emerged was an inarticulate stream of noises.

If I'm gonna die, then I'll die fighting, and take that thing down with me.

He raised the short-sword and pivoted on his heel in a side-step as the creature bore down on him, slashing at its throat. The blade skidded off its brown scales, jarring his arm. He cursed.

Leveling her spear, the petite rider laughed. "Nice try, little squire. A Dagger-tongue's skin is as hard as tempered steel."

"I'll show you who's little," Thomas growled, cutting aside her spear jabs. It was awkward with half his body gone numb.

"I'm surprised you can still move. Ah, well, it makes the fight more interesting." The rider's feral grin was visible through the helmet's cut-out; her round face and small frame reminded him of Annabelle. She barked out a command and the Dagger-tongue swept around to threaten him with its wicked claws.

Thomas staggered as he backpedaled. The ground shook. His knee buckled and he fell, his entire left side useless. The laughing rider drummed her heels against the Dagger-tongue's sides, and it lumbered after him.

Blast it all to perdition! Orders be hanged; I must do it.

Extending his kythim, he reached for his flame-pot, then cursed. The embers had died. He turned to the torch-flames, their signatures bold and bright like beacons in the darkness. The torches flickered and dimmed, then brightened again. The mercenary captain shouted. Warmth and life flooded into Thomas, and he drank it all like a starving man. All numbness receded. In its place, an idea arose. Could he do it?

Nearly upon him, the creature reared up and readied its claws. *Here goes nothing. Murder Stick don't fail me now.* The short sword's blade glowed white-hot. As the animal descended, Thomas angled the weapon toward its chest and the blade penetrated the tough scales as though they were butter. Flesh sizzled and the stench of scorching filled the air. The animal gargled, leaning back as if trying to escape from inevitable death.

It worked!

Extracting the sword, Thomas rolled out from under the collapsing beast before it crushed him, bisecting the rider's spear as she thrust, the point catching on his right pauldron and slicing through. He felt a hot sting and switched Murder Stick to his left hand.

"What did you do to her?" the rider shrieked, leaping from the saddle. "How?" Axes in hand, she flew at him like a berserker. Too much emotion. She flailed at him. It was like fighting a little kid. Thomas evaded her blades and blocked her attacks without much effort. On an upward block the tip of his sword caught on her helm and knocked it off, revealing the round, tear-streaked face of a young girl. She stumbled back with her axes raised in a cross-defense. Thomas froze. She couldn't be more than sixteen, just a child. Like Annabelle.

He recovered, settling into a defensive stance. "Back off, kid. I don't want to hurt you." His boot contacted something hard. He spared the slightest glance. His longsword. Hooking the hilt basket with his toe, he flipped it up and caught it with his right hand. A grin twitched at his mouth.

Heh. Now we're cooking with gas.

Wide eyed, her face contorted by grief and rage, the girl screeched and charged at him, swinging her axes. "You killed my baby!"

Thomas switched his blades around just in time. "What baby?" he retorted, deflecting her wild swings and sidestepping her charge. He jerked his head toward the fallen Dagger-tongue. "That thing's your baby?" He grunted. "I don't want to know who the father is."

Her only response was an incoherent scream and a flurry of ax blows.

Guess I struck a nerve.

Crazy kid. He needed to put her down, fast, before he ran out of energy. And before she hurt someone—namely, him. He drove her back, until she was right beside her fallen mount. Finding an opening in her clumsy swings, he sliced at her fingers.

She dropped the axes and fell to her knees, sobbing, "Just kill me." She seemed so vulnerable, huddled there. It was like seeing the kiddo in pain.

I can't kill her. Just a kid. I know I should ... this is a battlefield ... but I can't. The Code says to show mercy.

Thomas shook his head, scanning his periphery as he circled her, then smacked the hilt of Murder Stick against her head. She fell to the ground with a groan. Well, that took care of that. Hopefully the bulk of the Dagger-tongue protected her from trampling. Blade at the ready, he glanced around, seeking his next opponent.

The ground shook. Before his eyes, the dirt was moving in a slow wave. Dinah's head surfaced briefly, she took a gulp of air, and then she submerged in the earth once more. He caught a glimpse of Commander Storm battling two Dagger-tongues and their riders and moved to assist the evainghir.

From her perch on a buttress root, Wuya called, "Jacinta—ware the ground. Stonesingers!" Shadows flickered, and suddenly the black-armored mercenary was there, brandishing axes, to engage the Commander.

The rider tried to fall back. Then the ground under the creature's feet became like liquid, and the animal began to sink. Extensions of the earth resembling a jagged, gaping maw rose from the main mass, seizing the Dagger-tongue. It squealed and thrashed, sending dirt flying, but couldn't stop the earthen hands from dragging it—and its screaming rider—under the ground. It halted at the rider's shoulders, leaving her head and the creature's snout exposed. The rider let loose with a stream of curses.

Whoa. Nice attack. Like some kind of land shark. But how would you coordinate with someone while they're underground?

Wuya screeched the rider's name, redoubling her assault. She seemed a difficult opponent despite Commander Storm's greater size, strength and prowess. Every time the evainghir was about to land a blow, Wuya slipped into a shadow and then popped up again, just out of reach, although the Commander turned in the correct direction every time.

While the Commander and the mercenary captain fought, Thomas sheltered by the corpse and caught his breath, surveying the battlefield. He watched as another Dagger-tongue and rider were pulled into the ground. After the stunt with the fiery blade, his wyld was nearly exhausted again, and his strength was fading. Good thing there was plenty of fire around.

I wonder why Commander Storm told me not to use my wyld. I would've died otherwise.

He sipped more of the torch-fire, but not as much as before. Again, the flames flickered and dimmed. "What in perdition?" Wuya snarled, ducking and raising her axes to catch the Commander's downward stroke. "Torchbearers, don't extinguish the flames yet!"

I should do just that. Extinguish the flames and then maybe she can't use the shadows.

He reached out with his kythim again. From the edge of the wood, something made a burbling noise. Thomas glanced up and met the eyes of the wyrmkin, then froze. Instead of blank white, they'd become lambent gold. It stood with feathered wings partially unfurled and toothless mouth agape. Locked in its gaze, he felt energy humming between them and a pull, like from the torches, but this time it flowed in the opposite direction.

A cheerful feminine voice spoke into his mind: "You cannot hide from Gehenna, Caster of Flame. Gehenna was tired; thank you for the special treat."

Did that thing just talk?

In the midst of rising, Thomas rocked back on his heels as if struck by a blow. What the ... He was suddenly dizzy, weak, and cold. Had that blasted thing drained his reservoir? How?

Glowing eyes still fixed on Thomas, the wyrmkin hunkered like a cat preparing to spring. "Gehenna is a good girl. Gehenna will catch the wyldling for Mother. Mother will be pleased. Mother won't mind if Gehenna takes a bite." The wyrmkin uttered a burbling coo, then launched herself into the clearing straight at Thomas with hand-like talons extended.

Thomas stumbled back, tripping over the Dagger-tongue's tail and sprawling on the ground. It knocked the wind out of him. Gasping for air, he raised his swords and watched in horror as the feathered reptile bore down on him with gleeful eyes and hungry mouth. This time pointed teeth glinted in the torchlight.

Can't move ... Face death with eyes wide open ...

A wave of stony soil rose between him and his attacker. David emerged, dark eyes alight and his black hair disheveled. He thrust with the rock-spear in his hands and impaled the wyrmkin as it was about to descend upon Thomas.

The creature's eyes widened, and it spoke inside his head one last time. "Muh ... ther ..." Golden light went out like a snuffed candle. The wyrmkin slumped and David grunted as he shunted the body aside. His face was a mask of sorrow as he released the spear.

Heat punched Thomas in the gut, alongside a pang of loss. Although his power had returned, the wyrmkin's final mental cry haunted him. It had sounded ... human. He blinked at the scaled and feathered corpse. "Was that thing ... a person?"

"Yes." Trembling, David crossed himself. "Hardly more than a child. May Lord Yshua have mercy on her soul." He knelt and placed a hand on the ground beside the dead wyrmkin. The soil became like liquid, and the creature was swallowed up until not a trace remained. "That's the least I can do for her."

"Gehenna!" the mercenary captain wailed. Shoulders stiff and arms shaking, she stood upon another root buttress. Her beaked helmet turned in their direction. Jabbing a finger at Thomas and David, she snarled, "You'll pay for that."

David looked sick. Thomas sneered. "Take responsibility, *Captain.* I'm not the one who sent little girls into battle!"

"What have you done to them?" The crow-helmet swung as Wuya scanned the glade in the torchlight. She was the last Battlecrow standing. Here and there, a snout or a head protruded from the soil. Trapped, the soldiers squirmed and yelled for help, while worm-like tongues extended from tubular snouts and waved in the air.

Wuya brandished an ax. "May the Void swallow you, Stonesinger!" She continued to rave, raining calumny on them.

What a drama queen. Thomas grimaced, sheathing Murder Stick so he could take David's helping hand. He staggered, and the dwelfnhir steadied him. "You touched the Aethyr, didn't you?" David murmured in his ear.

The tightness in his throat made it difficult to swallow. "Yeah," he whispered. "It was life or death." But if he hadn't used his wyld, would the wyrmkin have attacked him?

Guilt curdled in his gut. *Maybe David wouldn't have needed to kill the poor thing—no, it was a* kid!

Wuya vanished, then reappeared in a shadow behind Commander Storm with axes raised. Thomas was about to shout a warning when the evainghir whirled, narrowly missing the mercenary with his blade-ringed tail. Cursing, Wuya hopped back into a shadow and popped out of another shadow on the edge of the clearing.

As if nothing had interrupted him, Commander Storm finished dispatching the last of the Dagger-tongues remaining above ground. He turned from his grisly work, flicking the blood from his swords. Somehow, he had found chinks in the animal's armor. "There is no need to continue this farce. Surrender now, and I'll see you have a fair trial."

Standing on a gnarled tree root, Wuya jerked her head to face the Commander. "No," the mercenary growled, stiffening. "I've never broken a contract."

"Well, harpy," Thomas muttered. "You'll have to break one now." He rolled the grip of the longsword in his hand. "Easy as breaking a nail."

"Insolent boy," Wuya scoffed, pacing along the glade's edge. "Once the contract is fulfilled, I shall enjoy watching my second cut that sly tongue from your mouth. Aha!"

With a cry of triumph, she crouched, seized Dinah's hair, and hauled the dwelfnhad up from the ground. Wuya pulled Dinah back against her, the edge of an ax-blade at Dinah's throat.

Eyes bulging, Dinah grabbed the other woman's arm, but it wouldn't budge. "Now, drop your weapons."

"Dee!" David moved toward Wuya and his cousin, then stopped when Dinah sniffed sharply. On her cheeks, moisture glistened in the torchlight. Her topaz eyes were wide and glassy with unshed tears, and she pressed trembling lips together.

"Let her go, Crow-face," Thomas snarled. "Only cowards take hostages."

"Be quiet, boy," Wuya snapped. The crow helm jerked to Commander Storm. "Take just one more step, Storm, and she dies. I know the weakness of a sourethol's armor. And you. Gehenna's murderer." Her voice dripped with venom as she confronted David, who flinched. "This one is dear to you, yes? Lay down your weapons. Release my soldiers and their mounts, or I'll lop off her pretty head."

Still holding his swords, Commander Storm narrowed his eyes. "You offer one life in exchange for fifteen."

"Two lives for fifteen," Wuya snapped. "Or do you not value your messenger? Rook holds him fast."

Perspiration slicked David's face, and he trembled as he glanced from his cousin to the evainghir. "Commander ..."

"We let them go, they'll just attack us again," Thomas muttered.

"Silence, boy!" Wuya spat. She barked out a phrase in a harsh-sounding language that sounded like a curse, then demanded, "Release my soldiers and their mounts from the earth, and I swear upon my contract they shall withdraw without reprisal."

Commander Storm replied calmly, "And then you will release the dwelfnhad."

"No. First, you will summon the wyldling. I know you have her with you." Her voice broke a little. "My Gehenna was on the trail when you killed her."

Thomas experienced a frisson. *Oh, crap. That's why the Commander warned me not to use my wyld. So the wyrmkin couldn't target me. Now that I think of it, he implied earlier that wyrmkin could sense wyldlings using their power.*

Commander Storm lifted his chin. "How many times must I repeat myself? The one you seek is no longer in our company, Wuya. Let the dwelfnhad go."

The mercenary captain growled, "Enough! Drop your weapons. The wyrmkin-murderer will unearth my soldiers or this one dies." Dinah whimpered as the captain's arm tightened. A dark line appeared and dripped down her neck. Hand extended, David made a sound of protest.

Commander Storm held Wuya's unseen gaze for a moment, then sheathed his swords and lifted his hands. "Do as she says, Shepherd. Sir Thomas, sheathe your blades."

Before he finished speaking, David was already on his knees with fingers dug into the earth. Inhaling sharply, he bent his head and murmured what sounded like a prayer. The soil and rocks began to ripple like water in spreading rings from the epicenter he formed. Slowly, the mercenary's soldiers began to rise from their dirt prison. More slowly, the earth drew away from the Dagger-tongues. Patting their mounts, the young women wept, their faces slack with relief.

This is not a sound strategy. Sidling further away from the scaled beasts, Thomas spluttered, "But Commander ..." Commander Storm's left hand twitched an order to sheathe his weapons. Swallowing a curse, Thomas obeyed.

Wuya cracked out with another curse-like phrase. What in blazes was the crazy crow-lady saying? Hopefully not an order to attack. Whatever it was seemed to bolster the soldier-girls.

"Sir Thomas, *attend,*" the Commander admonished, rotating his wrists and flexing his fingers. Thomas stiffened with hands still on the sword grips. Both words and gestures were signals. The evainghir's glance grew fraught with meaning. "Your tongue flaps like the *buzzard's* wings. Either reign in your *fiery* temper or take better care with *your targets.*"

He wants me to use my wyld? Something to free the Cat-Vulture ... While Thomas deliberated, the last of the daylight faded from the eastern sky and the shadows cast by the torchlight deepened. He'd better do something fast, before Crow-face decided to vanish into the shadows and take the Ambassador along with her.

Commander Storm faced the mercenary. "Wuya. Your ... warriors will soon be free. Release the dwelfnhad."

Thomas considered the two syraxim beneath the tree. The big one, Rook, lay atop Peter with his talons near his throat. Peter's eyelids were shut, and he made soft keening noises. Rook's dark gray tail twitched, the end tapping on the ground like a cat's. Thomas's gaze slid to their right. A torch-pole stood nearby. He suppressed a grin as a nasty idea took shape.

Hmmm. How to make it seem natural. After all, Crow-face is looking for a wyldling.

While everyone was distracted by the excavation of the soldiers, Thomas extended his kythim and coaxed the flames down the pole. Swiftly, he sent the line of fire across the ground toward Rook's tail. The hungry flames attacked, and the stench of scorched fur filled the air.

Springing backward off the smaller syrax, Rook let out a bellow that blended a raptor's shriek with a lion's roar. He stampeded around, screeching and chasing his flaming tail.

With a triumphant cry, Peter rolled over onto his paws and unfurled his wings. Commander Storm barked out: "To the Fortress!" And Peter leaped into the air, pumping his wings for all he was worth toward the southern mountain pass.

"Rook! What are you doing?" Threads of panic snaked their way into Wuya's voice. "Stop playing and secure the messenger."

Rook squalled and kept trying to pounce on his own tail. Changing tack, Wuya screamed, "Flee, my daughters!" Recently unearthed, the girls and their mounts scrambled from the clearing and crashed through the dark forest.

Shoulders squared, Commander Storm placed his hands on the pommels of his scimitars. "The wyldling you seek is not with us, and reinforcements shall join us presently. Release the dwelfnhad and withdraw. You have gambled and lost."

Wuya bowed her head. And then, she chuckled. "Oh, capturing the wyldling was only part of my contract, Storm. I have one more card to play. While we've been chewing the fat, my special forces surrounded the clearing." Taking a deep breath, the mercenary hollered: "Muertaka! Take them!"

Everyone froze, but then nothing happened.

A new voice, a woman's contralto, echoed around the clearing. "Is that so, Captain Wuya of the Battlecrows?"

Mounds of earth and stone rumbled into the clearing from every direction. Warriors stuck chest-deep in dirt struggled, gnashed their teeth, and shouted curses. Dwelfnim in rust-colored armor accompanied the prisoners with one hand thrust into their pile of dirt.

A statuesque woman emerged from the southern edge, riding a platform of basalt. "If you mean these special forces," the newcomer said, extending her arms to encompass the trapped soldiers, "then I am afraid they have been otherwise engaged."

Tall figures clad in red armor rose from the ground on either side of the mercenary captain. Wuya snarled. Lowering her ax, she thrust Dinah out into the clearing, then stepped sideways into the shadows before the dwelfnim could grab her.

"She's getting away!" Thomas yelled. The Battlecrows were after Annabelle, and he needed to know why.

Dinah stumbled, and the Commander lunged forward to catch her. "She has *already* escaped, Sir Thomas," the evainghir said. "Ware your tongue; doubtless the crow has spies listening."

If there were spies, then he could catch one and find out who Wuya was working for. "We have to find out where Wuya got her orders from!" Spluttering, Thomas moved toward the spot where the mercenary had disappeared.

Anger burned deep inside him, gathering into flame—

"Young man," came a woman's deep alto. "You are far too hasty and hot-headed for your own good."

A cold, massive hand seized Thomas. His concentration shattered. Sound fled to a dull hum in his ears. Darkness fell like a cool, velvet curtain and a scent like warm flint filled his nostrils.

Everything seems so far away ...

His eyes snapped open, then squinted as a bright light bloomed. Before him stood Commander Storm and an equally statuesque figure swathed in a crimson robe—the woman who'd rode the basalt slab into the glade like a cavalry charge. Their rescuer bore a more delicately featured version of Commander Storm's reptilian visage. Tight, black curls framed an oddly beautiful, brown-scaled face. Was this the elderly caretaker lady?

The two seemingly engaged in an argument. Both gesticulated and their mouths moved, but he couldn't hear what they said.

Thomas swallowed, and his eardrums popped.

"... took your dad-rotted time, Tanisha," Commander Storm growled. "You could not help but know we were coming."

Thomas blinked. *She* what *now?* He wriggled, but nothing budged. It was like someone had shoved him inside a boulder up to his neck. Shifting his eyes, he realized this was the case.

Criminy. I can't even move my head.

"Of course I knew, Daniel," the tall, reptile-lady replied dryly. "Evanrudhe sent me tidings of your impending visit a fortnight ago. Since then, I've been trying to locate the *talented* child you lost to the wilderness." Commander Storm sneered.

Sighing, the woman rubbed her temples. "I have not yet done so. Always, there are interruptions. Strange energy signatures in the earth-matrix. Nehmwights where there shouldn't be. But here I am. Captain Wuya scattered cadres of soldiers between here and the pass, or I would have arrived earlier." She arched a black eyebrow. "Surely, you would not expect me to leave enemies along your planned route?"

Commander Storm tensed and narrowed his eyes. "Be that as it may—"

Standing akimbo, the red-robed woman tsked, then spoke over him. "As usual, Daniel, you deflect from the real problem you face." Still glaring at the Commander, her tone sharpened as she pointed to Thomas. "How could you allow this untrained lad free reign with his *talent?* Even after what happened to Remiel, I expect better of you."

Commander Storm ... flinched.

What the heck? Thomas cleared his throat. "Excuse me, Sir? Um. Ma'am?" Two pairs of eyes—one steely gray and the other reddish-brown and hard as agates—turned to bore into him. "What ..." He licked his lips. They tasted like ash. "Uh. What's happening? Are you the Caretaker ... ma'am?"

Somber, the reptilian woman replied, "Aye. Greetings, Sir Thomas. I am Tanisha Delwyr, Caretaker of Y'Vasheirdenelle. As for current events, your messenger is safe. I sent him on to the fortress. Wuya and her Dagger-tongue Guard escaped, as far as I can ascertain. My Stonesingers are harrying all her surviving forces from the valley as we speak."

Does that mean she'll let me out of this rock?

He opened his mouth to ask, but the Commander raised a hand. "Rest assured, lad. The captured Battlecrows shall be interrogated." His face hardened as he looked past Thomas. "They will yield up any information regarding their employer."

Thomas slumped. That's right. Now he remembered. In his frustration at Wuya's escape, it had slipped his mind. The Stonesingers had caught some of her reinforcements.

A wan smile curved the Caretaker's thin lips and warmth entered her agate eyes. "I believe the youngling should be released. After all, he is not my prisoner."

Hey, I'm right here, lady. Aloud, he said, "Yes, Ma'am. Not that I'm complaining. It's a very nice boulder—comfortable, cozy, just right for taking a good, long nap—but I'm pretty wide awake right now and ... and my right foot itches." He cleared his throat. "Please. If you don't mind. Could you let me out, Ma'am?"

Approaching him, the Caretaker grinned. "What a delightful surprise. This one was raised properly, Daniel. Doubtless before you got your claws into him." Commander Storm's jaw clenched. She chuckled as she laid a hand on the rock near Thomas's left shoulder. Though smaller than the Commander's, the Caretaker had strong hands with a sword-wielder's calluses.

"Aye, Thomas, because you asked so politely, unlike *some* young men I know ..." Her eyes flashed red and the stone surrounding him disappeared. Thomas staggered into her, but she braced him up without budging. Or a grunt of effort. Thomas marveled. This reptile-woman—evainghad? —was solid. She was a warrior, like the Commander.

While Dinah conversed with the Caretaker, their heads close together like conspirators, Thomas and David rounded up their mounts. It felt good to have something to do.

He patted Tinker. "Glad you made it, Roast Venison." Nonplussed, the stag snorted and trod heavily on his left foot.

Biting back a curse, Thomas clambered into the saddle. One of these days ... He'd be happy to return Tinker to his true master.

The Stonesingers created shackles from stone for the twelve prisoners. Most of the dwelfnim then formed ranks around the Battlecrows and escorted them from the clearing. A few Stonesingers remained behind with the Caretaker to light their way with lumen crystals.

The remainder of the night passed in a blur as they left the forest and descended rugged terrain toward a ravine. When Klotho rose over the mountains behind them, Thomas gaped as her pale light touched massive towers, pointed spires, and arches like stone lace. Y'Vasheirdenelle formed a rocky island in the middle of a deep ravine, a broad eversteel bridge connecting it to the mainland. The Commander and the Caretaker resumed their bickering—this time concerning the best way for a sourethol to train a wyldling.

Sighing, Thomas exchanged a commiserating glance with David. He wondered anew what, exactly, had happened to create a rift between Commander Storm and the Eldest. Who started it? Probably he'd never know. He just hoped their family squabble wouldn't compromise the mission to rescue Enoch.

Masquerade

Nothing would compromise the barrier he'd created. William folded his wings and settled back on his haunches. He surveyed the work with pride. The castle he'd discovered provided the perfect setting for a collaborative exercise in conjuring warded shields. Even though his scales should provide protection enough, he'd warded this patch of the dreamscape against the knight with the golden aura and his blazing sword.

He congratulated himself for his cleverness. Water was the natural enemy of fire.

"Wow," said the maiden standing akimbo beside him, "the dome over the castle turned out great. It's solid, and I like the way the sapphire and violet weave together."

William grinned. "I do, too." Glancing down at her, he chuffed a laugh. Yes, yes. He'd had a little help from Milady Blue, and along with supplying the water for the spell, she excelled at delicate, detailed work. But she hadn't known where to begin. She'd woven her contribution to the fabric of the ward according to *his* direction and *his* calculations. Ward-weaving was ideal for testing how various aspects of Aethyr worked together. He'd taught Annabelle Arkhadic methods because it was the most efficient way to increase her strength, even though she griped about it hurting.

"Don't mind that," he'd told her. *"The pain goes away in time."*

It wouldn't—pain never did—but she'd get used to it. Annabelle would thank him later, when she was the most powerful wyldling on Tehara, and William was Varazslo in truth. William grinned. Oh, the things they could accomplish together!

But why would she thank you? Once she's strong enough, you're going to siphon off her ability which could kill her.

He raked his claws through the plush rug beneath him. There was no use worrying about that now. He *would* find a way to extract her wyld without killing her. Maybe, once she grew stronger, if he did it in trickles, gradually—

He squinted. Why was her kythim showing tiny ochre spirals of fear? No, wait, those meant she was confused.

Gazing at the ward, Annabelle frowned and tilted her head. "That's odd. Where did those little orange knots come from?" She giggled. *—They kinda look like Cheetos—*

"Orange?" William scowled and his tail lashed, its spikes shredding the velvet curtains behind them. "Well, er ... That's an inherent part of the dreamscape itself. As you gain proficiency, you start seeing all sorts of colors. Well done!" Quick! He needed a distraction. He shook a scrap of rug from his talons and nudged her hard enough to make her stumble.

"Hey! What was that for?" She scowled at him. Her sapphire aura did all sorts of interesting things with bright green that vanished almost instantly, rust-red wavy lines, and threads of lavender that had been growing in his presence. He *really* wanted to know what lavender meant.

"Oops. Sorry. Don't know my own strength sometimes. I was only playing." With a sheepish grin, William offered her a claw. In her aura, the rust died away and the lavender became more prominent again, joined by indigo ripples. A smile twitched at her lips as she grabbed a finger wide as three of her own. She was so blistering *small* for something that confused him on such a grand scale.

That reminded him. Their time was limited. She still owed him an answer to a question. Last night, she'd asked him what he thought 'leading people to glory' meant. A ridiculous question. Why lead other people to glory when you could claim it all for yourself? It felt like a trap, so he'd told her to ask a different question. But aside from that, he enjoyed their little talks. Conversations with Annabelle were ... enlightening.

William hauled her to her feet, shook off her grip, then rose. "Our ward should keep away anything nasty while you answer my question. But first, let's go check out the kitchen in this place."

Maybe there'll be a barrel of whiskey in there.

"Are you hungry?" She eyed him warily. "I don't ever feel hungry in the dreamscape ... I remember being thirsty, though."

"Nah, I ... I just want to see if there's a kadorei-style kitchen in this castle." William had an idea she wouldn't approve of him swilling whiskey.

"Ooh!" She clapped her hands. "Maybe I can bake you a cake. Even if it isn't real, it still would be fun. I'm good at baking and I bake for all my friends. But maybe dragons don't like cake? Raeden says he'd eat anything I made ..."

While she chattered about her spotted harkhurz champion—he'd heard all about Lord Raeden von Bleistaff and how 'awesome' he was—William gritted his teeth and padded across the grand hall, feet sinking into the thick carpet and snagging on his claws—who put such useless rubbish in a castle?

Inwardly he cursed himself for not being more cautious with the ward-weaving. When had the orange crept in? He could've sworn he hadn't touched the Arkhabadh. Annabelle noticed when he did and clutched her stomach like she wanted to vomit. She hadn't seemed ill this time, despite her kythim and unguarded thoughts revealing everything about her. Was the sneaky little tessaramint hiding some reactions from him while allowing him to read others? He'd observe her more closely.

Whenever she used her wyld, chills went through William straight to the marrow, but he'd grown accustomed to the sensation. It wasn't unpleasant—not at all, which surprised him— more of a fresh feeling like passing under a waterfall, the scent of citrus, or the taste of mint.

In the corridor, blessedly free of carpets and curtains, he shook the last of the rug scraps from his claws. Snickering, Annabelle pulled bits of burgundy velvet from his spikes. "You're like a porcupine dragon. This must be a pain in a dense forest. Did you ever wish you could change your shape, so you weren't so—I don't know—pointy?"

William stiffened, scarcely daring to breathe, panic scrabbling through him like a horde of rats. Varkrav's hairy ears! Did she suspect? Was she fishing, trying to catch him out? Quick, quick; think. What should he say? He had a contingency plan for this. Why couldn't he remember it? He gnashed his teeth. Argh!

Annabelle's eyes widened and she backed away, hands held out in a warding gesture. Pink jagged lines and orange spiraled through her kythim. "Oh, no! Did I offend you? I'm sorry, Varazslo. Um. Forget what I said." Her face went ashen.

—oh my god is he going to kill me—

Merciful Valeshka, she'll blast me with her wyld!

William reared up and scooted backward until his spikes grated against the stone. His scales should protect him from any of her attacks; he knew her capabilities. "Annabelle, wait! No, you didn't offend me. You startled me." He held up his hands. "I won't hurt you. Uh ... we're friends, remember?"

Staring at him, Annabelle took a shaky breath. Her kythim calmed down. "Yeah. I don't know what sore spot I hit but ..."

She bit her lip and looked down. "You're a handsome dragon, and I like you just the way you are."

William slowly lowered himself to all fours. "Handsome? Me?" He coughed out a laugh. *She ... likes me.* Behind his breastbone, a strange, warm tickle he only felt around her made it difficult to breathe. *No! Stop it. It's her spell again.*

She smiled, a dimple forming in her left cheek. "Sure. And your swirly markings are pretty." She spun a finger around to make a circle.

He squinted. Was she trying to cast another spell? She must be daft—or trying to lull him into a false security with flattery.

"Sort of like a mackerel tabby cat—only they *move* sometimes. Did you realize that?"

William grimaced. He scraped his claws along the stone floor. "Yes, of course they move. It's, uh, a dreamscape thing."

"Really? 'It's a dreamscape thing.' That's all you've got?" Annabelle's eyebrows rose. *—he falls back on that as a reason for everything—*

Quick! Change the subject! William blurted, "And I'm not like you. *You're* pretty. There's nothing pretty about me. And that's just the way I like it."

Annabelle's eyes went wider than before, and she covered her mouth. Her kythim flashed bright green, returned to blue, and then the lavender streaks lengthened.

—he thinks I'm pretty—

Void freeze it! He'd said that aloud. Even worse, he'd meant it and if anything, he'd understated. That must have been the spell she'd cast—to dig up his secrets. He stared at Annabelle. Now she was blushing, which made her even prettier. That warm tickle in his chest would drive him mad.

Just act like nothing happened. And if she asks—deny it!

—I embarrassed him. He's so weird. I never thought a dragon would behave just like a teenage boy—

He needed to find whiskey—and fast.

William shook his head to clear it. "You're wasting precious time, Milady Blue. I'm taking us directly there. Now, don't have a conniption ... I'm going to grab you." Opening his wings, he swept them around her and pulled her in close. "Hold on."

Annabelle gasped, but didn't struggle this time. She put her arms around his neck and went still. "Ready," she squeaked. "Are we teleporting?"

"Er, yes." William took a deep breath. She smelled nice, like spring rain and citrus, with a hint of cinnamon. The scent was richer and more nuanced to his dragon form. "Give me a moment." *To relish this.* He ground his teeth. "To concentrate! And you should hold on tighter, just in case." Murmuring agreement, she obeyed. A tremor went through his wings.

Liar. You fabricated an excuse for her to hug you!

William picked her up and stepped through the wall as if it was mist. Gray streaked around them, and then he stood in an expansive room with ovens set into stone walls, two fireplaces, a pantry, and a large wooden table. He set Annabelle on the table and backed off. His chest scales still tingled, and the fluttery feeling wouldn't go away. It seemed worse than before.

That's what you get for touching her!

Ignoring her inquiries whether something was wrong, he bolted straight for the pantry, which turned out to be the size of the kitchen. Inside, he found shelves of canned victuals, sacks of grain, a rack of huckleberry wine, stacked barrels of ale, and casks of ... brandy?

It would have to do. He bashed in the lid of one cask, hoisted it aloft like a large mug, and gulped down ruby-brown liquid. For a moment nothing existed save the pleasant, burning sensation of liquor traveling down his long throat. Once he finished, he belched. It was so loud it rattled the pantry shelves. He froze, then peals of mirth drew him to the pantry door.

"Excuse you!" Annabelle clutched her belly and laughed. "Totally rude, but that burp was epic. I guess you were thirsty."

"Very," he rasped, tossing the empty cask aside. It was an excellent brandy. "Er. Excuse me." She found loud belching amusing? That surprised him.

"What was that?" She wrinkled her nose. "It smells like—"

"Brandy."

"Oh." *Now* she looked disapproving. Rust-red joined the lavender in her aura.

—I hope Varazslo isn't an alcoholic like my uncle—

"I need it to settle my nerves." Why was he admitting that to her? And what was an alcoholic? Probably something bad, from her reaction. "Uh. It's a dragon thing."

Rolling her eyes, Annabelle snorted a laugh. "Sure. Whatever you say."

William sat down in front of her. He carefully wrapped his tail around where he could keep an eye on it. That appendage was a menace. "Now. We have a deal. Tonight, I taught you the basics of making a shield. Now it's your turn to share. I want to know where you're from."

Annabelle perched on the edge of the table, swinging her legs. She regarded him with strangely knowing, yet guileless eyes. "You're not used to being touched, are you, Varazslo?"

William lifted his chin. Good. Thanks to the brandy, he was back in control again. "No, Milady Blue, I'm not. And that's an extra answer you owe me. Because it's your turn to share."

"Okay." She smiled. "But tomorrow, we're talking about you. And I want to hear more about how Enoch's doing, too."

Northward ... William still hadn't figured out what happened during their fight, when the wyldling snare formed the brief connection between them. Whatever it was, Northward seemed less hostile than before. Pity tinged his glances and thoughts.

I'll show him *who's to be pitied!*

"More about Northward." He grimaced. "I suppose that's fair. Now, Milady Blue. Tell me about your home." He settled back on his haunches and waited for her to begin.

From Northward's unguarded thoughts, William gleaned that Annabelle was from somewhere extremely far away. Some mysterious realm called Wisconsin. As she spoke about school, church, her friends, and her family, he forced himself to pay attention to her words and not just her kythim. Eventually, she'd get to the important things—like how one advanced in the arcane arts and whether an Arkhadahn such as himself could become an overlord in her world.

Tomorrow, he'd ask a more specific question. For starters: what sort of magic did her people use? Were any of the people also dragons? Annabelle seemed fascinated with the creatures. It would be nice to become a dragon in the waking world instead of simply masquerading as one in the dreamscape. More and more, the dragon felt like his truest self.

Down By the Bay

Seated on an atoll rising from the crystal blue waters of Limani Bay, Annabelle and Rhiannon waited for Mordred and an escort of guardsmen to arrive. They munched on sliced watermelon; beneath the odd-looking blue rind the flesh of the fruit was a dark pink, just like watermelons she'd eaten back home in Wisconsin, and they tasted much the same.

Even Raeden found no fault with them as a breakfast addition. That morning, she'd told him about the last family reunion on her mother's side, when she and her five teenage cousins were scolded for an impromptu watermelon seed spitting contest that Annabelle had won. She was astonished when her champion laughed. It warmed her heart.

She looked forward to seeing Raeden at Lachesis-set, when she'd bring his evening meal. He still refused to eat anything his captors gave him and the fishing pond she'd created was proving difficult to maintain.

Annabelle touched the area over her heart. The Oathbond was quiet. She wondered what Raeden was doing right now. Probably watching the sea birds and wishing he could fly away from his prison islet.

White-feathered gulls and other winged animals darted and swooped over waves shimmering in the sunslight. She shaded her eyes and squinted. Were those gray creatures bats? No.

Their necks were too long, like cranes or herons, but with their long supple tails they resembled miniature dragons rather than birds.

Dragons. Heart racing, Annabelle's thoughts strayed from her champion to her dreams. There was someone else she looked forward to seeing. She still hadn't told Raeden about meeting Varazslo in the dreamscape, or the information he'd shared about Enoch. Until they had access to a waystone, she thought it best to keep quiet about it. Her champion would only worry if he knew about her nocturnal adventures.

After all, I'm being cautious. Nothing bad has happened. Varazslo seems harmless enough, as dragons go, and interesting to talk with. He puts up a front of omnipotence, but I think he's just lonely and needs a friend. Thinking about the dragon made her smile. *And here I believed I was socially awkward! There's actually somebody worse off than me.*

After Annabelle's morning visit with Raeden, the princepsa had offered to take her on a tour of the most beautiful sights of Ynys Lloches. She'd agreed, if only to keep from fretting about Raeden's situation. There wasn't much she could do for him—not when Morgan Brenin deftly turned aside any requests regarding the waystone or arguments she made to set Raeden free.

Her latest attempt to sway the monarch yesterday afternoon had met with failure.

"You must first fulfill the prophecy, Ahdmerel," Morgan Brenin had said, stern upon his throne. *He fingered his torc as he looked down on her. "That was the arrangement. Once my people have their glory, I will grant you access to the waystone."*

"But, Your Majesty," she'd protested, *"I need a clearer definition of what kind of glory you're expecting. If I'm supposed to 'lead' you, then that means leaving Ynys Lloches."*

Surprisingly, Rhiannon had supported Annabelle. "Surely," the princepsa had argued, "this prophecy is a sign that we must join the wider world. Trade with other nations. Sawel and I have long discussed the possibility—"

"Nonsense," Morgan Brenin replied with a dismissive wave. "What can other nations offer us but trouble? We are a peaceful race, and the outside world is rife with turmoil, war, and bloodshed. Our people are safest dwelling here in the sanctuary Rainblessed prepared for us."

From standing close beside her, Mordred approached the throne with his hands spread. "Father, how can we find glory here in Ynys Lloches?" he'd asked. "Glory is meaningless if no one beyond the gwerindawr know about it. I, for one, would like to visit other realms of Tehara."

The king's face had clouded with disapproval as he surveyed his son. "What I have decreed, I have decreed." Mordred flinched.

Rhiannon persisted. "Brenin... Father, with respect, please reconsider—"

Morgan Brenin cut her off. "When you sit upon this throne, Rhiannon, then you may dictate foreign relations. Until then, my word is law."

Reflecting on the trap she'd fallen into, Annabelle sighed.

Rhiannon touched her arm and startled her from her introspection. "No need to be glum, Lady Ann. My brother should arrive soon."

"It's not that," Annabelle replied. Heat rose into her cheeks. What did Mordred have to do with anything? She fidgeted with the watermelon rind. "I'm just confused. You see, my dwelfnhad friend, Dinah, visited some time ago in her capacity as an ambassador. Did you meet her? She's a Stonesinger and probably wore red robes."

The princepsa beamed. "Oh, Lady Ann! I do indeed remember meeting your friend. She was lovely and we had a nice chat about our present treaty. But what confused you?"

Annabelle fussed with the hem of the gossamer tunic Rhiannon had given her. She must choose her words carefully. "Well, Dinah told me the gwerindawr were a friendly and hospitable people. But the king seems dead set against communication with the rest of Tehara. What would you do if it were up to you?"

"I have all sorts of ideas ..." While they waited for the men, Rhiannon described her plans to open trade between Ynys Lloches and the outside world, with the dwelfnim gradually stepping aside in their role as intermediaries. "But it will have to wait until the torc of the Brenin passes to me," the princepsa concluded, stroking the abalone shells woven in the netlike necklace spread over her decolletage. Her expression sobered. "More of my people might have survived the pestilence if Grandfather had allowed the dwelfnim to visit more often and had been more accepting of Landbound medicine."

"Landbound?"

"That's what we call people who can't grow the galamerdhe." Rhiannon extended her swimming tail, lifting it from the water. The indigo and purple scales sparkled like gems in the sunlight. They felt like fingernails. Rhiannon had insisted Annabelle touch them when she noticed her staring the previous night.

Such pretty scales ...

Annabelle shook herself. "Um. Wait. You said there was a pestilence. Like, a plague?"

"Yes." Rhiannon let her tail flop back into the water. "Three Cycles ago, a fever swept over us like the tide, and when it receded several moons later, it had carried off a fifth of our people." Her voice grew small. "Sawel's parents, my grandfather, and my mother among them."

"I'm sorry for your loss." Annabelle swallowed. "That must've been so hard. How ... How old were you? And Mordred?" She imagined the princeps as a little boy, crying for his mother, and her eyes began to burn in sympathy.

Rhiannon gave her a gentle smile. "Thank you. It was a difficult time, but Dred and I weathered that storm and are the stronger for it. Sawel was there for us, too, as his archimandrite duties allowed. He'd come of age a season before the pestilence. I was thirteen winters when Mother went home to Yshua. Dred was only four, so I cared for him until he began his training as a guardsman at eleven winters." She placed a hand over the necklace and her eyes grew dreamy. "Shortly after that, Sawel offered me this betrothal net. He'd woven it himself, you know, once he had Father's blessing."

Annabelle was relieved that the conversation had shifted to a more positive subject. "Was it difficult to get his blessing?"

Rhiannon laughed. "Hadrien's tears! No. Father seized the opportunity to merge the archimandrite's family with the royal line. Our parents had been pushing us together since I was able to swim. We were best friends before we knew anything about our future obligations. Sawel was always so kind and forbearing. Handsome, too." She chuckled, a wicked glint in her eyes. "He had no chance, really. I'd cast my net for him even before my galamerdhe formed." Seeing Annabelle's blank look, she added, "It's the first harbinger of a child's transition to adulthood. One's galamerdhe grows in for the first time between the tenth and thirteenth summer. Mine grew in a moon before my tenth Nameday. Generally, it happens a little earlier for girls."

Like puberty. Annabelle smiled, thinking: *If I ever marry, I hope my husband is also my best friend. We'll be sharing everything. I don't see how the relationship would work, otherwise.*

"That's wonderful," she blurted to silence the thoughts of Sir Thomas her musings stirred. "That you and Sawel were good friends before you married. Are you planning to have any children? As soon as the words were out of her mouth, she knew it was the wrong thing to say, because Rhiannon's cheerful expression vanished. She recalled the room they'd given her for her bedchamber—an empty nursery with bright mosaic tiles creating colorful tableaux on the wall.

"I'm sorry!"

"No harm done, dear." The princepsa lowered her gaze to where her flukes churned the water. "We've been trying for Turnings, but ever since the pestilence, birth rates have been low all over the archipelago."

Fussing with her necklace, she raised her head and stared off toward the horizon, her face hard. "This is why I want to open treaty negotiations with the Landbound races. Certain commodities, like these shells and our coral bead tapestries, could be bartered for medical knowledge."

Annabelle grasped at a chance to cover up her faux pas. "Trading pretty shells for medicine is a great idea. Have you discussed it with the king?"

Rhiannon laughed. "Oh, I've tried! I explained *all* my ideas to Father. About how our people risk stagnating without the consistent flow of ideas and goods from other cultures ..."

Not to mention, Annabelle mused, *the risk of birth defects that come with inbreeding.*

With an exasperated groan, the princepsa raised her tail and slapped her flukes against the water. "But he won't listen, because he believes interacting with the Landbound will lead to our destruction. The funny thing is, he was much more open to the idea of trade with other races back when mother was alive. I distinctly recall him challenging Grandfather once when he issued a decree that our children must not be educated about the outside world. Fortunately, Father won that argument. But this was an indication that Grandfather's health had begun to decline. So, the torc passed to my father."

Annabelle stared down into the water. Near her submerged feet, Wesleyen and several other octopi crept out of the coral they'd hidden in and began playing a sort of chasing game. One of them—a large, older female called Delfie—was Rhiannon's companion.

Too bad Rhiannon isn't the Queen. I think she might've let Raeden and me go, if it was up to her. How long will she have to wait until the torc passes to her?

"Is there a certain age when a ruler has to abdicate? When did your father become Brenin?"

Rhiannon sighed. "There's no set age for a Brenin stepping down. It depends on their physical health and soundness of mind. Father is still in his prime. He donned the torc over four Cycles ago. And things were fine for five Turnings. But then the pestilence came. Although Father survived, he wasn't the same afterward. Mother's loss affected him keenly. He never laughs anymore. All joy has washed away from him. He's steadily grown more isolationist—just like my grandfather was as Brenin."

She bent and combed her fingers through the water. Delfie rose and wound tentacles around her wrist. Rhiannon lifted her and the octopus crawled up to her shoulder. "The past few Turnings, I've even heard him mutter about banning the dwelfnim from visiting us every autumn, but Sawel and I managed to convince him that would be a ruinous decision. Yshua be praised for that." She turned to Annabelle with a wry smile and patted her leg. "Once you've fulfilled the prophecy, perhaps Father will relent and allow the people access to the waystone."

Annabelle bit her lower lip and squirmed in her seat of ancient coral. "But what if I can't? Some of the tasks I think I've already completed before I even came here. Sawel agrees with me. But I still don't know how to bring glory to the gwerindawr without leaving this place."

And until she accomplished that, Morgan Brenin, reigning monarch of Ynys Lloches, wouldn't allow her or Raeden to leave. A circular argument.

"Don't fret, dear." Rhiannon put an arm around her shoulders and kissed her forehead. "I have faith that the Threefold One will show you the way. Sawel is helping you, and nobody knows the prophecy better." After giving her a squeeze, the princepsa let go and turned to murmur an affectionate nothing at Delphie.

"I've discussed this with your husband already, but what do *you* think constitutes glory for your people, Rhiannon?"

The princepsa paused, her expression pensive as she stroked the octopus between its eyes. "Prosperity for everyone. Great enterprises such as our ancestors undertook, but now lay at the bottom of the sea. The ability to learn new things from other people to improve our lot, so that we in turn may be a force for good in the wider world."

"Those are all good things and would bring glory to your people. I know you'll be a great queen." And yet, Rhiannon's answer didn't seem quite right.

Shrugging one shoulder, the princepsa laughed. "I will certainly do my best, as the Almighty gives me strength."

Annabelle watched Wesleyen capture a fish with wicked jaws—she thought it might be a young barracuda—and wrestle it into submission. She shuddered at the thought of those sharp teeth ripping into her little friend's expressive skin. Or her own.

"The prophecy also mentioned a curse, but Sawel said we should focus on the glory first." She frowned. "He didn't seem to want to talk about the curse at all."

Rhiannon took a deep breath. "That's because he doesn't have the authority to discuss such matters with others. But I do." She touched Annabelle's knee. "My father would not want me to tell you this, Ann; he forbids his advisors to share this information with anyone. But I have seen the records. There is something wrong in Ynys Lloches. The ocean yields less of its bounty as time goes on. The coral reef sickens and dies in the outer reaches and the blight creeps slowly inward. It's like something is sucking all the nutrients from them. On the furthest islands the freshwater springs have grown brackish. Cycle by cycle, our population ages and there are fewer children born." Her voice roughened. "I fear our race is doomed to extinction in a matter of generations if we don't seek out fresher water."

Is this the curse I'm supposed to break—the reign of a harsh king? But how? I won't hurt him. He's Rhiannon's and Mordred's father. But maybe the curse involves all these health and ecological issues. She preferred the second option.

Annabelle met the princepsa's golden gaze and took her hand. "If it's within my power, Rhiannon, I will figure out what curse is on your people, and I will break it."

"Thank you." For a moment, the princepsa looked as if she was about to cry, but then she shook her head and made an exasperated sound. "I wonder what's taking Dred so long. I'd have thought he'd be eager to join us." She raised her eyebrows. "Bide here a moment; I'll see what's delaying our princeps." With a flip of her tail, the princepsa dove into the water.

Annabelle stared after her, mulling over what she'd learned. If Rhiannon couldn't persuade her father to open their borders for the future of their people, then what could Annabelle possibly say to convince him to show her the waystone?

Raeden said none of the "water sprites" could be trusted. Despite her champion's suspicions, Annabelle was inclined to trust the princepsa, who seemed remarkably down-to-earth—or down-to-water, in this case—for someone born into royalty. She had to admit that Rhiannon was trying her best to be an excellent hostess.

And I like her. Mordred's lucky to have her for a big sister. She's a good person who cares about her people. She'll be a great queen someday. Too bad she's not the queen now.

Scanning the horizon, Annabelle's gaze settled on a forbidding dark lump. One of the outer islands? From what she could tell, it rose from the sea like a dark fortress. Something about it called to her, even as it repulsed her. Maybe Rhiannon and Mordred would take her to see it if she asked.

Rhiannon's head broke the surface a few feet away. She pushed a sodden lock of purple hair from her face. "Dred will be around with our escort in three flicks of a lightning bream's tail; there was a disturbance off the southern shore ... nothing to be worried about," she added with a bright smile. "The sponge harvest is going poorly this Turning, and several gatherers got into a bit of a kerfuffle over property lines."

"Oh," Annabelle remarked, uncertain what to say. "I hope it turns out all right, and no one got hurt."

I wonder if the bad harvest is a symptom of the "something wrong" in Ynys Lloches. The curse I'm supposed to break. But I don't want to upset Rhiannon by bringing that up again.

Floundering for a new topic, she turned her attention back to the distant island. "Rhiannon, what's that place?" She pointed. "Does anybody live there?"

Grimacing, Rhiannon heaved herself up on the atoll. "Nobody lives on that dark isle. We call it the Reckoning Point, where the Brenin sits in final judgment on the most violent criminals. Thankfully, it's been over a generation since anyone was murdered. We work hard to ensure any grievances are addressed before they devolve into violence."

Annabelle made a face. Had the king originally planned to send Raeden there? "So, this Reckoning Point is like a maximum security prison?"

"Guards are assigned to patrol its waters. I suppose it could serve as a prison, although the smaller islets work just as well." Rhiannon shrugged, her eyes on Delfie as she crawled out of the water and into the princepsa's lap. "Solitary confinement and being landbound for a moon or three is enough to convince lawbreakers to swim within charted waters. Father says he'll teach me and Dred about matters concerning the Reckoning Point as a final lesson before he steps down and I become Queen."

Shuddering, she rubbed her arms. "Those found guilty of murder are executed at Reckoning Point ... flung into the Depths and fed to the Abyss, where even a gwerindawr can drown. However, that last may be hearsay meant to frighten people."

"Gwerindawr can drown? But you have gills!" Yesterday Annabelle watched in fascination while the gills on Rhiannon's neck worked underwater. The opercula on either side lifted to reveal delicate gills the same hue as watermelon flesh.

"Perhaps their gills are sealed off before they're thrown in. You know about these here," Rhiannon tilted her head and indicated the edge of a scaled flap on the side of her neck. "But we also have gills on our galamerdhe." She raised her tail again to indicate opercula on the outside of both her knee joints.

Annabelle gaped, then shook her head. "However they're executed, that's horrible." She sent up a silent prayer of thanks that Raeden hadn't killed Mordred, or any of his guardsmen. Still curious about the dark island, she asked, "Rhia, have you ever been there?"

"I've never set foot on the island, but Father took me and Dred on a swim around the isle, to show us the entrances. It's difficult to get into and even more difficult to leave. Not that anyone would want to go there. Even from a distance, it exudes an unpleasant aura."

Rhiannon cuddled Delfie and the octopus draped her tentacles over the princepsa's shoulders. "I pray every day that when I become queen, I shall never need to sit in judgment on anyone or preside over an execution."

Experiencing a chill of foreboding, Annabelle averted her gaze from the Reckoning Point. It would be just her luck—that the waystone was there, on an island where no one wished to go.

Tiger, Tiger, Burning Bright

Resisting an urge to kick the darn thing, Thomas glared at the quiescent waygate that connected Y'Vasheirdenelle to the waystone at Ynys Lloches. When he spoke, his voice echoed. "What do you mean this thing is locked on their end, and it won't open for another moon?" He resisted a different, more pervasive and primal urge to whip around and run across the domed chamber to the waygate opposite. That was for later. Much later, if he had his way.

Once Commander Storm informed the Caretaker which waystone Annabelle and her champion had fallen through, that she held Daar-Lûsin, and her status as a water wyldling, the caretaker homed in on Ynys Lloches, the secluded archipelago of the gwerindawr. Within an hour, she'd confirmed the presence of a young female water wyldling on the main isle of the Ynys Lloches archipelago far off the continent's west coast. It took a little longer to pinpoint the kaenhir's location, but it appeared that he'd survived as well. Thomas felt relieved. And here he was, in the Nexus Chamber of Y'Vasheirdenelle, which served as the only direct route to the islands of the merfolk.

Now all that remained was to go get her. Unfortunately, that was easier said than done.

"There's gotta be a way to get through. A special command." He pressed both hands toward the polished surface of the sapphire glass set into the curved wall. Energy hummed and crackled, then a force repelled him before he made direct contact. With a growl of frustration, he switched to pushing the arch of dark gray stone surrounding the blue crystal. "C'mon, Dinah. Tell me. I need to get the kiddo away from neurotic fish-people. Abracadabra. Hocus pocus. Alakazam. Open, says me!"

Dinah sighed and rubbed her temples. While they stayed at the Fortress of the Living Stones, she'd exchanged her armor for a Stonesinger's rust-red and burgundy robes. "I'm afraid it doesn't work like that, Sir Thomas. The waygate arches won't open outside their normal schedule unless you have the vashenta keyed specifically to it. The Caretaker has a vashenta keyed to ten—including Y'Pohlzardenelle—but Ynys Lloches isn't one of them. The gwerindawr royal family has held all four in their keeping for over an Epoch. They allow only two dwelfnic ambassadors to visit every Harvest Moon, when the waygate opens for the span of three days."

Well, that sucks. Dinah had already told him about the merfolk, who seemed a bit of contradictory conundrum wrapped in an enigma. Welcoming to the dwelfnim, yet reclusive and secretive. Anyone they took off the isle with the waystone, they blindfolded until they reached the main island where the royal family lived. Dinah maintained that the gwerindawr would treat Annabelle hospitably because of her affinity to water. And despite their prejudice against the wensallen-kaen, they'd probably not harm His Excellentness out of respect for Annabelle. Thomas wasn't so sure.

I need to get the kiddo and her dog-man away from those fish-tailed jokers.

Straightening, Thomas ran his hands along the soot-gray stone of the wall on one side of the jewel-like gate, tracing the glyphs carved into the arch lintels. A few of them—like the twinned reversed fish-like symbols—looked familiar. "Isn't there some ... I don't know ... mystic universal key like the kiddo's moon dagger you can use to unlock it?"

"Daar-Lûsin is the only one such," Dinah snapped. Staring at the glyphs on the opposite lintel, she crossed her arms and lifted her chin. "Otherwise, the Eldest would've mentioned it as an option."

Thomas eyed her sidelong. The dwelfnhad sounded crabby. Was it something he'd said? She'd seemed fine up until a minute ago. When Dinah offered to show him the nexus while the Caretaker searched for Enoch and David helped Commander Storm interrogate the Battlecrows, Thomas had leaped at the chance. Part of him hoped beyond hope that he, as a wyldling, could do *something* to make the waygate to Ynys Lloches open. But the thing pushed him away. He glanced around the chamber, as if its features could provide a solution.

A hemispherical chamber at the heart of the Fortress of Living Stones, the nexus lay under a dome that somehow showed a clear, night sky full of stars no matter the time of day. An eerie glow emanating from the pale marble floor and walls provided enough light to see without dimming the starlight above. The Nexus Chamber was accessed through entrances at the base of a twelve-sided pillar that connected the floor to the starry ceiling. Set at intervals above the openings three wide metal rings etched with arcane symbols rotated at different rates. What appeared to be a giant broad-sword blade protruded from each ring like the hands of a clock. When the three sword-blade pointers overlapped—he'd been told—a chime would ring out and the waygate the pointers indicated would activate. Aside from their voices and the scuff of their footsteps, the place was silent.

A lop-sided grin tugged his mouth. "Heh. The kiddo would love this place."

"Yes, she would," Dinah replied with a wan smile, her gaze dropping to her bare feet. She hugged herself and rubbed her arms.

"Look, Ambassador." Thomas sighed. "I'm sorry if I said anything to upset you. Thanks for bringing me here."

"You are very welcome. Nothing you said upset me, Sir Thomas—only my own musings. Despite what I said about the gwerindawr being peaceful ..." She bit her lip. "I've been mulling over my past visits to Ynys Lloches. Thinking back, Morgan Brenin's increasingly isolationist attitude was ... concerning. I'm worried for Ann and Lord Raeden. Which brings me to the reason I brought you here." She straightened and turned to face him.

There was real danger to the kiddo after all—and she's only now telling me?

"Oh, so you admit you had ulterior motives?" Thomas strove for nonchalance while fire raged inside him, demanding to be unleashed. There was no point in yelling at Dinah for something she had no control over. He raised his eyebrows. "So now the truth comes out. No, wait!" He held up a hand when she opened her mouth. "Let me try and guess. You lured me here to bury me in stone because I made one too many rock puns this morning at breakfast."

Frowning, Dinah shook her head. Thomas forced a grin, nearly breathless from suppressing the anger boiling inside him. *It's not Dinah's fault ... don't take it out on her ...* He took a deep breath to calm himself, then snapped his fingers. "No, hold on ... I got it. You want me to go through the gate to Balthazar's Crucible." He jerked a thumb over his shoulder, toward the golden portal on the far side of the chamber, directly opposite the waygate to Ynys Lloches. His grin went crooked. "I can feel it pulling at me, by the way."

Like I feel the Ynys Lloches waygate pushing me away.

Dinah flinched. "No, Sir Thomas. I didn't bring you here to force that decision upon you. I ..." Her topaz-colored eyes grew round, pleading, as she held out her hands. "I thought it might be easier for you to find Ann in the dreamscape in the Nexus Chamber. Look!" She reached inside her robes and extracted a small, slim bundle. She smiled. "Praise Yshua! The Eldest had wyldhar'to'randhallienshah—" she grimaced. "Sorry, I lapsed into dwelfnic. I mean, she had wyldling dream-walker incense in storage. Breathing the fragrance should help your mind relax into a trance state so you can enter the dreamscape."

Thomas blinked. Great. Now he felt terrible. "Uh ... wow. Sure. I'd be glad to try."

Dinah offered him the bundle. "If you found Ann, I was hoping you'd pass along a warning to be careful around Morgan Brenin. He's grown paranoid. I fear what he would ask of her as a water wyldling, and she should be wary of making promises of service to any gwerindawr. Hopefully Lord Raeden is able to counsel her."

Thomas nodded. "Will do." At Dinah's direction, he removed his jacket and lay down in front of the sapphire waygate. He rolled up his jacket and tucked it under his head, then stared up at the star-crazed dome, naming constellations like he and the kiddo had done one night. There was Gideon's Sword, Ziggorath the Kraken, Omar's Battle Diadem, the Pearl-Net of Jedediah ...

Annabelle had traced out the shape of a frog among the stars. *"And your good friend, Jeremiah Bullfrog,"* she'd said, giggling, then sang a silly song she'd called "Joy to the World." It had been irritatingly familiar, like a word on the tip of his tongue.

Yes, there it was—Jeremiah the Bullfrog. Now he couldn't unsee it.

His throat thickened and his hands clenched into fists. The very next night, the waystone took her away.

I will *find you, kiddo. And I'll bring you back, if it kills me.*

Dinah knelt beside him, setting up small cones of incense the size of his thumbs around his head. She held out a length of straw, and he stared at it a moment before realizing she meant for him to light it. He chuckled wryly and concentrated. Golden sparks flared. Faint wisps of smoke drifted up from the merrily glowing tip. Dinah touched it to the incense. The scent of lavender, balsam, and something else he couldn't define wreathed his face. Stars danced overhead.

Thomas's eyelids drooped. He concentrated on the blue, spring rain and citrus essence of Annabelle, and then ...

... he stood clad in the gold-chased soot-gray armor the dwelfnim called sourekghar, left hand gripping the hilt of his fiery blade. Around him, the landscape shifted from arid scrubland to a rugged, stony terrain the likes of which he'd never seen.

The ground varied in color from drab browns, mottled with olive green to blue grays with streaks of black. Slender green stalks with translucent leaves thrust up from the ground in bunches but shattered like glass when Thomas kicked them. There were trees, of a sort, their black trunks shiny smooth in places but ridged in others with leaves that sparkled like cut emeralds or gleamed like polished jade. When he touched one, a sharp ridge of "bark" sliced the tip of a finger.

"Criminy!" Staring at the beads of blood welling up, Thomas raised his eyebrows and grunted. "Obsidian," he muttered. "What is this place—somebody's rock collection?" He sucked on his wound, then, after assuring himself there was no immediate danger, he sheathed his sword and dug out a handkerchief to staunch the bleeding.

He scanned his surroundings. More obsidian trees, glass plants, and huge boulders of various shapes seemingly grown from the ground. Silhouetted against the horizon, towering spires pointed toward the sky, gleaming like jagged, crystal knives in the light. He frowned at a blue sky devoid of suns and clouds. Why weren't the suns ever in the dreamscape? Sometimes clouds hid the perfect blue of the sky, and once or twice when it happened to be night, he'd glimpsed the moon, but never the suns. Shadows were also absent.

Thomas shook his head. If it wasn't a threat, then it wasn't important right now. He needed to find Annabelle. There was no other reason to linger in the dreamscape.

I'd better shake a leg. Get moving before I wake up. Or something jumps out at me.

Keeping an eye on the trees, Thomas gave them a wide berth as he jogged along between patches of the strange, glassy vegetation. Although everything seemed wide-open, there was a heavy stillness to the air. No birds called and no insects sang.

Friggin' eerie. Like the place was waiting for him to move on. To leave.

Thomas shivered. It wasn't as if he *wanted* to stay in this madhouse. He hadn't asked to be brought to a rockhound's dreamworld. Maybe his presence in the stronghold of Ebenezzar Earthshaker had something to do with it. He didn't care. All that mattered was finding the kiddo.

Without any trace of blue to fix on, Thomas ran toward the distant spires. Was it a city? He'd come across towns and villages in the dreamscape, but they were always empty. The land grew rugged and large, red crystals—rubies? —jutted from the brown, stony earth. Suddenly, a series of giant rubies burst from the ground right in front of him, cutting him off. When he moved to either side, more rubies sprang up like massive quills to create a fence.

"What gives?" he cried. "I'm just passing through." He rapped a gauntlet against the ruby pillar. Tink, tink. "Open up."

Nothing happened.

Thomas clenched his jaw, "Fine," he snarled through his teeth. "Prepare to be sliced."

Sinking into the riding stance, Thomas gripped the sword hilt with both hands and sliced sideways, golden flames streaming in contrails. Just as it had with the Dagger-tongues, his blade rebounded. His sword vanished. The armor encasing his arms shivered, flexing and contracting, as a shriek rang out, sounding like metal scraping against metal.

"What in blazes—" Thomas cursed and clapped his hands over his ears out of reflex even though his helmet already protected them. His suit of armor had absorbed all shock of impact and recoil. Backing away from the ruby fence, he pivoted, searching for the source of the cry, which still echoed all around even as the sound faded.

My sword!

Heart racing, Thomas checked the scabbard. Empty. Panic flooded through him. Why hadn't the sword reappeared? It always reappeared. Maybe he needed to *will* it into existence, this time. He concentrated with his entire being, calling to his weapon. Nothing. He panted. Every sense and nerve fired as he monitored the vicinity and waited for something to happen.

"Calm down," he hissed. "You're a friggin' knight. A trained warrior. You aren't defenseless."

As he scanned his surroundings, Thomas did a quick breathing exercise. *Good air in ... Bad air out ... You can fight hand-to-hand as well as with a sword, and you have armor ... Good air in ... Bad air out.*

Nothing changed. The ruby quills stood rigid, and the ruby pillars remained still. Nothing emerged to assault Thomas. With his final exhalation, the worst of the tension flowed from his body. But not all. Irritation still pulsed through him, igniting his wyld—he shook his head. No ... No. Shouldn't waste it. He glared at the ruby fence. A crooked smile twitched his lips. Let's test how strong this armor is. With a shout, he charged the red stone fence.

Thomas was thankful for his helmet. For a moment, he blinked up at the blue sky, then performed a kip-up. "Note to self," he said, patting at his armor, "rock-world doesn't like me." He barked a laugh. So, now he knew. This place defended itself. At least his armor hadn't disappeared like his sword. "Guess I'm not going to Spire City."

Shrugging, he turned back the way he'd come. Off in the distance, he glimpsed the snow-covered peaks of mountains. Maybe he'd find a trace of Annabelle, or information regarding Enoch's whereabouts in that direction. "And while I'm wishing," he muttered, skirting a large cluster of boulders, "I'd like a double bacon cheeseburger with extra pickles and a pile of salty French fries."

With a confused frown, he eyed the holes at the base of the boulders lining his path. What had made them? Ground squirrels that could burrow through solid stone? He hadn't seen any animals here. And where had that wish come from? Cheeseburger? French fries? He could picture the sandwich, and fried potato sticks in his head, clear as day, but he'd never seen food like that anywhere—

Shimmering with heat, orange salamanders as long as his feet emerged from the holes and swarmed the path, cutting him off. Thomas groaned and staggered to a halt. "Oh, for the love of all that's holy! Not again." He swung around, but the fiery creatures blocked him at every turn, bobbing up and down and squeak-squelching. If memory served, this was a prelude to attack. His hand flew to his hip, but the sword still hadn't returned.

And the last time, my flame-wall didn't deter the little critters for long. They ate it up, and would've eaten me, too, if Balthazar hadn't rescued me.

Oh, how that chafed! Thomas spun, monitoring as many salamanders as possible, his mind scrambling for a plan. Before his eyes, several of the creatures swelled to the size of his leg. What the heck? So far, the salamanders seemed content to remain in place if he didn't move.

He took a deep breath and addressed the largest of the salamanders. "Hey, Burnie. Balthazar said you guys represent my—" he grimaced— "feelings. Is that why you got bigger?"

The critter he'd dubbed Burnie tilted his head and chirruped an interrogative note. Around him, the other salamanders started squeaking and bobbing faster.

Thomas huffed out a laugh, and raised his hands, preparing for battle. He had no choice but to use his wyld and brute-force his way through the beasts and hope they didn't immolate him. The firewall hadn't worked before, but maybe ... The salamanders had eaten his defense, his fire ... Thomas narrowed his eyes. Could he summon another fiery entity to eat *them*? He reached down into his reservoir and grinned. Yes, he could.

He focused on the white-gold eyes of the largest salamander. "Hey. I'd like to introduce you to a friend of mine." Digging down deep, he tapped into boiling magma. Golden light suffused his vision as heat filled him. Burnie whistled, and all the salamanders rushed toward him. "Burnie!" Thomas yelled, bringing forth his defender. "Meet Tony!"

Made of gold lava and emitting a corona of flames, a tiger twice the size of Thomas burst into existence. The brown-striped beast roared. A shockwave bowled over the nearest salamanders and pushed them all back several paces. Burnie slid back, hissing, its claws leaving charred furrows in the rock.

Thomas sagged, drained and cold, managing to stay on his feet despite his shaking legs. "Hope you're hungry," he gasped, looking into the beast's white-flame eyes. "Go, get'em tiger."

Muscles bunched under golden fur, and the flametiger sprang into the mob, scattering the salamanders. He leaped upon Burnie and tore it to shreds, gulping down the salamander in three mouthfuls, then went after the rest. An opening formed. Thomas grunted a laugh; he didn't have the energy to do more. "Thanks, Tony."

Gotta get moving while the path is clear. Behind him, Tony roared, and salamanders squealed like eggs hitting a hot frying pan. As the salamander's cries diminished, the tiger's roars faded into satisfied growls and gulping noises. Eyes fixed on the mountain peaks, Thomas staggered, then jogged ahead as fast as he could on his trembling legs. It was such an effort to move now. He shouldn't have expended so much of his wyld reservoir on the flametiger. Oh well, lesson learned. Next time, he wouldn't invest so much energy.

But I must reach those spires while Tony deals with the salamanders. Once he's done, I'll send him back into the reservoir, and I'll have my energy back. Easy as pie.

Thomas cast a glance over his shoulder to check the creature's progress. Shock sizzled through him, radiating from his core to his extremities. Framed by the sapphire sky, his golden flametiger stood alone, the size of an elephant with a corona to rival that of Lachesis. Shading his eyes, Thomas turned to face him fully, laughing weakly. "Whoa! You're friggin' huge, Tony. I hope you're full, 'cause it's time to go back home to your nice, cozy, fiery bed."

White-hot eyes regarded Thomas, still burning with hunger. Tony licked his chops. Growling, the beast prowled toward him.

Thomas felt like the ground had given way beneath him. He should know better. As long as fuel remained to burn, fire was never satisfied. Maybe it was time to wake up ... No! Tony was his creation. He stiffened his spine.

Commander Storm wouldn't back down, and neither would Sir Rick. I'm Helzarvenn, the Caster of Flames. I need to master this Aspect before it masters me.

Thomas raised his hands with palms outward and mustered authority into his voice. "Tony! Stop. Right. There."

Tony hesitated. He shook his head, then narrowed his eyes at Thomas. Growling, the flametiger crouched, and smoke rose as the ground charred under his belly.

"Bad Tony," he snapped. "It's time to go home." His arms started shaking. He lamented the loss of his sword. "Stop playing around." Squinting against the glare, he forced iron command into his voice while speaking softly. "Go. Home."

I really could use a big stick.

Muscles bunched. The corona blazed pure gold.

Eyes wide, Thomas backpedaled. *Oh, crap, he's gonna—*

Stone rose in a wave and rolled over the flametiger just as it was about to leap. Tony shrieked and steam hissed everywhere, obscuring trees, boulders, and the heavens. Thomas stumbled back while shielding his face with his arms. The odor of scorched earth and burned stone made him cough and his eyes water. As the flametiger smothered, strength returned to Thomas in a steady trickle and his trembling subsided. He alternated between panting and coughing, grappling with a sense of loss and lingering shame.

Once again, he'd needed to be rescued from his own fire.

Thomas shook himself. No time for self-pity. Who or what had killed Tony? Were there Stonesingers here? Based on what he knew of David and Dinah's proficiency, it would take more than their strength combined to overcome his giant flametiger.

"Hellooo!" A male voice penetrated the smoke and steam. "Did I get it? You alright, sir?"

I know that voice from somewhere ... It made him think of picnics by a lake, and a single yellow sun shining overhead.

Earth? Blinking away tears and trying not to cough, Thomas oriented on the sound and pivoted on his heel. "I'm just dandy," he grated out. "Still in fighting trim in case you got any ideas. Who goes there?"

The fog dissipated, and a figure in rust-red and ruby armor emerged, waving its arms and coughing. Shock lanced through Thomas.

That armor ... What in blazes ... Another friggin' wyldling!

Thomas experienced another frisson as a young man of about Enoch's and Annabelle's age met his gaze. The newcomer stopped dead and stood staring at Thomas with his mouth hanging open and his green eyes bugging out of his pale face.

I know him.

Like a sword of jagged glass and flame, memory sliced into Thomas, burning him, consuming his senses. He stumbled backward.

A man silhouetted against reddish-orange fire licking the ceiling of a cabin, screaming: "Tom! Lily!"

"No!" He blinked, trying to clear his vision, but the burning building was all he could see. And then, it morphed into Balthazar's reptilian features.

Eyes brimming with sorrow, the Sage said, "Confront your inner demons, Helzarvenn."

No. I can't face this. There's no time. I have to find the kids!

Thomas clutched his head and screamed. Everything flickered. Golden mist swirled. An icy hook in his gut yanked ...

He opened his eyes to stars above and the visage of his commanding officer.

"Sir," he croaked. "I tried to find Annabelle ... but I failed."

Commander Storm frowned. "Tonight will bring another opportunity to try again."

Thomas accepted a hand up. As they left the Nexus Chamber, he reported on all he recalled from the dreamscape.

Fool in the Rain

When Annabelle arrived by coracle at her champion's prison islet, he stood tall at the foot of the pier, hands clasped behind his back, waiting for her. Relief washed over her. "Raeden!" She hopped out of Mordred's coracle, rushed down the pier, and embraced him, burying her face in his chest. Guilt gnawed at her heart for all she'd been keeping secret.

Should she report what she'd discovered about Enoch in the dreamscape?

"Good morrow, Freylin." As his arms encircled her, she breathed in his warm, peppery cardamom scent and relaxed. He'd grown more willing to accept her hugs lately, but he never initiated them and usually broke them off right away. This time, he held on for more than seven heartbeats and the Oathbond conveyed his own relief and contentment.

No. I can't tell him yet. He'll demand to know where this information came from. And I can't lie. If Raeden freaked out, maybe hurt one of the guards, then the king would have an excuse to execute him. Maybe once they had access to the waystone and could actually travel to Ingaraik ...

Yes, it would be better to tell Raeden everything then.

Raeden was always uneasy about her going to the dreamscape—where he couldn't follow—and talking to a Sage everyone believed dead. He'd be even more upset about her making deals with a dragon. But she could handle Varazslo. She'd never before met anyone who hung on her every word like he did. The poor dragon seemed starved for affection.

Her cheeks warmed. *Varazslo said I was pretty. Even Raeden hasn't told me that ...*

Giving her champion one last squeeze, she pulled away to look him over. "Good morning. How are you feeling?" Although she felt his ribs under his wrinkled tunic, his green eyes shone brighter than yesterday, and he'd made an effort to groom himself. A good sign.

Raeden bowed slightly. "Your servant is well, Freylin. He thanks you for asking. There is the scent of rain in the air, but he has built himself a shelter." He peered into her face. "How do you fare? The water sprites, do they still treat you well?"

"Yeah." She adjusted her glasses, which had gone askew when she hugged him. "They're really nice, and they threw a celebration last night to thank me for improving the filtration around the sponge bed. The next harvest should be better. Tomorrow I'm going to check out the coral reef to see what's causing it to waste away." She grimaced. "I just hope the gwerindawr don't expect too much of me."

And that the king sees I'm trying to break whatever curse is on his people ... by mending the things Rhiannon says have gone wrong over the past few years ... Cycle.

Raeden shook his head. "Freylin, your servant believes you do too much already. Yesterday, it was the sponges. The day before, you used your wyld to check all the children's health, and then the women. And even before that, you made the fishpond for your servant. You could scarce keep the eyes open in the evening—"

The pier creaked. Ears pinned, Raeden stiffened, a growl rumbling deep in his chest as he glared past her. Annabelle turned. Mordred stepped out of his coracle and started toward them carrying the basket Annabelle had left in the boat. The princeps hesitated midway and met the kaenhir glare for glare. At least his hands were occupied so he couldn't draw his knives.

Stiffly, Mordred said, "Lady Ann?"

"Oh, I'm sorry." Annabelle laughed, feeling sheepish. "I forgot our breakfast." She patted Raeden's arm, then went to collect the basket. Her champion muttered something in his native tongue she didn't catch.

"Thank you," she told the youth. "There's no need to hang around; I'll be waiting right here for you in two hours."

Please, just go, Mordred. Annabelle hugged the basket to her chest and backed away. On the way over, she'd begged Mordred not to mention his desire to court her. Although she kept putting him off, she hadn't told her champion about her deal with Mordred, and the longer the princeps lingered, the more she feared what he might reveal. And Raeden's reaction. Would he attack Mordred? She'd hoped setting the task of finding Daar-Lûsin would get him out of her hair during her visits with her champion. Thus far, Mordred and his Howling Tempest hadn't had any luck in finding the dagger. She both hoped for—and dreaded—his success.

The princeps shook his head, the glower clearing from his face, and smiled. "As I have no pressing obligations this morning, I shall stay." His smile grew hard as his attention returned to Raeden. "I understand your champion accounts himself a proficient archer and always hits his target."

Annabelle winced. She shouldn't have told Mordred about Raeden's bow last night at the fete. But the princeps extolled his own skill at hitting targets, and after a few mugs of cider, she'd felt obligated to knock him down a few pegs.

Why did I drink an entire pitcher of cider? Rhiannon warned me it was mildly fermented, but it was so delicious and made me relax after a day spent using my wyld. Maybe too much, in the case of my tongue.

She recalled telling the gwerindawr about her adventures in the dreamscape searching for Enoch; how much she missed Khinjara and wanted Daar-Lûsin back. Then she started blubbering, and Rhiannon carried her to bed. She remembered Mordred shouting after them that he would find her dagger if it was the last thing he ever did.

Unsheathing a dagger, the princeps made it dance across his knuckles, spun it around his fingers, and then put it away. "Perhaps he would like to pit his skill with the bow against mine with throwing knives."

So we can have a repeat of what happened on the beach? Heck, no! She inhaled sharply. "Mordred, I don't think that's a good—"

"He would, water sprite," Raeden snapped. He lifted his chin. "The bow he has made is inferior, but he can hit any target from here to the far end of this rock. For you, he would grant a concession. Twenty paces is a comparable distance for the throwing of knives."

Mordred's eyes gleamed. "Is that a challenge, sniffer of trees? I've hit targets at greater than thirty paces."

Annabelle stood between them, chewing on her bottom lip. "But, guys, what about—"

"Very well, stripling," Raeden said, his glare intensifying. "Thirty paces for you and your knives. The length of the island for this one and his bow."

Mordred snorted. "You need not shoot at such a great distance with an inferior bow. Reduce it to half of that, and we have an agreement. He who strikes true most often wins."

Raeden's eyes flashed and his lip curled away from his fangs. "This one needs no concession. No matter the distance, he will hit his target. What are your terms, water sprite?"

"Breakfast!" Annabelle raised the basket over her head, into the path of their locked gazes.

The two men looked at her as if startled she was still standing there. Raeden's ears drooped. "Freylin. Your servant has been dragged away. He makes apologies for his rudeness." He held out a hand, and she walked back to his side. "His honor was at stake," he murmured, taking the basket from her.

"I also apologize," the princeps hastened to add, the wooden pier creaking as he sauntered over to join them. "Lady Ann, we'll put off the challenge until after you've broken your fast."

"And had the devotion," Raeden added, and Mordred bowed. The kaenhir pulled out a prayer book from his vest. The cover was warped, and the pages all wrinkled from its dip in the ocean, but at least the ink hadn't run. His silver watch had also suffered from being submerged. Extracting the water had been a test of Annabelle's water weaving skills. *That* particular use of her ability pleased her champion.

Raeden glanced at her pleadingly. *Oh, he's still waiting for me to forgive him.* In a dry tone, she said, "I suppose, you're both forgiven—as long as you don't hurt one another in this silly contest."

"Silly?" Both of them spoke simultaneously, and Annabelle couldn't help but laugh. Suddenly, she had an idea.

Here's one way to make peace.

"And I'll set the terms," she added, crossing her arms. "If Raeden wins, then Mordred has to stop goading him. If Mordred wins, then Raeden will use his title when addressing him." She raised her eyebrows and shook a finger at them. "You have to promise: no more name-calling."

Mordred beamed. "Of course, Lady Ann! And you shall be the final arbiter."

Annabelle smiled. This was even better. While honest, Mordred was both reckless and arrogant. *I bet he believes he'll win, even without seeing Raeden's bow and arrows.*

Raeden led her to his newly assembled shelter, built from palm leaves and bamboo poles. Mordred followed. Setting down the basket on a flat stone he used as a table, Raeden eyed the princeps askance. His whiskers twitched; something had amused him. "Freylin, your servant agrees to the terms, and that you, in all your Cycles of wisdom, should be the judge."

Brow wrinkled, she regarded her champion. It was easy to forget the difference in their life experience, but now she wondered at her presumption in scolding a man more than twice her age. "Uh ... I'm glad that's settled, then."

Raeden nodded, his visage unreadable, and hunkered beside her at his makeshift table. "Take care, Freylin," he said. "A fool often stands in the rain, hoping to grow flowers."

She frowned, mulling over his words as she laid out a handkerchief for a tablecloth and arranged the food items. Wensallen-kaen proverbs didn't translate well into the trading language, and Raeden's grasp of idioms was ... tenuous, at best.

"Are you warning me not to interfere in this challenge, or what?"

He tilted his head. "Is that what he said? No. He warns you not to hope for too much, too quickly. The folken and the water sprites have a great divide between, for many generations."

He knows me too well. Annabelle hunched her shoulders.

Opening the prayer book, Raeden began reading Psalm sixty-nine. "Those who hate me without cause outnumber the hairs of my head; many are those who would destroy me—my enemies for no reason. Though I did not steal, I must repay. You know my folly, O God, and my guilt is not hidden from You ..."

Inwardly grimacing at the Psalm he chose for their devotion, Annabelle set a raw fish filet wrapped in a broad leaf in front of her champion. *And now I feel guilty for keeping things from him, and all the pain he's enduring.* But telling him about the dreamscape would only make him worry; he couldn't act on anything while they were stuck here.

And I'm afraid he'll tell me I can't go to the dreamscape.

If the princeps was offended by Raeden's choice, he gave nothing away as he listened.

While she ate her seaweed wraps—and Raeden picked at his share after eating the plain fish—Mordred walked Crescent Islet and chose targets. By Annabelle's reckoning, the prison islet was about the size of a city block in area but shaped like its name. The pier jutted out from the inner curve into a natural harbor and faced the main island. Mordred diligently measured out the paces to his target, a bulbous-trunked bromeliad, then cleared a path to a tree in the center of the thickest part of the island. He sliced away the bark to reveal the pale inner wood.

Overhead, the clouds gathered, and a fresh wind began to blow in across the sea. Raeden scented the air. "The rain comes sooner than your servant thought." He abandoned his meal and ducked inside his shelter to fetch his bow, made from a yew sapling, and arrows that were little more than long wooden darts fletched with seagull feathers. She'd watched him whittle and fletch them yesterday, taking mental notes on how it was done.

Mordred indicated that Raeden should go first. His expression grew smug when Raeden nocked an arrow to his rough-looking bow. That smugness disappeared after Raeden shot ten arrows, one right after the other, and Annabelle didn't need her glasses to know that each hit the target. Her champion hadn't missed any of his targets the previous day, or while they traveled together. Biting her lip to suppress laughter, Annabelle hurried over to the tree and verified that every bolt had struck true. Three had even split the shafts of previous arrows.

Annabelle extracted the intact arrows and then jogged back to where Mordred was checking the draw on his throwing knives. "Raeden's arrows hit the mark. It's your turn."

To his credit, the princeps seemed willing to take her at her word, or maybe his eyesight was keener than hers by a great margin. His smile oozed confidence. "Your champion is fast, I admit it. However, allow me to show you why they call me 'Quickhands,' Lady Ann." He rolled back his shoulders, cracked his neck, and eyed his own target - a white handkerchief stuck to the bromeliad's prickly trunk. Taking a deep breath, he exploded into motion, drawing his daggers two at a time and flipping them at the cloth in rapid succession until his bandolier of sheaths was empty. Bits of white shone through the forest of knives that sprouted from the trunk.

Annabelle blinked. "Wow. You weren't kidding about being fast. Your arms were a blur."

Mordred straightened, his smugness returned. "And each knife struck its intended target."

She nodded, then chuckled. "That they did. Well, it looks like you both won the contest. Or lost, depending on how you look at it."

"Two out of three?" Mordred suggested to the kaenhir with a gleam in his eye. "There must be a clear winner."

Raeden lifted his chin. "This one defers to the arbiter's final ruling. Freylin?"

"I say you both won, and that's that." Annabelle crossed her arms. "Which means you both have to be civil to one another going forward. No more provocation or name-calling."

Mordred puffed out his chest. "I will abide by your ruling, Lady Ann, and swear to keep a civil tongue around your champion and not provoke him to anger."

She turned to Raeden, who squinted at Mordred as if he suspected him of a trick. "Raeden?" she prompted.

Her champion shook himself, then bowed with his fist to chest. "Your servant promises also to be civil to the gwerindawr, so long as they do not threaten you."

"Good." Annabelle nodded. "And I must say, I'd like to learn how to throw knives like that—not that I'd ever be as fast as you," she added to Mordred, who preened.

"You won't need to learn any of that," Mordred replied. "I would use my exceptional skills to protect you, Lady Ann."

Annabelle laughed. "What do you mean? There's no danger on Ynys Lloches I'd need your protection from." At least, Rhiannon insisted there wasn't.

"Why, Lady Ann," he replied, widening his eyes and placing a hand over his heart, "surely you realize that I mean to accompany you wherever you go. In time, you will return to the wider world. You will need a stalwart defender."

Raeden bristled. "Freylin already has a champion ... Your Highness." The title seemed torn from him. He came to stand beside her. "She needs no other."

Annabelle nodded. *As much as I like Mordred and enjoy his company—in small doses—I must agree with Raeden on this.*

"Thank you, Mordred," she raised her voice just as he was opening his mouth. "I'm grateful for the offer, but I don't think that'll work out. Besides, Raeden is my champion."

The princeps gaped at her. "But do you not yearn for someone in your own cohort to converse with and be your confidant? Forgive me, but your champion is ..." he hesitated, as if choosing his words carefully, "rather older than you."

Crossing his arms, the kaenhir snorted. "This one is not in his dotage yet."

Heat rose into Annabelle's cheeks. "I'm fine with my champion as a conversation partner. I don't care if he's old enough to be my dad." The Oathbond tightened. "He's my friend—regardless of his age."

Eventually, I'll confide in Raeden about the dreamscape. Just not now.

Mordred stiffened. "We shall see," he said, then spun on his heel and strode toward the abused bromeliad.

While Mordred retrieved his knives, Raeden laid a hand on her shoulder. "Young men like that are fickle," he said softly. "They chase after all the butterflies and only listen to their own howling into the wind. Your servant will hear anything you have to say, Freylin." His fingers squeezed briefly, and a thread of expectant hope wormed through the Oathbond. "Anything at all. And he will not howl."

Annabelle frowned. *Mordred may be a bit arrogant, but I think it's too soon to call him fickle. And what's all that about howling? One of these days, I need to learn Raeden's language.*

Before she could ask Raeden to clarify, he brought out another, smaller bow and a handful of arrows. "Your servant knows how much you like to learn, so he has made you a bow of your own." His black nostrils twitched, and he peered at the overcast sky. "The rain holds back. There is time for you to practice. Your servant will instruct you, if you please."

Warmth filled her as she accepted the gift. "Thank you! Archery was always my favorite part of gym class." Her champion raised his eyebrows, and she laughed. "I guess gym class is what you'd call the Earth equivalent of battle training."

Raeden's ears lifted and he nodded with approval. "Try the bow. Your servant will observe what you can do. A little maiden should know how to shoot a bow, to hunt, and to defend herself from enemies before they come near."

"Well, I'm pretty sure that last isn't what our teachers had in mind." Annabelle tested the bow's draw. Her arm shook with the effort, but she managed to pull the string back to the anchor points Raeden suggested: cheekbone, cuspid, chin. She grinned at her champion. "Hey! That's just right. Nice work. I'll aim for Mordred's target." *Once he moved out of the way.*

The princeps sauntered over beside her, tucking the last of his knives into their sheaths as she nocked an arrow. He stared. "Lady Ann, what is this? Battle training?" He made a dismissive sound and waved his hand. "There is no need for you to fight while you have me around. And your champion," he added without missing a beat when Raeden scowled. "Perhaps the scout hounds are uncouth enough to require their women to fight, but we gwerindawr believe fair damsels shouldn't be burdened with the arts of war."

Lowering the bow, Annabelle quirked an eyebrow. *Really? He has to keep poking the wolf!*

"Good thing I'm not a fair damsel, then," she hurriedly replied, before Raeden could take umbrage. "I'm an *unfair* damsel. Right, Raeden?" Her champion tilted his head, looking perplexed. Mordred gaped, and she giggled at their expressions. Centering herself, she raised the bow. "And who says I'm fighting anyone? I happen to like archery for its own sake. Now please be quiet. It's been awhile since I last did this, and I need to focus."

Her arm trembled and the arrow's point jittered as she drew. She waited for a comment from Mordred, but he stood silent with his arms crossed, his handsome face pensive. Raeden knelt in front of his shelter, watching her. *Nothing from the peanut gallery, then.*

A cool breeze fanned her left side. Annabelle focused on the handkerchief, ripped and tattered from Mordred's knives, and recalled the mantra for using her wyld. Calm. The arrow's shaking slowed. Concentrate. The target became her entire world. There. That little flap hanging down in the middle. Commit. She loosed the string and let the arrow fly.

Caught by the wind, the arrow flew right past the bromeliad and disappeared into the greenery beyond.

"Cheese and crackers!" She let her arms fall. "Can I have another arrow?"

"Perhaps this is not the best time," Mordred began, but then his eyes widened. "Ah! It's raining." Spreading out his arms, he tilted back his head and sighed.

"Oh!" Cool droplets splattered in Annabelle's hair, and she chuckled. *Now I suppose I really am a fool in the rain.*

Suddenly Raeden stood beside her, holding a broad leaf over her head. "The lessons can continue tomorrow, Freylin." He squinted at Mordred and murmured, "Without the water sprite. He has odd notions of what females should and should not do. Your servant will gladly train you to throw knives, if that is what you wish."

Mordred straightened and ran his hands back through his damp hair. His head was high, and a confident smile adorned his face. "Lady Ann, I fear I must deprive your champion of your delightful company. But do not fret; you shall see him again at Lachesis-set."

Annabelle hugged Raeden, hating the way the Oathbond thrummed with sorrow. He held the leaf over her head as they walked along the pier and while Mordred helped her into the coracle. His eyes gleamed with an inner smile as he handed the makeshift umbrella to her. She took it, not having the heart to remind him she was a water wyldling and enjoyed the rain.

Annabelle turned so she faced her champion. "See you later," she said. "There's no need to stand there getting drenched."

Sodden with the steady downpour, Raeden stood at the end of the pier and raised a hand in farewell. She was tempted to try using her wyld to keep him from getting any wetter. But the stubborn kaenhir wouldn't like that.

Mordred sang a sea shanty in the gwerindawr tongue as he rowed quickly for the main island, his baritone voice perfect in pitch and beautiful to the ears. For once Annabelle didn't care to know the words. She watched as her champion grew smaller, until the sheeting rain hid him from view then dropped the leaf and let the rain soak into her. Why hadn't Raeden gone to his shelter? He hated getting wet. The Oathbond remained silent with distance.

An exclamation roused her from her contemplation. Mordred's song cut off. Wiping away rain, she peered at the approaching pier, where several of Mordred's men waited. An ochre-skinned man—Lladdhe—held something aloft while shouting.

Annabelle's heart caught in her throat at the familiar shape.

Rekindled Hope

Like the kid in the rust and ruby red armor he'd seen yesterday in the dreamscape, the place was achingly familiar.

Thomas stood in a glade. A bluish mist drifted along the ground, more vibrant than he'd ever seen. Hopefully that meant she was close. Trees vaulted overhead, and before him loomed a dark gray wall three times his height that somehow seemed more *there* than anything else.

Thomas's hand went to his hip. His fingers made contact with metal, and he glanced down. Relief flooded through him. *My sword's back!* A small noise made him turn, and he nearly swallowed his tongue.

Annabelle stood in the clearing, clad in dark blue armor and framed by lilac bushes swirling with that faintly glowing blue mist. Her blue eyes widened. Here in the dreamscape, her long hair hung loose and gleamed more golden than the blonde he recalled from the waking world. She stood frozen in place, seeming .... wrong, somehow. Delicate and small. And then he realized that he was used to looking up at her—not down.

Things have certainly changed. Pulse racing, he gripped his sword. It grounded him.

Hesitant, she whispered, "Sir Thomas?"

A tightness he hadn't been aware of in his chest loosened. *Finally! After two nights spent scouring the dreamscape—I've found her!*

"Kiddo," he said, striding toward her, then stopped when she leaned back on her heels. "About friggin' time I found you. I've been trying to find you in this freak-show of a place every night since you and his Excellentness vanished." Her mouth moved and his lips twitched into a ghost of a smile. "And before you ask, everyone's fine—even your stupid deer. Now, tell me where you are, and I swear by all that's holy, I'll move heaven and earth to get to you."

Inwardly, he groaned. *Criminy! Where'd* that *come from? Commander Storm would pummel any knight he heard spewing out such ... poetic tripe.*

"Oh!" Her eyes softened and a bright smile spread across her face like dawn breaking. "I'm glad you're okay. So. Were my eyes deceiving me, or are you back to your human form now? Is this what you really look like?"

He raised his eyebrows and rapped his right fist against his chest. "Just as you see, kiddo."

"That's awesome!" She bounced a little in place and Thomas pursed his lips to keep from laughing. A comfortable warmth filled him as she chattered. "I'm so happy for you. This is great ... what you always wanted, wasn't it? I've missed you—" she bit her lip, about to lunge at him, but then held back— "all of you. Do you miss me? Where are you guys? Did you make it to Y'Vasheirdenelle?" Her expression grew serious. "Have you had any trouble with nehmwights?"

Anger smoldered deep within at the thought of nehmwights getting their hands on her. He buried it, like the flametiger had been buried. He assumed a soldier's blank expression. "Like I said, everything's been fine with me. David's praying for your safe return. Dinah told me to tell you that she misses you a lot.

I, uh ..." He rubbed the back of his neck, resisting an urge to squirm. "We all do. Even the Commander, though he'd never admit it."

She didn't need to know about the attacks. It would only worry her. And talking about it would only stir up his rage.

Balthazar may have a point. I need to do something about my anger.

"Right now, we're at the Castle with All the Rocks." He offered her a wan smile, hoping to hear her laugh. "How about you?"

Covering her mouth, Annabelle snickered. Her eyes sparkled. "It's called 'the Fortress of Living Stones,' you dork."

Yes! Ever the know-it-all. I even miss that. He chuckled. "Tuh-may-toe, tuh-mah-toe. Now, your turn. The Caretaker says you and His Excellentness wound up on some islands I can't pronounce the name of. The place where the mermaids live." He edged closer and held her eyes. "Can you confirm that? More importantly, are you safe?"

Nodding, she toyed with her hair. "Um. Yeah. Raeden and I are okay. We're on an island called Ynys Lloches. That's ee-nus-loke," she said, stretching out the syllables. "With the gwerindawr. There's no nehmwights."

There better not be. Suppressing a burst of anger, Thomas recalled the message he was supposed to pass along. "Excellent. Now, this is probably behind the times, but Dinah asked me to warn you about the king of, er, Ynys Loches. She says he was acting weird the last time she visited. Paranoid. Are he and the ... islanders... treating you well?" No use in attempting the name; he'd only mangle it.

"Me? Yes." She moistened her lips and rubbed her arms. "The gwerindawr like me quite a bit. And yeah, I noticed King Morgan seems paranoid of the outside world. I was talking about it with his daughter ... Um." Her blush deepened and she spoke in a rush. "They have this prophecy the king wants me to fulfill and he imprisoned Raeden for attacking someone and I'm afraid he'll kill him unless I break a curse and lead them to glory ..." she took a shuddering breath "...they won't tell me where the waystone is and I kinda sorta promised Prince Mordred I'd let him court me when he found Daar-Lûsin but I don't love him and I don't think Mordred really loves me and Raeden'll go berserk when he finds out—"

"*What?*" Thomas burst out as he moved toward her. What in perdition? Whatever he'd been expecting her to say, it wasn't this. The king wanted her to fulfill a prophecy? Her champion locked up like a common criminal? That guy was virtue incarnate. Annabelle—courted by a fish person—named Mordred, of all things? He sounded like a clown of the first order. Thomas scowled. Oh, heck no. That wasn't happening. She was just a kid. Too young to be in a relationship.

He grabbed her shoulders. "Kiddo, slow down. I don't understand. Start from the beginning. Tell me what you need, and I'll do what I can."

Tipping her head to look at him, Annabelle placed her hands on his chest. Her eyes went glassy. "T-Thomas, please. The king won't let us go. I'm afraid he'll execute Raeden if I don't lead them to glory. The princess and her husband are helping me, but we don't know what the prophecy means by glory, or what curse I'm supposed to break. I don't know what to do." She refocused, holding his gaze as her voice broke. "I could really use a knight in shining armor right now." Her face crumpled. Ducking her head, she clung to him like a drowning person. "I'm sorry, I'm sorry," she sobbed. "I know ... you don't like ... to be—"

Thomas wrapped his arms around Annabelle and held her tight. He fought back an urge to cry along with her. Resting his cheek on the top of her head, he swayed in place, like they were dancing. Her hair smelled like spring rain, oranges, and something milky sweet. She shouldn't have to deal with ... everything she was dealing with. Wrath burned like a furnace inside him. His jaw clenched. After he found a way to that island, he'd make the gwerindawr king pay for every one of her tears. Maybe set him on fire. Just a little.

"You have nothing to apologize for, kiddo. Nothing."

This is all my fault. If I had been a little quicker to reach her at the waystone ...

He smoothed a hand down her hair and continued to rock her until her weeping subsided to sniffling and his rage ebbed away. Blue and golden mist swirled around them, streaming in ribbons side by side, but never quite mixing. Finally, he loosened his embrace and let his arms return to his sides.

With a sigh, Annabelle stepped back, wiping away tears. Her face was blotchy from crying, and her eyes seemed even bluer. "Thank you for hugging me," she said in a small voice, then gave him a watery smile. "My knight in shining armor."

Feeling heat rise to his face, Thomas managed a lopsided grin. "Uh, you're welcome? But I haven't done anything yet."

"Just being here means a lot," she said. "I was wondering. Could you help me figure out something about the prophecy?"

"I'll try to the best of my ability. But I'm not great with word puzzles."

"I just need your input." She paused. "What does the phrase 'lead to glory' mean to you?"

Thomas frowned and scratched his chin. "Maybe, help somebody become famous or renowned? Improve themselves? I don't know, kiddo. It's not something I ever considered. I'll ask David and Dinah and report back to you tomorrow night."

"Oh, yes! Please. Ask Commander Storm and the Caretaker, too. They've been around, so they'll have a broader perspective on things."

Thomas snorted. "Might as well call them old, kiddo. Anyways ..." He cleared his throat, adding, "It sounds to me like you and His Excellentness both need to be rescued."

Annabelle's eyes widened. "But Enoch needs it more. I'm going to try talking Mordred to put the courtship on hold until after Enoch is rescued." She hunched her shoulders and looked at her feet.

Thomas shook his head and ran his hand through his hair. "I'm not gonna let them force you into doing stuff by holding your champion's life over your head. That's downright dirty pool." He suppressed an urge to set something on fire. That would only frighten her. "Besides, the Caretaker hasn't even located the kid yet. So there's nothing we can do about it. In the meantime, there's a way for you to rescue yourself. If you and His Excellentness get to the waystone, I bet your moonlight dagger could bring you straight through to the Fortress of Living Stones."

"Yeah, thanks. I've already thought of that. The problem is, I can't reach the waystone. Nobody will tell me—" She paused, her eyes brightening. "Hey! Guess what?"

"Straw!" Thomas replied, smirking. He'd missed this. "And what?"

She bounced on her feet and clasped her hands beneath her chin like a giddy schoolgirl. "I found out where Enoch is."

"You did?" Thomas stared. Her excitement was contagious and seared through him like fire ant bites. A grin spread across his face. With a whoop of exhilaration, he lifted her up and spun her around. She squealed laughter as she gripped his arms. "Great job, kiddo!" He set her down and stepped back, then schooled his expression to a trooper's sobriety. "Where is he?"

Her cheeks rosy, Annabelle averted her gaze and fussed with her hair, tucking stray locks behind her ears. "Um, he's being held in a fortress somewhere out West, in the Ingaraik

Mountains. I still haven't been able to break through the wyldling snare's interference, though. Our connection is still … gone."

"The Ingaraik Mountains," Thomas mused aloud, scratching his head with a frown. "Commander Storm will know where those are, for sure. I'd better go give him my report … Hold on." He crossed his arms. "The Caretaker's been scouring the planet with her magic hoodoo for a trace of the kid, and I've been searching high and low for a clue in the dreamscape. So far we've both found nada." Leaning closer, he arched an eyebrow. "If that dagger you got in Treehome hasn't mended your bond with Enoch, then where did you get the intel?"

She offered a tremulous smile. "Um … snooping around the dreamscape?"

His brow lowered. "Annabelle," he replied in a reproving tone. "Did you figure out where he was on your own or did you have help?"

Biting her lip, she glanced at her feet. "Technically … I had a little help from a friend."

Oh, no. This could be bad. Annabelle would try to befriend a venomous snake or cantankerous porcupine, if she could. He grabbed her shoulders. "Kiddo, please. This is important. Who helped you? And when? Did you meet a guy in a cloak with a glowing purple sword?"

Annabelle giggled and shrugged out of his grip. "No, it was a *dragon* with glowing purple *eyes*. I met him three nights ago. He told me where Enoch was. I asked for proof of life, and he showed me an image of Enoch. And he passed the test when I tried to catch him in a lie." She sounded smug.

"A dragon?" Thomas felt some of his tension melt away. "You mean one of the Sages." Leery as he was of Balthazar, the kiddo loved her Sage, and Hadrien appeared to have her best interests at heart. So far. And then he tensed. *Purple eyes? Criminy!*

She hemmed and hawed. "Uh, no. At least, Varazslo told me he wasn't a Sage. But he—"

"Where did you meet this dragon fellow?" Thomas smiled grimly and placed a hand on the sword at his hip. "I'd like to have a chat with him. See if he can reproduce this 'proof of life' for me, too. Can you show me?" He needed to be sure the situation with this Varazslo was on the up and up. Things weren't what they seemed in the dreamscape.

The kiddo's naïve. Too trusting of strangers. She needs me around to watch out for her.

Annabelle's brow furrowed. "I don't know how to get to his tower. Actually, I'm surprised he hasn't come around. He always seems to find me, no matter when or where I arrive in the dreamscape. We've agreed to meet on neutral ground ..."

The dragon had a tower? Inwardly, Thomas groaned as she continued to tell him about her new "friend" and how he was teaching her magic in exchange for answering questions. Teaching him about friendship? Ha! That was a load of malarkey. He didn't like the way her face lit up when she talked about this stranger, and he was sure her champion wouldn't approve of her gallivanting around the dreamscape with a monstrous winged reptile that could eat her up in three bites. In all the stories, dragons were not a girl's best friend.

Thomas held up a hand to stop her chatter. "Whoa, whoa, whoa, kiddo. Have you told His Excellentness about ... any of this?"

That shut her up. Annabelle flushed, then looked away. "No, not yet."

He uttered a foul curse, and Annabelle squawked, "Language!"

Thomas scoffed. "I thought he was your best friend. Why the heck haven't you told him?"

"Raeden *is* my best friend." Annabelle threw out her arms and stomped around the clearing. "But he's also imprisoned on an island and surrounded by merpeople who hate him because of some dumb war a long time ago. If I told him where Enoch was, he'd get upset because we couldn't go rescue him." She crossed her arms. "He's got enough to worry about. I'm trying to keep him safe."

Thomas rubbed his forehead. "If you told him, kiddo," he replied gently, "it would give him hope about Enoch, who is *also* his friend. You're not the only one who lost him."

Annabelle flinched, and for a moment looked like she'd burst into tears again. Then she lifted her chin and glared at an unoffending tree. "I'll take that under advisement."

Silence pressed down on them. Thomas swept his hand through the gold mist segregated on his side of the glade. Further away the blue mist eddied around Annabelle while she examined the foliage of a nearby bush.

Thomas sighed. "Hey. Did Enoch ever show you Lilac Grove?" Eyes wide, she shook her head. He gestured toward an opening in the trees. "Let's go for a walk."

"M'kay," she murmured, falling into step beside him. Her hand crept into his, and he let it. Her skin was soft, but cold. "I remember being in these woods. With Enoch. In the dreamscape."

"Me, too—but in the waking world. Of course, that was back when I was a grumpy toad."

"I liked you as a grumpy toad. And now that you're a grumpy man, I like you that way, too." Annabelle laughed, squeezing his hand. Thomas smiled at her and squeezed back. The tightness in his shoulders receded. His anger was all but gone, dimmed to the faintest of sparks. Maybe there was hope for him. If not, then he'd enjoy this time here with her.

Thomas quickly found the trail that led back to the Darkenwood Forest's truncated road. When it grew too narrow to walk side by side, he made Annabelle use the path proper while he trod through the undergrowth. "You know what I think," he said, wryly. "I think you're afraid to tell your dog-man because he'll get upset that you've placed yourself in danger, and then forbid you from coming to the dreamscape anymore."

Annabelle lowered her head so that her hair hid her face. "Okay. I have more than one reason. So sue me."

He barked a laugh. "I'm not judging, kiddo."

"And I appreciate that, Sir," she replied loftily. After a pause, she asked, "Wanna know what I think?"

"Hmm?"

"I think you want to see Lilac Grove because you're hoping it'll bring your memories back."

Thomas stiffened. "Maybe. I'm not holding my breath, though." *Even so, it's better than facing whatever demons Balthazar says I have inside me.*

"Well, it can't hurt, right?" She hesitated, glancing up at him. "You know, I learned a faster way to get places in the dreamscape. If you don't mind me showing you something a strange dragon taught me."

"Go ahead, kiddo."

"Alrighty then. Hold on." A picture came into his head of stone walls flanking a portcullis. There was a twisting in his gut, a falling sensation, and then they were staggering before the Westgate. "Sorry about that." Annabelle giggled, letting go of his hand. "I'm still a novice at teleportation, and I only know about this place from bits of Enoch's memories."

You're a novice at a lot of things. And too young to have to deal with the sticky situation you're in. But at least the instant travel thing was legitimate. He'd seen and felt how it was done and was sure he could replicate it. Glancing around the empty courtyard, Thomas strode toward the manor at the end of a long avenue lined with lilac bushes. It looked familiar, but more like something that had been described to him than an actual memory. His shoulders drooped. "So much for that."

Annabelle patted his arm. "Maybe if you went to the garrison? Could you find it?"

"You mean you don't know where it is?" He feigned disappointment and said sarcastically, "Here I was counting on you."

She made a face and playfully swatted at him. "How should I know?"

"Okay, gimme your hands. Let's try your dragon friend's teleporting trick."

Closing his eyes, he tried thinking of the garrison, but then an open area like an amphitheater with benches surrounding a sand pit popped into his head. Annabelle's fingers tightened. There was a shifting sensation, and they found themselves in the place he'd imagined.

Thomas blinked. "This is the training arena."

Annabelle looked around. "You remember it?"

He wrinkled his nose. "Sort of?"

"Can we go sit down?" she asked. "I want to think about this. Maybe we *can* figure out a way to get your memories back using the dreamscape."

"That's not a bad idea," Thomas admitted. He followed her to one of the benches and they sat down. "But first, I want to make sure we understand each other."

"Oh?" She'd been looking up into the sky, as if seeking something, but now she faced him. "I thought we already did. But go on." She clasped her hands in her lap and looked at him with a quirky smile.

Thomas cleared his throat. "You have the information about Enoch, right?" She nodded, frowning. "And I'm gonna verify it with the Caretaker and Commander Storm. So, there's no need for you to see this Varazslo anymore. You have me, now."

Her eyes shone and her cheeks grew rosy again as she smiled. "Yes, and I'm so happy!"

Hoo boy. What's going through her head now? *Scratch that; I don't want to know.*

Rubbing the back of his neck, Thomas glanced aside to galvanize his resolve. "Anyway, I'll make sure you're safe here in the dreamscape, but you have to promise not to wander around unless I'm with you. And for the love of all that's holy, talk to your champion about these things." He grimaced at a sudden image of her holding hands with a fish-man. "And any problems you might be having with men bothering you to ... whatever."

Annabelle nodded, then saluted. "Aye, aye, Sir."

He snorted. "I'm serious, kiddo. We both just want to make sure you're safe."

She rolled her eyes, then smiled. "I know. You don't have to worry. Mordred is a gentleman. Oh! I want to show you something cool. You'll like it." Brightening, she held out her hands, palms up. "Watch this." Her brow furrowed as she stared intently at moisture rising from her palms. Sapphire light rippled, steadily intensifying and elongating until a short sword made of water materialized with its hilt resting on her right palm. Looking up at him, she grinned. "Just like Murder Stick."

Thomas chuckled. "Nice!" He held out a hand and summoned his fiery blade. It materialized with the hilt in his hand. "I've got one, too."

She gaped. "Wow. A flaming sword!"

He remembered his promise to train her in the dreamscape. "I bet you haven't had much time to practice the sword dance. How about a spar?"

Looking uncertain, she shrugged, glancing from her sword to his. "Sure."

Assuming the first position of Invitation to Dance, he nodded. "Ready when you are, kiddo."

Gingerly, Annabelle advanced with her translucent, rippling blade held at a diagonal with the tip raised. Thomas frowned. That was wrong. With his fiery blade extended, he opened his mouth to correct her, but then she rushed forward, and he parried instinctively.

Fire collided with water in an explosion of steam. He reeled back. The sword disappeared from his grasp. He landed in the sand with an "oof," then scrambled to his feet. Oh, no! Had he burned the kiddo? He squinted through golden mist, then sighed in relief. Annabelle was sitting in the sand, laughing, staring at something in the sky. As he staggered over to her, she pointed.

Thomas looked up and collapsed on his knees beside her. *Well, that's something you don't see every day. Did we make that by mixing our magic?* High above, broad ribbons of shining sapphire and gold wove an intricate pattern he couldn't decipher. It was beautiful, like the Northern Lights. He realized he was grinning like an idiot. Slinging an arm around Annabelle, he hugged her to his side, and they laughed together.

Hearts

Crouched beneath the mirror-maze's canopy of shifting rainbow colors, William chuckled and savored his own cleverness. Even though the hisanabyad wasn't around to guard Annabelle's dreamscape domain at present, he'd prepared for the creature's return by setting up traps around the forest glade and river. The Dreadlord's library yielded a surprising amount of information on manipulating the dreamscape's Aethyric essence.

William backed away from the mirror-maze, careful to tuck his wings in close, and inverted the surrounding energy field, rendering it invisible while disguising the snares as harmless-looking patches of zillah clover—the favored food of the hisanabyad. He'd learned that from a completely different volume than the one about mirror-mazes.

Too bad I can't tell Annabelle about this. She'd be impressed by my sheer genius. Maybe she'd even hug me again ...

Behind him, his spiked tail quivered and lashed in excitement. William let it. He enjoyed a brief vision of her hug as a reward for his impending success before locking the image away again.

You'll see her again in a few hours. Stop distracting yourself. There's work to be done.

As much as he'd enjoyed conversing with Annabelle the previous night, her description of her home had been ... dissatisfying. In between all her boring chatter about her education, her religion, and her family, he'd learned what her world lacked. Wisconsin had no wyldlings. No arkhadahns. No dragons. Her kythim had muted to gray with that admission.

From what it sounded like, no one in her world used either Aethyric or Arkhadic energy. What if there was *no* magic? Could he stand to live in a realm without it? Maybe escaping Tenebris to a place he couldn't follow would be enough.

William was prepared with better, follow-up questions this time. Certain things she'd mentioned about 'technology' and mechanical devices tantalized him. There had to be opportunities in her world. There, he'd be far, far away from Tenebris. If no one *else* in Wisconsin had magic, but he did ... Was there a way to carry it along with him in his arkhabala?

Work now. Speculate later! William growled. *Ugh! even my own inner thoughts sound like Tenebris.*

He shook his head and surveyed the four traps he'd designed to capture Annabelle's white-winged companion. Yes. They were now flawless; he'd added a built-in redundancy to capture a shapeshifter of variant forms. Not that there was any indication the traps had failed in their intended purpose—

Chills snaked through his arkhabala, and he tasted mint. One of his tell-tales had triggered. He froze. *Milady Blue's in the dreamscape ...* right now? Odd. What brought Annabelle to the dreamscape so early? After a cursory double-check of the mirror-mazes, he unfurled his wings and took to the sky.

During his flight, William extended his kythim and searched the vibrations in the dreamscape's fabric for the signatures of others wandering the realm. It wouldn't do for the Dream Traveler or anyone else to catch him by surprise. He homed in on Annabelle's sapphire bloom, radiating her fresh, sweet scent far and wide. Despite the warmth it kindled behind his breastbone, he groaned at her open, trusting nature.

I should teach her how to suppress her kythim before she attracts trouble, but its expanse does make it easy for me to locate her.

Inhaling the purple mist that always lingered nearby, he gathered Aethyric energy and winged his way to Annabelle. Before long he flew over a woodland that seemed familiar. Bright blue sparked amid the darker blue tendrils.

William narrowed his eyes. *What's she so blazing happy about? I'm not with her! Is someone else with her? Argh! I knew I should've taught her to restrain her kythim.*

Perhaps she'd finally succeeded in re-creating her dog golem, but better safe than sorry. He fashioned a shadow-cloak to hide himself from view, then sent out a violet tendril of his own to investigate ...

Gold flashed. Flame singed his questing thought-tendrils and the scent of wood-smoke stung his nostrils. *No!* He recoiled, wings faltering, and he nearly plummeted into the trees below. Frantically flapping, he caught himself, then ensured his magic cloak still covered his entire dragon form.

What's that burning knight doing here—so close to my wyldling? He'd better not hurt her!

Champing his teeth, William seethed as terror and anger fought for dominance. That knight had pursued him through the dreamscape, flaming sword in hand, until William learned enough about the dreamscape to avoid him.

William's clawed hands trembled, and his spikes bristled. The urge to descend, to rend and tear his enemy with his fangs and talons nearly overwhelmed him. He shook his head. No, no, no. That wasn't how an Arkhadahn operated. Armored though he was in fire-resistant dragon scales, he must proceed cautiously and use his head.

He breathed in more purple mist until his racing heart slowed and his brain cleared of primal noise. Tentative, he reached out. Annabelle was still in a wonderful mood—as shown by the bright blue and lavender in her aura. So ... the knight wasn't hurting her. That was good. Wasn't it? His stomach churned as foreboding sent a shiver down his spine. A sensation came, like feathers tickling the inside of his skull. He pushed it aside. Later.

William drifted lower, sailing just above the treetops. He'd recognized the woodlands, finally; this was the Darkenwood Forest, and the shield wall of the Lilac Grove garrison loomed ahead. Annabelle's kythim rippled above the wall. It drew him like a moth to a flame. He gritted his teeth. That cursed knight was there, too. He'd get to the bottom of this, and extract Milady Blue if it proved necessary. As he neared, a concussive wave of sapphire and golden energy flung him back, tail over horns, robbing him of breath. Wood splinters and dust eddied around him as his armored dragon form crashed into trees.

What in Varjev's name caused that explosion?

Rising, William shook himself, mended his tattered shadow-cloak with a thought, and looked up. Blue and gold waves rippled together above the garrison like an ethereal banner. No. That was impossible. Fire and water shouldn't blend like that. They were direct opposites. Blue and violet were much closer together. But when he and Annabelle had woven the shield together, their aspects had remained separate ...

His gut in knots, William snapped his jaws shut to trap the saurian bellow and black lightning that wanted to escape. Spitting curses, he galloped through the open gate, then realized his talons clattered against the cobblestones. He tried his wings. They worked. Excellent. The tickle inside his skull returned, but he shook it off as he flew through steam and the smell of ozone until he came to an amphitheater, then perched on the top-most tier of benches.

There they were, kneeling in the sand. The cursed knight had his arm around *his* wyldling, and she leaned against him. Laughing together. Bright blue and lavender shone in both their auras. William stared at Annabelle's kythim. The lavender was much more pronounced here, in the knight's presence, than it had ever been around him.

William's talons dug into the wooden seat. It felt like a giant fist was crushing his heart while the ground fell away from under his feet. He could scarcely draw breath. What were these *feelings* raging through him? They were so ... *strong*.

Fear that he was inadequate in some way, an urge to rip the knight to shreds, and a desire to weep coupled with the horrible sinking sensation that something belonging to him had been lost—or stolen—and he may never reclaim it.

Suppressing a howl, he leaped into the air and flew ... away. Just away. He needed to regroup. To plan. To *think*. The pumping of his wings and the breeze in his visage helped clear his head. It struck him like one of Tenebris's Pain Hexes. He finally understood what lavender meant. The knowledge seared him with the pain of seven circle etchings—but on the inside.

First the beguilement spell, and now she'd betrayed him. All this time, she'd been friends with his nemesis. Anger made sense, but why did it also *hurt?*

Tenebris is right. Women are *poison.*

He growled through his teeth. "Vorniad drag that thieving knight through the six abysses of perdition. I'll *not* be defeated by a meat-headed barbarian whom I once turned into a *toad*." He chuckled bitterly. "Oh, no, Milady Blue. This game is far from over."

William was diverted from further agonizing by the tickle he'd felt before, only this time it felt more like spiders crawling across his brain. He gasped. One of his mirror-mazes had triggered! He paid closer attention to his environment. Unconsciously, he'd headed toward Annabelle's little dreamscape haven. He grinned. His quarry was nigh.

Shifting glimmers of red, purple, and green overlaid on milky white caught his eye, and he began a spiraling descent. A scan of the area informed him that no one else lurked nearby. Doubtless Milady Blue was still with—

Enough of that. He shoved all thoughts of *her* into the chamber he'd created for that purpose, then quadruple-locked the door. There. Now he could focus on more important matters.

William landed beside the trap and prowled around it. Something had nibbled on the zillah clover. The flashes of color told him he'd bagged the hisanabyad, but loose threads drifted around it like the frayed edges of a linen napkin. As he watched, a few more gossamers peeled away. Clawing at the turf, he cursed. The creature was working its way free.

He inhaled sharply, pulling in as much of the violet mist as his form could hold, conjured an echo shield, then waded into the static to examine his catch.

Colors burst all around, and suddenly the hisanabyad reared before him, horn ablaze with light, pawing the air and struggling against a net made of rainbow lightning. White wings spread from its withers. He thrust the shield before him, and its clawed feet tore through the ethereal fabric like paper. A percussive wave buffeted the creature, and it dropped on all fours.

William fell back, furiously spinning another tether to replace the ones through which the beast had broken.

This thing is more powerful than I expected! At least the mirror maze keeps her from creating portals to escape.

Rolling its dark eyes at him, it shrieked with a woman's voice. "Infernal Hollow! How did you escape the Sundered Realms?"

Hollow? Is something behind me?

William risked a glance over his shoulder. Straining against the mirror maze, the hisanabyad lunged at him. The tip of her glowing horn pierced through the center of his seventh circle. An icy shudder swept over him and every scale on his body shivered, as if he'd fly into pieces. What was happening?

The hisanabyad seemed to grow larger. He gaped up at her in confusion, and she stared wide-eyed down at him. The horn pulsed in time with her words. "You're merely a ... youngling?"

William touched his face. No scales. *Merciful Valeshka! She's robbed me of my disguise and all my protections are gone!*

Desperate, William flung the tether at her horn, and she fell back with a scream. While she struggled against the violet strands of the tether covering her like a jeweled net, he shakily rose to his knees. He felt naked without his dragon form.

The creature's wings were hopelessly tangled in the net, and she blundered around, crashing into the conjured mirrors and shrieking in pain at flashes of blinding light only she could perceive. Eyes riveted to his prize, William gathered violet mists and braided a second tether. The idea to weave it like that had come from ... No. He would not think of *her.* She was poison.

William set his jaw and watched as the hisanabyad sank to her knees. She appeared to crumple and melt into a female form clad in white, hunched over and hugging herself. She lifted her head and frowned at him through strands of long black hair. "So that is your true shape," she murmured. "You are not a full-blooded nehmwight. Tell me, child, who are your parents?"

William scowled as his fingers wove patterns in the mist-strands. "Oi! That's none of your suns-blistering business, voidrunner."

The dwelfnhad's brown eyes turned white and several strands of his trap fell away. She began to rise, liquid opalescence pooling between her hands. He flung the second tether, and it wrapped around her, pinning her arms against her sides. She cursed in dwelfnic. The spell she'd been crafting fell at her feet with a splash, then evaporated into rainbow sparks.

"Ha! Got you." The hisanabyad should be out of tricks now. However ... Keeping his eyes on her, he drew in more Aethyr for constructing a third tether. Because a smart Arkhadahn always prepared for the worst.

Black eyebrows lifted and a crooked smile curved her full lips. "Do you, shadowspinner?" The dwelfnhad's body compressed into a ball of white light.

He threw his half-formed tether at her just as she reformed into a tiny bird with a long, skinny beak, its wings a blur. Evading the tether, it shot skyward.

Fiery suns! She had a *third* form. That hadn't been in the books. Reaching out with his kythim, William sent strands of the new tether chasing after the hisanabyad while reinforcing the mirror maze's ceiling. He hadn't crafted it with a hummingbird in mind, but it should slow her down. Good thing he had a final card to play. Thanks to the purple mist all around him, he had energy to spare.

He dipped into the pool of violet light at his core and dragged forth concentrated Aethyr. To increase its potency, he cycled it through his arkhabala. It hurt, but only a little. A bright sheet of light burst forth from his hands. Reinforcing the sheet with the stray tether, he folded it like parchment to surround the hummingbird in a crystalline cage. The resulting faceted gem fell to the ground. She'd be able to breathe—if such was necessary in the dreamscape for an hisanabyad—but the hollow amethyst's volume didn't allow for much movement.

Ignoring her frantic fluttering, beak hammering, and piping cries, William mended the damage she'd wrought on his fabulous trap, transforming it into a prison. Rainbow lightning crackled all around the amethyst globe in a second, larger cage meant to contain her dwelfnhad form, should the bird break free. A third layer of lightning interwoven with violet netting would keep her winged equine form contained.

William's hands shook and weariness sapped his strength. But there was still work to do. Cycling more Aethyr through his arkhabala, he summoned the other three mirror-mazes he'd constructed and added their might to a final, fourth layer shield wall, fitting it together like puzzle pieces.

"Once you're sealed away," he muttered, "That leaves the blazing knight to deal with. And then Annabelle—uh—*her power* will be mine to harvest."

"No!" Fluttering madly around her prison, the bird shrieked, sounding like a teakettle. "You stay away from her!" Her voice subsided into a moan. "Oh, Yshua have mercy! I knew something was wrong ..."

"It's too late." William grinned through the pain in his heart. "Annabelle likes me. She's my *friend*." If he kept saying it, then it would become true. "And you can't keep her away from me while you're trapped in there."

So what if Annabelle does like that wretched knight better than me? That's only temporary. Once she realizes I'm his superior in every way—

"Heartless sorcerer." The void-cursed bird had pecked a tiny hole through the amethyst. He'd need to patch that before he finished the fourth layer. "You know *nothing* about friendship. Turn from your current path, or you will die discontented and alone." Her eyes flashed. "And if you hurt Annabelle, I will see that it happens in short order."

Even though her words sent a frisson through him, William barked a laugh. "Ha! Bold words. I'm not the pitiful little bird caught in a trap."

The beady eyes regarded him. She whispered, "Are you not trapped, little wyldling? Trapped in servitude to the Evil One?"

William flinched. "Oi! What are you on about? I'm no suns-blinded kadorei; I can't be a wyldling. I'm an Arkhadahn. And I serve no one but myself."

Before she could reply, he cast another layer of amethyst around the bird and combined it with a muffling spell. He sagged, and his arkhabala prickled in warning.

Almost depleted. Need to ... finish this ... and get away from here before someone else happens along.

Panting, he slammed the last pieces of the fourth layer into place, then inverted the signatures to render the prison invisible to all senses. An illusion resembling an innocuous copse of trees was the final touch. There. It was done. He'd succeeded, hadn't he? So why didn't he feel exultant? Perhaps he was too tired.

With the last of his reserves, William transported himself to his tower. He collapsed at his worktable and hunched over, forehead propped on the edge of the table. Shaking, he thrust his hands inside opposite sleeves of his burkheld and dug fingernails into his arms. He wasn't ready to return to the waking world. Not ready to swallow whatever vitriol Tenebris fed him.

"Are you not trapped, little wyldling?"

William's mind boiled over with questions, and his heart ... Well, no point in pondering *that*.

"Half-wit murder pony," he mumbled. "A nehmwight can't be a wyldling. An Arkhadahn doesn't need a heart. Women are poison. Milady Blue is my ..." Biting back a sob, he banged his head on the table. "I'm not trapped. I'm *not*."

And if he was, then he'd find a way out.

Beyond the Sea

Like a colorful trap the walls of the guest bedroom closed in around Annabelle. Friendly mosaic tableaux of gwerindawr going about everyday activities now seemed garish and threatening. It felt like an eel was twisting in her chest. Dressed for the day in a gauzy tunic and skirt over her undergarments, Annabelle sank back down on the edge of her bed she'd risen from only moments before. She concentrated on breathing normally. A comforting voice—one she hadn't heard in too long—echoed in her memory: "Good air in, bad air out. Thus begins the sword-dance."

Enoch's voice. Staring at a depiction of gwerindawr harvesting sponges, she struggled against tears. What if she never got out of this tropical paradise to resume her quest? Not for the first time, she wished she could communicate with Raeden using their Oathbond.

I need my champion ... my friend.

"Ann, are you ill? I'm so sorry if my news upset you, but my father says it must be so."

Slowly, Annabelle turned her head until Rhiannon's concerned expression filled her vision. "I don't understand. Why has the king forbidden me to visit Raeden for the next three days? He'll be expecting me. Is this some kind of punishment?" *For me or for Raeden?* She glanced at her weapons-belt hanging from a coral peg on the tiled wall. Raeden's sky-iron knife, which he'd entrusted into her keeping, was tucked into the sheath attached to the belt. "I'm working on fulfilling the prophecy as fast as I can."

The princepsa's eyes widened. "No, of course not." She sat beside Annabelle, causing the kelp water mattress to undulate and gurgle. Putting her arm around Annabelle, she continued, "From the moment you arrived a week ago, my father began planning a gala festival in your honor. He simply wants you close at hand, because people have traveled from as far as the Outer Reaches and the Lonesome Atoll to meet the Ahdmerel."

"What?" Feeling unmoored, she gripped Daar-Lûsin as a fierce wave of longing for her friends swept over her. It was bad enough she'd failed to find Thomas or Varazslo in the dreamscape last night—strange especially in Varazslo's case, because the dragon had seemed eager to hear more about Earth—and Khinjara was still missing despite the return of the dagger. Bad enough that she'd awoken from nightmares about nehmwights. But now she couldn't see Raeden ... for over three days? All for the sake of a celebration she wanted no part of? Visiting her champion was like being in the eye of a storm, a break from studying the prophecy and being whisked from place to place, a time when she could relax and just *be*.

Naturally, Raeden knew she'd met Thomas yesterday. With the dagger back in her possession, she'd chosen to try finding Enoch during her early evening visit with Raeden. Instead, she'd found Sir Thomas. Ecstatic, she'd told her champion when she woke and also taken the opportunity to inform him of Enoch's whereabouts. Her champion assumed she'd received this information from Thomas. She hadn't corrected him. That fact lodged like a bit of celery stuck between her teeth.

Today, she intended to risk Raeden's temper by asking for his advice on how to handle Mordred's courtship. To confess everything about meeting Varazslo in the dreamscape. But now that wouldn't happen. Because of a stupid party.

Annabelle hugged Daar-Lûsin. "I don't mind meeting people, but not all day for three days straight. Plus ... today I was supposed to scope out the parts of the coral reef that are dying and see if I can cure it. Isn't that more important?" The king had known her plans. Didn't he care about breaking the curse as quickly as possible? She looked pleadingly at the princepsa. "Please, Rhia, can't you intercede with the king for me? You're his heir."

"I'm very sorry, dear." Rhiannon squeezed her shoulders. "What Father decrees, he decrees. There's no going against him. Even when I'm resolved, the moment I come face to face with him, I just ... *can't.* No one can."

No one could refute the king? Annabelle found Morgan Brenin intimidating, but he was no Commander Storm. If she hadn't seen for herself how everyone—even the confident princepsa—quailed in this presence, she would have scoffed at Rhiannon's statement.

Stroking Annabelle's hair, the woman sighed. "Don't think I haven't noticed how all the socializing saps your strength. Sawel and I will try to hold back the tide of adoring supplicants for as long as possible. And of course, Dred will be at your side the entire time to shield you."

Mordred would always be at her side? Annabelle tried not to think about why that was. At least they'd all promised not to spread the news that she and Mordred were ... courting.

She blurted, "Supplicants? Holy cow." That didn't bode well, either. Wyldling powers notwithstanding, she was a plebeian sophomore in high school, not brought up as a noblewoman or to be a celebrity. Even if Mordred *did* intend to go beyond courting and marry her someday, he wasn't even in line for the throne. Cheese and crackers! She hadn't asked for any of this.

Bitter regret tightened her throat. *And I totally blew my chance to talk with Raeden about it.*

She swallowed. "What do these 'supplicants' think *I* can do to help them with whatever? I don't even know how I'm supposed to bring glory to your people."

"What can you do?" The archimandrite poked his head around the corner. "You've already done quite a bit—and the people haven't stopped talking about it. Your good work brings us hope, Ann. Like a spate of fresh water where before was only bitter brine. A cool spring on a desert isle."

"Careful, Sawel." Rhiannon chuckled. "Those are compliments to turn a damsel's head. You're fortunate I'm not a jealous wife, and that Dred isn't here to challenge you." Annabelle squeaked in protest, and the princepsa shook her a little. "I'm teasing, Ann."

Grinning, Sawel raised a ragged scroll that appeared to be made from the fibrous bark of a tree. "I didn't mean to interrupt you ladies, but Orcwith just delivered a message for Ann from her champion. Said he'd be back in ten minutes if you'd like to send a response."

With a wordless cry, Annabelle jumped up and ran to accept the scroll from Sawel. It *was* made of bark, scratchy against her palm. "Thank you."

Sawel stepped back from the door, allowing her to exit. "Thank Orcwith when he returns. He told me to pass along that your champion accepted the fish he brought for his breakfast quite graciously despite being informed you cannot see him today, and he's keeping busy making improvements to his shelter. Fortifying it against the weather, it seems. It'll be typhoon season in another two moons."

God forbid we're here that long!

Annabelle started unrolling the letter, and he patted her shoulder. "Go on, child. We don't have much time. Use my desk to compose a response."

"Oh, fish piddle. Ten minutes is plenty of time." Rhiannon sidled past Annabelle. She leaned against her husband, and he snaked an arm around her waist. His burgundy skin complemented her sky-blue complexion. They looked pretty together.

"If you don't complete your note before Dred arrives, I'm sure he'll wait. I'd offer you my desk, but alas! It's in disarray, as usual."

Smirking, her husband tickled her ribs. "Ten minutes is plenty of time to tidy up a desk."

"Oh! Stop that, Sawel. You know it makes Ann uncomfortable." She giggled, swatting playfully at his arm.

There they go again. It's the same thing every morning. Rolling her eyes, Annabelle grimaced. *I'm surprised they don't have a dozen kids, the way they carry on.* The princepsa seemed perfectly healthy and ready to bear children when she checked her with her wyld.

Sawel kissed Rhiannon's cheek and murmured something into her ear. She laughed.

Annabelle blushed. *I wouldn't mind it if Thomas tickled me the way Sawel tickles Rhia. Or kissed me ...*

"Um, see you in a few." Her face burning, she scooted past them with Daar-Lûsin in one hand and the scroll in the other. So what if Thomas hugged her in the dreamscape and swore he'd move heaven and earth for her sake? It didn't mean he was in love with her.

Focus on Raeden and his message, Annabelle!

"Ann," Rhiannon's voice floated after her. "I'll send Portia in to put up your hair in a mo—Yeek!" Her words dissolved into peals of laughter. "You'll pay for that, Sawel!"

"You are my sweet anemone, Rhia. I would endure your stings forever."

"Oh, stop, you silly cucumber. That's exactly what you told me when you proposed."

"It's still true."

Who calls their husband a cucumber? Snickering, Annabelle pushed through a curtain of shells and beads into the airy chamber they both used as their study. Klotho had risen, and her silvery-white light filled the room from a west-facing window. Sawel and Rhiannon still teased one another. She smiled at the cuteness—now that she didn't have to watch.

Unrolling Raeden's missive, she headed straight for the archimandrite's desk of polished coral that looked as if it had grown from the floor. She climbed up on the stool. Meant for a much taller person, her feet dangled like a child's. Sawel kept his work surface clear, aside from a copy of the prophecy scribed on a wax tablet. They'd been studying it together the day before, in between her attempts with the newly returned dagger to find Enoch in the dreamscape.

Being aquatic folk, the gwerindawr had little use for paper or ink. They carved figures with a stylus on wax tablets, wrote with grease pens on the durable leaves of the llenor tree, or wove shells and coral beads into patterns for their record-keeping and correspondence. Detritus in the form of half-finished bead weavings was scattered across Rhiannon's desk on the opposite side of the room, just as she'd warned.

Annabelle sat on the stool. She nudged aside the tablet and flattened out the sheet of bark. Doubtless using his claws, her champion had scratched out an epistle to her in capital letters:

"FREYLIN,
YOUR SERVANT PRAYS FOR YOUR HEALTH.
HE REMINDS: TRUST IN THE ALMIGHTY

A WAY WILL BE FOUND
LORD YSHUA THE CORNERSTONE
WILL CALM WATERS FOR ONE TO WALK UPON
BEYOND THE SEA IS A RECKONING
IT POINTS OUT THE PATH TO GLORY
YOURS ALWAYS,
RAEDEN VON BLEISTAFF"

She smiled at Raeden's poetic and rather cryptic verbiage. It was sweet how he was always so concerned about both her health and her faith. It reminded her of the many letters he'd sent to her while she'd been ill and sequestered in the Women's Quarters of Treehome. Then her eyes fastened on the words "reckoning" and "point." Their proximity to one another niggled at her mind. Eyes widening, her breath caught in her throat at the image the words conjured of a dark, forbidding island on the horizon. Rhiannon said they executed prisoners there. Had Annabelle mentioned it to him on an evening visit during one of her rambling recitations of daily activities? If so, then no wonder he remembered it.

Morgan Brenin could send Raeden there at any time.

I won't let that happen. Even if I must use my wyld to stop the king.

Two nights ago, Varazslo showed her how to create an impenetrable dome. If she had to ...

Swallowing past a lump in her throat, Annabelle allowed the bark to roll up, then reached into separate pigeonholes for a grease pen and a llenor leaf. Raeden deserved a response.

"Dear Raeden,

I'm healthy and Sawel leads us in prayer every day, but I miss you. Hopefully I can convince the king to let me visit you tomorrow. This morning after breakfast I'm going with

Rhiannon and Sawel to see the underwater ruins of an ancient city from before the Oblivion Wars, back when Hadrien was still around—She was looking forward to that, if not the party afterward —*Sawel believes it could help me figure out the rest of the prophecy, about breaking the curse and leading them to glory. Maybe if I solve the mystery today, the king will let us go tomorrow—*"

Beads clattered. "Lady Ann, I'm here to—"

Annabelle jumped with a gasp, covering the missive with a spare leaf. But it was only Portia. Apologizing, the teal-skinned handmaid came over with a comb and swiftly braided Annabelle's hair. She praised the silky smoothness of her tresses and its unusual golden-brown color. Annabelle held her tongue; in a society where vibrant orange, blue, green, pink, or purple hair abounded, she couldn't help but feel like a ruffed grouse amid peacocks.

"There we are," Portia cooed as she tied off the end with a colorful band. "Now you're all ready for your expedition with the princeps."

"Also Rhiannon and Sawel," Annabelle interjected. She wasn't going anywhere with Mordred while unchaperoned. "They're going, too. Along with a plethora of guards."

"Of course, Lady Ann ... Er, a what of guards?"

After Portia left, Annabelle was just finishing the sentence with "*and we can meet up with the others and resume our quest to rescue Enoch*" when Mordred's greetings to his sister and brother-in-law intruded upon her awareness from the common area. Darn it! She had so much more to say, about the Reckoning Point, the prophecy, and maybe warn Raeden that she needed to tell him something—about the promise she'd made to Mordred—but her time had run out. Hastily, she scrawled out her conclusion.

"There's something I need to tell you, but I'd rather do it in person. I'll write more tonight—" if Morgan Brenin gave her time to herself— *"Thank you for your kind message. I will ponder your wisdom."* She hesitated. Raeden was all alone and surrounded by enemies. He needed some encouragement, too. *"You've always been my best, truest friend, and I love you.*
Sincerely, your Freylin,
Annabelle Leigh Wells"

It wasn't perfect, but it would have to do. She'd just finished tucking the blotted leaf inside a larger leaf envelope when someone slipped through the beaded curtain. Whirling, she clutched the dagger, her leaf packet, and Raeden's message to her chest. "Um. Hi, Mordred."

"Good morrow, my little damselfly," her boyfriend said, bowing slightly. With a confident smile, he held out a hand to her. "Would you like me to carry anything? Breakfast awaits, if you care to join me."

Annabelle left the lagoon with the others and slipped into the warm embrace of the sea. She relaxed as the water closed over her head and reminded herself that she didn't need to hold her breath as she followed Rhiannon and Sawel. Mordred swam alongside Annabelle, with Wesleyen and Delfie jetting ahead and then speeding back as the fancy took them. Their escort of guardsmen spread out to flank them.

When she'd asked, the princepsa said there was nothing to fear under the sea near Ynys Lloches. The guards were more for show than anything. Sawel had been excited to show her the ruins of the ancient gwerindawr capital. He often went there to pray, and claimed he'd had a vision of Hadrien there, once.

"And if I was blessed to see Rainblessed in a vision," the archimandrite had said, *"perhaps the Sage will speak to the*

Ahdmerel directly and impart wisdom to help you fulfill the prophecy."

I sure hope so, Annabelle mused. *Prophecy aside, I miss Hadrien.*

Rhiannon's long braid trailed out behind her and the gossamer fins of her galamerdhe undulated mesmerizingly as she porpoised along. A vibrant coral reef loomed ahead, teeming with colorful fish, anemones, and crustaceans. Annabelle glimpsed several octopi peeking out of nooks and crannies in the coral beds. Wesleyen stayed close beside her.

Is he afraid of the other octopi? I wonder if the wild ones would go after him if I wasn't here. Or maybe he just likes me. That thought made her smile.

Mordred, her *boyfriend*—that fact still astounded her—took her arm, drawing her from her introspection. They'd left the shallows and come upon a minor drop-off. He pointed below. Annabelle adjusted her glasses and squinted. Rows of structures spread out across the ocean floor that bore the shape of homes, albeit crusted in coral and barnacles with beds of seaweed in place of lawns. Delfie circled a structure and then went to Rhiannon. Wesleyen jetted into one "building's" window and then crawled out another before rising to wrap blue tentacles around her wrist. The water cooled slightly as they descended. The scene looked familiar ... like something from a half-forgotten dream.

This must be the ancient capital. Did I see it when I visited Hadrien for the first time?

She met Mordred's golden gaze. He grinned, then jerked his head toward his sister and brother-in-law awaiting them in what appeared to have been a town square with blue-streaked marble pavers. A statue of Hadrien stood in the center. Rhiannon beckoned Annabelle with a smile while her husband investigated an alabaster plinth, his chartreuse-streaked burgundy flukes stirring the bottom sediment.

Annabelle allowed Mordred to convey her down to the plinth. Sawel moved aside, gesturing at a symbol engraved on the marble surface and inlaid with lapis lazuli. She drifted closer. Her eyes widened. It looked like the astrological sign for Pisces, only flipped 90 degrees. *That's my birth sign,* she wanted to tell them, but only bubbles emerged. Wesleyen detached and perched on the edge of the plinth. His tentacles crept toward the symbol but avoided touching it.

Smiling at the octopus, she traced the stylized fish with her fingers. What did it signify? They didn't see the same constellations on Tehara as on Earth.

"Ahdmerel ..." A presence settled around her and a voice spoke directly to her mind.

Annabelle stiffened, then her tension receded. The presence was comfortingly familiar. Cautiously, she reached out with her mind: *"Hadrien, is that you?"*

"Indeed, little one." A pause. "You have found Ynys Lloches."

"Yeah, I did!" Excitement sent a frisson down her spine. *"I'm so glad to hear from you. How is it that I can talk to you outside of the dreamscape? Are you here in Ynys Lloches—in the flesh?"* Hope filled her. The gwerindawr venerated the Sage. If she could find Hadrien, then maybe *he* could convince Morgan Brenin to set Raeden free and let them both leave.

Hadrien's gentle response dashed her hopes. "I remain in the Sundered Realm and cannot be there in the flesh, chained as I am. However, Ynys Lloches is the one place on Tehara's material plane where the water-attuned may communicate with me in the waking world. It has been a very long time since anyone has. You must have found the plinth engraved with my sigil."

"Yes!" She described the Pisces-like symbol and Hadrien confirmed it was his sigil. *"Right now,"* she added, *"I'm here with the gwerindawr royals, looking at some ruins of the gwerindawr capital at the bottom of the ocean."*

"Ah, the gwerindawr are like my own children," Hadrien replied. "Many of them were my students. Their capital was destroyed during the Oblivion Wars. To ensure the safety of the survivors, the royal family begged me to sunder their waystone from all but the dwelfnic nexus. I did as they asked, but I gave the gwerindawr a solemn charge to be hospitable to those seeking refuge. I trust you have found safe harbor, then. And mentors to train you."

"Mentors?" Annabelle frowned. *"To train me in what? No one has taught me anything since I got here."*

"No one has instructed you in the discipline of your wyld?" Hadrien sounded shocked, almost scandalized. "How can this be? In my day, the gwerindawr were the most powerful of the merellein souretholim. They should all be vying for the honor of teaching a wyldling."

Annabelle gaped. *"The gwerindawr are water mages, like me?"* She turned to stare at Mordred, then Rhiannon and Sawel. *"But ... I've never seen them do anything magical. Unless you count being able to shift their legs into swimming tails—the galamerdhe."*

"The galamerdhe is merely the sign of their power," Hadrien replied. "Like all souretholim, they need contact with their attuned Aspect to manipulate it, but this should not be an issue. Water is all around the gwerindawr; it is why they chose an archipelago as their sanctuary. Something is wrong here. Very wrong." He chuffed. "This is highly irregular. No wonder I have not heard from anyone. What has happened to my gwerindawr this past Age?"

Tracing the symbol, Annabelle furrowed her brow. *"I don't know if this means anything,"* she said. *"But the gwerindawr have a prophecy about the Ahdmerel they expect me to fulfill. The king won't tell me where the waystone is until I do, and he's imprisoned Raeden. They hate the wensallen-kaen."* She swallowed. *"I'm afraid he'll execute my champion if I don't 'lead the gwerindawr to glory!' The prophecy also mentions a curse that I'm supposed to break. Maybe the gwerindawr losing their magic is the curse?"*

She had the impression of the Sage rising to his feet amid the rattling of chains. "What is this, child? Tell me about this prophecy." Just as it had in the dreamscape, it seemed the fleshy, spade-shaped tip of his tail enfolded her, like a mental hug.

Comforted by his phantom support, Annabelle recited what she could remember, and told Hadrien the prophecy had come to their archimandrite in a vision over a moon ago. Wesleyen stared up at her from his perch on the plinth. His pulsating siphons were the only parts of him that moved. Everything an arm-length away from the plinth seemed cloudy. Odd. While she described the ruins and her gwerindawr companions, Annabelle scanned their positions through the murk. Balanced on his flukes at her side, Mordred hovered near, his brow furrowed. The others watched her with perplexed expressions. Unmoving.

Are they frozen by a spell? Or am I *in a high-speed time bubble?*

"Troubling," Hadrien said when she finished. "The wensallen-kaen's plight complicates matters. My apologies, but I shall need to think about it, little one. This 'curse' you mention disturbs me greatly. If my gwerindawr have lost their connection to the Aethyr ... Hmm. Yes. Perhaps that is the curse you are meant to break."

"There's also other things wrong." Annabelle related what Rhiannon had told her of her people's tribulations. *"I'm doing my best to help fix the problems,"* she added. *"But how do I get to the root of the curse so I can break it?"*

"These are all ailments that could have been mitigated if the gwerindawr retained their powers. Unfortunately, pervasive as it is, a curse could be tied to any object or a location in the archipelago. You will know it by a sense of *wrongness* in the waters. But beware: a malecto grammerye should not be taken lightly—especially if its originator is who I believe it is."

"Who do you think cursed the gwerindawr?" Feeling vulnerable, Annabelle peered over her shoulder. *"And are they still around?"*

Hadrien sighed. "No, he is not. Ask me another time, little one, and I will tell you a very long and sorrowful tale from the Ages past. Presently, you have enough to occupy your mind. And I would not have you face danger unprotected. I see one course of action you must take: claim the sourekghar for your own protection, because there is no one there to train you. It will give you the strength to break the curse. Then be firm with the gwerindawr regarding your demands. You must leave if you are to resume your quest. Prophecy or none, only possession of the sourekghar will convince them of your authority as Ahdmerel."

"But first I need to find *the sourekghar, Hadrien. Where in Ynys Lloches is it?"* She scanned the ruins of the capital and her frozen companions. Frustration simmered inside her. *"Provided that my 'hosts' allow me the opportunity to search for magic armor. They rarely leave me alone. Unfortunately, it's not spelled out in the prophecy as something I need to accomplish."*

"Mayhap one part of the 'glory' the gwerindawr achieve is in helping you claim the sourekghar," Hadrien suggested. "Although the existence of this prophecy does not sit well with me—only prophecies concerning Lord Yshua truly matter—it seems innocuous enough, and perhaps it truly comes from the Almighty Threefold One for your benefit."

Annabelle was about to repeat her question about the armor's location when Hadrien continued, "I am not certain of the sourekghar's exact location, only that it is somewhere in the archipelago. You will feel a pull when it is near. The last Ahdmerel, Jedediah sel Drayven, hid it at the close of the Oblivion Wars. Jedediah the Faithful. After so many wyldlings ... and others ... fell away, he remained true."

There'd been a previous Ahdmerel ... It appeared she wasn't so special, after all. Pushing aside her disappointment, she asked, *"Why did he bring the sourekghar here?"*

Sorrow colored Hadrien's reply. "It was his final mission—cleansing Ynys Lloches of the enemy and securing it for the gwerindawr. They raised him as one of their own and he loved them greatly. The sourekghar served as the central node of a wardspell network. Leaving the armor ensured they would be protected against future raids.

"After Jedediah succeeded in his task and we set the wards, I brought him back with me ... though he was gravely wounded and did not long survive. Mere days after he died, the realms were sundered, imprisoning me and my brethren."

"I'm sorry." Annabelle swallowed past a knot in her throat. She wished she could hug Hadrien. And then something occurred to her. *"Wait. If I take away the sourekghar ... doesn't that mean the gwerindawr lose their protection?"*

"The wards were not meant to last longer than an Age," Hadrien responded. "Even with copious water to energize them, the weavings would succumb to attrition in time and unravel. Physical separation is their best security. If the face of Tehara has not greatly changed since the wars, then the archipelago of Ynys Lloches still lies far distant from the Imerinthian continent. You may claim the sourekghar without guilt. Tell them ... it is time they rejoined the wider world." The Sage's presence faded, his mental voice a whisper. "Trust in Lord Yshua, little one."

"Hadrien, wait! Where is the waystone on Ynys Lloches? And how, exactly, do I break the curse ..." Her question trailed off.

Aching silence was her only response. She stared at Wesleyen, who pulsed a paler blue and reached out to twine his tentacles around her wrist. She'd allowed her curiosity to derail the conversation. Vexation left a bitter taste in her mouth as she whirled to view her frozen companions.

Please, God, let them be okay!

Mordred, Rhiannon, and Sawel abruptly became animated once more. Relief filled Annabelle with a warmth like the breaking of dawn as they drew near with inquiring expressions. Once they surfaced, she had much to discuss with them.

Fuel for the Fire

Second-dawn broke and Lachesis spilled golden light across the rugged terrain. Much like the twittering birds, Thomas had already been awake for several hours. The scent of sage and lavender fought for precedence in the still, cool air as he jogged laps around the circuit of Y'Vasheirdenelle's highest balcony, which hung over a sheer drop to the ravine below. Each time he passed the statue of Ebenezzar Earthshaker, he dropped to do twenty push-ups or crunches.

Exercise helped clear the fog of sleep from his mind. Two nights ago, he'd found Annabelle in the dreamscape—or she'd found him, depending on whom you asked. Despite himself, a rueful smile quirked at his lips as he recalled their nearly disastrous attempt to combine water wyld and fire wyld. He thought his heart would stop when her watery sword exploded into steam. But neither of them suffered any harm.

And the strange fusion of our magic created something beautiful.

It had settled something deep in his soul to see Annabelle. To be there as a man, so he could hold her when she cried. To laugh with her under the swirled banner of sapphire and gold.

The kiddo sure had been excited to share what she'd discovered about Enoch. Ingaraik was a small section of a larger mountain range in the Western Marches. Several waystones could bring them there within six weeks, perhaps a moon, based on the schedule carried in the Commander's mind. They only awaited the Caretaker's report later today.

What worried Thomas—and concerned them all—was the source of Annabelle's information about Enoch's location. Though he hid it well, Thomas could tell Commander Storm was troubled to hear she'd been meeting someone calling himself Varazslo, which was a title reserved for the most powerful nehmwight sorcerer.

Shaking off his astonishment, Thomas had made sure to confirm with the Commander that nehmwights couldn't enter the dreamscape. "Because, sir," he'd said while they stood examining a map of the continent, "things aren't always what they seem in that crazy place."

Commander Storm had frowned, and his craggy features settled into pensive lines. "Nehmwights simply cannot enter the dreamscape. Arkhadic magic and Aethyric magic are like oil and water. For lack of a better description, the dreamscape *is* Aethyr. And a nehmwight arkhadahn does not possess the connection to the Aethyr that both wyldlings and souretholim enjoy." Tapping his fingers on the pommels of his scimitars, the evainghir shook his head. "Nay, lad. But it disturbs me that someone claiming this title is in contact with the womanchild."

The cold steel blades of his gaze pierced Thomas. "You mentioned meeting a young man in red armor who manipulated stone and earth. Your suspicions that it may be another wyldling hold weight. I have given this much thought and discussed it with the Eldest. She has noticed ... resonances. It is possible other wyldlings roam the dreamscape—and are playing at silly buggers. Sir Thomas, you must see to the womanchild's safety in the dreamscape while she remains on Ynys Lloches."

"Of course I will, sir," Thomas had responded in an even tone, though he felt irked. The Commander made it seem as if he hadn't already planned to do that!

When Thomas returned to the dreamscape last night to check up on Annabelle, he hadn't been able to find her, aside from lingering traces. She'd been back, but he'd missed her by hours. There'd been no sign of her suspicious dragon friend either.

If only we could open the way to Ynys Lloches! Thomas grunted as he finished a set of crunches, performed a kip-up, and resumed his jog. *The kiddo has too much on her plate to deal with alone, and His Excellentness is a prisoner.* A snarl twisted his lips. *That Mordred fellow better be the gentleman she says he is, or he'll have to face me in the combat arena.*

He rounded a curve passing an herbal garden and the cloying scent of lavender made his nose wrinkle. His thoughts swirled. Ynys Lloches proved distressingly distant—an archipelago in the middle of a vast ocean, far off the western coast of the Imerinthian continent—with a waystone that only connected with the nexus at the Fortress of Living Stones during the autumnal equinox. Three moons from now, leaving Annabelle out of reach both physically and temporally.

Unless she managed to open the way from her end. Now that she had that moonlight dagger back, she seemed confident that she could rejoin them once the gwerindawr king granted her access to the darn waystone. Everything hinged on that.

The gwerindawr prophecy was concerning though. She needed to get away from those crazy fish people before something bad happened. Because sure as frogs croaked, they had it in for His Excellentness, and that king sounded like a piece of work. If only Thomas could go there! He'd convince His Royal Fishiness to let Annabelle go immediately.

His fingers curled into fists, and he shook them out. *Sad to say, it's probably a good thing I'm not there on Ynys Lloches. A knight should be disciplined and demonstrate self-control at all times. And I can't vouch for my temper lately.*

Case in point: he'd incinerated all those nehmwights at Fort Arwydd. Dinah had been horrified, and David's censure shone in his face. Shame burned throughout Thomas's body. He must get a handle on this.

Before I hurt someone I care about.

Feet pounding on the stone battlements, Thomas rounded another bend where a fruit orchard grew. Heads bowed in prayer or meditation, David and Dinah knelt across from one another in an adjacent garden that seemed to be dedicated to rocks of all varieties, as did nearly everything in Y'Vasheirdenelle. It was a little jarring, seeing the cousins in red and burgundy tunics and baggy trousers like the resident Stonesingers wore instead of their armor. A tea tray sat on a raised section of stone between them, decked with tea fixings and fist-sized buns in three colors—pink for meat, yellow for custard, and pale purple for a sweet bean paste filling. Thomas's mouth watered. They were all delicious, but after his exercise he craved a meat bun.

Looking up, Dinah smiled and waved. David raised a hand in greeting and nearly smiled. Despite his worries, Thomas grinned. Perhaps a spar later that day would lighten up the Shepherd's dour mien. *And help center me.* He swerved and took a path that cut through garden beds of red flowers and aromatic herbs. The cousins rose as he approached.

"Good morrow, Sir Thomas. Unfortunately, you missed the prayer," David said. Thomas read a rebuke in his tone.

His grin dwindled to a tight smile. Nothing would come of any prayers he offered, even were he so inclined. He'd given up on God, and God had given up on him.

Expression placid, the dwelfnhir indicated the tray, which held enough food for four people. "Please join us in breaking our fast. There's plenty."

"Don't mind if I do," Thomas replied, and the three of them settled on the turf. He wiped his brow. "Pardon my sweatiness."

Raising his eyebrows, David cracked a wan smile. "I'm afraid it's inevitable, when one runs drills in the summertime."

Thomas snorted. "Or any time of the year, if it's me. No matter what, you guys always look fresh as daisies."

"We availed ourselves of the baths earlier," Dinah remarked, then grinned. "You should as well, Sir Thomas. Here," She held out a plate containing one of each bun type and a teacup. "You must have worked up an appetite."

Wryly, Thomas thanked her, and half-listened to her prattle while he devoured the spongy buns—grabbing three more—and washed it down with the pale green tea, grimacing at its astringence and the grassy flavor.

If I wanted to drink 'Essence of Lawn,' I would've been born a cow. It must be an acquired taste.

David ate and drank at a more sedate pace, dividing his mute attention between his meal and his cousin's rambling narrative about her last visit with Count and Lady Dulciber. "It's a shame about Rachel," Dinah said, shaking her head as she looked into her teacup. "Before the madness took her fourteen Turnings ago, she was such a lively young lady."

"Huh?" Thomas furrowed his brow. He couldn't remember much about his past, but certain facts from his professional life remained in his memory. "What madness? And I thought Lady Dulciber's name was Pansy, Posy ... something flowery like that."

"Petunia," Dinah corrected him. "But I was referring to the Count's daughter, Rachel. You wouldn't have met her. They keep her out of the public eye." Biting her lip, she turned her cup in her hands. "Rachel and I were friends ... back when she still recognized me. Although it pains me to see her as she is now, I make it a point to visit when my ambassadorial duties bring me to the County of Mirrors." She took a sip of tea.

Not knowing how to respond, Thomas shifted uncomfortably. David cleared his throat. "And regardless of what we discover here about young Enoch's location—the County of Mirrors will be our next stop."

"Because the Commander plans to muster the counts and marshals," Thomas added, on firmer footing now that David had deftly changed the subject to military matters. He chuckled. "And we'll all have a nice long talk about how to go about rescuing Enoch without losing too many men. I can't wait to see Annabelle's response to that. I can imagine it."

Rolling his eyes, he raised his voice an octave to mimic her: "Oh, no! Please just let me go save Enoch by myself, so nobody gets hurt!'" He snorted. "Naïve kiddo. She's too tender-hearted for her own good."

"You do realize," David murmured into his tea, "that the waystone leading to the Dulciber estate opens tomorrow. She's not likely to win her way through before that. Fortunately, the Caretaker will be here to receive her in our stead."

Tomorrow? Thomas's eyes widened. Criminy! How could he have forgotten? Urgency filled him at the reminder. He rocked up to his feet. "I've gotta speak with the Commander. See if there's any way we can delay until we get the kiddo back. She negotiated access to their waystone. Hopefully, it should only be a few days!"

If it were possible, Dinah looked even more miserable. "You know he won't," she whispered. "But I shall pray for a miracle."

Fat load of good that'll do.

Thomas laughed bitterly. "Have fun with that." At her scandalized expression, he grimaced and wiped a hand down his face. In a milder tone, he added, "Sorry, Ambassador. That was out of line." He managed a smile. "Thanks for breakfast."

Dinah's answering gaze was solemn. "You're always welcome, Sir Thomas." She paused. "Remember, David and I are your friends."

"Er, yeah." Thomas chuckled. "And I appreciate you putting up with me."

"Your company isn't the burden you believe it is." David rose, brushing off his trousers. "The Commander is probably in the Farseer Chamber with the Caretaker. Since I'm heading to the library, I'll accompany you down the lift."

The western horizon reddened as Atropos rose. Leaving Dinah to appreciate the gardens in solitude, Thomas and David made their way to a platform made of dark gray basalt. Once aboard, the dwelfnhir did ... something ... and the platform descended through a tube made of banded stone like agates. Watching colorful strata flash by, Thomas shifted his weight from one foot to the other and yearned for unmoving ground.

I don't think I'll ever get used to this.

The platform came to a halt, and they exited the tube. David led the way through a cavernous chamber lined with red-streaked pillars seemingly grown from the ceiling and floor and joined in the middle. Everything had a pinkish or reddish hue and light filtered down through openings high above. Lumen crystals mounted on pillars cast a gentle white glow.

"I feel like I'm inside the belly of a huge beast," Thomas muttered as they strode along the marble floor.

"Much like Jonah," David remarked beside him, "who spent three days inside a great fish after trying to flee from his duty and the task set before him by the Threefold One."

Had that been a reproof? Thomas cast him a sidelong glance. "You got something to say to me, Shepherd—about Balthazar's Crucible?"

David arched his eyebrows. "I believe I already made my view clear. It is in your—and everyone else's—best interests that you undergo the Sage's trial and confront your own issues before rushing to the aid of others."

Thomas sighed. "Let's at least confirm where Enoch is and get the kiddo back before I consign an entire moon of my life to wandering aimlessly in a desert—all to hang out with a grouchy old reptile who generally disapproves of me."

He touched his chest, tracing one of many scars concealed under his cotton tunic. *I'm not so sure I want to remember whatever gave me these.*

"Take heart." David offered a wan smile. "Surely, the journey won't last a moon. You won't travel aimlessly, for I shall be there to guide you to the Crucible."

Despite himself, relief rushed over Thomas, and he stopped in his tracks. He'd been half-convinced David was sick to death of his stubbornness and would be glad to leave him behind.

And let's not forget my *grumpiness; Balthazar doesn't have the monopoly on that.*

Thomas swallowed thickly. "Well, I appreciate it. Be glad to have you along ... if it comes to that." But he wasn't going to risk getting stuck in the Evergold Desert of Losaridos until the nearest waystone decided to activate. He had his duty to the Northern Marches, and Enoch ... and the kiddo.

For the love of Jeremiah Bullfrog! He wanted to rip out his hair. There were too many places he needed to go, and not enough paths available to reach them. He scoffed. "Why couldn't the timing work out better?"

David's topaz eyes softened. "All will work out according to the Almighty's will—which is always for the good of those who love him. Do not worry about Annabelle. The Caretaker will send her in the proper direction after she arrives from Ynys Lloches. Whenever that may be." He clapped a hand on

Thomas's shoulder. "Here I must part ways with you until main-meal. Walk with Lord Yshua, Sir Thomas."

Throat tight, Thomas nodded. "You, too." The man deserved that much. With an answering nod, David pivoted and ducked into an access corridor that ran between the cathedral-sized rooms.

If only I had faith like him, Thomas thought as he turned toward the Farseer Chamber. *Or even the kiddo. With faith like that, maybe I'd finally tame the inferno raging inside me.*

Thomas heard the Commander and the Caretaker long before he saw them. Voices raised in anger carried from the vast, red-stone room that housed the Farseer. Amazing, how the statuesque woman could march into verbal battle against the evainghir and emerge victorious more often than not. It amused Thomas to see his Commander taken down a peg, even as it unnerved him.

"... impossible," Commander Storm snarled. "The Evaingynon are either dead or confined in the Sundered Realms. How could they touch the waking world in this way?"

"That is what I am telling you," the Caretaker snapped. "Something is obstructing my view of the Ingaraik Range. Impossible as it seems, the resonance bears Shadowveiled's signature."

"You must be mistaken, Tanisha," came the cold response. "Either age or wishful thinking has befuddled your wits."

"For shame, Daniel! That blow is beneath you. I may have changed your diapers, but a mere generation separates my age from yours."

His superior officer ... wearing diapers? Thomas supposed such a thing had happened, once. But still! Speaking of impossible, Commander Storm as a baby was almost impossible to picture. Almost. Thomas drew up short, choking back a laugh as he leaned against a marble pillar carved with serpentine and winged figures.

"... cannot fathom what Jethro could want with an air Aspect-attuned wyldling, or why he would stoop to abducting the sel Drayven heir."

"Why do you ask me?" the Commander fired back. "I cannot speak for him or ascertain a probable motive. It remains as much of a mystery to me as it does for you. Even more so, for I have never met my father."

"Count your blessings, Daniel," the Caretaker retorted. "Praise Yshua, you did not experience the pain of losing your parents." Despite its volume, her voice quavered. She cleared her throat. "Not that you have acknowledged the Threefold One since you were a boy throwing mud pies at my garden wall."

Despite his unease, Thomas bit back a grin, picturing a miniature version of the Commander slopping around in the mud. That was easy enough to envision.

"It has been an Age since I was that boy," the Commander growled. "Take care, Tanisha."

"How well I know." The Caretaker laughed humorlessly. "Unfortunate indeed that Remiel isn't here. If he were, he would—"

"Enough." Commander Storm's voice held a cold finality that made Thomas shiver. "My brother is not a subject I wish broached."

Commander Storm had a brother? Thomas experienced another frisson. Stray memories drifted like smoke. Something about a duel with a cloaked man holding a guitar-like instrument ... Sharp pain as a sword nicked Thomas's chin ... A scarred face sneering from beneath a cowl. *"And who do you think helped teach him the sword dance?"* ... And then Balthazar's basso rumble: *"Never mind Jethro's wayward firstborn."*

It was all a muddle, confusing him ... And then the memory was gone, drowned out by the two Sages' children sniping at one another, their voices ever clearer. Didn't they care that everyone could hear them? Embarrassed on his commander's behalf, Thomas reached the entrance to the Farseer Chamber. A forest of joined stalactites and stalagmites separated him from his goal in the center of the cavern.

"... your fault Remiel was lost in the dreamscape." The Caretaker sounded on the verge of tears. Framed by a pair of pillars like stone ribbons joining the ceiling and floor, she stood straight-backed, a monument of reptilian womanhood in her flowing red gown and ruby-decked headdress. Dangling rubies flashed as she trembled, and her hands fisted at her sides.

Man, she looked pissed. Thomas swallowed. *I'm not sure I should interrupt their shouting match, but I've gotta speak with Commander Storm.*

Unseen behind one of the pillars, the Commander groaned. "Must we re-chew old soup, Tanisha? There are more pressing matters to discuss."

"No," the Caretaker demanded, raising an arm to point. "Nothing is more important than family. After all these Cycles, I shall finally have my say, because you would not listen to me then. You were supposed to provide back-up for his efforts in locating your father—"

"A fool's errand," the Commander muttered.

"But as usual," she spoke over him, "you failed to heed my warnings. Instead of standing beside your brother, you went gadding about the continent on some fool errand of your own, and then turned up too late to save him—"

"Enough!" Commander Storm unleashed a bellow, and Thomas flinched against a ruby-veined stalagmite. "That 'fool errand,' as you call it, prevented a new nehmwight Dreadlord from arising to plague the continent. I had my duty ..." A sharp inhalation echoed through the chamber, and the Commander spoke in a bleak tone. "And I reckon you have forgotten—or it never mattered to you from the beginning—that my attempts to retrieve Remiel's mind destroyed my ability to enter the dreamscape ever after."

Great blazing balls of fire! Thomas's heart beat a staccato of trepidation as he wended his way around a forest of pillars. No wonder the Commander never looked for the kids himself in the dreamscape—he couldn't. How that must have irked him. No wonder he never talked about it.

Rounding a final column, Thomas halted beside it, unwilling to leave its meager cover. An oblong ruby crystal twice Commander Storm's height dominated the center of the room, illuminated by a shaft of yellow sunlight. The crystal resembled the waystones, only red instead of milky or colorless. Comparing the crystal's size to Commander Storm's was a simple matter, because the evainghir stood beside it while gripping the hilts of his scimitars.

Thomas steeled himself. *At this rate, I'd better intervene before they kill each other.* "Sir?" The word emerged as a breathy whisper.

As one, two brown-scaled visages snapped toward him. Ruby-red and storm cloud-gray eyes narrowed in identical expressions of censure.

The Caretaker crossed her arms and glared down her flat nose at him. "How much of that did you witness?"

He suppressed a titter. *Enough to know that everyone's family is dysfunctional.* He said, "Um, the first thing I heard was about your view of Ingaraik being blocked."

Commander Storm harrumphed and shot a glare at the Caretaker. "We need not speak about the rest. Doubtless, Sir Thomas is here to learn the whereabouts of the lad." He beckoned Thomas with a jerk of his head.

"I wish I could state with absolute certainty that I succeeded," the Caretaker said dryly. She moved closer to the Farseer and gently flattened a palm against one of its many facets. Her eyes glowed red and the huge crystal came alive with light and movement.

Like a television ... only everything was pinkish. Thomas furrowed his brow. Television? Where had that thought come from? Sooner or later, he'd need to get his memory back. Unease curled in his belly. *Just not until after the kids are safe.*

He came up beside the Commander, who stared into the crystal's depths with a frown. Each facet showed a different moving image. Except for the largest one, front and center, which rippled with light but no coherent picture. Grumbling, Commander Storm stepped closer and tapped it. Violet and ruby light zigzagged across the surface from the point of contact.

The Caretaker tsked. "I've told you not to do that, Daniel."

Commander Storm cast her a disgruntled look but withdrew his hand.

Stepping closer, Thomas frowned. "What's up with the wonky one? Is that the interference you were talking about?"

Crossing her arms, the Caretaker smiled wryly. "Indeed, Sir Thomas. This facet shows—or rather, doesn't show—the ruins of Ingaraik. I followed the barest traces—echoes, really—of a wyldling signature from the Darkenwood Forest to this place." A frown wrinkled her forehead. "No other location on Tehara defies my earthsense. Therefore, I conclude that Ingaraik is the best candidate for your baron-knight's location."

She shot a sidelong glance at the Commander, who stood rubbing his chin and glowering into the troublesome facet. "You are welcome to parse out the signature yourself, Daniel." She waved a hand. "Prove me wrong, since you believe it is impossible."

"Hmmm." Commander Storm touched the blank facet. Violet sparked in his gray eyes. "I am sensing a resonance here ..." His eyes widened and he stepped back, looking shaken. "Tanisha, I ..." He cleared his throat and lowered his head, mumbling, "I apologize."

Huh? Thomas felt like the floor had fallen out beneath him. The great Commander Storm ... *apologizing?* This was like watching a dog stand on its hind legs and preach a sermon. But considering His Excellentness, Lord Raeden von Bleistaff, maybe that was a bad analogy.

"Sir? Is it ...?" *Your father.* His voice trailed off before he finished, confused by the deep sorrow threatening to engulf him. Had something happened to his own father? *Do I want to know?*

"Indeed." Commander Storm ground his teeth. "These energy signatures originate from Shadowveiled."

Shoulders drooping, the Caretaker sighed. She rubbed her forehead. "Part of me hoped I was wrong. It makes no sense. Unless ..." She stiffened, her eyes widening as she placed a hand over her heart. "By all the stones of Tarrindor. Jethro's vashryu."

Face wooden, the Commander slowly turned to her. Their gazes locked. "You think?"

"I'm afraid so," the Caretaker replied, grim as a funeral dirge.

Thomas winced. Now what conflagration did they have to put out? Vashryu. That was some sort of gem the Sages used to focus their phenomenal cosmic powers. Balthazar had all but promised his vashryu to Thomas, should he pass the trials. He hadn't really considered it before, but that must amount to more power than a man could shake a stick at. A shaky exhalation became a whimper.

Well, that figures. More fuel to add to the fire threatening to consume me. Fear clawed his insides like a cat trying to escape. His brain offered up white noise in lieu of coherent reasoning.

Thomas glanced between his superior officer and their hostess. For the love of all that's holy, why weren't they explaining it to him? Didn't the Commander have orders to give him?

His throat suddenly dry, he rasped, "So. Jethro's vashryu is at Ingaraik. Uh ... what exactly does this mean for our mission to rescue Enoch?"

The evainghir looked at him. "It means our time has run out. We must assume the lad's captors have suborned his mind and plan to use him against us." His voice faltered and he blinked. He coughed, then lifted his head, his visage wiped clear of emotion. "I have no choice but to prepare for an all-out war. Against a wyldling."

"And perhaps more than one," the Caretaker whispered. "Only the Threefold One knows how long our adversary has been ... collecting wyldlings."

Fixing Thomas with a cold stare, Commander Storm clasped his hands behind his back. "Sir Thomas, if my fears prove true, then you must be prepared—by any means necessary—to kill Enoch sel Drayven on the battlefield."

Flood

The banquet for the noble gwerindawr took place in a lagoon off the Limani bay, on a seven-tiered coral platform resembling half a wedding cake. Each successive terrace was smaller than the one below and culminated in the throne at the top, where Morgan Brenin sat.

Annabelle and Mordred reclined at a low table on the sixth level. The princepsa and the archimandrite lounged on the other side of a path leading up to the seventh tier that held the Brenin's throne. Although Rhiannon beamed at her and waved, Sawel wore a concerned expression.

Annabelle frowned. Was something wrong? The archimandrite had skipped the play preceding the banquet and only just arrived from researching the gwerindawr's earliest historical records.

She turned to Mordred—her *boyfriend*—and asked, "Do you know what your father has planned for his speech?"

Probably more propaganda about how dangerous the outside world was, that they were better off staying in Ynys Lloches, and the Ahdmerel would lead them to glory ... right here at home.

The princeps looked up from scanning the lower tiers of the banquet platform. "No, little damselfly." He smiled. "But I would assume most of it will be more singing of your praises for all you've done to help the people since you've arrived."

Annabelle winced. "I could do without the public recognition. I didn't accomplish much. It's not like I managed to break the prophesied curse. I don't even know what it might be." Sighing, she glanced at Sawel, hoping to catch his eye. Presumably, his research had been in aid of finding information on the curse.

Mordred chuckled. He patted her arm. "You're too modest. Don't worry; I promise I won't embellish this time. I'll translate every word true."

Despite herself, Annabelle laughed. Few gwerindawr outside the royal court spoke the trading language. That morning, Morgan Brenin's inaugural speech to welcome everyone and present the blessed Ahdmerel to the people had been entirely in the gwerindawr language. Mordred served as her translator. The king's praise waxed flowery enough to choke her, but Mordred had slipped in phrases about her battling sharks, washing away a plague, and diverting a typhoon. He claimed it was part of a new ballad he was composing in her honor, and he only wished to cheer her up because she looked sad.

I'd be less sad if the king would let me visit Raeden, Annabelle mused as she surveyed the activity in the lagoon.

Down below, octopi towed floating platters of seaweed salads, watermelon slices, and kelp-wrapped barley nut cakes to the lowest tier where servants waited to take them to the diners. Courtiers in their assigned seats chattered about the meal or speculated on the subject of the king's speech. Often they stared at her, though many were friendly and had greeted her kindly after her presentation to the wider court.

The common folk thronged the lagoon where decorated barges heaped with the same food items circulated, a susurrus of conversation in the air, but nobody was eating. They all waited on Morgan Brenin to open the banquet with a speech.

Morgan Brenin waited on the third sun. Chin held high and shoulders back, the king sat ramrod straight in what Annabelle thought of as his declaimer's pose, surveying the populace. The bronze torc resting upon his collarbones seemed darker than before. The torc was an ugly thing; Annabelle averted her gaze.

Atropos attained her zenith. The king clapped his hands. A sensation like thunder without sound spread from the throne in a ripple moving outward, through the air and disturbing the water. The first time he'd done it, Rhiannon had explained that it was one of the small bits of magic bestowed by the torc meant to gain an audience's attention.

Everyone hushed and stared at the king.

Then he glanced at her and Mordred. For some reason, his warm smile made her blood run cold. If whatever the king was going to say made him happy, then Annabelle didn't think she'd like it.

Please, God. Don't let him say he'll execute Raeden. Please. Anything but that.

"My people!" Rich and resonant, his voice rang out into the silence. Mordred whispered a translation into her ear. "Before we thank the Almighty Threefold One for his gracious benevolence and the bounty spread before us, I have wonderful news for all of you. Not only does the blessed Ahdmerel of prophecy share our waters and swim among us, soon to restore us to our former glory—and this should be enough for a celebration—but there is more." He paused and made a sweeping gesture in their direction. "It involves my beloved son, the Captain of the Howling Tempest, Mordred Twywysog."

Sounding confused, Mordred's breath hitched while translating the words "beloved son," and his voice faltered as he spoke his name, which needed no translation. Morgan Brenin's voice boomed as he continued his speech. Beside her, Mordred stiffened. He stopped translating and instead muttered something in his native tongue. He sounded ... nervous.

Annabelle turned to the wide-eyed princeps, whose blue skin had gone pale. "Mordred? Are you okay? Do you need something to drink?" She concentrated, and a small globe of water appeared above her palm. He ignored it, staring past her at his father, whose voice rose in a triumphant tone, followed by something that sounded like an invitation, and then fell silent.

The people applauded.

What did he tell them?

Annabelle trembled. The water globe collapsed and dripped between them. She scanned the crowds, the tiers filled with gwerindawr nobility. Many of them smiled, but several young women scowled, and one haughty, green-skinned beauty outright glared at her. What had Morgan Brenin said to upset *them?* Hastily, she glanced at the princepsa. Rhiannon was clapping and cheering. Sawel was frowning at the king. The king was grinning at Annabelle and Mordred like a doting father.

Confusion and fear wrenched her gut. *What is going on?*

She turned to her ... boyfriend, who blinked like he was coming out of a dream, then grabbed his shoulders, shaking him. "Mordred!" Panic strangled her voice. "What did he say? Please tell me!"

"He said ..." He took a deep breath. "Forgive me. He said we're betrothed. The handfasting ceremony takes place at moonrise."

Annabelle stared at Mordred. *Not my boyfriend. My fiancé, now. Oh, fudge!* She felt as if she teetered over an abyss. Mouthing the word, "No," she whirled to face the king, to say something about not being ready for marriage, but Morgan Brenin had resumed speaking to the crowd.

Why make this declaration now?

Her eyes burned as she turned back to the princeps. "Why ... How?" She wished she was with Raeden on Crescent Islet. Or better yet, gone from this place through the waystone. She gripped Daar-Lûsin. "Mordred. Did you tell him about us, after I *begged* you to keep our courtship a secret?"

Her fiancé blanched. "Lady Ann, I apologize," he whispered in a rush. "Yes. I told Father we were courting—before you asked me to keep it a secret. And he was so *pleased* with me! But I never imagined ... this."

Mordred's voice broke and for a moment he looked lost. Then his face hardened and his eyes blazed as he cupped her cheeks, brushing away tears with his thumbs. "Do not weep, my little damselfly. I vow I'll make it up to you, once we are wed." He leaned closer. "Perhaps Father will be so pleased to have you bound to our people, we could ask him to grant a boon. To release the scout hound. Or allow you and me to leave Ynys Lloches together. To seek glory. And to find your brother."

For a moment, Annabelle wavered, but then she recalled the king's adamant refusal to take her and Raeden to the waystone. His disdain for Rhiannon's ideas regarding trade with other nations. His dismissal of his son's aspirations.

No. We're all stuck here so long as Morgan Brenin is in charge.

Annabelle jerked back, away from Mordred's warmth and his golden gaze before she relented. "No. I ..." *I can't marry you. I don't know if I love you.* She knew she must tell him. But something kept her from saying it aloud. What if marriage to the princeps was what God planned for her? Could she try to love Mordred? She wasn't sure of his feelings. And if they didn't love one another, then they'd both be miserable. But if there was a slim chance that Mordred could free Raeden, that they could all escape Ynys Lloches and then rescue Enoch ...

She bit her lip, then asked, "Mordred, do you even love me?"

Mordred hesitated, glancing at his father expounding from his throne before replying. "That's not the point of a ... union such as this. Father says we must wed. Lady Ann, you are a fine woman. People adore you. I ..." He swallowed, looking uncertain, then sat up straight. He took her hand in his and held it against his cheek. "I am ... fond of you, little damselfly. Perhaps love will come in time. Likely not a grand passion, but ... you are to be my wife. I will always take care of you and remember my duty. With me for a husband, you'll have no reason for complaint."

No reason, except ... you're not Thomas! Her chest tightened. "I don't—"

Sudden cheering drowned out her voice. Forcing a grin, Mordred looked past her. At his father, who held out his hands.

Morgan Brenin smiled, benevolent as a shark. "Come to me Ahdmerel, my daughter." Striations in his bronze torc glinted orange in the sunslight. It seemed ... wrong.

A wave of nausea rippled through her. *I need to get away. The dreamscape ... Thomas ... Enoch ... Khinjara ... Varazslo ... The king can't obtain my consent to hand-fasting while I sleep, can he?*

With the roar of applause thundering in her ears, Annabelle lurched to her feet. She swayed, her vision tunneling until the king's triumphant expression was all she could see. Her hand sought out Daar-Lûsin as she stepped toward her future father-in-law. Before he could grab her, she dashed past him, pushing behind Rhiannon and Sawel. The applause dwindled, becoming gasps and shouts of astonishment as she unsheathed Daar-Lûsin and teetered at the edge of the banquet platform. She set her mind in the pattern Khinjara had taught her and prepared her consciousness to flee into the dreamscape. Once she touched water, the passage from waking to dream world would be easy.

Her stomach clenched. The water seemed so far below.

My knight in shining armor, please be there!

Clutching Daar-Lûsin, Annabelle leaped.

The wind roared as shining wavelets rushed up to meet her, and a flood of gray fog swept her away.

"Annabelle!" Her name echoed throughout the mist.

That voice ...

"Enoch!"

Had she found him at last?

She opened her eyes to snow-capped mountains shrouded in silver mist. It reminded her of a picture she'd seen once of the Rocky Mountain Range. Her heart lifted. This was the place she'd been seeking. Enoch's domain. His presence was diffuse, but it was the most she'd felt since he'd been abducted.

"Enoch, I'm here."

The silver mist coalesced into a ghostly human figure and assumed her heart-brother's features. Instead of the silver-chased armor, he wore a light gray jacket with black embroidery, brown trousers and tall leather boots. Dark gray metal glinted around his neck—the wyldling snare. His kythim was subdued. An image of a silver diadem appeared on his brow, then winked out. He looked much as she remembered, but with a new gravity and sorrow in his eyes, and his shoulders slumped as if he carried a heavy burden.

"Annabelle." His face lit up as he reached for her.

She ran into his arms and hugged him with all her might. It was like hugging a snowman, but she held on. "You're okay, you're okay! I've missed you." His arms were like ice. "Enoch, why are you so cold?"

"Missed you, too," he murmured. "I don't know. Maybe because I'm fighting the snare to be here." He shuddered.

Annabelle wrapped her kythim around him. She thought about tropical weather and Ynys Lloches, where she would be hand-fasted to Mordred at moonrise ...

"Ah, that's better. Nice and warm." A blissful expression passed over Enoch's face. Then he frowned. "Annabelle, are you well? You're all flushed."

"Yes, I'm fine." She pushed away thoughts of her betrothed. "Forget me, how are ..."

Enoch flickered. His eyes widened. "Not sure how long I can stay—" Images flooded her brain too quickly to make sense of them, but with them came an underlying dread and a warning.

She responded in kind with a barrage of memories and images. "Enoch! Raeden and I are stuck in Ynys Lloches ..."

"—just wanted to make sure—"

"... Can't get to you until I fulfill the gwerindawr prophecy..."

—you were alive and well—"

She sent more images of her meeting the dragon in the dreamscape. "... And get to the waystone to travel to the Ingaraik Mountains, if what Varazslo says is true—"

Shocked recognition, then panic lanced through their entwined kythim. The silver mist convulsed. "Ann! That was no dragon. Don't trust him! He's the one who abducted me—" Soot-gray bands engulfed her heart-brother like a set of snapping jaws, yanking him from her grasp into the nothingness.

Cold emptiness punched her in the gut like a fist made of ice. Her shredded kythim stung and leaked blue mist. Enoch was gone again. She wailed, clutching her head which reeled with a tornadic bombardment of memories not her own.

Enoch's memories. Several images rose to the forefront. One kept trying to resolve—of someone he called "the Dreadlord"—then fluttered away like newspaper pages in the wind. But she glimpsed Enoch's primary jailors, and his voice whispered their names. A sneering, bearded nehmwight in black robes—*Yvres Tenebris*—a powerful sorcerer. A burly, brown-furred kaenhir with fierce yellow eyes—*Zakaar Ravenos*, who'd murdered Enoch's friends. And then, a tall, gray-skinned youth in brown robes with dreadlocks, orange eyes, and an insufferable smirk—*William Dulciber*—

Wait. She knew that guy from somewhere.

Annabelle seized the last image before it escaped on the wind with the others. She held something like a full-color newspaper clipping in her hands.

"Call me Varazslo," the youth in the picture said.

As she stared, the smirking youth morphed into a skinny, gray-scaled dragon with thirteen horns on its head and black swirls on its flanks. It had the same smirk on its visage and its eyes glowed orange, then purple, then back to orange again.

"Call me Varazslo," the dragon in the picture said.

Ice crystalized her core. The youth and the dragon spoke using the same voice. She remembered. The boy in the tower, orange eyes wide as he stared in shock. And recognition, she now realized. He'd known her name—who she was—from the beginning.

Orange eyes. He had orange eyes. The dragon did too, at first.

Nightmare images assailed her. The nehmwight warrior at the waystone. Coming for her with orange eyes ablaze and Raeden's blood dripping from his blade.

Fingernails tearing into the newspaper image, Annabelle panted. Her throat was dry. "Oh, my ... a nehmwight. God, help me. I hugged a *nehmwight.*"

But he never hurt me. He saved me from my rogue kraken. And he was rather gentle—

Dear Lord. That didn't matter! She'd been meeting *Enoch's captor* in the dreamscape. A nehmwight sorcerer who'd lied to her about who he was. Teased her with information about Enoch. Taught her magic that made her sick. Manipulated her by saying she was pretty ... He probably didn't even mean it. Had Varazslo ever been her friend, or was it all pretense? She fought back tears. "Was any of it real?"

How could she be such an idiot? In the dreamscape, people could assume any semblance they wished, if they had the power and force of will to do so. Maybe if she had talked about it with Raeden, he'd have helped her see the truth.

But would you have listened to him? You thought you had it all handled. You wanted *to believe Varazslo was your friend.*

Annabelle's hands shook as she wadded up the image. "I *liked* him! I thought maybe he liked *me*. He certainly acted like he did, hanging on my every word and staring at me ... But all this time, he was a smug, conniving ... mendacious ... *noodlehead!"* She hurled the newspaper ball into the swirling winds. "What the frumious bandersnatch is the jerk after? Some sort of sick game? Why did he come after me—"

She froze. Varazslo—no, *William*—knew who she was. He knew she was a wyldling, like Enoch. He also knew when she was in the dreamscape; he'd bragged about setting up wards to alert him to her presence.

The sorcerer-dragon would come for her.

Annabelle shivered, hugging herself. She couldn't leave the dreamscape yet. She must stay asleep past moonrise. *Let's see ... Oh, cripes!* Full dusk was at least five, six hours away at Ynys Lloches. Moonrise was even later.

She couldn't evade the nehmwight sorcerer forever. He knew the dreamscape better than she did.

Besides, I have to confront him. Demand the truth. Maybe she could pretend she didn't *know*. Could she fool him? *No, he*

seems able to read me, somehow. Concealing something this big ... he'll know something is up. Keeping away from him until she figured something out would be best. There must be some secluded corner of the dreamscape where she could lay low.

Khinjara would know where to hide. The dreamscape was her home. Khinjara might even take her to Hadrien.

Annabelle screamed for Khinjara. No answer. Why wouldn't the hisanabyad come? She had the Dagger of Moonlight back. Annabelle's heart sank. More and more, she feared something had happened to her winged unicorn friend. But Khinjara was wise and powerful. What could harm an hisanabyad?

Terror flooded her entire being. There had to be someone who could help her confront this William Dulciber. She had no idea how powerful he really was, or what he was capable of. What if he had done something to Khinjara?

I need to find Thomas!

Even if he teased her about being a silly, naïve girl, he would still protect her. She could trust Thomas. He was a knight, and her friend. He'd always been honest with her. Unlike Varazslo, he was always exactly what he appeared to be.

Annabelle concentrated on the knight in the gold-chased armor, picturing his lopsided grin, the scar on his chin, and the way his eyes sparkled when he laughed. She recalled the strength of his arms and his warmth when he held her.

The mountains fled. Suddenly she stood on a dusty ridge overlooking sand dunes and brown lands. Although no suns shone in the clear, blue sky, the air baked her, sucking moisture from her being. *I can't stay here long ... this hot, arid place is hostile to water wyldlings. But it's just right for a fire wyldling.*

Pivoting in place, she scanned the empty desert. "Thomas!" Fear roughened her voice as she screamed his name over and over. Hurry ... Hurry ... Tears of frustration evaporated as soon

as they formed. Lethargy settled into her bones. She was weakening. *I need water!*

Annabelle fled the desert wasteland for her comfortable glade, slowing long enough to assure herself that Varazslo hadn't beaten her there. He hadn't. Their arrangement was to meet in neutral territory, agreed upon beforehand. But he hadn't kept their appointment last night, and he'd proven himself a filthy, deceitful snake. So all bets were off. She needed to prepare.

Annabelle sank into her river. Fear hollowed out her bones despite the water energy filling her reservoir. Of course, Thomas wouldn't be in the dreamscape. Why had she expected to find him? It was late morning in Y'Vasheirdenelle. The absence of Khinjara shook her to her core. Before Ynys Lloches and losing the dagger, she'd always come.

Staring up at the patches of blue between the tree branches and foliage, she whispered, "You can't worry about that now, Ann. You have a dragon to contend with. So what if you're not as strong as he is? You still have to face him. Make him tell the truth and freaking explain what he wants from me."

I won't be fooled again!

Anger filled her faster than the water soaked into her. Fear receded. Her fingers curled into fists. How dare he kidnap Enoch? How dare he pretend to be a dragon and then befriend her? Was this mighty sorcerer such a coward he couldn't approach her as himself? What was he afraid of? Annabelle was no warrior. There was nothing remotely scary about her!

Why was she so afraid of a boy who hid behind dragon scales?

Annabelle barked a laugh. This was the dreamscape. *If I wanted, I could become a dragon, too.*

Even as the thought occurred to her, water flowed over her body, and Annabelle began to change.

Clue

Trying not to think about Annabelle laughing alongside the knight with the golden aura, William removed the latest batch of Zakaar's elixir from the flame just as it began to boil. He extinguished the flame and removed his heat-resistant gloves. Then he dropped a handful of dried chamomile into the steaming black liquid, and it began to fade to brown. He placed the lid on the cauldron and wiped sweat from his forehead. The difficult work was done. Now the elixir needed to steep for eighteen hours before he distributed it among the fourteen vials lined up on the laboratory bench.

William exhaled noisily, then turned to regard his companion. The black thorny threads that used to twist in his kythim had gradually disappeared over the past moon. *At least the harkhurz is still my friend. I can rely on his loyalty—so long as the elixir continues to stave off his madness.*

Zakaar leaned by the door, one foot propped against the wall as he trimmed his claws with a paring knife. "You have changed," he murmured, raising his eyebrows.

William snorted. "That's rich, coming from you. I'm not the one who *was* going mad, and now isn't, thanks to my special formula." He paused, narrowing his eyes. "What d'you mean, I've changed?" *And is it something Tenebris would notice?* His master would be there shortly to bind William's arkhabala for the next battle training session.

"For several days, you smelled of honeysuckle alongside the blood and lightning-scent. Now, you smell more than ever like the master." He grimaced, baring his fangs. "Of persimmons, chicory, and vinegar. It has grown most unpleasant to be in the same room with the both of you."

"Oi! You're ... *unpleasant*," William muttered, but his heart wasn't in the insult. His hands shook. *I need my whiskey.* However, Tenebris could come in at any moment. He began cleaning up and returning implements to their proper places, making more noise than strictly necessary. "Who blistering cares what I smell like?"

Zakaar kicked off from the wall. Sheathing his knife, he sauntered over, then lunged forward to catch a glass retort before it hit the stone floor. "Something is very wrong, my friend."

William snatched the vessel and tucked it safely into its pigeonhole. "Nothing is wrong." *Suns scorch it!* Reaching into his burkheld, he pulled out his flask and took a hasty swig—then nearly choked on the liquor.

The harkhurz pounded his back. "Something is wrong," he asserted, his furred visage grim.

In between coughs, William spluttered, "It's nothing."

A faint chime rang, and they both froze, staring wide-eyed at each other.

William blinked. *My tell-tale wards. Tenebris is coming.*

"The master," Zakaar rumbled. "I will stall him." He moved toward the door, placing his burly frame right in front of it.

Like that'll work for longer than two seconds. Tenebris could blast him with a thought.

Gratitude warmed him along with the whiskey despite the harkhurz's misplaced valor. William cleared his stinging throat and jammed the flask into an internal pocket. He found a sprig of mint in another pocket. Chewing it, he sealed his notebook and was tucking it into his burkheld when the door latch rattled. He'd locked it, of course.

"William!" The wood muffled his master's voice as he pounded on the door. "I know you're in there. Don't make me disintegrate this door."

Zakaar gave William a questioning look.

"Just let him in," he grumbled. Tenebris could do what he threatened, as William knew from experience. There was no escaping the man when he'd decided his apprentice needed an "object lesson."

The harkhurz shot the deadbolt back and stepped aside. Tenebris barged in without sparing him a glance, black burkheld billowing behind him. His eyes flashed. "Let's make this quick. I have work to finish before I retire for the day. Give me your hand."

William considered disobeying him. Having his magic sealed away disturbed him as few things did. But he was no coward. Jaw clenched, he held out his left hand. A minor defiance.

"No, your dominant hand, you bumbling fool. I'm binding your arkhabala, not bolstering your capacity."

"Yes, Master," he replied in a flat tone, switching hands. He avoided looking at Zakaar.

Eyes glowing, Tenebris seized his hand and dug his thumbnail into William's palm. William focused on the energy flow. It happened quickly. The tattoo on his master's hand swirled, a thread spinning off and circling his thumb. Icy agony plunged into William's hand and shot up his arm to embrace his torso. He hissed. His arkhabala convulsed like a beast under attack, everything prickled, and then it went numb and still.

I think I know how he did it. Sealing away power is like a temporary version of my mirror-maze trap on a smaller scale.

After applying some modifications, Tenebris's spell could be useful in the dreamscape.

"That'll wear off in an hour, Acolyte." His master faced the harkhurz. "I have a job for you. Report to me immediately after the training." Tenebris sneered. "Don't go easy on him. Otherwise, the lesson won't sink into the imbecile's thick skull." And with that, the Arkhadahn swept from the room, slamming the door behind him.

Massaging his aching palm, William stared at the place where his master had stood. Imbecile. No matter how many times Tenebris said it, that word still had the power to wound him. He wished his heart was as numb as his arkhabala and as silent as his skin. Reaching within to find the amethyst glow reassured him. Although he was less certain of his command over it in the waking world than he was in the dreamscape, his connection to the Aethyr brought comfort.

At least it would be Zakaar teaching him today, and not the Golorum. Or Northward. Or Incendo, for that matter. Mother of the Outer Darkness! Hopefully he never had Incendo for a teacher.

He shuddered, then stomped to the door, beckoning Zakaar. "Let's get this over with." He yanked the door open. "Time for this imbecile—" he spat the word— "To get the rocks knocked from his thick skull."

The harkhurz accompanied him down the corridor. After a moment of silence, he said, "I do not think you are an imbecile, William. You are the cleverest man I know. Only you could find the cure to my madness."

William kept his eyes straight ahead. Most clever. That was a compliment. It felt ... good. And rather embarrassing. Like gifts, he wasn't accustomed to receiving them. His fingers twisted inside his sleeves. Normally, he would've retorted "of course I'm clever," but for some reason it no longer felt proper to do so.

Now what? I believe I'm supposed to say something pleasant in response—but what? Quick, think! What would Milady Blue say?

He winced. As much as Annabelle was a tender subject, he dredged up her lesson in friendship. *"When you're friends with someone, you need to show your appreciation for their kindness—"* Kindness? Ha! There was a term he'd always equated with weakness and stupidity— *"with gratitude and encouraging words. If you're grouchy and nasty all the time, then they won't stick around. And then you won't have any friends. You'll be alone."*

It struck William, then, that he didn't much care for the idea of being alone. Not anymore.

Suns curse that maiden! She'd ruined him with her beguilement spell. Despite her betrayal, he yearned to see her. He'd returned to the dreamscape, of course, but stayed hidden in the shadows while Annabelle ran around, calling for Varazslo. He was tempted to go to her, even then, except she called the name "Thomas" more often. That cursed knight. His nemesis. Why hadn't the man stayed a toad?

At least I still have Zakaar.

William hunched his shoulders and walked faster. "Thank you," he muttered.

Zakaar kept pace with him. "Pardon, Dulciber?" He sounded shocked.

"I said: 'Thank you!'" William snapped. Why was this so difficult? "For ... being my friend. You've served me well."

From the corner of his eye, he glimpsed pale lavender tones blossoming in the assassin's kythim. It worked!

"I am glad to serve, Dulciber. You are a kind master."

Me? Kind? Had the suns turned green? William staggered to a halt. "Being kind ... this is a good thing? Tenebris says it's a sign of weakness."

Zakaar's ears lifted, and his eyes brightened. "Not at all. It is a sign of your strength growing. My mother always said to me: 'Zakaar, to lure the desert fawn, you must spread the sweet grass instead of the nettles.'" He paused and glanced at the floor, shrugging. "Of course, we would then kill the fawn and eat it, but clever as you are, surely you know I am making a picture with words and not advising you to kill your friends." He grinned.

"Huh?" Was the assassin joking—or was this a new form of madness? Perhaps William needed to adjust the elixir's potency.

"That is to say," Zakaar continued, "if you are sweet—kind—then others will enjoy to be near you."

Like Annabelle, William realized. His brow lowered. Oh, she was a sly one, luring him in with her sweetness. "If I am kind," he began, slowly. "Others will want to be with me." He took a deep breath. "Others like ... maidens?"

Merciful Valeshka! Did I really say that out loud?

Eyeing him sidelong, Zakaar tilted his head, then chuckled. "When did you begin to care for such things? I thought you only cared for gaining all your circles."

They resumed their walk at a more leisurely pace. "I *do* only care about my advancement as an Arkhadahn," William grumbled. "It was ... There was something Northward mentioned, and I wondered ..."

Zakaar's ears went back. His eyes glinted and black threads twisted through his kythim. "You spend too much time listening to the warlock. He cannot be trusted."

Good. He'd covered up his slip. Given Zakaar's ... *history* with maidens, the longer he kept the harkhurz ignorant of Annabelle's existence, the better. Despite his faith in his elixir's efficacy, he'd devised plans based on five possible scenarios of Zakaar meeting Annabelle and how to prevent the harkhurz from killing her. But why tempt fate?

"I'm just learning more about the enemy," William said. They turned a corner and entered a low-traffic section of the fortress where empty alcoves interrupted the corridor walls. He wanted to access the training hall via the back entrance today. Less chance of encountering Northward. "Like you do, when you're scouting for your, uh ... work."

"Yes. But when I scout, the enemy does not see me. If I must get in close—but not kill—then I put on a disguise."

"Excellent idea. In fact, I made a disguise for myself under the same principle." He grinned, as excitement shot through him. *My arkhabala might be bound, but the amethyst power inside me is undamped.* "Would you like to see it?"

Zakaar paused beside an alcove, eyes wide. "You would show me your disguise?" His ears lifted and the lavender replaced the black threads. "I am honored" He bowed.

William shrugged. "You're my ... friend. I can trust you." His dragon was sheer genius. He'd been wanting to show the Dreadlord for days, but there hadn't been an opportunity. Zakaar was loyal and would be properly impressed by his skills. Like Annabelle had been.

"Hold on, this will take a moment." Pushing the maiden from his mind, William concentrated on his image of Varazslo. He knew the dragon's appearance better than his own. His mind went sideways as he reached down into the reservoir of purple light. A ghostly image of the dragon began to coalesce in front of the nearest alcove.

"Dulciber, what is happening to your eyes? They change color." Then Zakaar growled. "Wait. Someone comes."

William ignored him. He gave a little push with his mind, and Varazslo appeared in all his dark and spiny glory. "Ah," he sighed, slumping. That had taken more out of him than he expected. He should practice creating illusions outside the dreamscape to increase his stamina.

Cursing in his native tongue, the harkhurz drew his long knives and lunged at the apparition. William held Varazslo in place, leaning against the wall and laughing as Zakaar slashed at the dark gray dragon. His blades went right through the conjured image as if it was smoke.

The assassin retreated. "Dulciber, what ..."

"Oi!" William cackled. "You should see your *face*."

"What in all the nether perditions is *that* abomination?" A woman's voice shrilled.

Snarling, Zakaar whirled from the illusion. William's laughter cut off. Incendo stood at the end of the corridor, Northward at her side. Both were sweaty and wore battle leathers. By some miracle, the Marshal's pet wyrmkin wasn't with them.

The youth's eyes were wide. His gaze shifted from the dragon, to William, and then back again. "Did you make that with your sorcery?"

"Yes." William shot a glare at Incendo. All his good cheer had evaporated. "And for your information, it's not an abomination; it's a creature of myth called a *dragon*. You'd be amazed at the things I can create, Northward." His mouth snapped shut before he revealed any more. Northward seeing his disguise made him uneasy. With a surge of intent—and a wave of his hand, for the sake of drama—William dispelled the image into gray mist.

The wyldling snare *should* keep Northward away from the dreamscape. William's gaze dropped to the soot-gray metal around Northward's neck. His stomach churned as he recalled his bungling attempt with the snare during his first training session with Northward. He still couldn't figure out which memories Northward had seen, but the other youth seemed less hostile since their altercation. He hadn't called William "son of a goat" or "nehmwight filth" for days.

Likely it's all pretense, meant to lull me into a false sense of security.

William stalked down the hall, hands fisted at his side. "Would you like another demonstration?"

Northward shook himself. His kythim betrayed wariness as he stared into William's eyes. *—Just what are you capable of, sorcerer? Come on. I* know *you're reading my mind—*

Face tight, William stared back. He refused to take Northward's bait.

Incendo sneered. "Further demonstrations of asinine tomfoolery won't be necessary, boy. Now hurry along to your daily chastisement." She looked Zakaar up and down. "Bringing your bodyguard won't save you from the Golorum."

Zakaar growled. "I will be his trainer today, devil woman." His glare passed over Incendo, his malice settling on Northward.

"You're being unfair, Lady Marshal," Northward said with a chuckle. "Dulciber holds his own during battle training. He's a lot tougher than he looks." Turning to William, his gaze sharpened. *—You need to be, given how much your master tortures you—*

William swallowed. He'd wondered what Northward glimpsed. There was his answer. *Probably he's just biding his time, waiting for the opportune moment to use it against me.*

"The boy has yet to prove himself to me." Incendo snapped, eyes narrowed. Then her burnt visage twisted into something resembling a smile. "Perhaps I ought to take a turn with his ... training."

Valkor avert! She'll kill me for sure.

William clenched his jaw and faced Incendo—then looked down. The crown of the blistering woman's head barely reached his armpit. She wasn't much taller than Northward, come to think of it. *What am I so scared of? I'm still an Arkhadahn, even with my powers bound.*

"Bring it on, Marshal," he replied, biting off each word. He held her gaze, refusing to be cowed by the fury blazing within her pale blue eyes. He thought he smelled smoke. No, he would *not* be distracted by thoughts of that cursed knight!

Incendo snorted, breaking the spell. "You aren't ready for me, boy. Perhaps after another Cycle puts meat on your bones. Good luck, then, Ravenos. Try not to eat this arrogant twit for breakfast. He'll give you indigestion for sure." She jerked her head. "Come along, sel Drayven."

Zakaar flinched, then redoubled his glare at Northward, who gave him a wide berth as he passed by. "Let us go, Dulciber. Time is flying. Soon, you will want to chase your dreams."

He has no idea how right he is, William mused as they entered the training hall. *Today, I confront Annabelle regarding her other "friend" who wants to kill me.*

Trailing purple mist, William flew through the dreamscape over grasslands, lakes, and forests. The hisanabyad was still safely ensconced within her prison. Annabelle wasn't at their agreed-upon meeting place, but that didn't matter. He knew where she'd be. The little maiden was nothing if not predictable in her habits—even if her notions regarding social interactions did make his head spin.

Ha! But I have a surprise in store for her this time.

Before long, he circled above Annabelle's glade. Instead of a maiden in dark blue armor, a blue-scaled dragon sat on its haunches beside the stream, wings neatly furled, neck elegantly arched. Her tail extended behind her into the water. Sapphire eyes blazed with inner fire as they tracked his progress. A magnificent blue aura shot through with red sparks and gray lines shone around the reptilian figure.

She's even beautiful as a dragon. William's wings floundered, nearly dropping him like a stone instead of spiraling grandly into the clearing. *Milady Blue figured out how to change her shape! But what is* she *so angry about?* I'm *the wronged party here.* His emotions swung like a pendulum between vexation at her betrayal and pleased astonishment at her resourcefulness.

A pity I'll be sealing away her wyld.

On the way over he'd rehearsed how this conversation would go—how he'd scold without alienating her, even offer to lead her directly to Northward if she'd agree never to meet the knight with the burning sword again—but now all his careful planning had washed away like chalked runes after a rainstorm.

Heart racing, he landed across the clearing from her and mimicked her posture. Was he bigger than her? Yes, and by a fair margin. Good. "Annabelle," he began. "I see you—"

She cut him off. "Shut up." Her voice was cold and hard, like an icicle down his spine. Oddly, this thrilled him, and his arkhabala flexed like a beast rising from slumber.

"You've been lying to me, Varazslo." The red sparks in her aura thickened and the sapphire glow in her eyes intensified. "Or should I say ... William Dulciber."

Shock ripped through him and his jaw dropped. Whatever he'd expected her to say, it wasn't this. He'd been so cautious. *Suns burn me to ash. She knows.* Should he deny it? No. The crimson fury in her aura made it clear that would only make things worse for him. *Can I salvage this?*

He wracked his brains for a plan, but with her eyes on him, his thoughts whirled in a maelstrom instead of falling neatly into place like they usually did.

"How ... Who ..." He swallowed thickly and dug his claws into the soil, tearing up sod. Yes, she'd caught him. However, he must mitigate this situation, somehow, or he'd lose her completely. If he hadn't already lost her to that cursed knight ... No. He'd win back her friendship. Annabelle was *his* wyldling.

You're an Arkhadahn. Don't stammer like a blithering imbecile. That won't impress her. Be dignified!

William lifted his snout and tried for nonchalance. "Clever maiden. It appears you've finally pierced my disguise. How did you discover my real name?"

Annabelle's wings rattled and her fan-shaped ears flattened. "Why should I give away my secrets to a lying fraud? I know you're a nehmwight, though God only knows how you're able to access the dreamscape."

She slammed her tail into the stream behind her. Water sprayed. "Of course, you knew exactly where Enoch was," she interjected, her voice shaking. "Because you're the one who kidnapped Enoch and put the wyldling snare on him!" Moisture welled and dripped from her glowing eyes. Her kythim dulled to gray around the edges.

Were those tears? Was she crying? Panic quivered under William's scales. How did he make this stop? Villem's spear! He needed to bind her wyld. He opened his jaws, but the cantrip jammed up in his throat, tangled up with all the things he wanted to say to her.

Annabelle shook her head. "I'm such an idiot," she choked. "Your eyes really *were* orange. All that tripping over your own tail. Then whenever you used magic, it made me sick ... The clues were right there, right in front of me. This whole time, you've been laughing at me—haven't you?" Her chest heaved. "If you really were my friend, then you'd have told me who you really were from the start instead of playing this wicked game."

Blinking away tears, she bared her teeth and rose on all fours, lashing her tail. She wobbled, and bright yellow panic briefly shot through her kythim, although it subsided as she widened her stance and lifted her head.

William fought for composure. *She's not used to that body. I can use that against her if she attacks me. No ... when she attacks me.* Eagerness filled him. It would be nice to fight someone he could defeat, for a change. Zakaar's grappling techniques were fresh in his memory. No, no. First, he must seal her magic.

"Drop your illusion, *William.* I know what you are."

—*Or is he afraid to face me as his true self?* — Her voice echoed through his head.

Sneering, he stood and shook out his wings. Didn't she realize Varazslo *was* his true self? As galling as it was to be accused of cowardice, he shouldn't let on he could read her mind. "I think not, Milady Blue. Not unless you drop yours first." Now how to rile her up so she unleashed her wyld on him? What were her weak spots? Ah, yes ...

"No way, José," she growled. "I prefer being a dragon." Uncertainty rippled through her aura, and she trembled.

She has to know she can't beat me in a straight-up fight—in any form. And who in perdition is José?

William shook his head, chuckling. He emulated Tenebris, voice dripping condescension as he cooed, "And what a pretty little dragon you make, Milady Blue. I could pick you up and put you in a jar. Add you to my collection."

She stiffened, more red sparking throughout the blue and drowning out the gray. Excellent. He grinned widely. "Maybe I should take you back to my tower and teach you how to use your wyld properly. Your weavings are *so* clumsy." They weren't at all, but she didn't know that; her confidence was eroding along with her emotional control.

"Tell me," he drawled, stalking nearer, claws squelching in the sodden moss. He paused one dragon-length away and lowered his head to meet her gaze, then let the orange creep back into his eyes. "Were you ever able to conjure up your pathetic water-dog again? Or did it prove too difficult for a daft maiden who was too blind to see clues dropped right in front of her?"

With a snarl, Annabelle pounced. Astonishment ripped through William. He'd expected an arcane assault. But he was ready for this, as well. *Thank you, Zakaar!* Bracing himself as Zakaar taught, he reared up and embraced the little blue dragon, pinning her arms and wings. It was almost as pleasant as hugging her. The silly fool had made herself sleek and smooth rather than prickly and spiny like him. Doubtless trying to emulate Hadrien Rainblessed—minus the whiskers. As enjoyable as this was, he needed to seal her magic—

"You fork-tongued ... supercilious ... noodlehead!" She screamed, thrashing in his arms. "Khinjara! Help!"

William roared with laughter. Warmth grew behind his breastbone. He wasn't sure what a noodle was, but *that* was a proper insult. Northward should take lessons from Annabelle. "Holler all you like, Milady Blue. Your pet hisanabyad isn't coming."

"Smarmy jerk! What did you *do* to her?" She head-butted his chest.

He grunted. "Nothing lethal. Trapped her in a mirror-maze."

"Why are you so ... *awful?*" Growling, she kicked his belly, and he felt the sting of her claws. A thin tendril of fear coiled at the base of his skull. His mirth subsided.

My armor isn't proof against her claws?

"Oi! None of that, now, Milady Blue," he chided, blocking her feet with his spiked tail.

—Ouch!— She yelped and tried to roll up into a ball.

And my spikes can damage her. Better take care. He didn't want to actually hurt her. He wanted to—

Out of nowhere, her spade-tipped tail smacked his snout, jarring him. He shook his head, then laughed. "So weak. Barely tickled." Tenebris's casual slaps stung worse. He needed to concentrate on the seal.

"Let. Me. *Go.*" Snarling, she began thrashing around again. Moisture collected between them. A cool, fresh feeling like spring rain washed over him.

What the ...! Now *she chooses to use her magic?*

William began intoning the cantrip to bind her. His grip loosened as Annabelle grew more slippery. Her wings broke his hold. *Oh, no, you don't Milady Blue!* He seized her arms, his claws penetrating her scales. He winced at her pained cry. No time to worry about hurting her now. He couldn't let her escape.

Shrieking aloud as her mind bombarding him with insult after insult—most of which he couldn't parse—Annabelle slashed at William. Her claws scored his right cheek. Three-quarters finished, the cantrip died on his tongue. He jerked his head back, then felt ten separate daggers plunge into his chest. Right into his seventh circle. It *hurt.* Worse than his etchings. Worse than a Seventh Order malecto grammerye.

Her claws were firmly embedded in his chest. "Let. Me. *Go.*"

William smelled honeysuckle. From the recesses of memory came the sound of a woman weeping.

The mysterious phantom woman's sobs blended with Annabelle's. A tiny voice, barely a whisper, tickled in his mind. *—Please, stop. You're hurting me. Let me go—*

"No," he snarled. He'd lose her. She'd run straight to that cursed knight. "I won't let him take you away. You're mine!"

—I don't belong to you ... I belong to Christ!—

William's vision went blue. Mint flooded his mouth, and he smelled citrus. A cold deeper than the arctic sank into his bones. Panic tore away reason as his dragon form melted away. His wings became his brown burkheld and his spiked tail, his trousers. Horrified, he watched as the claws gripping her morphed into gray fingers slick with her blood. He fought nausea as his own blood trickled down his chest. His scales were gone.

Merciful Valeshka! I'm vulnerable. I must bind her wyld. Turn her back to a maiden before she rips through to my heart. Now.

His vision cleared and he found himself staring into blue eyes darkened by pain.

—Even after all you've done ... I can't make myself kill you. I only wanted to be your friend. Were you ever mine, Will? —

Her words rang with truth. Shock seared William from the inside out. Intent surged and crackled across his skin like black lightning. *Bind her wyld.* Before he could pick up the melody of the cantrip, his arkhabala struck. Infused with the Aethyric magic of his ruptured disguise, inky dark vines streaked with purple writhed down his arms. They delved inside Annabelle.

Gasping, the blue dragon arched like a bow and puffed into blue mist. It evaporated. Milady Blue, the maiden, stood before him. Her dark blue armor receded where his grasping hands sank in just beneath her shoulders. Smeared in his blood, her pale hands were like ice against his chest. The wounds she'd inflicted stopped bleeding and closed. Cold pulsed through him. It was her wyld, pushing inside him even as it struggled to pull free from entanglement with his arkhabala.

Freezing void! Their magic was ... *melding.* How could that possibly have happened? Tenebris said the Arkhabadh and the Aethyr were incompatible! Yes, he'd planned to siphon her power from her, but into focus gems—not directly into himself!

He yanked back, but his arkhabala resisted. *Why won't it obey me? Is she trying to* steal *it from me? I must subdue this!*

Face ashen as the moon, Annabelle stared up at him, lips trembling, eyes red-rimmed and leaking tears. "Please, William," she whimpered. "It hurts. Let me go."

—I'm sick to death of lies and secrets and being used and boys thinking they own me oh my gosh what is that crawling inside me I'm gonna freaking barf—

Her mental barrage disoriented him. It reminded him of the wyldling snare debacle with Northward. Why did he have such a strong connection to these wyldlings?

What if the hisanabyad was right, and he was one himself?

Now is not the time to think about that!

William tried to let go of Annabelle, but he couldn't move his body. His insides were frozen. "I ... can't ... let ... go."

Ebony tendrils crept up Annabelle's neck. Her eyes widened. "St-stop it!"

"I'm trying." He tugged harder. "*You* stop taking my arkhabala."

"I'm not ... doing ... anything!" She panted, writhing. So, she wasn't intentionally stealing his power. Was this *his* doing? William could *feel* his arkhabala burrowing through her like worms, the darkness spreading inside her, and how she fought against the invasion. But she was losing. The inky vines of his arkhabala curled over her jawline, reaching up into her face. The sapphire of her kythim faded to a dull gray. No, no, no. This was wrong. He'd never wanted to extinguish her light.

Tears like ink slid down her cheeks. "Will," she gasped. "Please. Stop."

—It's too strong! God, help me—

How did he make it stop? Could he entice his arkhabala back to where it belonged? William focused on her wyld, a ball of icy water inside him. *There's enough here for study!* He shouted at his arkhabala. *If you extract everything from her now, there won't be any for later. We need to safeguard what we've already taken.*

For a moment, he despaired, but then his arkhabala paused in its ravaging. Slowly, it retreated. The inky black receded from Annabelle's face and neck. She wilted with a shuddering sigh, her hands sliding from his chest to flop at her sides. William grunted, recentering himself to counter-balance her weight. He held on to her arms. In a moment, the last of his tattoos should return to him and then he'd let go. Maybe.

Annabelle seemed to gather her remaining strength. William braced himself for a last assault. His arkhabala hadn't yet completed its transfer. Purple mist swirled around them. He breathed in a portion. It smelled like honeysuckle. Annabelle inhaled it, too. Her eyes widened and her armor shifted to dragon scales, but they were darker than before, tinged violet.

She shuddered, staring up at him. "Will ... what do you *want* from me?"

William hesitated, staring into her eyes as she transformed from maiden to dragon. "I ... I want ..."

The obvious answer: *Your power.* But that no longer seemed the full truth. What *did* he want from her?

Burning Bridges

Sir Rick said that what one wanted often conflicted with what needed to be done.

Pondering this painful truth, Thomas strode through the dreamscape. It was up to him to warn Annabelle about Enoch. He was still reeling from the Commander's assertion that the kid could now be their enemy based on what they'd sensed in the Farseer crystal. Even though Commander Storm himself admitted he could be wrong, it was obvious he didn't think so, and, despite their differences, the Caretaker backed him up. Neither David nor Dinah would admit what they believed, but both of them were probably praying for Enoch's soul right now.

Shadowveiled's vashryu held enough power to warp the perspective of even the most strong-willed folks, given enough time. Enoch had been missing for weeks. His captors had had ample opportunity to bend his mind to whatever worldview they embraced. Even to the point of abandoning all the principles he'd once held dear. Or loved ones.

Thomas wasn't as certain that Enoch's fall was inevitable. It didn't match up with the kid he'd known. Enoch was tougher than that.

He swallowed, suppressing an urge to vomit. "Better to prepare for the worst while hoping for the best." When they'd met, the kiddo had been optimistic about reaching Enoch in the dreamscape. Hopefully, she hadn't yet.

She might think of Enoch as her brother, but even brothers who cared for their sisters could still hurt them.

Thomas shuddered. Where had that thought come from—his past? If so, then he really didn't want to remember anything about it until he averted this present crisis.

Coming upon a copse of trees beside a river winding through a grassy plain, he paused to reconnoiter. Who the heck dreamed up this weird realm—some half-blind person who'd lost their glasses? Everything appeared out of focus, as if someone had colored the landscape using pastels and then blurred the lines. It was difficult to parse out human energy signatures from that of other life forms when it all blended together.

I could've sworn I detected Annabelle's energy signature somewhere around this place. She was here a little while. But where did she go?

He'd also sensed the purple energy signatures—Shadowveiled's signature. It made him think of music. "Ashes, ashes, we all fall down ..." Softly singing, he fingered the scar on his chin. *What am I doing?* He paused, forcing his hand back to his side. The children's song faded. Where had that come from? Another hidden memory? He ran a hand back through his hair.

I have far too many of those.

Purple meant mind and illusion magic. He knew that now. Grimacing, he slashed seed heads from grass stalks to disintegrate into orange embers. Someone in the dreamscape was messing with his head, and when he found out who ...

What if the threat stalking Annabelle in the dreamscape was the wielder of Shadowveiled's aspect, all this while? Commander Storm suspected there were other wyldlings besides Thomas, Annabelle, and Enoch. One of them could be a mind mage. Even worse, whoever had taken the kid might have brainwashed him into leading Annabelle into a trap so they could nab her, too. Could the "Varazslo" dragon she'd met be Enoch in disguise? It made sense, in a sick way. Someone had hired Captain Wuya to capture Annabelle in the waking world, so why not have agents here in the dreamscape?

Thomas clenched his jaw. Either way, the two kids meeting could spell a disaster. He'd better find Annabelle, and fast. And if this dragon fellow hurt her, then God help him, because Thomas was not in a forgiving mood.

There! A glimmer of blue. He charged ahead, leaving the pastel world behind him.

Violet mist swirled amid the gray, mingling with that tantalizing swath of blue. Scenery grew even more indistinct as he plunged forward, following those telltale tendrils of energy. The violet was nearly overpowering, suffocating the blue, but the blue held on strong like a stalwart soldier standing his ground despite overwhelming odds on the battlefield.

Battlefield? Criminy! Annabelle wasn't a fighter. Why couldn't he find her earlier? Anxiety sliced a ragged path through Thomas as he broke into a run. Was he too late? He was supposed to protect her in the dreamscape.

Plants resembling black vines sprang up, weaving like serpents. Cursing, he summoned his blade and slashed through them. The acrid stench of burnt vegetation made his nose wrinkle. He extinguished the fire with a thought. A shabby wattle and daub hut emerged through the mist, but when he pushed his way inside, there was nothing there but moth-eaten blankets and broken-down wicker furniture. He cut through the rear of the building, following that piquant sense of blue. It grew stronger.

The gray mist thickened, and the dark silhouette of a stone arch appeared looming over him like a hammer ready to fall. Beyond the gateway, the purple and blue energies beckoned. Purple. He cursed. *I knew it.* He was ready to tear apart anything purple. The sound of snarling beasts permeated the mist. How far away? He thought he heard Annabelle's voice like a tickle in his brain.

Narrowing his eyes, Thomas paused and tried to peer through the mist. Dare he burn it away? He didn't want to risk harming Annabelle. He continued forward warily, sword held before him in a guard position. Trees resolved from the murk. Like a shining strand of sapphire, Annabelle's energy trace strengthened. Everything in him screamed to rush forward, but he held himself in check. He needed to be cautious. Whoever else was involved could mess with minds. He didn't want to come out of this believing he was a tap-dancing rutabaga, or something equally ridiculous.

Again, Thomas sensed Annabelle's voice; it held a tone of desperate pleading, almost like she was sobbing. "... don't know what you want, then let me go!"

Had that joker—the wielder of purple magic—snared her? Wrath inflamed Thomas and caution flew to the four winds. "Let her go, or I'll blast you to perdition!"

With a cry of rage, he charged headlong into the forest, hacking and slashing his way through dense underbrush until he arrived at a clearing and a stream. The mist thinned out while becoming more agitated, a maelstrom of purple clouds streaked with orange and black lightning. For a split second, he glimpsed two shapes inside struggling—one larger than the other—but then the larger form vanished, as did the orange light. Purple mist streaked with black remained, surrounding a hunched bestial shape.

He staggered to a halt, peering into the fog. *Where's Annabelle? Whoever just took off couldn't have been her.* He summoned fire to his blade, then called to her.

"Thomas!" Joy filled Annabelle's mental voice, all garbled like it came from underwater. But all he saw was the hunched, winged creature—a wyrmkin? —with dark scales amid the purple clouds. The reptilian beast faced him, fanged mouth agape. A keening wail emerged from its throat as it opened its wings and reached out with muscular forelimbs.

Panicked rage filled Thomas. Had the blasted thing eaten Annabelle? He'd cut her out of it before it killed him! Grasping the sword hilt in both hands, he plunged the fiery blade into the creature's chest, cutting through the scales like a melon's rind.

Got you!

Satisfaction purred inside him like a cat licking cream from its whiskers. It was cut off as a woman's agonized scream rang out and a shockwave punched him backward. His sword disappeared in a puff of golden smoke.

What the—

Sprawled on his backside, Thomas braced himself up on his hands and steeled himself for its inevitable charge. The reptilian creature warped and shrank into a familiar, blue-armored form clutching her middle.

A pile of rocks crushed his chest. *Did I just ... Oh, God! Kiddo ... no ...*

Panting, he pushed himself to his feet. He had to help her. Somehow. This was the dreamscape. There had to be something he could do to right this wrong.

The vibrancy of Annabelle's armor had diminished, the plates flaked and cracked, with the worst damage just beneath her breasts, where cracks spread out from a smoking rift. Black tears streamed down her ashen cheeks, leaving dark paths like runny tar in their wake and her lips trembled. Her wide blue eyes met his, filled with terror. He choked when she flinched away and stumbled back from his reaching hands.

"Annabelle!"

Oh, God, what have I done?

An iridescent form coalesced just in time to catch Annabelle as she fell. A brown-skinned dwelfnhad clothed in white cradled the shuddering girl. She shot an accusing glance at Thomas, and he felt it like a lance to the heart. "How could you, Helzarvenn?"

"Who're you? I didn't know ... Is she ...?" He took a step toward the two women, but Annabelle cowered away and the dwelfnhad scowled. A large feathery wing swooped out from behind the dwelfnhad, curled around them like swaddling clothes, and then they vanished into a shrinking dot of white light. Thomas gaped, his heart racing.

"She lives," a familiar voice said. "For now." Strong hands grabbed his shoulders and spun him around. He stared up into the mismatched eyes of the Dream Traveler. "You have done enough damage here, Caster of Flames."

You!

Thomas jerked out of his grip and turned to stare at the place Annabelle had been. His senses reeled. "How," he choked, clutching his head. "Jeremiah bloody bullfrog! I friggin' stabbed her." He whirled to glare at the tall, cloaked figure. "How do you know she'll be okay?"

And why didn't I remember this guy existed until now?

The Dream Traveler stood with his hands at his sides and his scarred face placid as a still lake. The neck of his musical instrument jutted up over his shoulder. "Worry not, Helzarvenn. The hisanabyad will take the womanchild to Rainblessed for healing. Threefold One willing, Ahdmerel will survive to waken from this dream."

Sinking to his knees, Thomas choked back a sob. His eyes and throat burned. "I was supposed to protect her. What a nightmare." His gauntleted hands formed fists. *Get yourself together, soldier! Enoch may be lost to us, but the kiddo needs your help.* Lifting his gaze to the Dream Traveler, he demanded, "Take me to Annabelle, Mr. Cowl. Right. Now."

The Dream Traveler's eyes hardened. "I touched the poor child's mind, and I do not believe she desires to see you ever again. You have burned that bridge behind you. If you had sought out Balthazar's aid, mayhap this," he swept out an arm, "would not have come to pass."

"Just what I need: an 'I told you so' from Mr. Cowl." Thomas spat, then narrowed his eyes. "Wait a minute. You 'touched' her mind? You're a mind mage. The purple mist is yours!"

"'Mind mage?'" Crossing his arms, the Dream Traveler snorted. "How gauche. I prefer the term randahllein sourethol, but, aye, my affinity centers in that aspect."

"I saw purple smoke everywhere." Thomas jabbed a finger at him. "That was *your* mind magic, wasn't it, Mr. Cowl? For all I know, you set all this up! How long were you watching before you decided to waltz on over? Something had a hold of her, then she was that ... thing. Before ... before ..." His throat constricted.

The Dream Traveler regarded him without expression. "Before you attacked her." He blinked, then shook his head. "As for whatever you saw—or believed you saw—I had nothing to do with it. In fact, I was bound by honor not to interfere. I have intervened on Ahdmerel's behalf enough already. She must learn to fight her own battles, Helzarvenn. Both here in the dreamscape and in the waking world." One black eyebrow arched, he leaned forward. "After all, that which does not kill us makes us stronger, does it not? I believe you told her that, once." A faint smile curved his lips, and his scarred cheek twitched. He chuckled as he pulled out his instrument. "A sentiment my brother would applaud."

Rage filled Thomas. *Annabelle could've died!* How dare this ... this *coward* throw his own words back in his face at a time like this? Heat built up inside him, and the flametigers roared, demanding release. He glowered at the smug bard with the weird eyes. "I don't know where you get off—or your blasted brother, whoever he is—but you can both go to perdition."

While laughing outright, the Dream Traveler plucked out the first line of Ring Around the Rosey. He shook his head. "Oh, you are well acquainted with my brother. More's the pity."

Thomas struggled to reign in the flametigers. They wanted out. Scowling, he said, "I seriously doubt that."

"Which does not surprise me in the slightest," the bard retorted with a manic grin, "for there are many truths you doubt. In any event, it is time for you to awaken. Try not to burn any more bridges. Send Commander Daniel Storm my regards—if you remember."

"What?" Shock sent Thomas reeling. *Commander Storm?* Could the Dream Traveler be the brother the Commander had lost in the dreamscape? In that moment, he lost control. An inferno burst forth from his hands in the shape of a great cat.

Laughing like a madman, the Dream Traveler strummed a wild chord, then disappeared in a flash of violet light before the golden flames consumed him. The two energies clashed, creating a shockwave that sent Thomas spinning into the void. The flames rushed after and surrounded him like a corona.

"Get back here, Mr. Cowl," Thomas shouted.

I'll remember. Commander Storm's brother. Criminy!

A comet ablaze, Thomas flailed like a man drowning, trying to reach somewhere, anywhere solid. He landed with a jerk. Peering through flames, he glimpsed orange eyes glowing in the darkness. Had the nehmwights found him?

Someone grabbed his shoulders and shook him. Garbled voices called out, saying things that made no sense. The nehmwights were there, with their grins and their knives ...

Panic jolted through his body.

I won't let them hurt me again!

"Get off me!" Thomas summoned the flames, and they pounced like hungry tigers on prey.

A voice cried out in pain, jarring Thomas. *David? What's he doing in the dreamscape?*

The stench of burnt flesh and fabric filled his nostrils. Thomas opened his eyes. The curtains around his bed dangled in tatters, smoking and smoldering in the steely light of firstdawn.

David staggered back while covering his face, his left hand reddened and steaming. In a billowy red robe, Dinah cowered with an arm around her cousin and shouted at Thomas to stop. Thomas stared at her. Why was everything on fire? His gaze fixed on raised hands still aflame. Struggling to clamp down on his wyld, he forced them down.

I can't ... I can't ... Oh, God!

David ... The burning blade! Annabelle! Had that really happened?

What have I done?

Horror strangled him with icy claws, but it failed to extinguish the inferno blazing inside. He shook with the effort of shutting down the conduit to his reservoir and yet the energy gushed forth in a golden torrent. A wall of flames surrounded the bed.

Put it out! Why can't I make it st—

Dinah's shriek tore through the white-hot clamor in his mind as a heavy and cold wave of stone rose up to engulf him. The fire went out.

Get up, soldier! Inertia means death.

Thomas groaned. Ugh. His skin itched and his entire body felt like it had been smashed by a battering ram. Or the Commander's tail. Herbal scents flooded his nostrils as he inhaled. An infirmary. Huh. What had happened to him this time—a training exercise gone wrong and a tumble into a patch of poison ivy? That didn't track, unless he had also eaten the poison ivy, because his insides were smoldering like a stampede of fire ants.

Something nagged at him. Something very important.

A whiff of burnt cloth, and his heart skipped a beat. He saw it again in his mind's eye. The burning sword plunging into an armored chest. Annabelle's blue eyes wide in a face ashen with shock and pain. Flames in the darkness, the stench of charred flesh, and David stumbling backward—

"David!" The word came out as a croak, and for a moment he wondered if he'd become a toad again. It would serve him right if he had, after what he'd done to his friend and—*oh, God!* Not Annabelle. He was supposed to protect her. That dragon-thing had come at him, and he'd thought ... But it didn't matter. He hadn't paused to wonder why he heard her voice coming from it. He'd assumed. He'd stabbed her. A sweet girl who'd looked past the warts of a surly toad and seen someone worth caring for.

And he'd *stabbed* her.

Moisture flooded his eyes in a hot, salty wave. "Oh, no. Kiddo."

It should've been me with a blade in my chest. Why couldn't it have been me? I'm the monster who can't control his wyld. Or his temper.

He recalled a tall figure in a dark cloak swooping in to pull him away from the kiddo and the ... whatever woman-creature that was who took Annabelle away to be healed. Hadrien *better* have healed her. Ice crushed his heart and lungs even as rage stoked his inner flames. He clenched impotent fists.

That blasted Dream Traveler! I remember now. He was the one who cut my chin.

Thomas could never recall him, but he was there the whole time watching everything. And if that smug bard really was

Commander Storm's brother and made him forget things ... Then he had mind powers.

Jeremiah bloody Bullfrog. That guy could have something to do with Enoch's abduction.

He needed to speak to the Commander. Pronto.

Thomas rolled from a soft mattress and landed in a crouch on a cold, hard surface. Quivering, he blinked away tears until a pinkish blur under his nose resolved into the sparkling, red-veined stone that comprised much of Y'Vasheirdenelle's structure. Human fingers splayed before his eyes. Thomas bit back a sob as tears splashed his hands. He might be a flame-throwing, kiddo-stabbing wretch with anger issues, but at least he wasn't a toad again. There was a chance he could still make a difference in the war looming ahead. But first he must make what amends he could. He needed to learn control.

"After I see the Commander," he rasped, "I'm leaving for Balthazar's Crucible."

Soft, scuffing sounds drew his attention to the room's only entrance and a blurred human shape hove into view. His muscles and joints moaned in protest as he scrambled to his feet and into a battle-ready stance. He reached for the fire within, and then recoiled. No. Never again would he bring forth flame without thought.

"Commander Storm left for the County of Mirrors yesterday with my cousin and a contingent of Stonesingers."

It was David. Thomas blinked. Stupid eyes, getting all watery when he needed to see. *Shepherd, I'm sorry,* he wanted to say. *What in perdition are you doing here, in the same room with me? I friggin' burned half your face off.*

"Shepherd," was all he could choke out.

David gazed solemnly at him from the doorway, right corner of his mouth twitching. Bandages covered the left side of his head. "Would you embark on a journey to the Crucible without me, Sir Thomas?" He raised his left hand, also wrapped in gauze. "I may be hampered as a warrior, but I can still guide you. Show you the way."

Thomas stood at attention and saluted his friend. His vision blurred. He bowed his head to hide the shame brimming in his eyes. The shame that ripped into his heart with fiery talons and would soon reduce him to ash.

Let Me Drown

Flames ripped Annabelle apart with insatiable maws. Fiery worms spread throughout her body, concentrating in her chest, her shattered heart. A cold ache settled in her stomach. She struggled to breathe as Khinjara fled with her through galaxies and past rainbow nebulae. Away from Varazslo—no, William—who had played her for a fool. Away from Thomas, who was supposed to be her valiant knight. Her trusted friend.

He was supposed to save me from the dragon!

Why had he stabbed her? Had he gone crazy? Did he hate her? Would he come to finish the job? Terror ignited her frayed and tattered awareness. *Mom ... Dad ... come chase the monsters away!* She wanted someone to banish the evil and then tell her everything would be all right. Where was Raeden? He'd sworn a vow to protect her. Why hadn't her champion come?

Nothing made sense.

Khinjara's opalescent glow enveloped Annabelle. At least her friend had returned. One shining star in a bleak and featureless void. The hisanabyad cradled her. "All will be well, Ann. Bide a moment longer. I'll send you to Rainblessed." Khinjara spoke in a murmur underlain by threads of panic. Her words jumbled and vanished into a maelstrom of pain, pain, and more pain.

Flashes of blue intruded. Annabelle floated on an endless sea beneath a sunless sky, but everything still burned. Chains rattled. Something scooped her from the water. Hadrien's visage resolved from the inferno, sorrowful eyes pouring tears to dampen the flames consuming her from within. The Sage rumbled what sounded like a prayer. Coolness spread over her like a dark blue balm. The worst of the agony subsided, leaving behind nausea. A wrongness coiled like a snake made of dark fire lingering in her gut.

I want to wake up!

Hadrien vanished into a glowing blue fog, and Annabelle spun out into the void. Panic crackled as she curled into a ball. Where had her Sage gone? Annabelle's head reeled sickeningly in the opposite direction from her body ... or whatever manifestation she possessed in the void place. Was she completely forsaken? She screamed for Khinjara, but no sound emerged, and the hisanabyad didn't reappear. Could anyone be trusted? She should have known. In the end, there was only one being to whom she could turn for help.

Please, God, help me ... Save me. I'm so sorry I didn't rely on you for help before. Please ... Don't let me drown. Wake me from this nightmare!

A point of pale blue light emerged from the blackness surrounding her. Sobs of relief shook her entire form. God had answered her prayer. He was faithful. He kept his promises to protect his beloved children.

Thank you, Lord.

Annabelle flung out her kythim in desperation. The tendrils of her terrified thoughts found purchase. The radiance grew as she dragged herself toward the light and frantic voices calling her name. Gravity asserted itself. Her stomach felt heavy with an alien fullness, dragging her down into watery depths. Was that despair? No. She couldn't die yet. Enoch needed her. She must make it to Ingaraik and free him from the monsters. Praying with all her might, she clawed her way upwards and into a humid, sweet-smelling brightness.

Blinking, Annabelle took in the dimly lit chamber. She recognized the princepsa's room. Soft hands grasped her shoulders. "You're finally awake," Rhiannon cried. A relieved smile spread across her beautiful, sky-blue features as she cradled Annabelle. Behind the princepsa Portia hovered, holding a steaming bowl. The cloying aroma emanated from whatever she held, conjuring a memory of a woman crying out for the child ripped from her arms.

That's not mine ... or Enoch's! Whose is it?

The heaviness in Annabelle's gut increased. Something squirmed. *Oh, God, is there really a snake inside me? Get it out!* Annabelle lurched, heaving. Portia shouted something at Rhiannon. The princepsa sat her up and bent her over the side of the bed, rubbing her back.

Acid burned as something boiled up her throat. Annabelle vomited. Black, sticky tar splatted upon the mosaic tiles. Flinching away, the two gwerindawr shouted in horror and disgust. Annabelle stared at the mess. At least it wasn't moving. Maybe she'd been imagining things.

It does resemble a snake, she mused blearily. *Yikes. I barfed up a tar-snake. That can't be good. Was I munching on asphalt?*

She hiccupped a brief laugh, then touched her left temple. Mild nausea lingered and her head felt heavy as if stuffed with extra memories, but at least she thought clearly again. She wondered about the illness.

And then she remembered. The bright agony of claws digging into her flesh as Varazslo—no, William—grabbed her arms. His tattoos somehow *moved* from him to inside her. The invading darkness, scorching her insides like caustic lye, entangling her wyld and the terrible *pull* of her essence outside of herself. Her magic resisted the extraction even as it dragged William's essence deeper inside to her reservoir. Despite purging herself a mote of his darkness lingered, brooding in the midst of her sapphire pool, a tiny black hole. Had William cursed her, somehow, while she'd fought to escape him?

Could he do that from the dreamscape—make the effects last in the waking world? Oh, dear. If I can't get rid of the black hole, then I need to somehow contain it. Keep it from sucking up my wyld.

She recalled how oysters formed pearls as a defense against foreign substances. Perhaps she could do something similar. She envisioned coating the black mote with layers of dark blue nail polish. It worked. The queasiness diminished to mild discomfort.

A sweet-smelling warmth touched Annabelle's face. Why did it remind her of honeysuckle and crying women? Rhiannon was wiping her skin with a damp cloth. "Annabelle, are you feeling better now?" She eyed the black tar on the floor. "I sent Portia to fetch a bucket and mop."

Mortification heated Annabelle's cheeks. "Ugh. I'm sorry about this. Let me help." With a thought, she tried summoning water from the pool to wash the mess over into the waste pit in the opposite corner. Fatigue and dizziness struck, and she sagged into Rhiannon's arms. Her stomach also made its displeasure known with a brief surge of nausea.

I guess I'm not feeling better.

"That won't be necessary." Alarm filled the princepsa's voice. She placed the cloth on Annabelle's forehead. "You aren't well, Ann. Whatever possessed you to throw yourself from the banquet platform? The people are still distraught. Father ... He ... had a fit. Just like Grandfather near the end. That torc ..." She shuddered. "Oh, Ann. Before the banquet, Sawel warned me, but I wouldn't listen."

"What do you mean? Is the king ..." Annabelle couldn't finish the sentence. Even after all Morgan Brenin's scheming to trap her on Ynys Lloches, she didn't wish him dead.

"Praise Yshua, Father's recovered, and I calmed the assembly. Sawel led them in prayer. Dred carried you back here after the doctor assured him you lived. For the past half hour, you'd been tossing and turning. Even yelling. Sawel prayed over you, but we couldn't wake you, no matter what we did. Portia said you had a fever ..."

She nattered on, but Annabelle only half-listened. She knew what Rhiannon said was important—the detail about the torc nagged at her—but her own ailment consumed her thoughts. This weakness and pain was not normal. Her chest tingled. She frowned. Was she going to be sick again? No. She wasn't going to vomit. This was something else.

Annabelle tore at the laces of her nightgown, exposing an angry red scar just beneath her breastbone. Horror rippled through her. *That's where Thomas stabbed me.* She poked at the puckered flesh. It was numb. Inside, she felt like she was burning alive.

Rhiannon gasped. "Hadrien's tears! Ann, what happened? That looks like someone stabbed you!"

"Yeah," she replied, covering up again. "I got stabbed in the dreamscape. It doesn't hurt. And I'm fine now." No, she wasn't. The tingling and burning around her heart wouldn't relent. Yes, she'd found Enoch, but it didn't feel like a victory. Too much else had gone wrong in the dreamscape. She stiffened, patting her hips and her legs. "Where's Daar-Lûsin?"

"Your dagger is safe in the other room with Sawel," Rhiannon said, smoothing Annabelle's hair from her brow. "Now, lie still and hush. You need to rest. Once you're better, you *must* tell me more about the dreamscape ..." The princepsa's voice droned on.

Rest. That would be nice. Annabelle needed a body of water, perhaps the pond she'd created for Raeden, to wash away the queasiness still roiling inside her. Floating in a pool while discussing everything with her champion might grant her clarity and a measure of peace.

The tingling surrounded her heart, intensifying. Feelings not her own twisted into spiny knots of white-hot rage. Annabelle's eyes widened. In all the tumult, she'd forgotten that whatever powerful emotions she felt, so long as her champion was within a certain distance—he became aware of it. And she'd just been more terrified and in more pain then she'd ever been.

"Oh, no! Raeden ... He's coming. And he's—"

Shouting erupted from outside Rhiannon's chambers. Portia ran in, breathless, with Sawel close on her heels, face contorted in a mask of horror. "Rhia!" he cried. "I've just received news. The scout hound's gone mad. He's escaped Crescent Islet and killed two of the guards!"

"What?" Annabelle gasped. How could Raeden escape? He couldn't swim. First heat flared and then cold chills shook her frame. She had to get to her champion before ... before ...

Annabelle lurched to her feet, swaying. Rhiannon put an arm around her just as Mordred burst into the room. He skidded to a halt, his golden eyes wide as he looked her up and down. "Lady Ann," he gasped, approaching her. "Are you well? Were you injured in the fall? The doctor said you weren't harmed, only sleeping, but I—"

"I'm fine," Annabelle lied, waving away his concern. The Oathbond felt like rusty barbs in her chest. "Tell me, please. What happened with Raeden?"

The princeps grasped her shoulders, and she suppressed an urge to pull free. Golden eyes—*not* orange. This wasn't William; it was Mordred. Her friend.

"Your champion made a raft from his shelter," he said, expression haunted. "Got past the patrols, somehow, and across the channel. By the time I reached the pier, he'd torn out the guards' throats." He shivered. "With his teeth."

The others cried out in horror.

"No. Raeden would never ..." Agony pierced Annabelle's heart, as if Thomas stabbed her all over again. She'd already witnessed her champion's swift and violent reaction when he believed her to be in danger.

Raeden's held himself in check for days, but he still sees the gwerindawr as his enemies ... And mine.

"Oh, my poor little damselfly." Mordred hugged her, and she sagged against him, her cheek resting in the V created by the straps of his bandoliers. She could hear his heart racing. "I needed to subdue him—it took all of us to bind him—then I brought him before my father. He sent your champion to the Reckoning Point. He killed five guards, and three of my men suffered grave injuries." *No, no, no.* A whimper escaped her. She gripped the leather crisscrossing his chest.

Mordred rubbed her back. "Our laws are clear. There's nothing that can save him from the Depths now." He paused, and there was sincere regret in his voice. "I'm sorry, Lady Ann."

Annabelle sagged, and the princeps braced her, holding her at arm's length. She peered up into his face. "The Depths?" Alarm bells rang in her mind. No. That was where the gwerindawr executed murderers. Her voice grew shrill. "Will he be ...?" She couldn't finish.

Mordred sounded grim. "He's to be executed at firstdawn."

"That's three hours from now." Sawel frowned. He'd calmed down, but his expression was tight as he met his wife's eyes. "No time for a fair trial. Rhia ..."

"Fed to the Abyss," Portia breathed, her eyes glazed and her hand over her heart. She leaned against the arched door frame and stared at her mistress. "Oh, your Highness ... I prayed this would not happen during our lifetimes."

No! Annabelle bent double, and retched, dry-heaving. Mordred grabbed her arms. She gazed up at him. "Please ... You have to take me to the Reckoning Point. I can stop this!"

Mordred blanched. "I cannot, Lady Ann. My father expressly forbade it. Looked right at me and said the Ahdmerel must not watch the execution. His word is law."

Annabelle trembled. She turned to the princepsa and the archimandrite. "There must be some way ... I have to save him!"

With Sawel's arm around her, Rhiannon stood tall. "Our father's word may be law, Dred, but I know all the loopholes. I am his heir. Captain, I order you to escort me and my companions to the Reckoning Point. Portia, fetch my scarf. If Ann must not watch, then we'll blindfold her."

"Rhia," Sawel said gently, rubbing his wife's shoulder. "We should tell her."

"Tell me what?"

Rhiannon lifted her chin and met Annabelle's gaze. "Ann, I must apologize. I've been withholding information at the Brenin's command. But this cannot continue. After his fit this afternoon ..." Reaching up to grip Sawel's hand, she took a deep breath. "As you suspected, Ann, the waystone is on the Reckoning Point island." Her voice trembled. "I'm sorry I deceived you."

Annabelle stared. Instead of anger—she was too weary for that—she felt relief as everything clicked. That's what Raeden's message meant! *I wonder how he figured it out?* She shook her head—slowly, because it still felt weird—and forced a wan smile. "It's okay. You were only following your father's orders. I forgive you, Rhiannon."

The princepsa blinked. "Thank you, dear," she whispered, then smiled. "Quickly. Come with me to my room. I had new clothes made for you. I meant to present them as a betrothal gift, but ..." Sorrow filled her eyes, then she shook her head. "Never mind. Only The Almighty knows what the future holds."

Rhiannon offered her arm. They left Portia to clean up Annabelle's mess while the two men looked at a map and discussed logistics. The new clothes proved to be a long sleeved, form-fitting top and a pair of snug breeches with stockings attached. *Like footie pajamas.* Seemingly made of tiny scales, the material was thin and stretchy like a leotard. And it was the same dark blue as her armor in the dreamscape.

With a gasp, Annabelle held it against her. Tears stung her eyes. "Oh, it's so beautiful. Thank you."

The princepsa smiled. "A bolt of this fabric has been in our treasury for ages, along with a sewing pattern. I hadn't planned it this way, but this uniform—it's called a wyldcham—should fit underneath the sourekghar when you claim it." Annabelle started, and Rhiannon chuckled. "Sawel dredged up some of his father's old records. Apparently, our people once gifted the wyldcham to visiting kadorei. In other words, wyldlings like you."

After that, there was little time for planning and none for argument. The Reckoning Point was an hour's swim from the main island. Annabelle was surprised at how quickly Mordred, Rhiannon, and Sawel agreed to help her save Raeden. Portia hadn't seemed happy about them rescuing a "murdering scout hound," but she went willingly enough when Rhiannon sent her off on an errand to smooth their way.

Once Annabelle donned her new garments and buckled on her weapons-belt, attaching both Raeden's knife and Daar-Lûsin, the princepsa led them to the pool in the royal suite common area. From there, they had access to the tunnels leading out to the ocean.

As Annabelle dangled her feet in the water, some of the weakness receded. "I don't understand," she said, running her hands along the strange fabric of her new breeches. "Don't get me wrong, I'm grateful. But Raeden's people are your enemies. Why are you helping me save him?"

Seated beside her with his galamerdhe in the water, Mordred touched her cheek. "If you are to be my wife," he murmured, "then it is my duty to stand up for you." He swallowed. "Even against my father."

Annabelle stared at him, but her response stuck in her throat. *Doesn't he realize that I'm leaving as soon as I rescue my champion? The waystone is on the Reckoning Point.* The warmth in the princeps gaze was melting her resolve. *Stop it, Ann! There's no time to flirt with handsome princes. You and Raeden both have a quest to resume.*

Rhiannon sat on the pool's edge and took her hand. "Forgive me, Ann," she replied. "I go not for the sake of your champion, but for my people. It's past time I confronted my father. You and Sawel have both helped me realize that our Brenin may no longer be fit to lead the gwerindawr." Pain twisted her beautiful features as her legs fused and transformed into her cobalt-scaled galamerdhe.

Mordred's eyes widened. "You mean to challenge Father ... wrest the torc from him?"

"You mustn't!" Ready with his swimming tail, Sawel held out his hands. "Remember, Rhia, what I said—it's cursed!"

Mordred gasped, and Annabelle nearly toppled over. "The *torc* is the source of the curse I must break? How'd you figure that out?"

And how the heck do I destroy something made of metal?

Rhiannon held her husband's gaze. "Don't fret, love. Even if it wasn't cursed, I'd refuse to wear that torc. It's a relic of a past Age. The Ahdmerel will destroy it." She nodded at Annabelle, who gaped like a fish, then continued. "Her coming heralds the dawning of a new Age ... new glory ... in a new world. Our people need a fresh symbol of leadership. We'll discuss it later." Her face hardened. "It's time to drown tyranny." She slipped into the water. After a meaningful glance at Mordred, Sawel followed.

Staring after them, Annabelle clutched her stomach. The nausea had returned. "But how do I ..."

Mordred grasped her chin and turned her head to face him. "Our new queen just issued an order." His gaze softened. "Don't worry, little damselfly. You are the blessed Ahdmerel. It has been prophesied. The Almighty will show you the way." Putting an arm around her, he pulled her into the water.

As they all swam toward the forbidding isle, Annabelle's mind spun with what she'd just learned. The Brenin's torc was the source of the curse! It made sense; she'd felt a wrongness around the king since she'd met him. Why hadn't she questioned it more?

Stop beating yourself up. You can't change the past. Right now, you need to figure out how to break the curse.

But what if she needed to hurt ... or kill the king to break the curse? Jerk though he was, Morgan Brenin was Rhiannon's and Mordred's father. And maybe the curse was to blame. Annabelle clung to Mordred as he rocketed toward the Reckoning Point. They were nearly there.

In self-defense, she'd once killed a nehmwight with her wyld. Could she end someone's life in cold blood? The notion made her feel like vomiting again. If there was any other option, she'd gladly take it. However, if worse came to worst ...

Oh, God, help me. Let me drown before that happens!

For the gwerindawr—for Raeden's sake and her own—she must steel herself to commit regicide.

Sorry

He's killing my wyldling!

Safe within his hiding place, William fought to control his arkhabala while it ran riot across his skin, shrieking at him to commit murder and save Milady Blue so it could eat her magic. He wanted to. He really did. But his battle with the spelled tattoos left him standing transfixed, unable to tap into the Aethyr, while the knight with the golden aura thrust a burning sword into the purple dragon's chest. Into Annabelle's chest.

"Oi! Stop it," he growled, digging his fingernails into his forearms, picking away the scabs from his wounds. The pain helped center him. "Stupid arkhabala. You took enough of her wyld. I need to *concentrate,* so I can get rid of that suns-cursed knight once and for all."

Part of William was prepared to run out there, transform that crazy knight into a worm, and then stomp the worm into mush. The stomping could wait until after he saved Annabelle, of course. She wasn't dead. And if he reached her quickly enough, then she wouldn't perish. Probably. No, definitely. She'd live.

A larger part of William—the part that respected the lethality of the knight's fiery blade and his combustible wyld—kept him rooted to the spot and hidden behind a veil among the trees surrounding Annabelle's meadow.

Hands shaking, William pushed back his sleeves to reveal a row of reopened wounds like vermilion frowns in his gray skin. *But maybe I can cast a paralysis spell from here. And if that doesn't work, then I can transform back into the dragon and—*

A spider-web made of razor-wire and broken glass enveloped his brain, and everything went white.

Music slithered into William's ears like an eel and slapped him back into lucidity. His head throbbed and a ball of ice had taken up residence in his gut. Someone was dragging him across damp stone. Had his master devised some new form of punishment?

He groaned and blinked away blurred vision. "Master Tenebris? I swear I used up all that kaiber power in Zakaar's elixir. I wasn't snorting it again." He stopped moving and then a familiar figure loomed over him.

William scrambled to his feet. "Burning suns! What're you doing here?" He reached inside for the amethyst light. His reserves were dangerously low. Extending his kythim, he found nothing to feed on.

Where's the purple mist? Is the Dream Traveler blocking my access?

Eyebrows arched, the Dream Traveler, Remiel, regarded him while rubbing his chin. "Interesting. Had I known releasing the hisanabyad from your trap would have this effect, I would have done it sooner."

William stiffened. "You did *what?*" Merciful Valeshka, if that thing was loose ... She'd come after him, and most likely kill him. Remiel obviously was not to be trusted. And William had next to nothing left in his energy stores.

I need to leave.

"I needed to free the hisanabyad to bring Ahdmerel to Hadrien Rainblessed for healing. I'll admit, twas a clever trap for a novice wyldling such as yourself, but—"

"Oi! You prattling string-tickler! I. Am not. A. Wyldling!" He screamed as he fled the dreamscape.

William opened his eyes to the waking world, wet-cheeked, throat raw, and his arkhabala writhing, its hunger unsated. Lamps bathed the room in blue-green light. Wiping his face on the burkheld hanging on his bedpost, he lurched from his bed toward his bookshelf, where he'd hidden his emergency whiskey bottle and the portrait of Annabelle.

Him, a wyldling? Ha! That was as ridiculous as him fancying Annabelle. Vexatious beguilement spell ... William choked back a sob. She *would* be alright, wouldn't she?

First the cursed murder pony, and now the blistering Dream Traveler. Was this some sort of cruel joke they'd hatched between them? And yet, he'd used the Aethyr in his spell work on multiple occasions. It rarely hurt him anymore. Nehmwights couldn't enter the dreamscape, but he could. He thrived there; tapping into the pure essence of mental magic. Both here and in the waking world, he'd crafted illusions and read minds. Well, two minds, but that was two more minds than the vast majority of people could read. And those two minds belonged to wyldlings. He possessed an uncanny connection with Northward and Annabelle. The evidence that he was a wyldling far outweighed evidence to the contrary.

Is it possible to be both an Arkhadahn and a wyldling?

He'd ponder that later. More pressing matters demanded his attention. That flame-casting moron stabbed Milady Blue! Wasn't the knight supposed to be her friend? They'd seemed pretty cozy when he saw them together. Or maybe the knight hadn't recognized her because she was a dragon?

William clutched fistfuls of his dreadlocks and groaned. All his carefully laid plans were unraveling. Not knowing Annabelle's fate was like a fist crushing his heart. But he couldn't go back and search for her in the dreamscape. The hisanabyad was loose.

Vorniad drag that suns-burnt bard to the Outer Darkness!

Hands shaking, William pulled the false book from its shelf and opened it. Yes, whiskey would help silence the weeping in his head and melt the ice in his belly. He stared at the nearly full bottle of amber liquid. The good stuff. Khalad had smuggled it into Fastness for him in exchange for a vermin repellent charm. Thankfully, the portrait was face down behind the bottle, so he didn't have to look at it. Unless he wanted to. He brought the portrait out along with the bottle and set it where he could see it while he drank.

Looking at her portrait tore up his insides, but it hurt less than knowing it was there and *not* looking at it.

Other than the bit of her wyld, this may be all I have left of her. No, better not think that.

He'd popped the cork and just taken a swig when the werelights in his lamps changed from blue-green to silver. William frowned. That meant Northward approached his door. Odd, but it was better than Tenebris—not that he needed to worry about that for a few days. Instead of going to bed between first and second dawn like he normally did, his master had departed on the Dreadlord's business. Since William was in disgrace, he'd left his apprentice behind and taken Zakaar.

What in perdition could Northward want? It better not be a sparring session. I'm not in the mood to be pummeled.

Grumbling, William returned the portrait, bottle, and hollow tome to their place and went to the door. He put his eye to the peephole. No one was there. He glanced at his werelights. They still glowed silver. Perhaps the tell-tales were malfunctioning. He'd need to reset them. Or Northward was too short for him to see through the peephole. William muttered curses as he unlocked his door, then opened it to find the other youth standing akimbo.

"Oi! You'd better have—"

A fist flew up and connected with his chin. William's head snapped back. White lightning and black stars filled his view as he backpedaled. Quick! A spell. He needed a spell.

Northward came after him, swinging, landing blow after blow. Red sparks and gray lines overwhelmed the silver of his kythim. "William Dulciber." His voice was as cold as the arctic wastes. "What in perdition." A punch to the ribs shattered William's concentration. "Were you doing." He tried to block it. Pain blossomed in his jaw, and he saw stars again. "Messing with." A hard shove to the chest, and William's back met the bookcase. "My heart-sister!"

Merciful Valeshka! How did Northward *find out? The wyldling snare should keep him from the dreamscape. Has he learned to read minds?*

"I don't know who—" A blow to his midsection left him unable to draw breath.

"Deceitful snake!" Northward snarled, spittle flying. "You know exactly who I'm talking about." Tears stood out in his eyes. "You pretended to be Annabelle's friend, then you betrayed her. I'll make you sorry you hurt her, Dulciber." Another fist flew toward his nose.

Enough! Face and ribs aching, William lashed out with a repulsion spell he'd once seen Tenebris use on Zakaar. Unable to speak, he couldn't cast any spell higher than the Fourth Order. Northward grunted and his eyes widened as he skidded backwards halfway across the room.

William struggled to breathe. Tears left scalding tracks down his cheeks. Eyes blazing with fury, Northward pushed forward as if he waded against a strong current. William strained to hold him in place, but a Fourth Order repulsion spell decayed rapidly when pitted against a strong-willed opponent. And he still couldn't talk.

Void freeze it, Northward! William raged, meeting the other youth's gaze. *I didn't betray Annabelle.* She *betrayed* me. *But I didn't harm her. I would never, ever ... She was fine until that cursed knight stabbed her with a burning sword.* He grimaced at a sudden freezing sensation in his gut.

Chest heaving, Northward stopped and stared at him. "So you really *can* talk to people in their heads on purpose ... Wait a minute. Annabelle was ... *What?*" Then his dumbfounded expression twisted into anger. He took one step forward with fists clenched. "You'd better not be lying to me, Dulciber."

William finally caught his breath. Panting, he clutched at his middle. It was a toss-up which was worse—the ache in his head or the pain in his abdomen. But he'd had worse beatings from Tenebris. He felt his teeth with his tongue. Northward's fists hadn't loosened any, but there was blood in his mouth. Nausea roiled in his gut.

I will not vomit!

Shuddering, he swallowed the blood. "I'm not lying. The knight stabbed her."

And I couldn't stop him. William suppressed a desire to weep. He pushed it down and locked it away inside the deepest dungeon in his mind. *Annabelle's not dead. She can't be. The hisanabyad took her to the Sage to be healed.*

Northward took another step toward him. "What knight? Who could possibly want to hurt Annabelle?" Orange anxiety spiraled in his kythim. "Is she okay?"

"I don't know. The knight's a crazy fire wyldling. He's been rampaging through the dreamscape for the past fortnight. I heard Annabelle call him Thomas."

Northward jerked back as if he'd been struck. "Sir Thomas?"

—has Thomas been in the dreamscape this whole time? —

William tasted more blood. He touched his face, then winced. Sure enough. He'd bitten the inside of his cheek. "Yes. That's the one. Thomas stabbed Annabelle."

Blame him, Northward. It's not my fault at all. No need to mention that he'd inadvertently turned the man into a toad. Why complicate matters further?

Northward scowled. "No. You're lying. That makes no sense. Why would he do that? The Sir Thomas *I* knew would never stab an innocent maiden like Annabelle. And in the dreamscape, she said ..." He shook his head, then frowned. "Not all of it's clear to me, yet, but she's been traveling with Sir Thomas and considers him a friend."

William coughed a helpless laugh. "Oh, yes. She's quite fond of *him*," he said bitterly, and Northward narrowed his eyes. "But he attacked her. As for why ... I'm just as boggled as you are by it." At least now he knew how Annabelle discovered who he was. And how Northward knew William had been meeting her in the dreamscape. Somehow, Northward communicated with her despite the wyldling snare.

How did he do it? And what does he know about my meetings with Milady Blue?

"Tell me what happened to Annabelle," Northward demanded. "Is she okay?" He lifted his chin. "Or don't you know because you ran away and left her like the coward you are?" Despite his inferior height, the kadorei youth seemed to loom over him.

William retreated until his back met the wall, the stones chill against his bare skin. What could he do? He'd wasted too much energy on the repulsion spell. Casting any other spell would wipe out all the reserves in his arkhabala. Then he remembered the soot panther fang talisman sewn into the waistline of his trousers.

"You're assuming things," William snapped as he prepared a Third Order shield against physical attacks. "Believe it or not, I've no desire to hurt her. I *wanted* to protect her, but I was outmatched—"

"Stop making excuses!" Crimson flared in Northward's kythim like blood-roses. He spoke through gritted teeth. "Explain what happened to Annabelle. And every word had better be true."

William muttered the activating phrase of the defense spell, and a shield crackled to life around him. Eyes wide, Northward retreated with his fists raised.

Swallowing more blood, William grimaced. "It's only a shield, Northward. That's insurance you won't pummel the shesm from me ... you aren't going to like what you hear. But I'll tell you anyway, since you asked *so* politely." Then William relayed an abridged version of his last meeting with Annabelle while monitoring Northward's kythim and facial expressions. Lies wouldn't benefit William now; he hadn't time to concoct convincing ones. And if Northward could enter the dreamscape again, then he was more powerful than formerly surmised.

Securing him as an ally has become top priority. But how do I do it? Northward hates me nearly as much as Zakaar hates him.

Careful to speak the truth—although he left out the part of Annabelle's transformation back into a dragon at the end—William told Northward that he and Annabelle had met to exchange information about magic and then argued until the knight appeared with his burning sword.

"He's always tried to kill me, so I left her—only because I believed him to be her trusted ally."

Red intensified in Northward's kythim. "Then you watched him run her through and did nothing to save her."

Frustration raked at his insides with fiery talons. "What was I supposed to do, Northward? It all happened so quickly. And then I was incapacitated by that Dream Traveler—a blistering pillock of a bard in a cloak with a powerful musical artifact."

"Oh, really?" Northward sneered. "And the great sorcerer William Dulciber couldn't defeat a mere bard." Uncertainty and confusion flickered in his kythim. *—there's something disturbingly familiar about this Dream Traveler; maybe Dulciber's telling the truth—*

"I *am* telling the truth!" William seethed. "As galling as it is to admit, there are powers greater than I dwelling in the dreamscape. By the time I recovered from whatever he'd done, Annabelle was gone. Taken away to be healed—or so that meddling musician claimed. I ... I think she's still alive."

"She'd *better* be alive, you festering pile of cat puke!"

"Oi! What happened wasn't my fault. I want her to be alive, too! I didn't stab her—"

"I don't care." Northward clawed at the band of dull, soot gray metal around his neck. "Take this infernal thing off—only for the space of ten heartbeats—and I'll be able to tell if she lived."

William gaped. "Are you totally gone? I can't do that."

"She's my heart-sister," Northward hissed. "Just for a second, Dulciber, act like you're a halfway decent human being with a *heart* and grant me this one. Simple. Request." He shuddered. *—Almighty, please be with me and Annabelle—* "You've already got your blustering shield, but I give you permission to immobilize me with your magic while the snare's off."

"As if I need your permission," William muttered. A Fourth Order paralysis spell should do the trick—if he possessed the energy for it. The shield would suffice if Northward tried anything. He'd need more than ten heartbeats to muster his wyld. Probably.

Am I actually considering the removal of the wyldling snare from Northward's neck—all for an iota of a chance to learn whether Milady Blue survived?

Yes. Yes, he was. He must know.

William stepped away from the wall. He felt his shield flow to close around him. "Make one twitch and I'll zap you with a Pain Hex that'll leave you piddling yourself." William couldn't deliver on the threat, but Northward had no way of knowing it.

"I won't move," Northward replied. "You have my word." His silver kythim rippled opalescent through bright yellow jagged lines. He was afraid. Good.

William kept the triangular key to the wyldling snare in his left trouser hip pocket. Monitoring his prisoner for any sign of duplicity, he pulled back the shield to expose one vertex of the key, then touched it to the collar. He told the snare to expand its circumference for ten of his heartbeats.

Northward inhaled sharply as the snare pulled away from his skin. His eyes glowed silver. William tensed, prepared to slug him—the shield would make it hurt more—but the kadorei youth kept his word.

One ... Two ... Three ... Four ...

Northward's kythim pulsed a bright blue as a grin spread across his face. "Annabelle's alive! She's upset, but okay—"

William sent a command, and the snare snapped back around the captive's neck. He stepped backwards. Out of range of Northward's fists. "She'll be fine, then?"

"Hey! That wasn't ten heartbeats."

"That was ten of *my* heartbeats, you miserable cretin."

Ochre confusion spiraled in Northward's kythim amid gray lines. "I don't understand." He shook his head "I saw it in her mind ... Sir Thomas *did* stab Annabelle. But why?"

"I don't know," William snarled. It wasn't his fault. *It wasn't.* Trembling with a fresh onslaught of rage, he growled, "Believe me, Northward, I would have *obliterated* that swordsman for what he did to Milady Blue, but he'd disappeared by the time I recovered from whatever that cursed bard did to me."

Northward stared, blinking, then his eyebrows shot up. "Kaspar's Breath, Dulciber. You have a nickname for Annabelle. And it isn't an insult." He barked a humorless laugh. "So *that's* how it is."

William scowled and blood pooled in his mouth. He swallowed it. Sooner or later, he'd be sick. "How *what* is?"

"The very idea of it's disgusting, but ..." Northward made a face. "You're sweet on Annabelle, aren't you?"

William opened his mouth to deny it, then hesitated. As humiliating as it was to admit a weakness, allowing Northward to believe he had *pleasant feelings* concerning Annabelle would reduce his suspicions. Fortuitous, really.

"I don't know about 'sweet on,'" he muttered, wishing he could sink into the wall, "but, yes. Her presence is more tolerable than most, and I'm ... favorably disposed toward her."

Northward grunted. Indigo amusement chased by opalescence rippled through his kythim. "You weren't planning to do anything that would hurt Annabelle?"

Not anymore, he wasn't. Extracting her wyld for his own use could be disastrous. It was all he could do to contain the icy ball of her wyld his arkhabala had stolen. Besides, the pain he'd seen in her eyes haunted him.

"No," William replied. He scoffed. "That's what I've been trying to get through your stubborn skull, Northward. All I wanted was an opportunity to study her power."

Northward stared at him. "And when the knight—Sir Thomas—attacked, you were willing to put yourself in harm's way to protect her?"

Why was Northward being so obtuse? William wanted to throttle him. Of course he'd protect whatever belonged to him! Annabelle might hate him now, but she was *his* wyldling. He'd find a way back into her favor. It shouldn't be too difficult. Hopefully she hated that Sir Thomas more than him now ...

William took a deep breath. "Yes, you mule-headed ninnyhammer. I was preparing to do so, when others ... intervened." Dare he admit his fear? He swallowed more blood. "Milady Blue and I ... I wanted her for a friend. I only disguised myself because I was afraid she'd hate me if she knew I was a nehmwight."

"Sweet Yshua!" Northward stared. "I want to believe you, Dulciber." Picking at the wyldling snare, he grumbled, "Annabelle liked you well enough to call a friend."

—Maybe there's still hope for an alliance with this snake ... so long as I take care—

William kept his face blank. Was that a stray thought, or an intentional sending?

Northward's lips thinned. "Drop your shield."

"I'm not an idiot, Sir Fancy-Jacket." Warning tingles radiated from his arkhabala, indicating his power was low. He'd be dropping that shield soon whether he liked it or not.

He rolled his eyes. "I promise I won't hit you."

"I'm not afraid of your little love-taps, Northward. My master, Tenebris—"

"You don't need to remind me," he murmured. "I know from your memories he's often beaten you to within an inch of your life, Dulciber."

Ugh! Those shared memories. Stupid wyldling snare ... William stiffened. "Enduring pain is part of an Arkhadahn's training. All masters beat their apprentices to toughen them up."

"That's what your master told you." Northward shook his head. "But I bet he's lying about that. You want to be free of him, don't you?"

He's trying to play me. William searched Northward's kythim for the plum-colored clouds of deceit, but he saw only brown outlining the silver tendrils and occasional opalescent ripples. He still wasn't sure what the opal meant. Odd. The anger was gone.

"You want to make a deal with me."

Northward nodded. The colors of his kythim didn't waver. "Primarily for Annabelle's sake."

For Milady Blue? Yes, he would risk it.

Time to roll the bones.

William allowed his shield to fizzle out. His energy was nearly depleted, anyway. Crossing his arms, he snorted. "Alright, I'm game. But don't ask me to remove the wyldling snare. That's more than my life is worth."

Northward's lips twitched into an almost-smile. "I did consider it. No, I propose to help you break free from Tenebris."

"In exchange for what, exactly?"

"You swear blood oath to—"

"Shut your gob, Northward! Nothing doing. I'm not forswearing one master only to gain another." His skin crawled, recalling the blood oath he'd sworn to Tenebris—in essence, to serve his master until capable of defeating him in the Arkhadahn's Challenge.

Northward groaned and rubbed his forehead. "If you'd let me finish, you'd know it wasn't *that* kind of oath. Since I can't trust anything you say, and you refuse to believe anything I say ... In place of real trust, a blood oath contract is necessary. Here, Dulciber."

He pulled a bit of folded parchment from his belt pouch and held it out, pinching one corner between thumb and forefinger. "After the Dreadlord proposed we work together, I figured drafting a contract would be wise. I've been working on this the past few days. When I saw Annabelle and found out you've been meeting her ..." Vermillion sparked in his kythim. He took a deep breath, and the sparks lessened. "I decided it was time to move forward. My terms are clearly laid out, and there's space to add your own. The first two terms are non-negotiable. I understand if you balk at the third."

William eyed the missive like a venomous serpent. He touched the parchment with a strand of his kythim. No mundane traps. He snatched it from Northward and scanned three lines of painstakingly neat script. His eyebrows rose. Northward had put a lot of thought into these ... demands.

First, William promised never to harm Annabelle or by inaction allow her to be harmed, to protect her to the best of his abilities, in any realm. That would be ... difficult. However, it was what he intended to do anyway, and it implied permission from Northward to be in her company. In both the dreamscape and the waking world.

She'll be my friend before the moon wanes ... not that I care about that wager with Remiel anymore.

He suppressed the grin twitching at his lips, forcing it into a pensive frown. Even that hurt his face. "The first condition's acceptable, so long as we specify a narrower frame of time than 'never,' clarify the definition of 'harm,' and limit 'inaction' to intentional ... er, negligence on my part."

Northward snorted. "Did you read through to the end? The term of the contract is fairly standard based on the regulations set forth by the Dwelfnic Council. It clearly states that it expires one Turning from today." His expression hardened and the opalescent ripples widened. "One way or another, this should all be resolved by then."

—I'm glad I added that clause about him helping me find my surviving sister. I wonder if she's a wyldling like me and Annabelle—

Trying to ignore Northward's musings about his kin, William read to the end, then bit back a laugh. He'd seen a loophole. A tiny one, but it left enough wriggle room for him to arrange matters more to his liking. He pretended to hem and haw for another moment, then sighed. "Very well, Northward. I'll play your little game. Now, in the interest of establishing *real* trust between us, there's something you should know about swearing blood oaths with an Arkhadahn ..."

He allowed himself a wan smile. Although the circumstances weren't ideal, things were falling back into place again. Northward would become William's ally, bound and sworn. He'd have Northward's blessing to see Annabelle again ... not that he needed it. Best of all, he possessed hope of escaping indefinite servitude to Yvres Tenebris.

And if Sir Thomas ever went near his wyldling again, then William would ensure the knight was sorry.

Heat Exhaustion

Even though he knew it must be done, Thomas had never been more sorry to step through a portal. Activating the waygate proved a simple task with the vashenta he and David wore like pendants. As he walked through, he brooded on his apology to Annabelle. He'd left it in a brief message for Peter to deliver.

I wish I knew for certain that Annabelle survived what I did to her.

Thomas pushed that aside. There was nothing he could do about it. He needed to concentrate on the task ahead of him. The waygate opened behind a caravanserai where David procured mounts and supplies for their journey to Balthazar's Crucible.

Being in the Evergold Desert was like walking inside an oven. Everything tasted like ashes and the very air singed his nostrils. Brown, suns-baked rocks and hard-packed sand stretched in every direction, studded by clumps of hardy vegetation: sage brush, Joshua trees, cacti, and whatever other sort of devilish plants grew in the God-forsaken Evergold Desert of Losaridos.

It's almost second-noon. We must be getting close by now.

Adjusting a moist wrapping over his mouth and nose, Thomas sat hunched over on his giant camel under an awning attached to the saddle. The awning blocked the worst of the suns' rays. Without it, the heat struck with hammer-like fists and his skin would be lobster-red inside of an hour. Even for fire wyldlings, there was such a thing as too much sun.

On his right, David rode a similar mount, his head swathed in bandages securing a poultice to the left side of his face. Another bandage obscured his left hand and forearm. He could still use it, but just barely. The Caretaker and Dinah had treated David's injuries as best they could, but the dwelfnhir's only hope for a full recovery was the phoenix aloe that grew in the center of Losaridos, where Balthazar's Crucible lay. Even after receiving the aloe's palliative and healing properties, David would bear awful scars for the rest of his life.

Thomas flinched, averted his gaze, then forced himself to look. *I did that. My lack of control, and the inner demons I've refused to confront.* Despite his companion's present stoic demeanor, the pain had been—and was—excruciating. The way David screamed ... Thomas's stomach still knotted, recalling his glee when he incinerated nehmwights. They screamed in the same way, as they cooked ... *And I laughed!* Thomas shuddered. He shouldn't wish that agony on his worst enemy, let alone someone who had only ever shown him kindness. A man who had become his friend.

Friend. Ha! Some friend I've been to him. He should hate me. Why doesn't he hate me? Pretty sure Annabelle does, after what I did to her. If she survived ...

A massive fist squeezed Thomas's heart, and his mind threatened to fracture. He pushed away the thought before he spiraled into the same madness that had nearly taken David's life hours earlier. Enough was enough. The time had come to face Balthazar. Confront his inner demons. Become whole again. Or he'd never be able to look the Commander in the eyes again. Let alone David.

As if sensing Thomas's regard, David turned to meet his gaze with one clear topaz eye. Half of his face was unmarked and perfect, handsome as ever. The other ... Well, under the bandages lay a reddish, cracked, and blistered landscape of ruin. At least his left eye would escape permanent damage. If they treated it with the phoenix aloe within the next twenty-four hours.

"You're brooding again, Sir Thomas," David murmured. The right side of his mouth twitched upward, and he lifted his bandaged arm. "Don't let this trouble you."

Thomas returned his attention to the path. His mount ambled toward a clump of something green and spiky. Most likely cactus. "I ruined your face and maimed your guard-hand. It would trouble me less if you'd demand a duel for satisfaction." He sighed. After what he'd done, he'd stand there with both hands tied behind his back and let David add to the scars all over his chest without interference. He eyed his companion sidelong. "Or even just yell at me, Shepherd."

"And what would that solve?" David asked. "It would neither assuage my pain, nor bring about absolution for your sin. Which you already possess but refuse to receive." His visible eye narrowed. "You never did explain what occurred in the dreamscape that precipitated ... this." He waved his injured hand in the direction of his face.

"Trust me. Talking about *that* will only make matters worse." Thomas swallowed. His throat was dry. He took a sip from his waterskin. Hopefully those plants meant a source of potable water. David assured him their water would last until they reached Balthazar's Crucible, where they'd refill them from a deep well and the giant camels could drink their fill, but Thomas wanted to ration their on-hand resources, just in case the well was dry, or didn't actually exist.

David didn't press; he drank from his own waterskin. "We should reach Balthazar's Crucible in six hours—midway between Klotho-set and Lachesis-set." He shot a glance at Thomas. "Phoenixheart will help you, Sir Thomas, but you must meet him halfway."

"It's just Thomas," he muttered.

"What?"

"Stop calling me 'sir.' Anyone who puts up with my crap as long as you have is automatically on a first-name basis with me. Hell, I burnt your face off. You can call me whatever you like."

"And here I thought only Annabelle had that privilege." David's mouth twitched again in an almost-smile. "I'll address you as Thomas only if you call me by my name, as well."

He had to mention the kiddo. Thomas glanced away to hide his grimace. "Sure, David."

When they reached the stand of fat, barrel-shaped cacti, the two men dismounted, leaving the protection of their awnings. It was now second-noon and the suns' heat buried Thomas like an avalanche. He unsheathed his new longsword. In hope that Annabelle survived, he'd left Murder Stick at Y'Vasheirdenelle to be claimed by its rightful owner—and skewered a cactus, starting a cut he could widen until the top fell off, allowing his camel to feed.

David did the same with another cactus. Though hampered by his wounded hand, he managed to expose the succulent's flesh for his mount. Thomas wanted to help, but didn't offer. *That'll only add insult to injury.* Instead, he sawed open another cactus and scooped out the nourishing pulp to slake his own thirst. He offered the rest to the dwelfnhir. After they'd both had their fill, they climbed up on their satiated camels and continued.

Golden, winged figures shimmered on Thomas's left. *Are those birds?* Shading his eyes, he frowned. *Can't be ... They look like they're on fire. I must be seeing things.* He rubbed his eyes and the avian shapes vanished. Softly, he snorted. Mirages. He'd better not be coming down with heat exhaustion. He drank some water. It tasted flat and tepid, but it soothed his raw throat. He replaced the wrap over his nose and mouth, freshly moistened with cactus pulp.

Four hours later, they approached another clump of cacti. No ... it was the same place; he recognized the plants they'd sliced open and plundered. Thomas snarled. "Jeremiah roasted bullfrogs on a stick! Weren't we just here?" His mount grunted. It sounded like a reproof.

Great. Just what I need. Sass from a camel.

David pulled back his cowl. Surveying their surroundings, he frowned, then winced. "How peculiar. We appear to be traveling in circles."

Thomas growled. "I thought you knew the way."

The dwelfnhir dismounted. "I did." Kneeling, he crossed himself, closed his exposed eye as he placed his right hand on the parched earth, and mouthed a prayer.

Really? Like that's going to accomplish anything! God abandoned me. Why would he help us now? Well ... Maybe he'll answer David's prayer. Rolling his eyes, Thomas heaved a sigh, then nearly coughed at the burnt flint tasting air. "Give it to me straight, David. Are we lost?"

David inhaled sharply. His eye flickered open and he examined the dust on his fingers. "Not exactly. However, something is interfering with my senses. We are being led astray."

Did the Almighty Threefold One whisper that in your ear— or is that just a guess?

Feeling ashamed, Thomas swallowed his aggravation. David didn't deserve his sarcasm even if it was only in his thoughts. "Led astray by what?" he asked. "Is this something new since you were last here?"

"All I know is this didn't happen before." David rubbed the dust between his fingers, nodded, then rose. "Then again, Helzarvenn—the Caster of Flames—wasn't with me." Flashing a half smile, he pulled his cowl up to cover his head. His camel knelt and he hopped up into the saddle. "Tell me; have you seen or heard anything?"

Thomas shook his head, watching as the camel lumbered to its feet. "This place is deader than a doornail. Nothing aside from cactuses. And some mirages."

David hummed pensively. "Mirages. What kind of mirages?"

He'll never believe me. Thomas barked a laugh. "You'll think I'm crazy."

David raised an eyebrow. "Humor me."

"I thought I saw birds made of fire. They looked kind of like peacocks. Almost like .... No." He shook his head. "Impossible. Those don't exist. They're just a legend."

I thought Balthazar used that name as a metaphor. Him being the fire Sage and all.

"Don't be so quick to claim something is impossible, Thomas," David replied. "With the Threefold One, all things are possible."

Thomas squinted out into the baking desert. He thought he glimpsed a flicker of red-gold flame. "Things like phoenixes?"

David chuckled. "Indeed. You should feel honored. I've never seen them. The phoenixes don't reveal themselves to just anyone."

"I don't feel honored," Thomas scoffed. "I just feel confused. And sweaty. And ticked off." *And guilty as hell.* Grasping the hilt of his sword, he glared out at the shimmering air. "You hear that, firebirds? I'm getting angry. And you won't like me when I'm angry."

David shook with quiet laughter.

"What?" Brows lowered, he stared at his companion. "Are you laughing at me?" *After what I did to him, he can still laugh?* Despite himself, a grin tugged at his mouth. The dour Shepherd still had his sense of humor. Maybe he'd be okay after all.

David drew his mount in close beside Thomas's until he could smell the medicinal herbs of the poultice. "This is meant to be, Thomas. Don't you see? You must petition the phoenixes to lead us the rest of the way."

"Of course I must," he muttered, toying with the camel's reins. "All part of the trial, I'm sure. Unless it's heat exhaustion." He barked a laugh. "Ask the imaginary phoenixes for permission to travel through their territory. I wonder if I'll need to beg them for those healing aloes, too."

"A polite request would suffice, Helzarvenn."

Orange-gold flames burst into existence between them and the cacti. Thomas flinched, his hand on his sword. Heat surged through him in sympathy. His wyld flared, stretching like a tiger waking from slumber. *Oh no, you don't!* Thomas slapped it down. The saddle lurched as his camel shied with a growling wail. *Not you, too!* Thomas cursed, clinging to its hump.

A plumed bird with feathers shifting through the color spectrum hovered in the midst of the conflagration. The size of an ostrich, it had broad wings, long, draping tail feathers and scaled legs. It moved off to one side, and another emerged from the fire, followed by a third.

The trio morphed into tall human forms with umber skin—two males and a female. They were clad in metallic gold armor with scales stylized to resemble feathers and gripped spears tipped with obsidian blades. Wearing an elaborate helmet like a flame-hued feathered head-dress, the woman in the center regarded him with eyes of molten gold. She arched a black eyebrow, and her full lips curved in a smirk. "Do you still believe we are imaginary creatures of legend, Helzarvenn?"

"Heck, no!" Heart pounding, Thomas finally wrestled his wyld into submission even as he struggled for control of his mount. "Lady, what're you trying to do—kill us? Maybe warn a fellow before you make with the pyrotechnics." The woman frowned, but the men on either side of her chuckled.

Beside him, David soothed his own beast. Wide-eyed and panting, he seemed to have lost his customary aplomb. "Greetings, Warriors of the Undying Flame. I am called David, and I believe you've already recognized my companion." He bowed, tracing the sign of the cross. "We come in peace, in Lord Yshua's name."

The woman lifted her chin. "Yes. We know why you have come, Stonesinger." She struck the ground with the spear butt three times. "I am called Fiamma, and these are my sons, Moeru and Jalin." Both men dipped their heads and thumped their chests with their right fists. Turning her burning gaze on Thomas, Fiamma added, "If this youngling could remember his manners, we might be convinced to escort you to Lord Balthazar's Crucible and mitigate the damage he wrought upon your hand and face."

I'm not a child. Thomas flinched and swallowed a smart-aleck retort. David needed whatever aid these warriors could provide, and as soon as possible. For David's sake, he could be polite for the span of a conversation. Placing a hand over his heart, he said, "My name's Thomas. I, uh, apologize for any rudeness, Lady Fiamma. You're right; my friend's in a lot of pain and needs healing. Could you please lead us to your aloes?"

Fiamma smiled, then bowed. "Gladly, Helzarvenn." She slammed her spear-butt against the ground twice, and the men burst into flame, transforming to phoenixes. She struck the hard-packed earth a third time. Fire erupted around the woman and her eyes flared incandescent as she assumed her bird form. Trailing colorful sparks, the three phoenixes circled Thomas and David, then hovered before them. "The deception glamourye is nullified," Fiamma said. "Follow us. We shall lead the way to the Crucible."

The firebirds led Thomas and David deeper into the baking desert, trailing golden sparks and a fragrant smoky scent. Thomas felt fine, but he observed David carefully because the dwelfnhir's strength seemed to flag. He sat hunched over on his camel with his injured arm pressed against his middle and his cowled head lowered. Thomas cajoled David into drinking water every quarter of an hour. Far ahead and to the southeast, he glimpsed towers of stone rising from the heat-shimmering horizon.

That must be where we're headed.

Klotho's actinic glare was just above the eastern horizon when the camels' feet thudded against chalk-pale stone emerging from the sand—a road—and the towers in the distance resolved into a forest of buttes and pinnacles with brown, red and golden strata. After they passed by a handful, Thomas noticed some of the shorter buttes were actually statues of phoenixes paired with humans. David's sigh of relief echoed off the buttes as thick shadows fell over them. Even Thomas was grateful for the coolness of the shade the towering stone figures offered. Succulents of all shapes and sizes grew at the base of each landform, many displaying yellow or pink flowers.

The camels caught up to the phoenix trio, who hovered above the road, flapping their wings almost lazily. Grunting, the camels came to a halt several strides away and refused to move further. With all those sparks flying, Thomas couldn't blame them.

Fiamma's voice came from the central phoenix. "Wait, Helzarvenn. Rest, Stonesinger. The remedy you seek grows here. My sons will attend you. I must fly ahead and prepare my people for your arrival."

Thomas frowned. "Prepare them how?"

Rising into the air, Fiamma chuckled. "We don't often have visitors, Helzarvenn. I wish to insure you are received hospitably."

Thomas snorted. "That doesn't sound worrisome, or anything."

"Do not be concerned," the phoenix replied. "Despite our prowess as warriors, we are not prone to quarreling. Nor do we attack strangers without provocation."

While their mother flew ahead to announce their presence to the phoenix community at large, Moeru and Jalin shifted to human form to collect plump, spear-shaped leaves and golden tubular flower clusters until they each filled a handkerchief.

"Is that the phoenix aloe?" Thomas asked. It had better be. He tugged on the reins, and his camel swayed as it knelt.

One of the twins—honestly, he couldn't tell them apart—nodded as he tied the ends of his handkerchief to create a little sack. "Yes, Helzarvenn. Our healer, Grandmother Sikha, will make a tincture from the flowers and sap for your friend's injured eye. The pulp can be applied directly to his burns."

"It'll take about a week," his brother added, wrapping his own bundle. "Maybe two. But so long as you use these several times every day, and keep the wounds clean, your burns will heal completely—"

"Although there will be scarring," the other twin warned, approaching David with the other pile. "I'm afraid that can't be helped."

David accepted the bundle. "Thank you, Jalin," he replied, his voice sounding thick. He turned to nod at the other twin. "I thank you both."

How did he tell them apart? Thomas slid off his mount. "Can we start the treatment now?"

"Of course," said the twin standing beside David. "Stonesinger, if you would dismount, I'll begin with your arm."

Turning away, Thomas saw to his own mount's comfort by removing the awning and saddle. The beast immediately lurched to its feet and trundled off to nibble on a cluster of miniature spineless cacti with pale green rinds. "You're welcome," he muttered. When he spun on his heel to go take care of David's camel, he nearly collided with the other twin, who dropped his handkerchief sack of aloe spears.

"Criminy!" Thomas held up his hands. *This guy is sneaky. I suppose he needs to be—a fiery bird patrolling a desert without much cover.* "Sorry about that ... Er, Moeru, right?"

The phoenix-man laughed. "Yes, I'm Moeru." He removed his golden-feather plumed helmet to reveal close-cropped black hair and a pair of pointed ears.

So, these phoenixes are dwelfnim, too? Interesting.

Moeru scrubbed a hand through his stubble. "The way to tell us apart is by our hair. Jalin is far vainer than me and keeps his longer. Almost to his shoulders—though you can't tell with his battle helm on." Grinning, he donned his helmet, then picked up his collection. "Here. You may wish to hold on to this," he added, handing Thomas the bundle of aloe spears. "For future misadventures. The leaves eventually desiccate, but their potency won't fade for over a cycle."

The edges of the fat leaves prickled through the cloth. "Future misadventures, eh?" Thomas managed a lop-sided smile. "I suppose I deserved that." He raised the package briefly in a salute. "Thank you for this." He tucked the aloe into his belt pouch.

"You are welcome," Moeru replied. "I'll gather more for the Stonesinger." With a bow, he went to harvest more leaves from other phoenix aloes around them.

David sat braced against his kneeling mount, which had been divested of its riding gear and provided with a pile of the pale succulents to munch. Clenching his jaw, Thomas forced himself to watch Jalin squeeze clear jelly from the leaves and spread it over David's raw-looking burns. To see how it was done. If David agreed to travel with Thomas ... after ... then he needed to know how to best help his friend.

At first the dwelfnhir flinched when the other man touched his arm, then sighed and leaned his head back, murmuring, "Praise the Almighty for his mercy." Catching Thomas's eye, he smiled. "I shall be well, Thomas. Now, I expect you'll be able to concentrate on your trial."

Swallowing with difficulty, Thomas ambled over and hunkered down beside him. "Thanks for the help, Jalin. I'll take it from here."

Jalin grinned, looking exactly like his twin as he relinquished the aloe spears. "As you wish." Hopping up, he strode away.

As Thomas squirted aloe sap on the red, raw skin, David raised his remaining eyebrow. "You do realize I can take care of this myself?"

Thomas snorted. "Yeah. But I have to confront what I did." He squeezed the next spear too hard, and the gel splattered against David's chest. Thomas grimaced. "Sorry."

With a soft wheeze of laughter, the dwelfnhir scooped up the wayward glop and shoved it under the wrappings on his face. He shuddered.

"Hey." Thomas scowled. "Aren't you supposed to clean the wound before you do that?"

"I suppose I need your assistance." David huffed another laugh. "But you should know: Phoenix aloe also has antiseptic properties."

"I'm surrounded by know-it-alls." Thomas rolled his eyes, then finished squirting the healing goop all over David's arm. He smiled slightly but remained silent, staring off into the distance over Thomas's shoulder while he slathered the gel until it covered the dwelfnhir's injured hand and forearm. *Yes. This is something I can do. Something not destructive. I can help make amends for what I did. Just a tiny flame in a vast darkness ...*

But no amount of phoenix aloe could heal the terror and pain he'd glimpsed in Annabelle's eyes or reconstruct the bridge between them he'd incinerated.

Pulling out a roll of clean bandages from a saddlebag, Thomas paused. "Do you think ..." He cleared his throat. "Do you think I can pull this off, David? Succeed in Balthazar's trials?"

His face blank, David blinked at him. "I don't think you'll succeed," he said slowly, and Thomas's stomach clenched. And then the unmarred side of the dwelfnhir's mouth twitched into a smile. "But I believe you can overcome anything, with the help of Lord Yshua."

"Why would he help me now?" Thomas scowled as he bound up David's freshly treated burns. "After what I did to you ... To Annabelle ..." Again, the fiery blade plunged through the dark blue armor just under the kiddo's breasts. He saw her cringing away from him—terrified—in the arms of the white-winged woman-creature who took her away. She'd been alive then, but how could he be certain she'd survived? Even if she did, he wouldn't blame her if she never wanted to see him again.

What good is a knight who harms the ones he's meant to protect?

The bandaged arm blurred, and grief crushed his chest. "David, I'm sorry!" He bowed his head as a sob ripped free from his throat. "Annabelle ... Oh, God, I'm so sorry! I stabbed her, David. Right through her armor. I could've killed her! She'll never forgive me ..."

If Hadrien healed her ... For the love of all that's holy, what if I killed her?

And then David's whole right hand gently rested on Thomas's head. It burned like a brand to his soul. "Again," the dwelfnhir said gently, "I forgive you. Seventy times seventy-seven times, I forgive you, Sir Thomas, Baron-Knight of the Northern Marches. In time, so too will Annabelle. And unlike mortal forgiveness—which has limits—the forgiveness of Khristos Yshua is boundless. His mercy is an undying flame that will resurrect your heart from the ashes. This is what will save you, in the end, my dear friend. I am certain of it."

Thomas closed his eyes. If only he could believe that.

Into the Depths

Annabelle trembled. If only she believed she could do what needed to be done. No, that was the wrong way to think about the task ahead of her. God was with her. She closed her eyes and prayed: *Please God, help me find the sourekghar and break the curse. Without hurting anyone.*

There was one way into the Reckoning Point, and it was guarded by four men loyal only to Morgan Brenin. Annabelle peered around the dead coral heap at the green-skinned mermen treading water beside the underwater arch at the base of the sheer-sided island. They were larger than Mordred, heavily muscled, and armed with wickedly barbed tridents. Annabelle felt vulnerable in her form-fitting wyldcham, even though Rhiannon asserted the thin fabric was tougher than silk.

I'll feel better once I find the sourekghar.

Sand, rocks, coral beds—everything around the island appeared dead and grim in shades of gray. No glimmering fish shoals in sight. No crabs or other invertebrates crept along the ocean floor. Resonating with the mote of darkness in her belly, a sense of corruption emanated from the darkness behind the guards. Was that the curse? How could the guards not feel it?

Calcified knobs dug into her palms as she gripped the edge of a reef crest. Coupled with the repulsion was a terrible attraction toward the island, which had only strengthened as

Annabelle neared it. Hadn't Hadrien mentioned something about a "pull" when she was in proximity to the sourekghar?

No way. It can't be here. My champion, the waystone, the curse I'm supposed to break, and the sourekghar—all in one place? That seems too easy. Not that I expect this to be easy.

Swallowing, she glanced at the couple across from her, peeking out from behind a separate mass of ghostly coral. Back in the royal suite, Rhiannon had seemed confident she could convince the guards to let them pass. Now, hiding behind a coral reef to the north of the entrance, the queen-to-be exuded uncertainty. A blue scarf was wrapped around her left arm, meant for Annabelle's blindfold once they reached the Circle of Judgement inside. A trident leaned against the reef. Sawel perched on a reef flat beside his wife, and the two gestured in the underwater sign-language of the gwerindawr. From the agitated flicker of their fingers—too fast to interpret—Annabelle assumed they argued.

A hand fell on her shoulder, and she flinched. Mordred rubbed her back. She turned to him. He looked odd with violet and dark green hair floating around his handsome face like a mane. It was moments like these when she wondered if they really could fall in love with each other. She couldn't marry him, of course, but it warmed her heart that he was still her friend. *He wants his father's approval so badly, but he's willing to support me against him. Because his father says we're betrothed. What a contradictory mess! Oh, God ... What if I need to kill the king?*

Lips quirked in a lopsided smile, Mordred jerked his head to her right. A familiar blue octopus bobbed up from behind a dark gray rock behind them. *Wesleyen!* Affection for the cephalopod swelling her breast, Annabelle held out a hand for her little friend as he jetted to her. She cuddled him close. He perched on her left shoulder, two tentacles wrapped around her throat. He tugged, then jetted away on the other side of

Mordred, following the coral bed. *Wes, no, come back.* Mordred tailing her, Annabelle followed the octopus, then gasped as the pull of the Reckoning Point strengthened, drowning out the repulsion. Could there be another way in? She beckoned Mordred. He scrunched his brow and made signs with his hands that she couldn't parse, then pointed back toward his sister and brother-in-law. Shaking her head, she grabbed his arm, then pointed at Wesleyen, who waited at the terminus of the coral bed.

Come on!

Looking perplexed, Rhiannon and Sawel swam over. Mordred signed at them and their expressions cleared. They all followed Annabelle. Maybe sometimes it wasn't so bad being the blessed Ahdmerel.

Wesleyen led her around the base of the fortress island out of view from the guarded entrance. Tentacles arrayed in a star around him, he suctioned himself to the basalt. Between his two front tentacles was a familiar sigil, the Pisces-like symbol inside a flat circle. The source of the pull. Wesleyen detached and jetted away to rest on a small ridge of coral. Annabelle placed her hand on the sigil, then spewed out bubbles in a scream when it depressed. Mordred pulled her back against him and pivoted to shield her as the stone split into two slabs and slid to either side. Bits of rock crumbled and fell. Silt puffed from the ocean floor.

Annabelle peeked around Mordred at the arch-shaped opening in the island's base. The urge to enter made her shudder, but it was so dark. The underwater tunnels the gwerindawr used to travel around Ynys Lloches all had bioluminescent algae on their walls to provide light. Only God knew how long it had been since someone used this one, and what lurked inside.

Biting her lip, she met Mordred's wide-eyed gaze. He glanced at the black maw. A slow grin spread across his face. He made a sign for her to wait—*that* one, she recognized—then swam over to the arch and beckoned the octopus. Without hesitation, Wesleyen jetted to the opening and entered the tunnel. Cyan light flared in rings around his head and tentacles.

Annabelle nearly choked on inhaled seawater. *Wes can fluoresce. Awesome! I didn't know octopi could do that.* Rhiannon and Sawel joined them. The princepsa touched Annabelle's arm, gave a slight nod, then swam toward the new entrance.

Please, God. Be with us. Please, God. Keep Raeden safe. She closed her eyes and trembled. *Please God. I don't want to hurt anyone.*

Taking Mordred's hand, Annabelle followed.

Stars still twinkled above, but the black sky had paled to indigo. Klotho would rise soon. Annabelle bid Wesleyen farewell. As she emerged fully from the water into the open air, a wave of Raeden's despair and anger thrummed across the Oathbond. The same dark resonance she'd sensed below struck her like a punch to the gut. She wilted. Mordred grabbed her before she fell.

Raeden's tension spiked and a wave of warning swept over her. He wanted her to leave him? Fat chance! *I'm here to save you, Raeden von Bleistaff, whether you like it or not!*

Annabelle tried sending him calm and peace—a pale blue sky over a stand of silver barked trees and green leaves whispering in the wind—but her own insides were in turmoil. What would comfort Raeden? Quickly, she sorted through her emotions, channeling the negative, tumultuous, and downright confusing ones off to the side. That left only one she could send. She took a deep breath, then opened the floodgates to her pure love for her champion.

Shocked silence was his response.

"I'm with you, little damselfly," Mordred whispered in her ear, startling her out of her interior world. "You'll break the curse. We'll find our glory in opposing Father's tyranny alongside Rhia." Despite his shaky voice, his hands were steady.

The men had left the water first to reconnoiter. Further up the stone landing, Rhiannon regained her land legs while Sawel stood guard, trident in hand. Annabelle wondered if he even knew how to use a weapon, but she didn't doubt his fierce devotion to his wife. Then her gaze lifted. Behind the archimandrite a circle of dark gray monoliths and dolmen loomed, surrounding a tall, milky crystal.

His hand enfolding hers, Mordred gaped. "Hadrien's tears! Is that ...?"

Annabelle experienced a frisson. She nodded, squeezing his hand. "The waystone ring."

Morgan Brenin's voice echoed from beyond the stone circle, listing off reasons for sentencing Raeden to death. "Who is he talking to? I thought nobody was allowed here."

"The Guardians of the Gate," Mordred replied, his voice strained. "Your champion. Maybe his most trusted councilors. Anyone the Brenin invites is exempt from the rule."

With Sawel's assistance, Rhiannon stood and the two stalked around the waystone ring to the Throne of Judgement hidden on the far side. Annabelle followed alongside Mordred, reaching inside for her wyld, then grimaced through a bout of nausea. The plan was for Rhiannon to confront her father first, accuse him of tyranny, and challenge his ability to lead based on his collapse the day before. Sawel would cite historical precedence and scripture to back her up. After that, Annabelle would come forward with Mordred—without the blindfold, she'd decided. She'd tied the scarf over her hair. While the princeps fended off the Guardians of the Gate, Annabelle would rescue her champion, announce her intention to break the curse from the prophecy, and ... then she would break the curse. Somehow.

Apparently, the princeps hadn't appreciated the idea of waiting until his sister and brother-in-law finished their presentation. Jaw clenched, he strode behind them and Annabelle hurried alongside, jogging to keep up.

Yeah, I agree. Let's get this over with before they shove Raeden into the Depths.

Or she chickened out.

Posts with glowing lumen crystals surrounded a circular expanse half the size of a football field. Beyond the posts the ground sloped down into a moat. Morgan Brenin sat on the Throne of Judgement, a rough-hewn stone bench on a platform made of the same dark basalt as the rest of the island. And the waystone megaliths, Annabelle realized. Even though the lumen crystals shed white light, the king's torc was cast in shadow. Two gwerindawr warriors with faded red skin stood on either side of the king. Like the four at the entrance below, these men were huge and tough-looking.

In front of the Throne was a circular pool the size of her parents' living room. An arched peninsula of stone jutted like half a bridge over the still, black water. Wrongness radiated from it like the foul stench of something rotten, and for a moment Annabelle's steps faltered. *That must be the Depths. But I thought it was the torc that was cursed.*

At the bridge's foot with his hands bound before him, Raeden stood ramrod straight, his emerald gaze fixed on Annabelle. Two dull-skinned, burly gwerindawr—one orange, the other purple—menaced him with spears.

Annabelle covered her mouth to stifle a cry and lunged forward. Mordred held her back. Her champion's tunic and vest hung from him in tattered rags. Bloody welts stained the white fur of his torso pink. His hair straggled like copper wire around his shoulders. Despite the spears prodding his back—this close, she sensed the painful pricks and his stifled rage—he refused to budge from his spot. As she and Mordred approached, his gaze dropped to their joined hands, and a feeling she could only describe as frustration mingled with disappointment surged along the Oathbond, then abruptly cut off.

She'd worry about that later. For now, she needed to concentrate on her wyld. Avoiding contact with the central pool, Annabelle extended her kythim toward the moat. That water still felt *wrong*, but at least touching it didn't make her want to gag.

Rhiannon and Sawel stood before the king. Either she'd missed Rhiannon's entire speech, or Morgan Brenin interrupted, because he was on his feet, shouting at them. Orange sparks flared on the black surface of the torc. "What baseless accusations are these?" the king ranted. "You betray the very waters of our people, Rhiannon. The vile beast is a murderer and must be fed to the Abyss!"

"Father, please listen!" The princepsa cried. "You are not well. I beg you, remove your torc. Just for a moment—"

"So you can lay claim to it and overthrow my rule?" Eyes blazing, the Brenin placed a hand on the torc. "Never!" The guards began creeping toward Rhiannon and Sawel.

"She doesn't want it," Sawel bellowed in a voice meant for preaching to vast crowds. "Your Majesty, Lord Yshua as my witness, you are under a curse." Pulling Rhiannon behind him, he leveled his trident at the guards. "Touch her and die!"

Annabelle stared. *Wow. He sounds just like Raeden. Maybe he* can *hold his own in a fight.*

"Free your champion, Lady Ann," Mordred hissed. Suddenly, he held a knife in each hand. "If the guards come after us, then I'll ... dissuade them."

"Thank you." Managing a smile for her would-be betrothed, Annabelle marched toward the pool and Raeden on the far side.

Swallowing bile, she pulled water from the moat. Her stomach roiled. She grit her teeth. *First, make a wave to push away the two guards, then create a shield around my champion.* His eyes locked with hers, Raeden stepped onto the half-bridge. *What is he doing? Oh, he's making space so Mordred can throw his knives at the guards.*

"I believed you fit to follow in my wake," the king raved, "but now I see I was mistaken. Your mother would weep with shame, were she here."

Beside her, Mordred stiffened. "Mother *would* weep in shame," the princeps roared. He pointed a knife at the king. "But not on Rhia's account. No, Father! She would weep because *you* have abandoned all honor!"

Morgan Brenin's burning gaze settled on them. Annabelle suppressed an urge to vomit.

Oh, no ... Mordred, you reckless idiot.

The king's face twisted. "My own spawn rises against me and corrupts the blessed Ahdmerel! Guards, seize these traitors!"

Screaming past the agony in her middle, Annabelle drove a sheet of water into the two men after Rhiannon and Sawel, bowling them over. Two of Mordred's knives took down a guard who left off menacing Raeden to charge toward them. Another pair struck Raeden's other guard; he dropped his spear, then collapsed, clutching at his throat.

Weakness turned her legs to jelly five steps from the pool. The water rippled, and a wave of wrongness swept from the Depths, driving her to her knees. She stared into the pool. Was something moving?

"Freylin! Are you well?"

Annabelle looked up and met Raeden's concerned gaze. Then a monstrous black tentacle shot from the pool, seized her champion, and dragged him into the water.

Crucible

When Fiamma returned, she led Thomas and David through the stone pillar forest until they reached a mesa even broader than the enormous, conjoined baobabs in Treehome. However, Thomas didn't need the direction; he felt like a fiery tentacle grabbed hold of his heart and pulled him toward the mesa. Fiamma called the landform Balthazar's Crucible and explained that it was a dormant volcano.

"A volcano. Why am I not surprised," Thomas muttered as he approached a wide stair at the base of the bluff-colored rock wall. His gaze traveled up the steep incline to an opening framed by an arch of dark gray stone. Apparently, what he needed lay within. He snorted and shook his head. It would be funny if, once he reached the cave, all he found was a scroll containing a message that the solution to all of his problems was to jump into a volcano. Sure, a normal person would be instantly immolated, but he was Helzarvenn, the Caster of Flames. Perhaps a volcano's cleansing heat was necessary to purge him of his inner demons.

Wasn't that the point of a crucible—to burn away the dross until pure metal remained?

That's what I'm gonna find out.

Leaving David in the phoenixes' care—and his vashenta in David's hands—Thomas began his ascent. Wind-borne sand eroded the steps and the edges on either side appeared to be crumbling. He stayed in the middle where the rock was whole and seemed solid enough to bear his weight. Though two could walk abreast, he couldn't fathom anyone wanting to because no railings lined the stair to guard against falling. Bent nearly double, he clambered up, making use of his hands. He arrived on the top landing just as Lachesis touched the horizon and the daylight took on a sanguine hue.

Thomas regarded the opening that lay before him. Like a black curtain that his eyes couldn't penetrate, it didn't seem particularly inviting. Golden runes adorned the dark gray stone of the arch that framed the opening. A stylized phoenix design adorned the apex. The arch reminded him of the Wall in the Darkenwood Forest and the monoliths that surrounded waystones. Obviously, this was the place he was supposed to enter the Crucible. Were there traps? Most likely. He'd proceed with caution.

Well, here goes nothing. Puffing out his cheeks in a long exhalation, Thomas drew his sword and approached the entrance with the weapon held in a diagonal front guard. The golden runes flashed as his blade met with resistance. He backed off with a grunt. What in blazes was this? Frowning, he lowered his sword and reached out to touch the blackness with his right hand. It was like pushing against a brick wall. Why didn't it allow him to enter?

"Was I supposed to knock and say 'open sesame' or something? Or do you not like my sword? Fine, I'll put it away." He sheathed his weapon and crossed his arms, examining the runes along the vertical supports. "I have no idea what these say," he muttered, then scrubbed his hands through his hair, growling, "A little guidance would be appreciated, Balthazar!"

He smacked a rune, then gaped when it began to glow with a steady golden light. The other runes all lit up. Cold stone warmed beneath his palm, and he jerked away, shaking his hand. Immediately, the runes went out. A glance at his hand revealed no damage. And it felt fine.

Rubbing the divot in his chin, Thomas stared at the arch. It responded to his touch. He placed his hands on it again, but nothing happened. Should he try using his wyld on it? After all, this *was* supposed to be the stronghold of a legendary fire mage. It would make sense if the key granting admittance was the type of magical energy that Balthazar commanded.

He raised his hands, then hesitated. The last time he'd summoned fire, he'd lost control and burned his friend. "But this is just rock," he said, looking from his hands to the arch. "I won't be hurting anyone. Right?" Who the heck was he asking? It's not like Balthazar would answer him out here. A sigh escaped him. His eyes fell on pictographs near the base on either side. His breath caught in his throat. *Those designs look like tigers.*

"Okay, that's gotta be a sign. I suppose knocking might do the trick." He chuckled, then added, "time to bring out a pair of fire kitties." His humor faded as he recalled the way his flametiger had grown beyond his control. He shuddered. "Small ones, this time. Maybe even flame *kittens.*"

Thomas closed his eyes and reached inside to the magma boiling at his core. White-hot feline eyes glared back at him surrounded by molten gold fire, and he nearly pulled back in astonishment. There were at least twelve cats down there—quadruple the number he'd perceived before—and none of them were kitten-sized. Probably because he'd been soaking up solar radiation all day long.

And haven't run into any nehmwights.

He shied away from the memories of human torches shrieking in the darkness and concentrated on the flametigers. "You guys gobbling up anger and shame salamanders down there?" He grunted a bitter laugh. "There's been no shortage of those this past week. A regular smorgasbord of salamanders. And I bet they were plenty big. Okay, here we go."

Inhaling deeply, Thomas cracked his knuckles and summoned the two smallest flametigers in his reservoir. A pair of great cats, golden-furred with brown stripes, materialized between him and the entrance. The flametigers' heads were at the level of his waist. Coronas of fire, flickering yellow and white, surrounded the muscular beasts as they regarded him, tails twitching.

Are they awaiting my command? Ordering them around didn't feel right. How should he deal with them, then? Had the kiddo been here, she'd suggest befriending the beasts and asking them for help. Suppressing a pang, Thomas snorted.

That's crazy enough it might just work.

Heart racing, he extended a hand to each cat, palms upward. "Hello, kitties," he said. Perhaps he should name them. Were they male or female? Unsure how he knew, he sensed the tigers were both young males. "Okay, guys. I guess I'll call you Righty," he told the beast standing to his right. Turning to his left, he said, "Which makes you Lefty."

I feel like an idiot.

First Lefty, then Righty, approached and snuffled at his hand. Their moist exhalations tickled. Heat radiated from them, but nothing beyond what was normal for a large animal. They made chuffing sounds, then rubbed their cheeks against his hands. Thomas sighed as his heart rate slowed. Maybe they wouldn't devour him after all. Marveling, he ran his fingers through their soft cheek fur and stroked their silky, rounded ears. Golden sparks drifted like glitter from where he touched them.

Both tigers grunted, their eyes slitted half-closed. Thomas grinned. "You like that, huh? Well, there's more where that came from." He scrubbed his hands through Lefty's ruff, then patted Righty's shoulder. More sparks descended and flickered out on the buff-colored stone at his feet. "But first, I was wondering if you guys could lend me a hand ... er, paw?" He waved at the arch. "Can you two get me through that gate?"

The flametigers blinked, then sauntered over to sniff at the arch. Lefty pawed at the base. Thomas sucked in his breath when the runes glowed in their presence. He felt a surge of hope. This might actually work. Now if only they agreed ...

Righty chuffed and glanced at Lefty. Both cats faced him and bobbed their heads.

Relief filled Thomas as tension oozed from his frame. "Thanks, guys." He took an uncertain step toward the arch. "Um, go ahead and do your thing."

On either side of the arch, the tigers reared up and planted their massive paws over a rune near the top. Huge claws sank into the stone and they both roared. All Thomas's muscles clenched and for a moment he couldn't move. His heart hammered. Every rune, including the phoenix emblem at the apex, flared with bright flames that consumed dark gray stone until only an arch of fire remained. The fire climbed the vertical supports and concentrated at the apex. The phoenix blazed like a miniature sun and bathed them in golden light.

Able to move again, Thomas shaded his eyes against the glare. The tigers slashed at the black curtain across the opening with burning claws, then dropped back on all fours. Flames ate away at the shroud to reveal a tunnel leading deep inside the bluff. Grunting, the tigers padded toward Thomas and rubbed their cheeks and flanks against him.

Checking his balance, Thomas laughed and petted them. "Good job, guys." As one, the flametigers moaned and began to fade. Regret dampened his spirits; he'd hoped the beasts would accompany him into the Crucible. "Wait. You don't have to—"

The transparent flametigers elongated, became ribbons of fire, and spiraled into the miniature sun. "Jeremiah Bullfrog!" he cried. *That thing ate my flametigers!* Its brilliance increased, and Thomas shielded his face as a heatwave washed over him.

The light winked out and the heat died, leaving Thomas alone in the red gloaming. He shivered at the sudden chill. Lachesis had set. Thomas sighed and slowly lowered his arms. Without his flametigers, he felt ... diminished. Inadequate. But he must go on. He'd come too far to turn back now.

He placed a hand on the longsword's pommel and glared at the portal yawning before him, and then the phoenix design. He recited aloud one of the first lessons Sir Rick had taught him.

"A knight faces his fear and overcomes it for the good of those he serves."

His eyes widened as the emblem's lines filled with a gentle glow. As he watched, a bird emerged from the emblem, leaving the apex of the arch blank. A phoenix surrounded by yellow-white flames hovered before the opening, its wings and long tail feathers eclipsing the darkness beyond. Sparks descended as it flapped its wings. It was twice the size of the phoenixes he'd met in the community below.

Drawn by its gaze of molten gold, Thomas approached until he stood an arm's-length away. Furnace-like heat radiated from its golden feathers. "Are you ... Will you ... What ..." He stammered, his fingers curling around the hilt of his sword. *You're a blazing knight—not the village knucklehead. Think. What would Sir Rick or Commander Storm say?* He swallowed and tried again, speaking with authority. "Who are you? What happened to my flametigers?"

"I am Garutha," a contralto voice murmured in his mind. It sounded female. "Your constructs are within me, fueling me. Tis the price that must be paid for passage. But never fear. The beasts will return to your reservoir and be renewed once my task is completed."

Good. His flametigers would survive. "Your task," Thomas repeated, squinting. "Are you here to guide me?"

Garutha nodded, then back flapped to put distance between them. Hot air fanned against Thomas, and he automatically leaned away. Garutha crossed the threshold, then paused, glancing back at him. "Welcome, Helzarvenn, to Balthazar's Crucible."

"Criminy," Thomas muttered. "This is really happening." He blew out his cheeks and stiffened his spine. "Okay. Lead on, Garutha, and I'll follow."

He passed under the arch in Garutha's wake, her form incandescent in the darkness. A grinding rumble had him whirling with his sword in hand. He blinked at the wall of dark gray stone now obscuring the outside world. He barked a laugh, shaking. "Ha! Should've guessed I'd be trapped here until I finish the trials." As he watched, runes appeared in the stone.

Warmth baked him from behind. Oddly, it reassured him, like a mother's presence. "Not trapped, Helzarvenn," Garutha replied. "You may leave the same way you entered. But you will forfeit a portion of your strength." She paused. "And you may never return."

"No second chances, eh?" Thomas gripped his sword and faced his guide.

"'Tis always another chance," Garutha said. "However, should you try again, your capacity would prove insufficient to open the way. You would extinguish yourself in the attempt. Either way, the sourekghar would be lost to you." Crest fluttering, she turned.

"More bad news. That tracks." Thomas huffed a laugh. "Aren't you a ray of sunshine?"

Garutha's feathers drooped. "Sunshine." Sorrow filled her voice. "'Tis what Balthazar called me. Before ..."

Now he'd put his foot in it. He seemed to excel at making females cry. Thomas cleared his throat. "Sorry, lady. I didn't mean to stir up bad memories."

But isn't that exactly why I'm here? To remember what horrible things happened to make me this way?

"You are forgiven," Garutha replied stiffly. She craned her neck around, and her tone softened. "Come along, child." She picked up her speed. Orbs set into the stone walls came alight with golden fire as the phoenix flew past them.

Funny. Garutha calling him a child didn't bother Thomas. He had the impression she was quite old, though not elderly. Was his guide somehow related to the phoenix community below—perhaps a revered ancestor? The phoenix-people seemed in awe of this place. Thomas shook his head. Never mind; it was probably none of his business. Besides, he had other things to think about. Such as potential enemies.

Gripping his sword, he trotted after Garutha. He wasn't sure if there was anything to fight in these passageways—doubtless the great flaming bird in front of him possessed her own protections—but having the weapon in hand comforted him.

The tunnels were made of the same buff stone, and meandered steadily downward, with occasional pathways branching off in other directions. Good thing he had a guide, or he'd easily lose himself down here. No one accosted them, but Thomas didn't let down his guard. He was supposed to be tested. It grew warmer as they descended. Sweat popped from his pores, and he drank from the small canteen he'd hung from his belt.

After what seemed an eternity of wandering, Garutha hovered beside another golden rune-inscribed arch with a black shield concealing whatever lay beyond it. "'Tis the entrance to

Balthazar's Crucible," she intoned, then gestured with a claw at his canteen. "You cannot carry a vessel of pure water beyond the portal. Drink it down. Also, you will not need your weapon. Leave it here."

Thomas obeyed. He wasn't too worried. His skill at fighting hand-to-hand was one reason Sir Rick had agreed to train him as a knight in the first place—

His eyes widened. "I think I just remembered something from my past."

Garutha bobbed her head. "'Tis beginning, then. Place your right hand upon the gating-stone, child. Do not break contact." Raising her left foot, she flattened it against the gray stone. Thomas followed her example, and the runes burst into flame. He flinched at the heat, but it didn't hurt, and his hand stayed put. The black shield vanished, and broiling heat billowed forth. "Go, Helzarvenn," Garutha said.

"Aren't you coming with me?"

Head lowered, Garutha sank until she stood on the floor. Her feathers dimmed. "I cannot pass the portal into Balthazar's realm. I am cursed never to meet my husband, until that which was sundered is made whole again."

Criminy! She's Balthazar's wife? Who would've guessed the guy was married? Huh. A dragon and a phoenix. And to be separated for so long ...

"I'm sorry." Thomas blurted. "Is there anything I can do ..."

She shook her head. "Not as you are now. Maybe never. Go, child, and face your destiny." Voice fading, the phoenix grew transparent like his flametigers had previously, then became a cloud of sparks that whisked back the way they came on an unseen breeze. Her final words rang in his ears: "The way out is through. Walk with Yshua, Helzarvenn. Call upon his name, and he will deliver you."

Call upon his name. He's never answered me before ... Not that I remember.

But he was here to remember.

Shaken, Thomas stepped onto the threshold and surveyed a familiar vista. Heat baked him. The flaming trees were there, as was the strobe of lightning, and the caldera filled with lava. And from the center of the bubbling golden pool rose the platform. Upon the platform the Sage awaited him, still bound in his chains. Trepidation turned his gut watery.

Balthazar lifted his head. "So," he rumbled. "You have come at last to confront your demons." He beckoned with the tip of his tail. "Step forward, Helzarvenn, and enter the Crucible. Walk with Yshua."

Thomas looked down. Heat stole the sweat from his face. Beneath the arch was a sheer drop into the lava. "Walk with Yshua," he muttered. "Right. I heard Yshua walked on water, but did he ever walk on lava?" Thomas coughed out a laugh. Somehow, he knew it would be this way. It was now, or never. Trembling, he met Balthazar's measuring gaze. He managed a lop-sided grin. "The way out is through, eh?" His eyes never leaving the Sage's, Thomas gave him a salute and stepped over the brink. He plunged straight into the lava.

Song of the Abyss

Before she could second-guess, Annabelle dove into the Depths after her champion. The water grew pitch-black within a few body-lengths of the surface. All she could think was: *Raeden can't swim!* Followed by: *Was that really a giant octopus arm?* And then: *What the heck am I doing? I can't even see!*

Vibrations came from above, and then light permeated the murk surrounding her. Something violet, light blue, and cobalt rocketed past. The figure paused, cobalt fins stirring the water as it turned. It was Mordred, gripping one of the lumen posts in each hand. His eyes gleamed golden in the light as he gave her one. The white glare above intensified. Looking up, Mordred pulled her off to one side. Ten more lumen posts drifted down, down, down, until they settled as small globes of illumination scattered like stars in the darkness. Rhiannon and Sawel swam in their wake, both holding their own light, and paused level with Annabelle and Mordred.

Grim-faced, Rhiannon pointed at her and Sawel, gestured below, then mimed hauling something back up.

A thread of relief stitched through the anxious quiver in her belly. *Thank God! They're still helping me.*

Mordred pulled her close, then propelled downward with the lumen post held like a spear. Annabelle angled hers similarly. Porous-looking rock formations surrounded them as they descended. Some were pillars, some were lopsided tori, but most were amorphous piles containing caverns and crevices where anything could be lurking in ambush.

But where is Raeden? How long can he hold his breath? Annabelle fought panic. That wouldn't do anyone any good. Like Commander Storm had taught her, she trapped the terror inside a ball of ice. She already had a way to trace Raeden to wherever the black tentacle-monster had taken him.

Annabelle could still feel her champion like a faithful dog curled around her heart. The Oathbond was strangely quiet, but not the absolute silence she experienced in the dreamscape. Sensing him somewhere below and to her left, she pointed the lumen post in that direction. Mordred veered toward a dome-like and lumpy jumble of black stones. Nausea coiled in her stomach. The rock formation emanated corruption. Buried beneath the darkness, she also felt the pull, stronger than ever, toward something she could only describe as blue.

The sourekghar is down here, too! Did the last Ahdmerel, Jedediah, bury it under those rocks?

Something white protruded from under a curved, black stone in front. Raeden! She scanned the depths. Where was the monster?

Then the rock formation opened a pair of huge, orange eyes. Dark music flooded Annabelle like a requiem. Her heart skipped a beat. The tentacle monster was a giant black octopus the size of her house.

No. That's not a giant octopus. It's a kraken.

Mordred drew up short. He angled himself between her and the kraken. The massive beast blinked, its arms curling and writhing like a nest of serpents stirring up silt. *We need to act fast! It's trying to conceal itself while it escapes.* She wasn't sure how she knew the creature's intentions.

Annabelle tapped Mordred's arm. She pointed at him, herself, then Raeden. The princeps met her gaze, nodded, pushed her into Rhiannon's arms, and plunged at the kraken.

That's not what I meant, you impetuous knucklehead! Annabelle felt like smacking her forehead. *Crap. I suck at charades. Please, God, be with me. Keep Raeden alive. Protect Rhiannon and Sawel. Oh, and watch over that fool of a princeps, too. In case I decide to marry him.*

Heart racing, she pantomimed spreading out to distract the beast to Rhiannon and Sawel. Pointing at herself, she wriggled her fingers and pretended to tie a knot. The princepsa and the archimandrite exchanged glances, flickered fingers at each other, then dove in opposite directions.

Annabelle extended her kythim into the dark symphony of the Depths. The pearl of wrongness inside her resonated with the corruption of the kraken—two black drums pulsing in counterpoint. So far, the shield containing the dark essence remained strong. Good. Now, how did one immobilize an enormous octopus long enough to extract Raeden from its clutches? Could she freeze it without harming her friends?

Maybe if I touch it ... Should I try communicating with it?

Soaking up energy, she gripped her lumen post like a spear and *willed* herself toward the kraken. This proved easier than she'd thought, because her wyld wanted her to go toward it. The kraken must be sitting on the sourekghar.

The muscular rings around the creature's eyes scrunched. Annabelle sensed discomfort and anxiety. *It doesn't like the light!* It swatted at Rhiannon and Sawel, and it tried to grab Mordred, but it kept missing. Annabelle aimed herself at the muscular arm around Raeden, which coiled ever closer to the kraken's billowing web and underside. Once again, she saw the dreamscape Kraken stuffing her dog, Dallas, into its beaked maw. In her mind's eye, Dallas morphed into Raeden. Anger boiled inside her.

No. I won't let you eat my champion.

There was only an instant to save him. Fashioning a curved blade like a giant ulu knife between her hands, Annabelle rocketed forward and sliced into the kraken's tree-trunk arm. Momentum pushed the blade through. Dark blue blossomed from the wound. Shock and agony fractured her world. Her awareness split.

My arm!

Convulsing, she lost control of the water-blade. It dissipated. Annabelle pulled her seven remaining arms close, curling up into herself. She watched her severed arm spasm, revealing gray suckers as it dropped her prey. Sapphire fury radiated from an alien figure floating between her and her meal.

Astonishment slammed Annabelle back into herself, and she stared up into a glowing orange, slot-pupiled eye the size of a large beach ball.

What the heck *just happened?*

Similar shock immobilized the kraken, who regarded Annabelle through a haze of pain. Fear, anger, and curiosity raged in a tempest that mirrored her own. Colors and word pictures flooded her brain.

—my arm it hurts the white light it hurts what is this warm blue radiance crush it cold I hunger fill the hollowness—

Holy cow! Was she *empathizing* with the creature?

As if she moved in a dream, Annabelle reached through the blue fog of blood. With a funeral dirge filling her ears, she sent her wyld into the stump to mend broken vessels and calm the pain. In less than a second, the bleeding stopped, and the sorrowful music faded into a background moan.

What are you doing? This thing wants to eat Raeden. Stop healing it and save your champion!

The kraken snatched its severed limb and stuffed it under its rippling web. *—not enough the cold the hollowness must be fed—*

It shrank into itself, shielding its eyes from the lumen crystals wielded by the circling gwerindawr. With an eye on the kraken, Annabelle backed away until she reached her champion. Raeden had curled into a fetal position. Pink still leaked from his wounds.

Annabelle hugged her champion. From the Oathbond, she'd known that he still lived, but his body was cold. Normally he burned hotter than she did. Half her attention on the kraken, Annabelle delved Raeden with her kythim. His heart beat once every three seconds and all his body functions ticked along, albeit at a snail's pace.

Whoa. Did he slow down his metabolism and place himself into a sort of suspended animation? Incredible!

Whatever he'd done, it had preserved his life long enough to be rescued. Annabelle didn't have time to speculate. She needed to heal Raeden, get him away from the kraken and out of the water, then find the sourekghar. Within seconds, she'd managed to close up his open wounds. The rest could wait until they were on dry land. She looked at the circle of light far above. The sourekghar's pull felt like shackles on her limbs; too strong for her to drag him up there.

And I'm growing weaker. There's a limit to how much I can do. I shouldn't have wasted energy healing the kraken.

But it wasn't right to let it suffer. Despite the corruption pulsing through the beast, killing it seemed ... wrong.

There's a connection between us. It seems so ... sad. Hungry and alone. Besides, who knows what would happen to me if I hurt it again?

When Rhiannon swam by, Annabelle waved her down. The princepsa understood immediately. She signaled her husband and brother. Sawel porpoised over, but Mordred seemed too intent on tying the kraken's seven remaining arms into knots to notice. Rhiannon grasped Raeden under one arm while Sawel grabbed the other, and the couple swam for the surface with her champion in tow.

Thank you, God.

A black arm snaked toward her fleeing friends.

Oh, no, you don't!

Annabelle shot toward the tentacle, intending to knock it off course, but then it wrapped around her, suckers digging into the scaled fabric of her wyldcham, pressing her arms against her sides. It dragged her toward its underside. Another tentacle grasped a struggling Mordred. He'd lost his lumen post. His arms were trapped and he couldn't reach his knives. She met his gaze. Her stomach dropped.

We're going to be eaten!

She glanced up. Three tiny figures—two finned, one with legs—had reached the surface. At least Raeden, Rhiannon, and Sawel were safe. Now she could concentrate on saving the boneheaded princeps. And hopefully herself.

Wriggling, she mentally screamed: *Let us go, kraken!*

The kraken held Annabelle up to one of its eyes and Mordred to the other. Word pictures flowed in her head, then organized and translated into words.

A feminine voice spoke. "Radiance, you are not my prey. The other has killed. He is my prey. I must fill the hollowness."

Mordred was its—*her*—prey, while she was not? Thrusting aside her confusion, Annabelle concentrated on the awareness of ... The creature waited. She had given Annabelle a name. Now she expected Annabelle to name her.

This was no time to be creative. The gwerindawr had already given this creature a name. "Abyss."

Annabelle sensed approval. Mustering her resolve, she sent: "Please, Abyss. Let us go."

"No, Radiance. This other has killed, and it has been too long. I hunger."

Oh. I see. Abyss only ate murderers. "But he did it to help me. And ..." Annabelle felt sick. Cheese and crackers! She'd killed that nehmwight with her wyld. "I've killed someone. By that logic, you should eat me, too."

Abyss examined her. Annabelle felt the kraken slither through her head. She grimaced. *Oh, God, please ...*

"You defended yourself," the creature mused. "Also, you defended the other one—the prey you took from me. The one who slaughtered innocents." Abyss sounded disgruntled. "You should have let me eat him."

"But he's my champion! He thought he was defending me when he killed those men. You can't have him."

"You are not quite correct, Radiance," Abyss replied. "*Those* deaths are not counted against him." She paused, focusing upwards for a moment. The kraken's choice of words concerning Raeden's guilt troubled Annabelle.

"However," Abyss continued, "that murderer is now beyond my reach. So, I will feed on this one." Her tentacle coiled tighter around Mordred, and he struggled. "I must fill the hollowness."

"Please, don't."

Staring into Mordred's panicked face, Annabelle's mind reeled. What could she do? Attacking the kraken would only hurt herself. Abyss's mournful song swelled. The cold emptiness inside the creature gnawed at Annabelle as if it were her own. The urge to weep and give in to hysteria waited just beyond a thin sheet of ice.

Abyss hungered, but this *hollowness* went beyond physical necessity. It reminded Annabelle of William's dark magic that had tried to devour her wyld. She'd contained it, but the corruption inside her was a tiny speck compared to the massive black hole of the kraken's hunger.

Please, God, help me. What am I supposed to do?

From the depths of her memory, a verse from the book of Isaiah rose to the surface:

"If you spend yourselves on behalf of the hungry,
and satisfy the needs of the oppressed,
then your light will rise in the darkness,
and your night will become like the noonday."

Although it wasn't quite what she'd wanted to hear, the Holy Spirit had answered her. Like Morgan Brenin, Abyss was under a curse. And it was Annabelle's job to free them both.

Hopefully the "spending" of herself wouldn't result in death.

Annabelle shuddered. She couldn't dwell on that now. What would be, would be. "Abyss," she sent. "If you let Mordred go, I'll feed you. I'll ... I'll fill the hollowness." With what and how, she didn't know. She'd figure that out once Mordred was safe. Besides, she still needed to find the sourekghar.

The kraken blinked. "This is acceptable, Radiance."

Suddenly, they were ascending toward the circle of light. It was brighter than before. Klotho had risen. The black arm holding Mordred shot for the opening, then returned empty. Daylight receded as Abyss dragged her back down to the bottom. Oddly enough, throughout the kraken's movement, the pull of the sourekghar remained steady.

Annabelle stared at Abyss. Did that mean ...

Horror filled her at the thought, but she had to know. "Abyss," she asked, trembling. She sent an image of the dark blue armor she wore in the dreamscape. "Is that armor ... the sourekghar made by Hadrien Rainblessed ... inside you?"

Silt billowed in a cloud as the kraken settled on the ocean floor. "Yes, Radiance. Once I was inside it, and all was well. Then cold and darkness came. My Faithful was gone. I was empty. So, I filled myself." Abyss held Annabelle before her orange gaze. Suckers rasped against the wyldcham as the kraken adjusted her grip. She turned Annabelle this way and that, as if examining her for flaws. Abyss blinked. "Now Radiance will fill me."

A rushing sensation overwhelmed her, and then the creature's sucker-lined underside filled her entire world. The dark blue beak in the center began to open.

Is it my time to die?

Resigned, lethargy chilling her limbs, Annabelle watched the kraken's maw expand. The ice sphere containing her panic shattered, but she was too tired to be afraid or even cry anymore.

Heavenly Father, I'm a mess, but please accept my spirit.

Something small and blue jetted past her—straight for the kraken's open beak. *Wes? No!* At the last second, Wesleyen squirted ink—and something that glowed blue—into the gaping maw. Abyss shuddered. Her grip on Annabelle loosened. What had the little octopus squirted into its mouth? It felt like ... *herself.*

"Not enough," Abyss moaned.

Then the kraken's beak snapped shut on one of Wesleyen's arms. No! Her brain screaming at her to flee, Annabelle wriggled loose and grabbed the little octopus. She tore him loose, clamping down on his tentacle stump as she kicked off from the kraken's lip. *I need to save Wes!* While she mended leaking blood vessels, Annabelle *reached* for the water above.

Abyss opened her beak and pulled them both into her gullet.

Annabelle curled around Wesleyen and squeezed her eyes shut. Her wyldcham snagged on something prickly. She knew what came next; octopi had radula to scrape away flesh. Perhaps her wyldcham would protect them ... Right up until the acid and digestive enzymes melted them alive.

Oh, Wes. I'm so sorry you got sucked into this. She barked a humorless laugh. What a time to make a pun. She needed to find the sourekghar. Maybe the armor would protect her and Wes from being digested.

"Radiance." The kraken's voice surrounded her like a requiem, almost sobbing. "Fill me."

Wesleyen squirmed, and Annabelle stroked his mantle. "Abyss ... Please ... Give me a minute."

Abyss shuddered. Her beak clattered. "You have a minute."

Once again, Annabelle reached out with her kythim. Wesleyen's valiant, yet foolhardy act gave her an idea. Somehow, the little octopus had absorbed some of Annabelle's essence. Perhaps the best way to fill Abyss was to pour her wyld into the kraken while replenishing her reservoir using the water all around them.

I just hope I can fill my reservoir faster than I empty it into Abyss. She's freaking ginormous.

Annabelle formed a conduit between herself and Abyss, and another between herself and the Depths outside the kraken. *Please, God. Let this work.*

And then she began. The process required little mental effort once she set it up. Steadily, she pumped shining sapphire energy into Abyss while pulling energy from the water. The kraken drank greedily. Extending a thought-tendril, Annabelle explored. The sourekghar had to be in here somewhere; she no longer experienced the terrible pulling sensation.

Her questing kythim happened upon a web of familiar cold, consuming emptiness that stretched away beyond the Depths. The black pearl inside her shivered in sympathy.

The corruption! Is this the curse I must break?

Finding the heart of the darkness, Annabelle stopped feeding the kraken and poured all her energy into piercing through the web. Nothing. On impulse, she grasped Daar-Lûsin and thrust it into the blackness. There came a sensation of thunder without sound. Suddenly, she was elsewhere.

Ignition Point

Thomas stopped dead on the forest path. Hadn't he been elsewhere a moment ago? Someplace hot where he'd summoned forth tigers made of fire? He stared at his hands, then frowned. And why expect his hands to be on fire? That would be ridiculous; not to mention, impossible. He was a swordsman and martial artist, not a magic-wielder. He might not remember anything before the past six winters, but he knew that much. Snorting a laugh, he continued on his way after adjusting the torc encircling his neck. The Baron-Knight's symbol of office rested heavily above his leather breastplate. Sir Rick had given it to him only hours before. He wasn't accustomed to its weight. And he didn't intend to become so. Not for cycles.

Thomas still couldn't believe Sir Rick had raised him to Baron-Knight before he sent him into the Darkenwood to find the three lost children. From his bed, he'd summoned the stewards to witness the signing of his Last Will and Testament and the passing of the torc. Sir Rick claimed that if the illness took his life, then Thomas would be the Baron-Knight and needed the authority of the office to enact martial law if the disappearances pointed toward something larger that threatened the entire Barony.

After sending away the stewards, Sir Rick also charged Thomas with the protection and further training of Enoch

Northward when the youth returned from Treehome. Apparently, the kid was the last scion of a royal bloodline. It was supposed to be a great secret known only by the Dwelfnic Council, Commander Storm, and the Baron-Knights. Meaning him. His head was still reeling from that revelation.

Could I handle that sort of responsibility, on top of governing the Northern Marches?

"You'll do that yourself, sir," he'd said at the elder man's bedside while gripping his hand. "Rest easy. I'll find those girls, simple as pie, and bring the torc right back to you. Because you're going to beat this sickness and go back to doing what you do best—leading and protecting the people."

But it didn't work out that way, now, did it? His own voice whispered, caustic as lye, from the back of his mind. *Sir Rick dies while you're out here, a victim of conspiracy and murder. You never find those poor girls. And then—*

Where the heck did those thoughts come from? Was he going batty? Shaking his head to clear it, Thomas swerved off the path to where he'd seen broken twigs and wilted leaves. He knelt to investigate the anomaly. Sure as frogs croaked, something had pushed through the underbrush here within the past day or two. He plucked a scrap of black cloth stuck on a branch, then grunted. Animals didn't leave that sort of thing behind. No. A person had come through here—and recently. It had rained last night, and the bit of cloth was dry. Could it be one of the lost girls? Hope had never been part of his repertoire. They'd been missing too long. Trepidation churned in his gut as he slid between the damaged bushes. He suspected he'd be discovering their corpses. Poor kids.

Amid the chatter of birdsong, Thomas emerged into a clearing where a wardspell's stone ring loomed as the primary feature—six dark gray monoliths surrounding a seventh monolith of quartz-like stone. He froze in his tracks. Something was wrong. The Veil should've stopped him from penetrating this deeply into the forest. Unease prickled along his spine as he approached the stone ring, then stopped again to stare.

Thomas knew little about stone circles and magic, but he was pretty sure the central crystal of a wardspell shouldn't look like the melted stub of a burned-out candle.

He cursed under his breath. "What in blazes could do that to a wardspell crystal? Sir Rick said those things are supposed to be indestructible." His fingers brushed the pommels of his swords for reassurance. Also strapped on his hips were weapons from Earth, the place Sir Rick said Thomas was from. Thomas didn't remember how to use the weapons—or anything about Earth—but having the things brought him comfort.

Locating three missing children no longer seemed a simple excursion. Failed wards compromised the security of the entire realm. Suddenly, his priorities had shifted. The wardspells maintained the Veil that protected Lilac Grove from massive beasts roaming the wilderness beyond. Creatures like soot panthers, dire wolves, and giant bears that would happily devour livestock and people along with them. A ball of ice formed in his stomach. Thomas cursed again and checked the draw on his swords. Perhaps he should've brought men along with him instead of dispatching the troops to search for the girls elsewhere.

I should head back to the rally-point. Right now. Order the men to initiate lockdown procedures and send out the garrison messenger. The Commander needs to know about this.

But how far did the damage extend? He ought to walk the line and see if at least one more crystal had gone melty before he went back. It wouldn't take long. Scurrying home like a terrified green recruit at the first sign of trouble was not how a knight behaved—let alone an Acting Baron-Knight.

Thomas skirted the wardspell circle, feet squishing through the mud of a recent spring shower, all senses at work analyzing his surroundings. Oddly, there weren't any tracks besides the ones he left himself. After a short hike he came to a stand of mature trees where undergrowth was sparse, save for fiddleheads pushing up through last year's bracken. Birds continued to call, and wind rattled newly leafed branches above him. He glanced up; based on the light, Klotho would set in another hour. He needed to finish his investigation by then so he could make it back to the garrison before dark.

Halfway to a massive oak, the hairs on the back of his neck prickled. He hesitated. His nose wrinkled at an ozone stench. Magic? Sir Rick had warned him this wood was uncanny. And the Veil was down. Thomas narrowed his eyes. There—a weird marking near the base of the tree trunk. It looked like blood. Someone was injured. One of the lost children ... or an enemy?

Thomas brought up his weapon into a guard position. Placing his feet carefully amid the raised and twisting roots, he used the trunk for cover as he crept clockwise around the tree. He nearly collided with a tall, cloaked figure coming from the other direction.

"Hey!" Thomas barked, his heart kicking into overdrive. The cloaked figure cried out, arms pinwheeling as it stumbled backwards over a root and went sprawling. A wicked-looking knife fell and clattered between two roots. Fresh blood smeared the ivory blade.

Thomas's grip tightened on his longsword. *Has murder been done here?* He drew his right-hand blade. He flicked the trespasser's knife away with his longsword. Thomas growled, "Who are you? What in perdition are you doing here? Did you kill those girls?"

The stranger's hood had fallen over its face. It crab-crawled away, panting, black cloak flapping open. No armor underneath and no other apparent weapons. Just a brown robe and a tasseled sash. But he had a knife smeared with blood. Lunging after him,

Thomas hooked his right-hand blade under the hood and flipped it back. A pair of wide orange eyes stared back at him from a gray-skinned face, slack with terror.

A nehmwight?

The separate voice that was also his muttered, *"the same clown I saw in the dreamscape!"*

Confusion swirled. Thomas shook it off. In a blink, he had his longsword's tip at the stranger's throat. Commander Storm trained all the men to fight nehmwights, but he'd never seen one before. Supposedly the fierce warriors lived far to the north in ice caves and hid from the suns. What was one doing here—and out during the daytime, no less?

The nehmwight's voice cracked as he choked out, "Zakaar!"

This clown is no warrior. He's just a kid, scared out of his gourd. Thomas's eyes narrowed. *With a bloody knife. Didn't the Commander say they sacrificed for their magic?*

Keeping the sword where it was, he fixed the trespasser with his most intimidating glare. "Zakaar, eh? All right, clown. Talk. What did you do to the girls?"

The nehmwight's eyes shifted to the left. *Someone's behind me!* Thomas was in the act of pivoting when pain exploded in his head, and everything went black.

Did I just die?

Where was he now? Cold and darkness had become his world. Off to his left, water trickled down an unseen drain. Thomas grimaced at the moldy odor of damp rot as he assessed his condition and considered his situation. The back of his head throbbed. That's right; he'd been in the Darkenwood, confronting that nehmwight kid, and someone had struck him from behind.

Presently, he lay spread eagle on a smooth, hard surface tilted at an acute angle with his head above his feet. He imagined Commander Storm chastising him: "This is no time to rest. On your feet, soldier!" He struggled, but he couldn't move—something held him down. Even his head and neck were immobilized.

I'm trapped! Gotta move. Inertia means death.

Terror flared like a dying star under his breastbone. Jaw clenched, he recalled Sir Rick's lessons on breathing. Good air in ... Bad air out ... After his mind cleared, he continued cataloging details. His boots and stockings were gone. So were his swords and the weapons from his home-world. That gave him a frisson. Or maybe he shivered because he was naked from the waist up and cold metal confined him by the head, middle, wrists, and ankles.

Grunting, he strained against his bonds, but they wouldn't budge. Thomas went limp, gasping. His aching head pulsed in rhythm with his heartbeat. Nausea roiled in his stomach. Sooner or later, someone would come. And probably torture him. He swallowed the sob welling up his throat.

"Quit your dad-rotted puling, Sir Thomas!" Commander Storm's voice was like a whip-crack in his imagination. *"Are you a worm or a man? Ursanovir appointed you as his successor. You're the Baron-Knight of the Northern Marches. Act like it!"*

Thomas inhaled sharply through his nose. "Steady, man," he growled through gritted teeth. "Don't panic. Yeah, okay, you're trapped, and—based on your scars—about to be flayed alive. But you already survived this. Commander Storm trained you in what to do under these circumstances—how to build a fortress around your mind. Do it."

With his eyes shut—it was too dark to see, anyway—Thomas resumed the calming exercise and felt himself rising like a balloon. Something tugged at his gut as he floated and kept him from rising further. A tether? That was odd, but he'd wonder about it after he protected his mind. He constructed the Lilac Grove garrison around his consciousness and infused each brick with a golden seal of protection. It was an easy task, quickly done, and he'd always wondered why Annabelle had so much trouble— guilt slammed into him like a battering ram and for a moment he couldn't breathe.

I'd give anything to hear her complain about training again.

A loud *clank* intruded from off to his right, followed by metal shrieking. His eyes flew open as first a slit and then a wall of orange light flooded his prison, giving him a bird's-eye view of himself strapped on a tilted table with grooves running around its edges. The tether he'd sensed was a shining gold strand connecting him to ... His past self? Perhaps he should think of it that way, now that his present-conscious-self was separated from the man below.

As he watched, Past-Thomas's unscarred chest heaved, and he strained to move as his eyes rolled toward the source of the noise—a door slowly screaming its way open. The light pouring in revealed a stone chamber that resembled a dungeon with chains and manacles attached to its walls—there were no other prisoners—and Thomas made note of the drain to the left of the slab holding Past-Thomas, and a small table positioned between it and the door.

Suddenly, the light flickered out, and the door creaked shut. A masculine voice snarled something that sounded like coughing up gravel.

The door flew open wide as if kicked from the other side and a familiar figure burst into the prison with a large satchel clutched under one arm while holding up the source of orange light—a fist-sized lantern. Eyes wide and jaw clenched, the nehmwight youth pushed the door completely open using his back and then stood there like a doorstop. He appeared harassed and from the looks he cast toward Past-Thomas bound helpless on the table ... Criminy! Was the clown frightened of *him*?

"William," a man's voice echoed, then spoke again in a harsh-sounding dialect.

The youth cringed. The lantern winked out, then came back on again. "Ha-hanockt, Reshkhan Tenebris," he stammered, then scowled. Thomas recognized the frustrated rage darkening his features as the same emotion smoldering in his own soul.

"Hai-shen dhal, arkhasuhl." Preceded by an orange glowing orb, the black-robed owner of the voice swept into the room. The youth stiffened as he passed, and his expression instantly shuttered. The nehmwight paused a stride-length from where Past-Thomas lay. Slightly taller than the youth, he bore a close resemblance to him, though the man was older, and his bearded face was leaner, his eyes and nose narrower.

He held himself like one accustomed to issuing commands and being obeyed as he drew nearer to Past-Thomas. Stroking his beard, the man regarded his prisoner with a thin smile. He murmured something in dialect, as if to himself, then chuckled.

"Sorry, could you repeat that in Trade?" said Past-Thomas. "I don't speak gibberish."

The nehmwight's smile broadened into a shark-like grin. His orange eyes blazed like perdition as he gestured at the small table beside Past-Thomas. "William!" he barked, and the youth jumped. The nehmwight spat out a series of consonant-rich phrases that sounded like insults.

"Yah-krin, Reshkhan Tenebris!" The youth—William? That didn't seem like a proper name for a nehmwight—allowed the door to bang behind him, hung the lantern from a hook dangling from the ceiling, then scurried over to deposit his burden on the table. He opened the case with trembling hands and retreated to slouch against the wall. Thomas shuddered at the implements lined up inside. Most looked sharp and capable of delivering incredible pain.

Reaching inside his robes, the older nehmwight drew out a dagger with a hooked tip—the twin of the one the youth had dropped in the forest. He loomed over Past-Thomas and smiled in a friendly fashion, though its warmth didn't reach his eyes. "Greetings," he said in slightly accented Trade, his tone jovial. "Welcome to my humble home. You may address me as Tenebris. What are you called, kadorei?"

"Whatever you want," Past-Thomas quipped. "I'll answer to pretty much everything—except 'late to dinner.'"

"Late for dinner?" Arms crossed inside opposite sleeves, the youth snorted and rolled his eyes. "Pathetic. Is he trying to be funny?" He, too, spoke Trade with only a slight emphasis on the velar sounds.

"Can't you tell?" Past-Thomas laughed. "I'd've thought you'd know 'funny.' Just look in the mirror, you clown."

Glowering, the youth made fists at his sides as he straightened to his full height. "Oi! What's that now?"

Tenebris shot him a glare. "What have I told you, William? Don't allow a prisoner to rile you with insults. Any nonsense he utters is pure drivel. Warrior bravado." He faced Past-Thomas, slapping the flat of his blade into his open palm. "Tell me about the garrison's defenses and I'll let you go."

"What makes you think I have any information about that?" Past-Thomas demanded. "You're barking up the wrong tree."

With a smirk, the nehmwight said, "William, show our guest what you've confiscated."

The youth gaped at him, then rattled something off in the nehmwight patois. Tenebris glared and snarled something harsh-sounding in response.

William sighed, reached inside his robes, and pulled out the Baron-Knight's torc. He sneered. "This bit of jewelry says you know quite a bit about the garrison's defenses."

"Go to the devil," retorted his past self. "You won't get anything from me."

"Oh," Tenebris purred as he held up his knife. "I think you'll find my methods of persuasion quite effective." Smiling, he turned to his young assistant. "Pay close attention. I am going to show you how to break a man and empower a Greater Sending simultaneously." He waved the dagger, punctuating his words. "Waste not, want not. Once I have the information we need from our ... guest, you can prove yourself worthy of the Third Circle by dispatching this one into the Outer Darkness. Now, get to work on that spellform."

William lost his scowl and gulped. He reached inside his robes, then withdrew his hand empty, looking like he was about to vomit. "Y-yes, Master Tenebris." He knelt on the floor, drew his knife, and glanced aside with a grimace as he sliced his left forearm. Blood spattered on the floor, and he used it as ink to trace angular shapes on the stones. With a surprisingly melodic voice he chanted in his consonant-rich tongue. Orange lines appeared where blood touched and pulsed with eldritch energy.

Thomas felt stirrings of alarm while he observed. These nehmwights were the ones who had kidnapped Enoch. Was everything that happened Thomas's fault, like he'd always feared deep in his gut?

Did I give away vital information under torture—allowing them to capture Enoch?

The pain of the knife didn't register when Tenebris began cutting into his past self, slicing wounds that would become those ridged scars in his chest. Agony already consumed his soul. Was he responsible for Enoch's captivity and the war threatening the entire Imerinthian continent? Rivulets of his blood flowed from the incisions into the channels surrounding him on the tilted surface and then trickled into a reservoir at its base.

Past-Thomas attempted stoicism at first; although he flinched and trembled, he voiced nothing aside from nonsense phrases and garbled insults against Tenebris through gritted teeth. But the sorcerer kept cutting. He practiced the art of patience, allowing the pain to ebb, and then renewed it. Relentlessly. Endlessly.

Off to the side, the younger nehmwight's voice shook as he chanted the alien words of his spell and kept his eyes averted from Past-Thomas's suffering. And then, when Past-Thomas was on his last tether, the grievous blow came.

Tenebris bent and whispered: "Tell me what I want to know, and the pain stops."

He wanted to. Oh, how he wanted to. Sobbing, Past-Thomas uttered fragments of the Baron-Knight's Code. "Seek justice ... Show mercy ... Walk humbly ... Innocent ... protected."

Scowling, Tenebris carved another line into his captive's torso. And then another. "You will tell me ... everything."

"No!" Past-Thomas howled, arching his back. "Lord Yshua ... Jesus, save me!" For an instant, shining gold tendrils fanned out around, and an opalescent glow limned his bleeding form. Slack-jawed, the apprentice slowly rose from his work and stared.

Those golden streamers must be my kythim, Thomas mused. *Can that clown see them, too?*

Tenebris stumbled back. Fallen from his trembling hand, the knife clattered into the tray. "Useless." The sorcerer spat, then glared. "I would have dispatched you without further pain, had you only cooperated." A mirthless grin spread across his face. "But now I think I'll have my apprentice send you to the Outer Darkness."

Watching from above, Thomas shook his head. He hadn't revealed any sensitive information after all.

Was it because I prayed? Did God answer me?

"William," Tenebris barked, startling the youth. "I know you're done with the spellform. Stop gaping like a witless looby and get over here. I've wrung all I can from this mreeshgraf. Time for you to cut his throat while I set up the next phase to make use of his lifeblood."

Wide-eyed and tight-lipped, the nehmwight youth exchanged places with his master. He drew his knife, then stood there, staring at the man lying on the slab and bleeding from dozens of wounds. "Merciful Valeshka," he whispered. "How are you still alive?"

Good question, Thomas thought. His past self had lost a lot of blood.

Eyes glazed with pain, Past-Thomas bared his teeth. "I'm tougher than ... a streak of yellow water like you ... see you last this long ... under the knife."

Squaring his shoulders, the youth sneered. "You know nothing of what I've endured as an Arkhadahn's apprentice." The fear behind his eyes belied his bravado.

"Don't want to," Past-Thomas gasped. "You've ... never killed ... Have you?"

"Oi, shut it." William thrust the knife at him with a shaking hand but stopped short of his neck. He dipped it into the reservoir and flicked blood into Past-Thomas's face. "I can kill without a second thought."

Despite himself, Thomas snorted a laugh. *The clown's had time enough for* fifth *thoughts.*

"Suns burn it," Tenebris muttered. "Why am I burdened with a worthless apprentice? William, I told you to kill the kadorei filth, not shoot the breeze."

"Yeah," Past-Thomas coughed. "Worthless. Coward. Miserable little toad."

William's mouth spasmed. "I'll show you who's a blistering toad!" His eyes flared violet light as he shouted something incoherent. The blood on the table gleamed with purple light streaked with blackness.

Past-Thomas screamed. His body bubbled, pale skin turning brown and bumpy as he shrank into a toad the size of a large tom-cat. Horrified astonishment spread across the nehmwight youth's face. Had the kid not planned to do that, then? Blood evaporated into purple mist that swirled around the toad and rose to engulf Thomas.

Everything froze. For a perfect, crystalline moment, the shards of memory slid together into a picture window. Thomas glimpsed, beyond the agony-that-was, the event that had shattered his mind two cycles earlier ...

No!

He slammed the shutters. Time resumed. A backlash of violet energy exploded out in rings from the toad on the table, flooring the two nehmwights. Above, Thomas's mind fortress disintegrated.

The chamber spun as Thomas was sucked into his past toad-form. Blood and the stench of fear surrounded him. Animal terror upended all other senses. Instinct took over. He had to escape. He scented water. The drain! The toad leaped from the slab to the table, scattering implements in a clatter of metal, then to the floor and the damp opening. While one tall, dark form made loud, terrifying sounds at another, the toad squeezed down pipes reeking of wet mold and out into the more fragrant scents of an early spring rose-tinged evening. Hind legs pumping like pistons, he was away from the blood-reeking castle ruin in moments ...

... And the world tilted as he tumbled through dim caverns that echoed with murmuring voices he almost recognized. He came to rest in a seated position, his back supported by something solid and round. A fire danced and flickered in front of him and at first, he saw nothing else. Fresh air and wood-smoke flooded his nostrils when he inhaled. Nearby, crickets chirped steadily, grounding him. But the crackle of flames made his heart race and palms tingle with a mixture of apprehension and excitement. Heat bathed him, welcome after his ordeal in the cold dungeon.

Panting, Thomas blinked in the firelight as his hands flew to pat down his chest. Through the thin fabric he encountered a torso and skin devoid of scars. The planes of his chest seemed underdeveloped and when he held his hands before his face they were innocent of the callouses he'd earned over two cycles of sword training.

What's going on? Where are my scars and callouses?

"Are you afraid, lad?"

His head jerked up and he gazed across the fire at his companion, a middle-aged man with dark-skinned and weathered features. Kindness filled the brown eyes meeting his, and Thomas relaxed against the log at his back. Sir Rick was with him, and the campfire was contained within a ring of stones. Energy harnessed and not on the rampage. Its light and warmth kept the darkness at bay.

He rubbed his palms along his denim-clad thighs to rid them of their dampness. "I'm not afraid," he said, then added, "sir."

Inwardly, he frowned. His voice sounded less resonant. Was this his younger self? It must be, because Sir Rick was dead. He blinked back tears.

"A man needn't be ashamed of his fear," Sir Rick said, leaning over to adjust a burning log with a stick. Wood popped and sparks ascended in a whirling dance. "Fear's a natural emotion, Thomas. It alerts us to danger. Don't suppress it. Acknowledge it, and work with it to hone your skills as a warrior. Otherwise, fear may come to rule over you." He raised his eyebrows. "Rather like fire. Both have their uses. Both destroy when freed from their tethers."

"I know that better than most, sir." How did he know that? A memory tried to surface—a dead man and a girl screaming amid flames and darkness—but he pushed it down. Just a nightmare. His throat tightened. He didn't want to see that again.

"You must face your fear head-on." Sir Rick regarded him, his head wreathed by sparks and wood-smoke. "If you keep running from the past, then fear will take you down from behind and consume you when others are relying on your strength and self-control."

Shaking, Thomas pushed himself to his feet. He felt lighter than he should. Vulnerable. "I'm not a coward, sir. I don't run away from danger."

Sir Rick sat back, the shadows accentuating the lines in his face. He shook his head. "You allow your fear to chase you toward darkness and away from the light. Turn and confront your demons. Or be consumed by them."

With a groan, the Baron-Knight rose and dusted off his trousers. "It's time to get back to business, lad. You need to remember so you can understand." He gestured at the flames. "The way out is through."

Thomas felt like his mentor had punched him in the gut. He'd thought his anger was the demon he must confront, but all this time his anger had been rooted in fear. His hands balled into fists. *I must fight it!*

He reached for his swords, but they were gone. Then he recalled his past self wouldn't know how to use them yet. His mouth felt dry. The old knight began to fade from view.

Heart racing, he called out, "Wait. Please. Sir Rick, I don't have any weapons. How am I supposed to fight my fear?"

"By standing firm in the truth and trusting in the Almighty Threefold One."

Criminy. I'm toast. His mouth tasted like ashes. "Um. I mean, what should I *do?*"

The late Baron-Knight offered him a gentle smile. "Remember all your father taught you. Remember everything I taught you, Thomas, and put it into action. Seek justice. Show mercy. Walk humbly with Lord Yshua." And then, he was gone.

Thomas stared off into the darkness, hands shaking at his sides. "What my father taught me." Why couldn't he remember? Because the demons stood between him and that knowledge. There was no growth without pain. His gaze drifted to the fire blazing within its ring of stones. "The way out is through," he intoned. "Well, here we go again."

He stepped through the flames ... and into the past.

Turning the Tide

Piercing the web of corruption in the kraken's belly was like passing through a curtain of both fire and ice into a washing machine during its spin cycle. Annabelle tumbled head over heels, then crashed down into a dead calm sea. She floated face up on a hard, concave surface and stared up into a sky of brooding clouds the color of old bruises until her head stopped spinning. There was no wind. All she heard was water sounds.

Annabelle sniffed. It didn't smell like the ocean. More like fresh water. Where had she ended up this time?

It's not Ynys Lloches, yet it seems familiar.

Turning her head, she saw nothing but flat water in either direction over the lip of a dark blue ... raft?

What's this thing I'm on? She rapped it with her knuckles. It was solid, like wood, but felt more like a giant fingernail. Something squirmed on her belly. She thought she glimpsed Wesleyen's head. Was she seeing double? When she tried to sit up and get a better view, her head swam, and nausea assaulted her. She flopped back down with a grimace.

Guess I'll just float along for a while until my stomach settles. She hoped it wouldn't be long. Wherever this was, she needed to find her way back to—

Raeden!

Her eyes widened. The Oathbond was quiet and seemed ... diminished. Her champion still lived but was far away. She rubbed her chest. The scaly fabric of her wyldcham rasped against her palm. Something slithered onto her hand. She lifted it and smiled wearily at the little blue octopus. "Hi, Wes." She eyed the stump where a tentacle used to be. "I suppose you're a septapus now."

Then she frowned. If Wesleyen was on her hand, then what was that weight on her belly? Carefully, she raised herself up on her elbow to meet the gaze of a second octopus twice Wesleyen's size. Black splotches shifted across its light blue skin. Like him, it was missing an arm. And it had orange eyes.

"Radiance," a voice spoke in her mind.

Annabelle gaped. "Abyss?"

"Yes," the former kraken said. Her mental voice trembled, and her tentacles moved sluggishly. "Thank you, Radiance. You have banished the hollowness. I can sleep now in peace."

"Ahdmerel," another voice boomed across the waters. "Lie down flat upon the sourekghar."

"Hadrien! Wait ... what?" She touched the smooth surface of her raft. "*This* thing is the sourekghar?"

"Yes," the Sage rumbled. "But in its quiescent form. I must awaken it; prime it with pure Aethyr. Lie down, child, and I shall reel you in. I fear we have little time before the portal closes."

Annabelle obeyed, her mind teeming with questions. Hopefully the Sage would answer them. Wesleyen clung to her neck. There was a lurch, a rushing sound, and her raft sped along until something like a huge blue leaf came down from overhead and scooped them up, raft and all. Annabelle held on to Abyss, who seemed too weak to grip her wyldcham.

The raft—sourekghar? She still had trouble believing it— tilted her into a reclining position, and a familiar reptilian visage filled her view. Her mood lifted even as tears stung her eyes.

"Hadrien," she choked, placing a hand on his snout. "I'm so glad to see you again."

"And I am relieved to see you recovered from your wound," the Sage replied. "I've been praying since you left me in the dreamscape. I knew it would not be long before you found your way to me here." His brown eyes shifted to the octopi. "Ah. You have made staunch allies among the Khaverim. Do you know? The female resembles one I knew an Age ago—Jedediah's companion, Abyssalin."

Khaverim? Annabelle mused. *That's dwelfnic for "friends."*

Abyss's eyestalks lifted. "Rainblessed," she said listlessly. Pink, gray, and dark blue swirled across her skin. "Where is Faithful?"

Hadrien regarded the female octopus with a somber expression. If he was surprised that she could talk, then he gave no sign. "Jedediah has gone home, Abyssalin," he murmured. "And it will not be long before you join him and Lord Yshua."

Abyss gave a bubbling little sigh. "Good. I have been too long in the darkness. I yearned to join Faithful ... but I couldn't." She turned limpid orange eyes toward Annabelle. "But Radiance has set me free. Now I remember Lord Yshua. Thank you, Radiance."

Gently stroking the former kraken's head, Annabelle's throat thickened, and her eyes burned. Speechless, she reached out with her kythim to mend whatever was broken inside Abyss. There was nothing she could grasp—or rather, there was too much. The cephalopod was dying of old age.

"It is her time, little one," Hadrien said. "Just as it is your time to claim the sourekghar." The octopus and the Sage looked at one another, and Hadrien nodded; it seemed something passed between them that Annabelle couldn't hear.

Annabelle sniffled. "Does this mean the curse on the gwerindawr is broken? Sawel—their archimandrite—believed the king's torc was cursed, but all along it was poor Abyss." She lifted Abyss to rest on her shoulder, opposite Wesleyen, who reached around to entwine arms with the female.

"The hollowness," Abyss whispered in Annabelle's mind.

Hadrien's brow furrowed. "It appears the 'curse' of the prophecy was twofold." He shook his head. "The torc absolutely should be destroyed, but you must have the protection of the sourekghar to do so."

"How'll I destroy the torc?" She snorted. "I don't think water can shatter bronze."

One of the Sage's whiskers moved, poking at the dagger at her right hip. "You already possess the key to break the corruption's hold."

Annabelle's eyes widened. "That's how I broke through the curse on Abyss. I basically stabbed it with Daar-Lûsin."

Hadrien nodded. "My brother Melkior wrought seldom, but he always wrought well. That blade will turn the tide in our favor, before all is done."

Speaking of using Daar-Lûsin to break things ... Annabelle eyed the chains binding Hadrien to the dais, then rested her hand on the dagger's pommel. "Could I use this to cut you free?" Rescuing Enoch would be so much easier with one of the Sages at her side.

Hadrien jerked back, eyes wide. "You must not break my chains, Ahdmerel! To do so would precipitate disaster. My brethren and I remain bound in our Sundered Realms for the safety of all who live on Tehara." He paused, searching her face. "If Valkor still lives—and it is perilous to assume he or any of the others have perished—perhaps the safety of your realm hangs in the balance as well."

"What do you mean?" Annabelle's breath hitched. Who was Valkor? And these "others" Hadrien mentioned? Were her loved ones back home in danger from something on Tehara?

Hadrien sighed. "I would not burden you unnecessarily. Once matters at Ynys Lloches are settled, we shall discuss—"

Lightning flashed overhead. Thunder cracked, and Hadrien's dais shook. The Sage drew Annabelle in close, sheltering her against his scaled chest. "There is no time! The bridge between this Sundered Realm and Tehara grows unstable. Lie still and prepare to receive the sourekghar."

Annabelle did as he directed.

"Abyssalin, are you committed to this course?"

"Yes, Rainblessed. I am prepared."

"Prepared for what?" Annabelle asked the female octopus.

"For what must be done," Abyss murmured. Complex patterns rippled across her skin.

Lowering his head, Hadrien wept dark blue tears. They ran like paint down his snout, falling on Annabelle and the dormant armor, which softened and flowed swiftly around her body, covering the wyldcham while moving under her weapons-belt. It felt like being wrapped in a warm blanket. Wesleyen crawled on top of Annabelle's head to avoid being swept up into it, but Abyss slithered until she hung from Annabelle's neck like a pendant. Abyss's head rested over Annabelle's heart.

"Abyss, what are you doing?"

Thunder crashed. Clouds raced overhead.

Abyss replied, "Radiance ... the vashryu is within me. But it is broken. Half is missing. My arms will hold the sourekghar together until the rest of the vashryu is found."

Hadrien's tears continued to fall, engulfing the dying cephalopod. "The sourekghar will preserve Abyssalin until she has served her purpose."

He makes Abyss sound like nothing more than a tool! Annabelle's tone grew acerbic. "And then what happens to her?"

"Do not worry, Radiance," Abyss replied. She sounded stronger. "I will go to be with our Lord Yshua and Faithful."

She'll die as soon as I find the missing half of the vashryu?

Annabelle stared down at her chest. The armor began to resemble what she wore in the dreamscape, but unlike there this new breastplate bore the bas relief impression of Abyss with her seven arms spread. Where her head would be was a glittering sapphire in the shape of half Hadrien's sigil—the fish-symbol that stood on its tail.

Annabelle ran her fingers over the gem. Although it sparkled with facets, it felt smooth. "How do I find the other half?"

"The vashryu desires to be whole. It will lead you to its mate."

Lightning lit up the entire sky. The dais shook. She braced herself against the Sage. At least she stood on her own now.

"I feel stronger," she mused aloud.

"Indeed," Hadrien replied. "This armor both sustains and protects you, little one, but you must still take care. Until you possess the other half of my vashryu, you will not have access to the full potential of the armor, and we cannot communicate outside the dreamscape."

Hadrien's sending me out there with faulty equipment? Not wanting to sound ungrateful, Annabelle kept that thought to herself. Another quake caused her to stumble backward and Hadrien caught her with his tail-spade. "Whoa!" She stared up at him. "Is there anything I can do to ... compensate?"

"Immersing yourself in water should help compensate for any lack. It is time for you to return to Ynys Lloches." His tail pivoted her around to face a rippling blue portal. Lightning arched from its circumference up into the sky and down into the agitated waters of the freshwater sea. "Before you leave," Hadrien said, "I must give you one last warning. Without the full vashryu you will also be vulnerable to others with an affinity to the water aspect. Be wary whenever you experience a sympathetic resonance to your wyld."

Annabelle stood with one hand on the Dagger of Moonlight and the other resting on the armor covering her stomach. Deep inside her reservoir, the sorcerer's magic seethed behind her shielding. *That reminds me ...*

Why hadn't Hadrien mentioned the mote of darkness — either now, or before when he healed the wound from Thomas's burning blade?

Doesn't he sense it? Annabelle opened her mouth to ask, but then another powerful quake shook the dais. The portal's surface shivered.

"Go, child!" Hadrien nudged her forward with his tail.

Cheese and crackers! Annabelle stumbled, then ran for the edge of the dais. *Whoa. I'll need to get used to this armor.* She leaped farther than she ever had before, straight into incandescent light.

"Radiance."

Annabelle opened her eyes and clawed aside the sheer blue fabric of Rhiannon's scarf drifting around her face. She lay upon a slab of dark gray basalt and Wesleyen floated near her feet. Rock formations loomed all around, lit from below by lumen crystals scattered across the silty ocean bottom. A bundle of emotions not her own knotted around her heart.

Raeden ... Thank you, God.

She'd returned to the Depths, and Ynys Lloches.

Tension melted from her frame. She pushed up from the stone. Glancing toward the circle of light above, Annabelle sent a wave of reassurance along the Oathbond to her champion. The knots loosened and warmth bathed her heart. She touched the sapphire gem—the vashryu—embedded in the breastplate of her armor. "Abyss, why do you call me 'Radiance?' Not that I'm complaining, but my name is Annabelle."

"You brought me light in the darkness," Abyss replied.

Annabelle's cheeks heated. *I can't take all the credit for that.* She caught Wesleyen and set him on her shoulder. "Speaking of light ... It's time we blow this popsicle stand."

Gathering her wyld, she reached for the surface, then cried out in astonishment as she rocketed upwards without expending any effort. She'd definitely need to adjust to this armor.

Encased in a column of water, Annabelle burst from the circular pool. Sapphire light bathed the Circle of Judgement. She had an impression of colorful bodies scattered across gray stone, and then she hunkered upon the half-bridge as the waters receded. Water sluiced off her slick armor. She straightened, blinking until her vision cleared.

Raeden stood at the bottom of the half-bridge, eyes wide, hair disheveled, and his short fur standing up in twists crusted with salt. He'd removed the remnants of his tunic, revealing black spots speckling his shoulders and the healed lacerations on his torso. Uncertainty quivered across the Oathbond.

"Freylin," he rasped, looking her up and down. "What you wear ... Is all ... in good order?"

Annabelle's anxiety, confusion, and relief at seeing her champion came rushing forth like a geyser. With a sob, Annabelle ran to him and collapsed into his arms. She breathed in cardamom mixed with sea salt. Stroking her hair and murmuring in his natal language, Raeden held her close like Thomas had in the dreamscape.

Before he stabbed me!

Hurt and betrayal joined the tumult of emotions like scalding and bitter tea forced down her throat. Annabelle's heart felt torn in two, just like Hadrien's vashryu. She broke down into wrenching sobs. Wesleyen stroked her cheek.

"Hadrien's tears!" Mordred said, sounding awed. "Lady Ann. You found the sourekghar."

The Oathbond tensed. Raeden's arms loosened and he stepped back, but he kept one hand on her shoulder. Sniffling, she looked up. Her glasses had smudged, and everything was blurry. Stupid glasses. She pushed them up on her forehead.

Mordred gazed at her, his handsome features tight with suppressed emotion. He extended his hand. "Please." His voice broke. "My father is dying."

"What?" Annabelle took in the three figures at the foot of the Judgment Throne, then gasped.

"The hollowness," Abyss whispered in her mind. *"You must break the curse, Radiance."*

"Damselfly." The princeps approached, reaching for her, then pulled up short when her champion growled. His golden eyes flickered from her face to Raeden's hand on her shoulder, then back again. Mordred's lips thinned as his arm dropped to his side. He turned toward the Throne. "Father had another ... fit. He collapsed."

One hand on Daar-Lûsin, Annabelle followed the princeps with Raeden at her side.

Please, God, let this all work out for the good of everyone.

Rhiannon and Sawel knelt on either side of Morgan Brenin, who lay on his back with the remnants of Raeden's tunic tucked under his head for a pillow. His legs had shifted into his swimming tail. Foam flecked his beard, and his chest rose erratically in panting gasps. His golden eyes were unfocused.

Tears streaming down her blue cheeks, the princepsa stared into her father's face and held his hand between both of hers. "Father," she whimpered. "I'm sorry. Please come back to us."

Jaw clenched, Mordred hunkered beside his sister and put an arm around her shoulders. He blinked rapidly and his chin trembled as he gazed at his father. "We tried removing the torc. It won't come off."

"Restore ... glory," gasped Morgan Brenin. "Rhysedd ..."

"He's calling for Mother," Rhiannon said dully.

The archimandrite looked up as Annabelle knelt beside the prone king. "I've prayed over him. Can you break it?" Expression grim, he indicated the torc resting like a ring of darkness upon Morgan Brenin's collarbones, emanating corruption like a foul stench.

Annabelle swallowed and drew the Dagger of Moonlight. "I'll try," she murmured. Then she recalled Hadrien's warning about needing protection. "But there could be shrapnel. You guys might want to back away to the other side of the pool."

Sawel nodded, then rose. Mordred helped Rhiannon to her feet, and the gwerindawr left Annabelle with their king.

"Raeden, the armor will protect me. Could you take Wesleyen and go with the others?"

Her champion stiffened, and for a moment she feared he'd refuse. "Shach, Freylin." Wesleyen's suckers popped loose as he lifted the octopus from her shoulder. Raeden's breath puffed into her ear. "Remember, the glory of Lord Yshua is with you."

The glory of Lord Yshua ... of course! Annabelle hiccupped a laugh, swallowing the rest before she dissolved into hysterical giggles. That was what the prophecy meant by glory, all along.

The glory of God.

Quick as thought, Annabelle summoned a helmet with a clear face shield, then gauntlets and gloves for her hands. *That's cool.* She stared at Morgan Brenin. Unseeing, his golden eyes darted from side to side. He seemed so helpless despite his powerful frame. Before, she'd been a little scared of the king, but now she only felt sorrow and compassion.

"Must restore ... our glory," Morgan Brenin rasped. "My dear Rhysedd."

She took his hand. "I'll do my best to end this curse. But you know, true glory only comes to those who follow Lord Yshua."

Morgan Brenin's eyes stopped their restless wandering and settled on her. He gripped her hand. "Blessed Ahdmerel?"

"I'm here," she replied. "I'll break the curse on your torc."

"Praise the Almighty." He closed his eyes. "It's too strong. End it ... daughter, so I may ... join my Rhysedd."

Annabelle bit back a protest about marrying his son. She'd clear that up later. The poor man was dying. She squeezed his hand and let go. Concentrating, she wove a protective layer of her wyld over the king. Hopefully it would shield him from the worst of the backlash and any shrapnel.

Mordred called, "We're all clear."

Heart racing, she slid the opalescent blade under the curve of the torc, flat against the king's chest. "Please, God, help me break this curse and set this man free from its corruption." Turning the dagger, she brought its edge to bear against the torc.

Daar-Lûsin flared as bright as the suns and cut through the cursed ornament like a hot knife through butter. The two halves rolled off the shield to the ground. Annabelle flinched, bracing for an explosion, but the pieces shriveled up into orange dust, then vanished. She slumped in relief and dismissed the shielding.

Weariness weighed her down like a heavy blanket. "It's okay," she called. Raeden stood at her right shoulder before she finished speaking. Wesleyen crawled on her left shoulder. The royal siblings knelt on either side of their father, Sawel beside Rhiannon, and Mordred to Annabelle's left.

"Can you heal him?" Rhiannon pleaded.

Annabelle bit her lip. "I'll try." Taking a deep breath, she placed a hand over the king's heart and delved with her kythim. He was like a fruit that worms had devoured from the inside. Whenever she tried to mend his organs, the life force kept slipping from her grasp. Like water through a sieve.

"Radiance," Abyss whispered in her mind. *"The hollowness took too much of his essence. Let him go home."*

Annabelle whimpered. "I'm sorry. I can't heal him."

Morgan Brenin stared up at her. He seemed different; his face softer, his eyes kinder. She could imagine Mordred becoming like this man. "What you have done is sufficient. Time I departed." He coughed. "Thank you, blessed Ahdmerel."

I am so tired of being the blessed Ahdmerel!

Raeden hunkered beside her and placed a hand on her shoulder. She sniffled. "It's just Annabelle, Your Majesty."

"You are not 'just' anything, Lady Annabelle," he rasped. "My daughter." Raeden's grip tightened on her shoulder, and he growled softly.

Morgan Brenin's expression grew mournful. "Scout hound ... Lord von Bleistaff. Had I allowed Ahdmerel to visit you as promised, those men would not have died. I hereby pardon and release you." Mordred frowned, but after a sharp intake of breath, Rhiannon nodded.

Her champion tensed. The Oathbond sang with guilt that quickly went silent. "One is grateful, Your Majesty," he replied stiffly. "He will not long trouble your people with his presence."

Then the king smiled as his gaze wandered to take in his family. "Rhia, forgive me. You have long since been ready to lead our people. Lord Yshua be my witness: I commend the gwerindawr kingdom into your care."

He reached out to her and Rhiannon grabbed his hand. "Father." She'd stopped crying, but her lips quivered, and her eyes were wide like a frightened child's. "Not like this. I still need you. I can't do this alone."

Morgan Brenin chuckled weakly. "You have your husband and your brother to counsel and support you." He exchanged nods with his son-in-law, then turned to Mordred. Sorrow filled his countenance. "My son."

Bent over the king, Mordred gripped his other hand. "Yes, Father?" His voice was eager, hopeful. He glanced at Annabelle, then returned his avid gaze to his father. "Do you have orders for me?" Wesleyen stroked Annabelle's neck. She swallowed tears. Even now, Mordred tried so hard to be the dutiful son.

"My dear boy," the king whispered, his voice faltering. "There is so much I want to ... say. For Cycles, I neglected you. Know that I am proud of the man you've become." He coughed. "Be a better captain than I was, Mordred." His trembling smile included Annabelle. "The blessed Ahdmerel shall keep you on a steady course."

Mordred looked at her, his expression haunted, mouth half opened to speak. Then his gaze flitted to her champion and his expression darkened. He faced his father and nodded. "All shall be as you wish, Father."

Annabelle shifted on her knees. *Should I say something? No. Let the king keep his dreams. Please God, ease his passing.*

Morgan Brenin closed his eyes. "Sing, my beloved children." Peace relaxed his features. Then he was gone.

As the gwerindawr lifted their heads and began their funeral elegy, Raeden tugged on her arm. "Come, Freylin," he murmured. "Let the family have their time to grieve."

Daar-Lûsin in hand, Annabelle stood before the waystone with Raeden at her side. The crystal's core glowed, steadily brightening. In a few moments, a portal would open to Y'Vasheirdenelle. Would Thomas still be there?

Fear twisted her stomach. *I'm not sure if I want to see him again. Not yet.* She touched the spot beneath her breasts, where Thomas had stabbed her. She couldn't remember exactly what happened after William's living tattoos retreated and the scent of honeysuckle flooded her nose ... Then the sorcerer was gone, and the burning sword pierced her. She shuddered.

"Freylin?" Head tilted, her champion regarded her with concern in his green eyes. "Are you ill?"

Rubbing her hand over the vashryu sapphire, Annabelle shook her head. "No. It's ..." She took a deep breath. "I'll tell you when we're at the Fortress of Living Stones." First things first. She needed to say goodbye.

Annabelle pivoted on her heel to face Wesleyen, Rhiannon, Sawel ... and Mordred. Emotion swelled behind her breastbone as the gwerindawr's new queen stepped forward with the little octopus perched on her shoulder. Wesleyen's dark blue skin rippled muted lavender, gray, and peach.

With a sad smile, Rhiannon opened her arms. "I hoped you'd choose to stay with us, but you're always free to come and go as you please." She laughed. "Once you rescue your heart-brother, bring him along, too."

I notice she doesn't mention Raeden. Oh, well. Now isn't the time to make a fuss.

Annabelle hugged the queen. She felt Wesleyen slide to her shoulder. "Of course, Rhia. I love you guys. I want to come back and see you all again. Thank you."

"No, thank *you*, Ann." Rhiannon held her tight and swayed. "I have so much to do—quite a lot—but when you return to Ynys Lloches, things will be different."

"*We* have a lot to do," Sawel corrected his wife. "Now that the curse is broken, the Aethyric powers should return to our people. They'll need guidance and reassurance. I've only skimmed the surface of my father's collection of historical records. It's time I plumbed their depths for information on our lost abilities."

"Once all this is resolved with Enoch," Annabelle said, "I'll do whatever I can to help you." The Oathbond prickled; she imagined Raeden admonishing, *"Do not make promises to the water sprites, Freylin."* Grimacing, she added, "God-willing."

"You will be in our prayers, Lady Ann," Sawel replied.

After giving Sawel a hug, Annabelle faced the princeps. Confusion warred with affection and regret as she gazed up into his golden eyes. Her breathing quickened. He'd been a friend to her, found the dagger, and risked his life to rescue her champion. Even though he was arrogant and reckless, she couldn't help but like him. Behind her, the waystone brightened.

From his bandolier, Mordred detached a pair of small daggers in their sheaths and offered them to her. "Lady Ann, I would like for you to have these, my best and truest blades. That way, a part of me will travel with you."

Annabelle accepted the knives and tucked them inside her belt pouch. "Mordred," she began. "Thank you. For everything. I ..." *Fudge!* What could she say?

He cupped her face in his hands. "I wish I could go with you," he murmured. "But Rhia needs the Captain of the Howling Tempest to help stabilize the kingdom. But know this: I shall come to your aid as soon as my queen gives me leave."

"What? How? The waystone's on a set schedule."

"I will find a way, my little damselfly," he murmured, peering deep into her eyes. "I solemnly swear it."

"Oh, you don't have to—"

Then Mordred bent and gently kissed her forehead.

Annabelle gasped as a frisson went down her spine. Was her wyld reacting to the princeps's vow? Her bond with her champion sprouted thorns, then flattened. Raeden growled.

With a smirk, Mordred withdrew and regarded her champion. "Take care of my betrothed for me ... old man."

Cuddling Wesleyen, Annabelle gaped at the princeps. *Wait, what? Does Mordred* still *intend to marry me?* Her protests stuck in her throat.

Raeden stiffened. "He will take care of her for *herself,* arrogant whelp." He narrowed his eyes and placed his right hand over his heart. "Unlike others, this one will always treasure Freylin's best interests in his liver."

I think he means that he has my best interests at heart.

"Um ..." Annabelle shook her head. She wasn't going to correct him in front of the gwerindawr. "Never mind." She stared down at Wesleyen, petting his slippery, velvet head. He stared back and continued to ripple lavender and gray. She touched the stump of his missing arm. Her vision blurred. "Oh, Wes. My little septapus friend."

Taking her arm, Raeden's tone softened. "Freylin, the little blue creature must stay here."

"I know." She kissed Wesleyen between his eyestalks. He caressed her cheeks and patted the sapphire gem in her breastplate, as if bidding farewell to Abyss. "I expect to see you again, little guy," she said as she handed him to Mordred. Her throat thickened as she drank in her friends' features, washed out in the waystone's glare.

Come on, Ann. We don't have time for the standard Midwestern goodbye.

"Bye," she choked out.

Suppressing an urge to weep, she walked into the waystone with her champion's arm firmly around her. "Daar-Lûsin, please take us to the Fortress of Living Stones." The white light turned pink. *I hope that's a good sign.* As they stepped into the light, Annabelle put her arm around Raeden's waist and held on tight—just in case.

What will I say if Sir Thomas is there? At least she had Raeden with her to act as a buffer—and protect her, if necessary.

They both staggered as their feet descended further than expected, but Raeden held her steady. The pink glare receded. They stood under a starry dome in a circular chamber with marble flooring and colored gates at regular intervals. A huge pillar dominated the center of the room. After the humid warmth of Ynys Lloches, the air felt cool and dry.

Peter, lounging at the base of the pillar, perked up. "Lawks!" he cried. "Hurrah! You made it to the Fortress of Living Stones!" Talons clicking, he leaped to his feet and spread his pink-feathered wings, cackling laughter. "Took ya long enough!"

While Raeden chastised the syrax, Annabelle held on to her champion's arm and scanned the room. "Hi Peter. Um ... Where is Sir Thomas?"

Peter pushed his feathered head under her arm, demanding pets. "Oh, he ain't here, Annie-O. But he left a message." Using his beak, he pulled a tube from his messenger harness.

Heart pounding in her ears, Annabelle accepted it and opened the tube. The scent of ashes and wood-smoke rose from the parchment. Suddenly her mind slipped into the past. A fiery blade plunged through her armor and straight into her heart. Tears filled her eyes and her chest tightened. She tried to focus on the message. The first line was written in a nearly illegible scrawl, but it was only three words.

"Kiddo, I'm sorry."

Weapon Reforged

Fragrant woodsmoke filled the air.

Glancing around, Thomas felt things click as memory returned. He was in his family's cabin, where his father often brought him and his twin sister on fishing trips. He knelt on a bearskin rug in a large room with knotty-pine walls adorned with pictures of men posed in military uniforms, a rack of antique rifles, the stuffed heads of deer, an antelope, and one snarling black bear. Drab brown curtains shut out the Wisconsin Northwoods winter night. A crucifix hung over the pot-belly stove, where a friendly blaze crackled merrily and heated the cabin's great room, though a chill still hung in the air. Several kerosene lanterns bathed everything in a warm golden light.

Before him stood a coffee table made of dark-stained oak. A broadsword with a long, golden hilt and bronze-gold blade inscribed with weird symbols lay on the scarred and water-damaged surface, atop the scattered cards of an abandoned euchre game. Its blade-edges occasionally caught the flickering firelight and seemed to glow. The weapon looked brand new but radiated the gravitas of age.

Closest to the stove, an auburn-haired girl in a green sweater and jeans knelt across the table from him. Head tilted and brow furrowed, her pale blue eyes regarded the sword. She traced the symbols. "Do you think these are magic runes? They look a bit like the Elf script from *The Lord of the Rings*." A wide grin dimpled her cheeks. "Wouldn't it be cool if that stuff was real? Just imagine! The powerful wizard who made our family the custodians of a magic sword could appear on our doorstep at any moment and sweep us off into adventure!"

"Yeah, right." Thomas rolled his eyes. "Dream on, Lily. I don't think Gandalf is gonna show up to claim it." He touched the hilt. It felt warm despite the chill in the air. His fingers itched to curl around the hilt. He wanted to lift the blade and swing it around, but his sister would just laugh and say he was no Aragorn. She'd be right. Although Dad taught them martial arts he'd learned from the Israelis, none of them knew anything about sword-fighting.

So what was the deal with the sword? Their family could trace their roots back to Scotland, but the sword didn't look like it originated in the United Kingdom. And it certainly wasn't native to Wisconsin. His cousin Neal would claim it came from another world entirely, like Eternia or Third Earth. That kid watched far too many cartoons.

"I can't believe this was hiding under that wonky floorboard in our bedroom." He shook his head. "How long do you think it's been in our family?"

Lily shrugged, her eyes reluctantly leaving the sword, though her fingers still idly traced the patterns on the blade. "Beats me. We don't even know if it *belongs* to our family. We should ask Dad when he gets back from town with the s'mores fixings." She frowned and waved a hand at the gun-belt he wore, and the pistols holstered at either hip. "Speaking of Dad, gunslinger boy, you'd better put those away before he gets back. Remember the last time he caught you messing with them." She grinned. "You couldn't sit down for a week!"

Averting his gaze, Thomas winced. That had been three years ago, and he could still remember the spanking. What Lily seemed to forget was that she'd dared him to remove the Desert Eagles from the display.

With a derisive snort, Thomas bounced up to his feet and crossed his arms. "Jeremiah Bull-crap. We're thirteen —hardly little kids anymore—and Dad taught us gun safety." He squinted. "Besides, who made you the boss of me?"

She smirked. "God did. I'm six minutes older than you. That makes me your big sister, so you'd better listen ... *Uriah.*"

Thomas smirked back despite his irritation. She knew he hated to be called by his first name. He lifted his chin. "Go ahead and make me ... Lily-dilly Weed."

Usually that was the opening gambit in a cascade of more and more ridiculous name calling, but his sister didn't rise to the bait and call him Tommy the tiny Tiger. Instead, her gaze dropped to the sword upon which her hand still rested, and then she looked up at him. A strange expression he couldn't parse crossed her face. Her right hand drifted toward the hilt.

"Oh, no, you don't! That's mine!"

Thomas lunged for the sword and seized the hilt with his left hand as Lily grasped it with her right. They staggered away from the table, tugging the sword between them, until its wide blade locked in place, pointed itself at the ceiling like a lightning rod, and refused to budge.

"What're you doing, Tom? Stop it."

"It wasn't me!"

Golden energy burst from the sword's tip and rippled out across the ceiling like liquid sunshine—then became a carpet of flame.

Lily gaped. "Holy cow!"

"Now look what you've done," Thomas shouted. "The ceiling's on fire!"

Dad's gonna kill us.

"It could've just as easily been you," she retorted, about to burst into tears. The sword poured out even more heat and light. "Oh, God, Tom! Magic is real. And it's *not* cool. We've gotta get out of here. Let go."

Glancing at the ceiling, panic filled him. The walls and curtains were on fire. It felt like a furnace. He tried peeling his fingers from the hilt, but it was as if they'd melded with it. "Criminy. I can't let go."

"I can't, either," she wailed, yanking backwards. The sword wouldn't budge, and neither would her hand. "It's so hot in here. Tommy—*do* something."

What should I do—chop off our hands? With what? My teeth?

He tried prying their fingers open with his other hand. That didn't work. They tried pulling together in the same direction, but the sword still wouldn't release their hands. He suggested gnawing off their hands at the wrist. Neither of them could bring themselves to do it.

Lily's blue eyes were wide and red-rimmed. Her lips trembled. "What do we do?"

We're gonna die, that's what. But he couldn't tell her that. She was already crying for Mom, for Dad, and for Jesus to come rescue them. Holding his twin close, he swallowed a sob and buried his face in her hair. They'd been together all their lives, so it only made sense that they die together, too.

Please, God, help us. Smoke filled the room. It stung his eyes. Stuck to the sword as they were, they couldn't lower themselves to the floor. Drooping in the heat, Lily sagged against him, wracked with a coughing fit. Thomas stiffened. Lily had asthma. Her lungs were weaker than his.

A white-hot rage consumed Thomas. He wasn't gonna let that thing kill his sister. "Let us go, you stupid sword!" he roared, shoving all his anger and fear at it.

Suddenly, Lily ripped away from him and Thomas went flying backwards, crashing into the smoldering couch with a grunt. He rolled to his feet. His head rang like a bell.

The sword ... it reacted to my anger.

Lily was screaming. He'd never heard her make sounds like that before—raw, ragged, and wild. They tore at his soul. He had to help her.

Across the room, she curled up and writhed on the floor. *On fire.* A hole yawned in the wall where the pot-belly stove had been, and that horrible, awful sword was still hovering in the center of the room, pouring forth a fountain of ruin.

And Thomas was to blame.

"Lily," he croaked, crawling toward her. His left hand throbbed. "Roll. Put the fire out." Coughs shook him, but he kept going. He had to get to her. Make things right again.

Dad rushed in, hollering their names, telling them to get out. He threw his coat over Lily, patted her down, and hauled her up. She screamed and thrashed. His head ached. The noise. He had to make her stop. Calm down. Be still.

Light burst forth from the sword. Gold lightning arced down to strike Lily. For a moment, her form was awash in light, and then nothing remained but ashes. His twin was gone.

No! I didn't mean to do that!

Thomas howled. Dad fell to his knees, his face stricken. His eyes looked like all the light had gone out of them. Slowly, he looked at Thomas and some of the light returned. "Uriah, get out of here before the Sword of Wrath takes you, too."

"Dad," Thomas cried, reaching for him.

A terrible groan shook the cabin, and the ceiling crashed down. On top of Dad.

No! Lord Jesus, please. Get us out of here.

The sword pulsed and an inferno engulfed Thomas. For an eternity, he knew nothing but agony and blindness. The flames became a horde of salamanders licking away at his flesh and bones, eating him down to the marrow. Soon, they would consume his soul. He deserved that. He couldn't protect Enoch. He'd stabbed Annabelle. He'd disfigured David with burns. He'd even destroyed his twin sister. Dad was gone, immolated under burning timbers. They were nothing but ashes. Just like Thomas would soon be.

Ashes, ashes, and we all fall down.

Helpless, he watched as the salamanders merged into one enormous salamander. Thomas recognized Burnie. And him without the strength to summon his flametigers! He had nothing left. Maw gaping wide to devour him whole, Burnie pinned Thomas to the ground. Then the salamander squealed as something pulled it off him.

"Uriah," whispered a still, small voice that filled everything. "You are my own dear child. I would never forsake you to perdition's flames."

Thomas couldn't move. He watched as a white pillar split the golden flames. Burnie cowered and sank to his belly, squeaking. The pillar resolved into a human form, a brown-skinned warrior clad in white armor and surrounded by a rainbow aura that extended out forever. His boot came down on the salamander's head, crushing it. Burnie flashed orange, and then disappeared.

A sense of familiarity tickled at his awareness. *Who's this guy? Why did he rescue me?* He still couldn't move.

The warrior approached Thomas. His arms were outstretched, as if to embrace him. Light gleamed through holes in his wrists, but that had to be a hallucination. His face beamed with a tender warmth that pierced Thomas through, like a sword to his heart. Thomas wanted to run from the man, but he also wanted to run toward him. But he still couldn't move. He might as well be dead, charred bones on dry and dusty ground.

The radiant man knelt beside Thomas and gathered him into his arms like he was a small child. He must be nothing but bones, greasy soot, and ash. And yet the white armor remained pristine. A scarred hand—yes, those were holes—descended and touched his brow. A searing heat, then coolness, spread over him like the phoenix aloe gel. "Remember."

"Remember what your father taught you," Sir Rick had said.

I remember I killed my dad. Lily. Annabelle. I deserved that nehmwight's torture. I deserve to be ashes scattered in the dust.

Thomas buried his face in the man's breast and wept. "I'm sorry. I'm sorry. I'm so sorry."

A gentle hand stroked his head. "Child, I forgive you. Forgiven. Forgiven." Brown eyes soft and crinkled at the edges, the man smiled down at him. "Now, Uriah-called-Thomas, I raise you up from the ashes." The man grasped his wrist, the scars rough against his palm, and Thomas stood, ashes slipping from his skin and falling in heaps upon the scorched timbers and rubble that had been his family's cabin. The scorched wooden floor was still warm under his bare feet. Unharmed, the crucifix lay at his feet.

The fire didn't melt it?

Thomas brushed ashes from his chest—the knife-scars had returned—and the light cotton trousers he wore. He picked up the crucifix. It nestled in his hand, like the hilt of a sword. He stared at it, then gazed, wide-eyed, at the man beside him. "It's you." His hands trembled and tears filled his eyes. "Lord Jesus. Or is it Lord Yshua?"

With a wry smile, the man patted his shoulder. "You may call me by either name—so long as you call me." He winked. "But don't call me 'late to dinner.'"

A laugh escaped Thomas. He turned the crucifix over in his hands and remembered sitting with his family in church, smelling beeswax as candles burned, the priest intoning the rite of the Eucharist. His own father, leading the whole family in devotion before bedtime.

In a wondering tone, he said, "You really did come and save me." His throat thickened, and he swallowed. "I'm sorry I ever doubted you, Lord. Is ... Is this visitation sort of thing normal?"

The man threw his head back and laughed. Thomas found himself chuckling along with him. Wiping tears from his eyes, the man replied, "I came because—like your namesake—it was necessary for you to see me so that your faith may be renewed." He raised an admonitory finger. "Do not expect this to become a regular thing."

Both relieved and disappointed, Thomas grinned. "I won't, Lord. And I'm not gonna ask to stick my fingers in your wounds." He made a face. *I always thought that was gross.* "Um, well. I know it sounds lame, but ... Thank you. For everything."

"Remain in my Word, and I shall remain in you, always." Smiling, the man held out his hand, and Thomas shook it. "I bid you farewell for a little while, Uriah-called-Thomas. We shall meet again. In the meantime, my peace, I leave with you." He breathed on Thomas and a new strength entered him. "Now, go, my child. Seek justice. Show mercy. And walk in my light."

I know I have to leave—to go back and fight—but I wish I could stay with him. The forgiveness he'd received wrapped around him, a tangible thing. Like armor. Thomas blinked away tears. *I wish I could've told Dad and Lily and Annabelle that I'm sorry, too.*

Golden light rolled in like fog, obscuring his savior from view. Lord Yshua said, "Uriah-called-Thomas, I will tell you three things to ease your mind: Your father dwells with me in paradise. Annabelle survived your blow and has returned to her quest. You will meet again. Lily still walks in the world. Soon, she will need her twin. In the fullness of time, you will find your sister on Lûsin."

"Lord, wait!" Thomas's breath caught in his throat and speech eluded him. He hadn't killed Annabelle! Lily was alive! But where was Lûsin, and how would he get there?

"Ask David." Even as the golden light blinded him to all else, Thomas felt Yshua's presence and heard the echo of his voice: "I will be with you, always. Seek me in my Word. Though the world may pass away, my Word shall never pass away."

Thomas shielded his eyes against a wave of blinding light.

When the light diminished, Thomas lowered his arm, and tensed, gripping the crucifix as he would the hilt of his sword. He stood on the dais surrounded by lava. The Sage crouched there, his chains keeping him from rising to his full height. He didn't seem as huge and scary as he'd been in the past. Perhaps it was only the mantle of Lord Yshua's strength and forgiveness that imbued Thomas, but Balthazar looked less like a disapproving judge and more like a benevolent commanding officer, or a comrade in arms.

Balthazar regarded him, the reptilian visage unreadable. Thomas cleared his throat. "Well, here I am, sir. Reporting for duty." He squared his shoulders, then saluted with the crucifix against his chest and head bowed.

How much of what happened during the trials did Balthazar know about?

"You have come through the Crucible, Helzarvenn," he rumbled. "What occurred during your final trial is between you and the Almighty, unless you choose to share it."

Can he read my mind?

The Sage huffed a brief laugh. "Only when you project." His tone firmed. "Now, lift up your head." Thomas met his gaze. Joy shone in Balthazar's eyes and his feathery crest lifted. "Lord Yshua's blessing is upon you. Praise be to the Almighty Threefold One. My prayers have been answered."

"Um. Mine, too." A lop-sided smile tugged at his lips. "So, what happens now?" Flat-out asking for the sourekghar felt gauche. *Although the armor seems less important now that I'm armored by faith.* His fingers rubbed the crucifix like a worry stone as gratitude warmed him.

Smoke puffed from Balthazar's nostrils. It smelled of beeswax and incense. "Helzarvenn. Sir Thomas, Knight of the Northern Marches."

Thomas stiffened to attention. "Sir!"

He held out a massive, clawed hand large enough to encircle Thomas's waist. "Your crucifix. May I?"

With a twinge, Thomas gave him the crucifix, all he had left of his family but memories.

"I shall return it to you shortly," Balthazar said. "You emerged from the Crucible a new man. As promised, receive the sourekghar I forged in concert with my brothers, and my vashryu to help guide you."

Opening his great jaws, the Sage exhaled golden flames. Thomas flinched but stood firm and stared into the conflagration as it swallowed him. Like before, the fire rolled over Thomas without consuming him, adhering to his body and flowing like molten gold to form a suit of armor covering him from head to toe. Unlike before, this armor felt *real.* Substantial. It hummed with power and purpose that concentrated in his chest.

He glanced down. What looked like a miniature of a long-hilted broadsword gleamed from the center of his breastplate. Disquiet filled him as he recalled the strange artifact that had destroyed his family cabin. But it also echoed the shape of a cross, the symbol of his renewed faith. One day, when he felt ready to talk about it, he'd ask Balthazar about the sword he and Lily found.

"Is that the vashryu?"

Balthazar nodded. "Tis my vashryu—my focus gem—through which I shall provide you consul. You need only ask, and I will answer."

"How convenient." His lips thinned as he nodded. "I knew there had to be an ulterior motive. I'm your ticket to ride out of here. Not that I blame you."

Amusement crinkled the golden scales around Balthazar's eyes. He grunted. "My motivation is to protect the people of the world, Helzarvenn. If I understand you correctly, the answer is 'no.' I am still confined here, in the flesh. The vashryu is merely a conduit through which we may communicate."

"Sorry, sir." Thomas furrowed his brow. "Is there anything I can do?" It really was too bad. The Sage would make a powerful ally in the battle to come.

"No," Balthazar replied stiffly. "My brothers and I must remain imprisoned here, if the balance is to be maintained."

"What balance?" Thomas frowned.

"That is a concern for another day. Focus on your current commission." The Sage waved the tip of his tail as if banishing all discussion of his freedom. "You are ready to venture forth. A weapon reforged."

A feeling of conviction settled over Thomas and complemented the strength he'd received from Lord Yshua. He raised his hands, admiring the gauntlets, hesitated to touch the sword-shaped vashryu, instead running his fingers over the smooth helmet. "Thank you, sir. I'm ... I'm honored." He saluted again, then lifted his chin. "I won't let you down." He thought of Lord Yshua as he spoke, and all he had done for Thomas's sake. He recalled the news about Annabelle's survival. And the sister he could now remember.

I have a twin. Lily's alive!

Holding out the crucifix, Balthazar breathed flame over it and Thomas cringed, suppressing a shout of denial. The crucifix glowed white hot and golden. "A Baron-Knight needs an emblem to proclaim his office. Stand fast, Sir Thomas, whilst I anoint you." The Sage pressed the glowing crucifix into the golden armor over his collarbones, then breathed fragrant smoke over Thomas. "I hereby formally raise you as Baron-Knight of the Northern Marches. And now, the code."

Placing a hand over the crucifix embedded in his armor—it was already cool to the touch—Thomas joined Balthazar in reciting: "Seek justice. Show mercy. Walk humbly with Lord Yshua. Protect the innocent and cast the evildoer into the light."

Afterwards, Balthazar breathed fire again. His clawed hands shaped the flames and formed a bridge that spanned the gulf between his dais and the gate. The gate back to the desert was open. "What?" Thomas joked. "You give me this armor that'll protect me from anything, but don't expect me to walk across the boiling lava lake?"

The Sage chuckled as he curled his tail around himself. "Do as you wish, Helzarvenn. However, the bridge is the fastest route to the exit."

"Sir! Before you send me back ... I thought you'd want to know. I met your wife."

Balthazar inhaled sharply and his fan-shaped ears trembled. "Garutha. Tell me, did she look ... well?"

Thomas snorted. "For a great, big fiery chicken who ate my flametigers for breakfast? Yeah, she looked spectacular." He grimaced, recalling the phoenix's loneliness. "Sorry, sir, for being flip. What I mean is, she's well, but she's a phoenix, and bound to this place like you are."

And forever separated from the one she loves most. God knows, I'm familiar with pain, but that is not a pain I'd ever want to carry around with me.

Balthazar gazed off into the distance, his eyes dark with sorrow, then shook his head. "If she is well, then I must be content. Whilst life remains, there hope reigns. I thank you, Helzarvenn. Your tidings uplift my heart." Somber, he puffed more fragrant smoke over Thomas. "Now you must return to the world and carry out your commission. Go forth with my blessing and prayers, Sir Thomas. Lord Yshua will be with you."

Yes, he will. He was there all along. The fire of my anger just blinded me to his presence.

A lump formed in his throat as he saluted. "Yes, sir." He pivoted and marched across the bridge, the heat rising from the molten rock below invigorating his strides.

Annabelle and Enoch were in trouble—and though it still vexed him—they were no longer his immediate concern. Lord Yshua assured him Annabelle had survived. One day, he'd kneel before Annabelle and beg her forgiveness. Just not on this day.

War lurked over the horizon. The world was about to go up in flames. As the Baron-Knight of the Northern Marches, Thomas had a job to do. Commander Storm had left standing orders to rally the troops. David waited for him outside in the phoenixes' village. As he passed through the gate, Lily's face flashed before his mind's eye. A grim smile stretched his lips. And then—after he fulfilled his duty—he had a sister to find.

Some Time Later ...

Where was the suns-cursed harkhurz when he needed him?

William slammed the door and summoned another werelight. "Suns burn it, Zakaar," he snarled, stalking across the chamber to his workbench. If Zakaar was nowhere in the fortress, then he'd need to activate another Seeker's Web. "Where in all the nether perditions are you hiding?"

"You won't find him here," a voice spoke from behind him.

Flinching, William spun on his heel. How did Tenebris do that? He could've sworn the room was empty; the wards he'd set should've at least warned him. "Master! I ... I thought you went into town this evening to buy more parchment."

"Acquiring parchment doesn't take all night," Tenebris replied dryly. His eyes narrowed as he fixed William with a cold stare but added nothing further.

Merciful Valeshka! What does he think I've done now?

William pursed his lips. His heart hammered. What did his master want? Tenebris often stared at him in silence when he wished to milk a confession of some wrongdoing, but William wasn't going to fall for it. Not this time. He had seven circles, a contract binding a wyldling as his ally, and claimed the dreamscape for his dominion. He'd wait out his master.

Crossing his arms, he slipped his hands into opposite sleeves and met the Arkhadahn's flat and expressionless gaze. Tenebris mustn't see them tremble. He schooled himself to patience even as his heart fluttered like a frantic moth, not daring to let his eyes stray to the shelf where he kept Milady Blue's jar.

I won't let you scare me anymore, Tenebris. Inside his sleeves, his fingernails dug into his forearms.

When Tenebris finally broke the silence, he spoke calmly, in an almost gentle tone. "William," he said. "Is there something you wanted to tell me?"

William froze. *He knows. He knows I've been digging through his Tenth Order spells, even though I've been so careful.*

"No, master," he replied in a tight voice. "What ... what is it you think I've done?"

In response, Tenebris reached inside his black burkheld. His eyes never leaving William's, he extracted something flat and square that fit in the palm of his hand. He held it up for William to see.

The blood drained from William's face, and he went cold. His heart plummeted to his feet as he stared at the portrait of Annabelle.

No. It can't be. When had Tenebris found the portrait? William hid it in his bookshelf since he'd removed it from his sakkhelt; it had been there earlier that evening when he checked on it.

A thin smile like the slash of a knife twisted his master's lips. "From the look on your face, you *do* have something to tell me."

William dragged his eyes from the portrait. "Master, it's not what you think. I took that from—"

"And how do you know what *I* think, Arkhasuhl?" Tenebris spat. "For the past Cycle, I've been shielding my thoughts and emotions from you."

That explained a lot. His eyes returned to the portrait. Tenebris must have searched his entire bedroom while Khalad ran him through combat drills in the training hall. How much did his master know about Annabelle?

"How ... How ..."

The Arkhadahn sneered. "How did I find out? I wondered why you've been so ... preoccupied as of late. Whatever project the Dreadlord gave you hardly accounts for the manner in which you've been mooning about." He tapped the edge of the portrait against the palm of his opposite hand and William followed the motion like the progress of a headsman's ax. "Being rather mystified about your behavior, I skimmed your journal and found references to a 'Milady Blue.'"

Ice coated his insides. William bit his lip. *Don't react.*

"At first, I believed your entries were plans for that hideous golem. But something didn't track." Tenebris narrowed his eyes. "Why would my apprentice need a disguise for a meeting with a golem when he could simply conjure one? Who was he meeting, and where? You haven't left Fastness. Naturally I went to inquire of your bosom companion, Ravenos—*my* servant."

William realized the cold, creeping sensation in his gut was fear. Oddly, the fear was not for himself. His terrified thoughts careened from Zakaar, to Annabelle, swinging back and forth between them like a razor-edged pendulum. Tenebris had done something, but his thoughts refused to coalesce into what that might be.

Tenebris laughed. "Can you imagine my surprise when the suns-burnt fool refused to comply? To answer me—his master—when I posed the simplest questions regarding your activities?"

Oh, no ... William rasped, "What did you do to him?" The torture methods of which Tenebris was capable sprang to mind. In graphic detail. He'd witnessed them often enough.

"I'm afraid I had to break his mind before he would confess what he knew—his suspicions, really—about why my apprentice was acting like a moon-struck fool. A pity, considering the lengths you went to enact a permanent cure for a broken tool. The level of his devotion to you was extraordinary. I cannot fathom what you promised him in exchange, but I'm impressed by how long he held out against my probe."

Tenebris broke Zakaar? What about ... William's heart plunged further into the icy depths which each sentence his master uttered. He swallowed, then tried to speak, but no sound emerged.

"Oh, my pet assassin is quite mad now." Eyes aglow, Tenebris bared his teeth in a shark-like grin, leaned closer, and whispered, "But he retains enough sanity to complete one last ... errand for me." He tapped the portrait against William's forehead in time with his words. "And provide an object lesson for you."

William flinched at each blow. They felt like knives carving into his soul. His mouth felt dry as dust. "Object lesson?"

Tenebris's grin vanished. His tone grew hard. "I warned you, William. Time and again, I warned you to avoid females and their ... allurements. You refused to listen." He raised the portrait and shook it in accusation. "Now one has entangled you in a web of delirium. But never fear, William." His expression softened. "I possess the antidote for this malady."

Malady? Oh, merciful Valeshka ... This is bad. Really bad. Tenebris, what did you do?

"Zakaar," he managed. "Where is Zakaar?"

Drawing back, Tenebris laughed. "I haven't the slightest idea. However, I do know that once Ravenos—mad though he is—is set upon a target, his focus never wavers. He never fails to ... eliminate it." His fingers clenched into a fist, crumpling the portrait, crushing William's heart along with it.

No ...

His master's eyes were hard as carnelian. "You see, my wayward Arkhasuhl? You needn't worry about your little problem. I took care of it for you." He let the balled-up portrait fall, and William's eyes followed it to the floor. As Tenebris stalked silently from the room, William fell to his knees beside the crumpled portrait, attempting to flatten it out with trembling fingers. Cracks ran all through the maiden's image. Miraculously, only her face was unmarred. It wasn't until the door clicked shut that the full import of his master's words struck home, stealing his breath.

Tenebris had destroyed William's most valuable ally. His friend. All his work, all the elixir he'd brewed, all for nothing. His hands formed fists and black energy crackled over his knuckles. He recalled Zakaar's amber eyes, clear and bright, while he taught William how to center his balance on the training room floor.

Suns burn Tenebris to ash—Zakaar was sane *again!*

But even worse, Tenebris had sent the assassin after Annabelle. A shudder wracked William's frame. He recalled the gnawed corpses of the maidens Zakaar had killed in his madness. Once Zakaar caught Annabelle, she'd die a horrible death.

No. I can't allow it.

As he stared at the pale, smiling face in the portrait, William felt the compulsion building in his seventh circle, where the blood oath was tethered. Like a ring of cold fire, it impressed an urge to leave Fastness and seek out Annabelle. The power it held superseded the oath he'd sworn to Tenebris Cycles ago as a foolish child.

"Are you not trapped, little wyldling?"

Annabelle's pet hisanabyad was right, after all.

A malignant hum filled William's mind, and his hands fisted in his robes. He snarled through gritted teeth. "Tenebris, you went too far. This is one object lesson I refuse to sit here and accept. I refuse to be trapped. Your oath no longer binds me."

Suddenly resolved, William's thoughts cleared like storm clouds from the sky. There was only one thing he could do.

He would go out into the world after his friend, restore his mind, and rescue his wyldling from certain death. The blood oath he'd sworn with Northward compelled him to do no less for her. And then, once he returned to Fastness with Zakaar and Annabelle, Tenebris had better watch out.

William tucked the portrait in his sakkhelt, leaped to his feet, and began snatching up spell components he'd require for his journey. He envisioned the list of things that must be done before he left. Pack spell components in his sturdiest satchel. Map out his route. Find provisions and coin. Borrow vashenta keyed to specific waystones from the Dreadlord's store. Trace Zakaar's movements using a Seeker's Web ... As he ticked down the list, his excitement grew alongside the ice of anxiety.

Finally, an opportunity to prove to Tenebris that he no longer needed a master. One way or another, William would soon be a free man.

END OF BOOK THREE
The adventure continues in *Wyldling Blood!*

Dramatis Personae

Annabelle Leigh Wells - 16yo girl from Earth, wyldling (water mage)

Balthazar Phoenixheart - the Sage (dragon) Thomas met in his dreams.

Daniel Storm, Commander - evainghir (half-dragon), warrior and leader of the group

David - dwelfnhir (male elf), warrior and pastor

Dinah - dwelfnhad (female elf), Annabelle's friend, a warrior and ambassador

Dreadlord, The - powerful dwelfnhir of unknown provenance; employer of Tenebris, William, and Zakaar.

Dream Traveler - a mysterious cloaked bard who haunts the dreamscape.

Ebenezzar Earthshaker - the Sage (dragon) associated with the stone Aspect. Co-creator of the Fortress of Living Stones.

Enoch Northward - 16yo boy, acting Baron-Knight of the Northern Marches, wyldling (air mage). His abduction is the driving reason for Annabelle's quest.

Hadrien Rainblessed - the Sage (dragon) Annabelle met in her dreams.

Khalad - Nehmwight male and squad leader of the Golorum—elite warriors.

Marshal Incendo – 19-20yo kadorei woman with burn scars; the Dreadlord's adopted granddaughter. Often accompanied by a wyrmkin called Friska.

Mordred - 18yo blue male gwerindawr (merman), princeps

Morgan Brenin - blue male gwerindawr (merman), king of Ynys Lloches

Peter - syrax (male griffin), messenger and scout

Portia - Rhiannon's handmaid

Raeden von Bleistaff - kaenhir (male dog-human hybrid), Annabelle's oathbonded champion and friend

Rhiannon - blue female gwerindawr (mermaid), princess and heir

Sawel - burgundy male gwerindawr, archimandrite and Rhiannon's husband

Tanisha Delwyr, Caretaker - evainghad (half-dragon) lives in the Fortress of Living Stones and leads the Stonesingers.

Tinker - a white-tail stag the size of a horse, originally Enoch's and now Annabelle's mount.

Toad/Sir Thomas - 19-20yo knight cursed into toad form, wyldling (fire mage)

Vespyrahl, Warlord - the most powerful nehmwight warlord

Wesleyen – a small octopus whom Annabelle befriends.

William Dulciber - 16yo male half-nehmwight, apprentice sorcerer (uses blood magic) with a thirst for arcane power and a desire to prove himself.

Yvres Tenebris - a very powerful master sorcerer and William's mentor

Zakaar Ravenos - kaenhir (male dog-human hybrid) formerly employed as a soldier of the Northern Marches but turned out to be a spy and murderer; one of Enoch's abductors.

Place Names

Fastness – the Dreadlord's stronghold in the Ingaraik Mountain range of the Western Marches.

Fortress of Living Stones – an edifice "grown" directly from stone and earth; part of Y'Vasheirdenelle.

Y'Dendordenelle – Dwelfnic for "tree home."

Y'Pohlzardenelle – Dwelfnic for "fire home."

Y'Vasheirdenelle – Dwelfnic for "stone home."

Ynys Lloches - "Sanctuary Isle," the place where the gwerindawr live.

Glossary

Aethyr - magic of an "elemental" variety, of seven "aspects," limited only by the imagination of the wielder.

Age - (time expression) roughly the same as 1,029 Earth years.

Ahdmerel - title referring to a wyldling attuned to water. High Dwelfnic term translating to "weaver of water" in the trading language.

Alarimet - "mirror twin" in dwelfnic; refers to a psychic bond between two wyldlings; the relationship is usually fraternal and never romantic.

Archimandrite -religious leader of the gwerindawr.

Arkhabadh - ceremonial blood magic used by nehmwight sorcerers, heavily reliant on symbolism and objects.

Arkhabala - nehmwight tattoos carved into skin of the back made from black ink and blood that store magical energy and aid in casting spells. Each "circle" is a higher level and greater capacity of magic unlocked. Tattoos expand on their own as the student advances and can be controlled with one's mind.

Arkhadahn - master nehmwight sorcerer, levels measured in Circles from 9 to 13

Arkhasuhl - student nehmwight sorcerer, levels measured in Circles from 1 to 8.

Aspects - Air (wind), Energy (fire), Flesh (shape), Mind (illusion), Stone (earth/mineral), Water (H2O), Void (space/time).

Atropos - The third sun, a red giant star.

Brenin - the gwerindawr king.

Burkheld - robe worn by sorcerers. Apprentices and Acolytes wear brown and masters wear black.

Crane Watch 11am-1pm

Cycle - (time expression) roughly the same as three Earth years; the time it takes for Tehara to make one complete revolution around the three suns.

Dolmagh - nehmwight word for skunk.

Dwelfn (s) **-im** (pl) - race of humans that resemble Tolkienesque Elves

Dreamscape - a changeable, malleable realm of the mind and pure Aethyr, accessible to wyldlings and souretholim.

Enlightened Faction - all Christian dwelfnim and their allies.

Epoch - (time expression) roughly the same as 147 Earth years.

Evainghad - the term used to refer to the daughter of a Sage.

Evainghir - the term used to refer to the son of a Sage.

Evaingynon - the term used to refer to the Sages; High Dwelfnic for "Wise Ones." Each is associated with an Aethyric aspect. It is believed that all perished in the Oblivion Wars. Annabelle refers to them as dragons.

Folken - how the wensallen-kaen refer to themselves as a people/race.

Frog Watch - 5-7am

Galamerdhe - the swimming tail of a gwerindawr.

Glamourye – an illusion spell to deceive that affects the receiver's perception.

Generation - (time expression) roughly the same as twenty-one Earth years.

Golor (s) **Golorum** (pl) - elite nehmwight warrior, one achieves this level for surviving pitched battle and is given a "blooding name."

Grammerye - a spell that directly impacts the item it's cast upon.

Gwerindawr - refers to what we'd call "merfolk" and are able to shift to fully human form (landbound) at will with great pain and effort. Skin and hair can be any color of the rainbow.

-had - female suffix

-hir - male suffix

Harkhurz - what the nehmwights call a wensallen-kaen.

Harrowdwelfnim - the term used by the dwelfnim to refer to nehmwights and their ilk, collectively.

Helzarvenn - title referring to a wyldling attuned to fire. High Dwelfnic term translating to "caster of flames" in the trading language.

Heron Watch 3-5am

Hisanabyad - a winged unicorn-like creature with both scales and fur, believed extinct.

Iqorasu (s) **Iqorasulim** (pl) - also called Sky-Dancers and believed extinct; refers to pygmy humans with wings who dwell in the Second Demesne, which can only be reached using a special artifact.

Jay Watch 1-3pm

Kaenhir - term used to refer to a male wensallen-kaen (man).

Kadorei - race of humans; what we would call a normal human here on Earth.

Klotho - The first sun, a white dwarf star.

Khaverim – Dwelfnic word for "friend."

Khristosian - a person of Christian faith.

Kythim - collective noun that refers to a person's "aura;" shows mood and mental state. Used to reach out mind-to-mind. Annabelle uses the word-picture "thought-tendrils."

Lachesis - The second sun, a yellow dwarf very similar to Earth's sun, Sol.

Lark Watch - 7-9am

Loricum - dwelfnic term for an expert in a particular field of science or an art; equivalent to a Ph.D.

Malecto-grammerye - curse magic.

Mreeshgraf - nehmwight insult

Nehmwight - race of humans that resemble Tolkienesque Elves (but more like drow), a subset of the Dwelfnim with gray skin and orange eyes. Sensitive to the sun but tolerant of cold.

Nightstalker - a nehmwight/kadorei hybrid that generally favors the nehmwight side. Those few born of a nehmwight mother are sacrificed to one of the various nehmwight godlings. Most often those born of a kadorei mother who survive to adulthood hire themselves out as mercenaries or follow other similarly violent professions.

Oblivion Wars - often mentioned, but little is known about them. Much knowledge of the past civilization was lost during these cataclysmic wars, when the Sages and their magically/genetically engineered constructs fought against the nehmwights and their allies.

Owl Watch 9-11pm

Panther Watch 11pm-1am

Princeps (masc.) - royal son; similar to prince.

Princepsa (fem.) - royal daughter; similar to princess.

Raven Watch 5-7pm

Sakkhelt - a multi-pocketed sash worn under the burkheld that holds components for spells.

Serpent Watch 1-3am

Shesm – a curse meaning "blood and offal."

Skelsdaran - title referring to a wyldling attuned to air/wind. High Dwelfnic term translates (roughly) to "master of the wind blades" in the trading language.

Skraeling - refers to human shapeshifter who can change into a single type of mammal, called one's totem; mass is conserved.

Sourekghar - magic armor created by the Sages for the wyldlings during the Oblivion Wars.

Sourethol (s) **-im** (pl) - Dwelfn who has an affinity for an Aethyric Aspect and can manipulate that Aspect in a limited fashion; confined to what they are in contact with, in many cases.

Sparrow Watch 3-5pm

Stonesinger - sourethol with a proficiency in the stone/earth Aspect.

Syrax (s) **-im** (pl) - race of humans permanently locked in a bestial shape. Refers to what we'd call a griffin, but the avian half can also be corvid, and the mammalian half can be something other than a great cat.

Thrush Watch 7-9pm

Tessaramint – a small, swamp-dwelling beast blending fox and cat characteristics, prized for its luxurious fur, notorious for being crafty and fickle in temperament.

Tradespeak - also called "the trading language." The common tongue used by the different races, cultures, etc. for diplomacy and/or commerce. Annabelle automatically interprets it as English.

Turning - (time expression) one turning of the seasons, roughly the same as an Earth year.

Varazslo – Title for the most powerful Arkhadahn; it means "highest."

Vashenta - High Dwelfnic term translating (roughly) to "key stone."

Vashryu - High Dwelfnic term translating (roughly) to "focus gem."

Wensallen-kaen (s) **-im** (pl) - race of humans with canine characteristics; High Dwelfnic for "scout hound."

Wren Watch - 9-11am

Wyld (s) **-har** (pl) - ability to use magic associated with Aethyric Aspects.

Wyldcham – a form-fitting, full body uniform often worn by wyldlings under their armor.

Wyldhar'ko'profides – Dwelfnic term for the wyldling snare.

Wyldling - a kadorei human born of the sel Drayven bloodline who can manipulate and/or utilize Aethyric Aspects.

Wyld'to'allein - Dwelfnic for "forger of bonds."

Wyrmkin - a winged, pony-sized dragon-like creature, of human intelligence and capable of telepathic communication, which can feed on and drain the Aethyric power of a wyldling.

<u>Wyldling Dream Series</u>

Wyldling Snare

Wyldling Trials

Wyldling Armor

Wyldling Blood*

Wyldling Courage*

Wyldling Dream*

*Titles forthcoming

Find out more:

About the Author

Born and raised in Wausau, Wisconsin, A.R. Grimes started writing "books" about dinosaurs in elementary school. She is the published author of the epic portal fantasy series, *Wyldling Dream*, and is furiously writing the fourth installment. Other than reading and writing, she enjoys singing in the church choir, listening to music, making fused glass art, drawing, daydreaming, and nature hikes. A.R. is married to a martial arts enthusiast and currently lives in Sun Prairie, Wisconsin. They share the house with two male offspring and three cats who—naturally—are the true overlords.

Find me here:

www.ingramcontent.com/pod-product-compliance
Lightning Source LLC
Chambersburg PA
CBHW061533190726
48289CB00004B/1025